THE HOT GATE

THE HOT GATE

JOHN RINGO

THE HOT GATE

Copyright © 2011 by John Ringo

A Baen Books Original

Baen Publishing Enterprises
P.O. Box 1403
Riverdale, NY 10471
www.baen.com

ISBN: 978-1-4391-3432-0

Cover art by Kurt Miller

First printing, May 2011

Distributed by Simon & Schuster
1230 Avenue of the Americas
New York, NY 10020

Library of Congress Cataloging-in-Publication Data

Ringo, John, 1963–
    The hot gate / John Ringo.
        p. cm.
    ISBN 978-1-4391-3432-0
    1. Soldiers—Fiction. 2. Human-alien encounters—Fiction. I. Title.

    PS3568.I577H68 2011
    813'.54—dc22
                                                    2011006288

10   9   8   7   6   5   4   3   2   1

Pages by Joy Freeman (www.pagesbyjoy.com)
Printed in the United States of America

For David P. "Thermal" Hartman
Died November 6, 2009
Long Beach, CA
RIP

✳   ✳   ✳

And
As always:
For Captain Tamara Long, USAF
Born: 12 May 1979
Died: 23 March 2003, Afghanistan
You fly with the angels now.

Lacadaemon (Lakedaimon):
Traditional name for the city-state of
Sparta in ancient Greece. Spartan shields,
during the Delphian League period, were
marked by the Greek symbol lambda (Λ)
as an identifier on the battlefield.

ONE

*Away to the darkness, cowardly offspring, where out of hatred
Eurotas does not flow even for timorous deer.
Useless pup, worthless portion, away to Hell.
Away! This son unworthy of Sparta was not mine at all.*

—Anonymous saying attributed to a Spartan mother

"Please take a seat and buckle in," the public affairs officer repeated. "We all want to get into space as fast as possible, don't we?"

"As a last gig, this purely sucks," Coxswain's Mate Second Class Dana Parker said, watching the group filing into her *Myrmidon* shuttle.

To say that the line between civilian and military was starting to blur in the war was an understatement. During the last battle around the gate, the *Troy* had suffered numerous casualties despite its kilometer-and-a-half-thick walls. The 142nd Boat Wing had lost five shuttles with their crews and in one case a consignment of Marines. Total losses were close to two thousand Navy and Marine personnel, mostly in the boarding action that had captured two Rangora space docks and their support ships.

On the other hand, the civilian repair crews of Apollo Mining had suffered over two hundred casualties doing repairs in the middle of a battle.

Thus when Apollo's owner, or at least someone close enough to the top to get away with using his name, asked if the Navy would be ever so kind as to lend Apollo a *Myrmidon* to pick up a group of space tourists, the Navy had been happy to oblige.

1

It was good press for the Navy and doing Tyler Vernon a favor was always a good idea.

Troy, the nine kilometer battlestation that, along with her sister station *Thermopylae*, had just smashed a Rangora fleet flat, was the brainchild of the Chairman of the Board of Apollo. Also his home away from home. The financier rarely left his quarters onboard. And when he did it was in his customized shuttle, *Starfire*, which could often be seen drifting across the main bay or observing some new construction on the battlestation.

It was often wondered who really commanded *Troy*, Rear Admiral Jack Kinyon, its supposed commander, or the reclusive tycoon.

The trip Dana had gotten stuck on was part of a contest to name Battlestation Three. The eight-kilometer ball of nickel iron was on its way inward from the asteroid belt, preparing to join the *Thermopylae* and *Troy* in guarding the Grtul gate, humanity's contact to the stars. Not that for most of Dana's life it had been much more than trouble. Her first memory was of walking out of the burning Los Angeles basin after a Horvath kinetic bombardment.

Her last visit to Los Angeles, one of many at this point, was to drop off more shuttle loads of Rangora prisoners. The survivors of the recent battle joined the more than ten thousand already in the camps built in the midst of the devastation. The ten-foot-tall lizards, whose labor could not be used for military purposes, were being used to strip the area clear of damage. Since the resulting superfires had burned everything from Glendale to Pomona to Irvine flat, it was also a convenient spot to stick them.

Her first trip to L.A. had entailed some really bad flashbacks. PTSD was considered the new normal, but returning to her birthplace had been a shock. By this point, it was just another destroyed city. Crawling with Rangora prisoners, who were not nearly the supermen they seemed when Earth first came to their attention as an easy conquest.

This trip was easier. The kids were among the thousands who had submitted names for the new battlestation. The requirement was that it be a battle in history where a group of outnumbered defenders fought a valiant battle, win or lose. Each kid had to submit an essay defending their choice. The winners were drawn by lot from essays or arguments of notable merit.

Thirty kids between the ages of six and twelve were chosen.

Along with them were six civilian chaperones and two PAO officers, and that filled the thirty-eight-person cargo section of the *Myrmidon*.

"And we're full up," Engineering Mate First Class Hartwell said.

Thermal had been her boss back when Dana was a newbie engineering apprentice assigned to the 142nd. During one of her first battles, several coxswains on their way back from Earth had had the bad luck to be on a civilian shuttle coasting between Earth and the *Troy* when the Rangora came through—a shuttle that the Rangora turned into debris during the battle. Thus the 142nd was left with a shortage of drivers just when they needed them.

Dana, as one of the engineer mates with a high rating in "flight cross-training," had been picked to drive a shuttle. Since she was a total newb, Thermal took her under his wing. They'd been partners for the last two years and in three days that was going to end. Dana was on orders to transfer to the 143rd Wing on the *Thermopylae*.

"Double-check the door," Dana said, watching the PAOs get the kids settled down. That wasn't going well, since the kids, all of whom were also crazy for space, were bouncing around like Mexican jumping beans. "The last thing we want to happen is the compartment to evacuate in orbit."

"That would be bad, yes," Thermal said, climbing out of his seat.

Generally a PO2 didn't order a PO1 around. But while Thermal "owned" Shuttle Thirty-Six, Dana was responsible for all actions during flight. Thermal was probably going to check the hatch anyway, but Dana hadn't survived this long by taking anything for granted. Space was a cold, unforgiving bitch and she wasn't going to have "killed thirty kids" on her resume.

Dana watched on the internal monitors as Thermal made his way forward. He had to stop from time to time to answer questions from the hyperactive children in the compartment but he finally managed to make his way back to the flight deck.

"Whoo!" Thermal said, dogging the hatch and leaning on it. "That was worse than a hot LZ! Those kids are going insane."

"We'd better get them to the *Troy*, then," Dana said, giggling. She hated when she giggled but it was her normal reaction to stressors. By now she'd had enough of those to get over it. And nobody in the 142nd said a *damned* thing about "Comet's giggle." They'd heard it too many times when the shit was hitting the fan.

"Please prepare for lift-off," Dana said over the internal speakers. It was the first time she could think of when she'd used them. Most of the time they carried Marines who had implants to receive broadcasts. And a good bit of the time the cargo compartment was evacuated so the Marines could unass quicker.

Which reminded her to check, for the fourth time, that all seals were tight and the compartment's air circulators were working. That was, technically, Thermal's job. And she'd seen him do it since he sat down and to her starboard from the flight control position. Didn't mean she wasn't going to triple check. And check again.

She pulled the shuttle up and around under moderate drive. She could pull up to four hundred gravities if she wanted to subject her passengers to a relative condition of three gravs of inertia. But not only would that unduly stress her passengers, it would heat up the shuttle as it rocketed out of the atmosphere faster than the most advanced air-breathing fighter. Then there was the overpressure wave, the sonic boom, the fact that STC had her on a strict flight path and the fact that Manchester field was busy as hell. All good reasons to keep her velocity down.

Two freighters were taking off to the east on the increasingly large tarmac and three more were inbound to the west. One of the ones to the west she recognized as the *Troy*'s milk run freighter, which carried up food and other consumables and carried back refined metals from the Apollo processors on the *Troy*. The metals would, in turn, be shipped to factories all over the world, and mostly be turned into parts and materials for the growing Terran Alliance Fleet and modules for the *Troy*, *Thermopylae* and Station Three.

At seventy thousand feet, ground control automatically handed off to Space Traffic Control. Dana noted it and decided to see if Athena was busy.

"Athena, Shuttle One-Four-Two-Three-Six," Dana said.

"*Comet*," the AI replied. "*How are you today?*"

"Milk run," Dana said. "Carrying kids up to the *Troy* to be all agog."

"*I'm aware of the mission*," Athena said over the hypercom. The FTL transmitter was one of a dozen alien technologies that Terrans, at this point, took for granted. "*I take it you don't care for it.*"

"Not my idea of vital support of humanity, Athena," Dana said. "Anything I should be aware of?"

"The usual mess of destroyed ships," the AI said distastefully. *"There's a large section of hull plating surrounded by a constellation of lesser damage moving through your route. I'll warn you when you're getting close."*

"Roger, Athena," Dana said, making a moue. "Seems like an odd place for debris."

"It's from the first battle," Athena commed. *"Portion of a Horvath destroyer. It was ejected into a retrograde orbit but it's become more of an asteroid at this point. Apollo keeps planning to smelt it and move it but there's always something else that comes up. There's a fair bit of small particles around it. I'll vector you wide."*

"Thank you, Athena," Dana said. "I'd hate to kill these kids. Take that back, I'd hate to be *responsible* for killing these kids."

"I take your meaning," Athena commed. *"Gotta go, kid. There's more fires than that to stomp out."*

"Thirty-Six, out," Dana replied, making a slight adjustment to her path. Deep space rubble from the various battles was bad enough. The orbits around Earth were just a *nightmare.* Many of the satellites weren't even in use anymore, being communications satellites that had been outmoded by the hypercom. But with everything else going on in the system, nobody was getting around to pulling them out of orbit.

"Can I let the kids unbuckle?" Thermal asked.

"Let me get out of the junk belt," Dana said. "I don't know when I'm going to have to pull a high G maneuver until we're beyond geosynch."

"Roger," Thermal said.

"And do you really want a bunch of space junkies loose in the cargo bay?" Dana asked.

"Better than squirming in their seats the whole trip," Hartwell said.

"They probably smuggled screwdrivers onboard," Dana said. "You know they did."

"You really don't like kids, do you?" Thermal said.

"I like them just fine," Dana said. "Preferably poached, but grilled is pretty good, too."

"We're going to be in this war for a long time the way things are going," Thermal said. "Where are we going to get the next generation of intrepid space eagles?"

"I wasn't interested in space," Dana said, sighing slightly as the last geosynchronous satellite was behind her. "I'm here to protect and defend the planet, just like it says in the commercials. And given Johannsen's, I figure we're going to have all the volunteers we need."

Earth's cities had been repeatedly hammered by orbital strikes to the point that of the "top one hundred" cities from before the war, only five were unscathed. That didn't even count the deaths from a series of plagues broadcast by the Horvath when Dana was a child.

One critical aspect of the plagues, though, was quickly refilling Earth's population. The Horvath had hidden a subtle genetic change in several of the viruses that were spread. The change had to do with female reproduction, especially in the "blonde" genetic subgroup. Women who were affected, and the spread had been very nearly one hundred percent, were subject to a "heat" cycle similar to male reproductive drive, and pharmaceutical contraceptives were then rendered functionally useless. The Horvath had anticipated their plagues essentially depopulating the planet and wanted to ensure a steady supply of new human slaves.

Friendly Glatun medical AIs and doctors had stopped the plague from killing most of humanity, but since most of the world's population was infected by the orbitally distributed plagues, they were left with the problem of what was called "Johannsen's Syndrome." The only way to fix the global issue was a reverse plague. But not only were the ethical considerations against infecting people without their consent, to stop the Horvath plagues they'd immunized most of humanity with advanced nanobots that stopped virtually any biological or nannite in its tracks. To undo the damage required multiple medical visits and advanced technology that, at that point, was fairly rare.

This left virtually every woman on the planet with so much as a trace of blonde gene as a baby factory. The first year after the plague, Germany had one birth for every reproductive aged female. Scandinavia at one point hit an average birth rate of 9.1, meaning that if the rate continued, the average Scandinavian—Dane, Swedish and Norwegian—woman would bear nine children in her life. The teen pregnancy rate got completely out of control for about five years before education and cultural effects started to get a handle on the new reality.

It was all very well to say "be fruitful and multiply." Johannsen's made the situation simply insane.

Most of those children from the first "baby explosion" were still below military age. The kids she was transporting were a good example. But between the damage to infrastructure on Earth, requiring nearly complete reindustrialization, and the critical need for Navy and Marine personnel, many of them were going to end up living, and fighting, in the reaches of space. Most industry, for that matter, was moving to orbital. Not only were there fewer environmental issues, it was simply easier with modern technology.

If these kids wanted to work in space when they grew up, the jobs were going to be there.

"We're out of orbit," Dana said. "You can let them undog if you want. But you'd better keep an eye on them or they'll have the hatch open to see if space is really vacuum."

"I've a better idea, Coxswain," Thermal said. "Since you're engineering rated and I am cox rated and this is a milk run, why don't you go forward and give them a class on maintenance of a *Myrmidon* shuttle. Start with the Sector Seven grav plates."

"You have got to be kidding me," Dana said. "That sounds like a job for the engineer."

"Sounds like a job for the junior PO, to me," Thermal said, grinning. "Seriously, Coxswain's Mate. Time to man up. Or woman up in your case."

"I hate kids," Dana said.

"I can make it an order if you want," Thermal said. "Take the tool bag."

"You are a vicious and cruel human, you know that, Thermal," Dana said, getting out of her chair and pulling the shuttle's toolbag out of its compartment. Mounted over the compartment was a racked crowbar. "I ought to put this crowbar to good work on your skull."

"Now, now," Thermal said. "*You* know the significance of the crowbar. Let it not be used for lesser purposes."

"Athena warned of debris up ahead," Dana said, temporizing.

"I heard," Thermal said. "I can fly this thing nearly as well as you can. Out! Away to your mission, Comet."

"Bastard," Dana muttered, undogging the hatch.

She was immediately assaulted by the sound of children. They weren't screaming so much as having to talk very loudly to be heard over the kids who were talking very loudly to be heard over—

"AT *EASE*!" Dana bellowed. "That means quiet *down*!"

"Coxswain's Mate?" one of the PAO officers said. He was a lieutenant, which meant Dana was seriously outranked. On the other hand, this was *her* shuttle.

"I'm going to conduct a class on *Myrmidon* maintenance, sir,"
Dana said, sliding around to the aisle. The *Myrmidon*, with all its
seats installed, didn't have much room to maneuver. "Since these
kids are into space and all that. It'll keep them from trying to
take it apart to see how it ticks."

"I *know* how it ticks," one of the boys said. "I made a complete
scale model of a *Myrmidon* last year, every part."

"Every part?" Dana asked. "Even the components of the Sector
Seven grav module?"

"No," the kid said. "I had to do that as one module. It was too
small to do all the components."

"Not in here," Dana said, hefting the heavy toolbag into his
lap. "So out of your seat. It's time to do some PMCS. And *you*
get to start. Where's the Sector Seven module?"

"Underneath her chair," the kid said, struggling with the twenty-
kilo bag.

"So how are you going to move the chair?" Dana asked.

"Uh . . ."

"Everybody up!" Dana said. "All the chaperones to the rear.
Unless you're *really* interested in space shuttles. It's going to
take at least four of you. Get the number three and four chairs
undogged and moved forward. Do not *touch* the hatch. It's locked
internally but God knows what you little demons could figure out."
She stopped with her hands on her hips looking at the suddenly
quiet group. "I said *get those chairs moved!* Move it! Move it!"

"And . . . fore!" Tyler Vernon called, swinging his golf club.

The club head connected with the ball and sent it out on an
almost straight trajectory towards the circle of red lights set up
a kilometer away in the main bay. The ball went left, a slice, and
lower than he'd expected, and nearly hit one of the gravity drives
on Horn Four.

"Damn."

Rising up from the interior of the six kilometer wide main bay
of the *Troy* were four three-kilometer-long "horns." They tapered
from six hundred meters wide at the base to two hundred meters
at their terminus. The terminus was ringed with grav drives larger
than any ship's.

Their purpose was to rotate the *Troy,* which they could manage at about ten meters per second. Given that they were moving

two trillion tons, that was pretty good. Archimedes, the father of leverage, once remarked that if he had a lever long enough he could move a world.

Tyler was quietly proud that he'd finally proven the old guy right.

They were also a convenient place to hang secondary systems. Horn Four, besides its grav drives and the massive matter conversion plants necessary to drive them, was home to four "small" one-hundred-meter fabbers, primarily used to produce missiles. There were more on Horns Two and Three while Horn One was home to the main ship fabber, Hephaestus.

Since *Troy* was full up on missiles again, all four hundred and fifty thousand in the two completed missile magazines, the fabbers switched to producing laser emitters and power systems, which was building up *Troy*'s onboard laser capability nicely.

"I've *got* to get rid of that slice," Tyler said, taking his next swing.

Golfing in space suits had a venerable history. Alan Shephard, commander of Apollo Fourteen, had hit two golf balls on the Moon. At that time, lifting the mass of his golf club and the two balls had cost nearly sixty thousand dollars.

Tyler's company had figured out how to give a two-trillion-ton asteroid an Orion drive that accelerated the battlestation at .2 G. Lifting his golf clubs wasn't a big deal.

What *was* a big deal was trying to hit the balls in microgravity. Tyler was in a space suit whose boots were grav-locked to the top of the *Starfire*. That meant that he couldn't rotate his body worth a damn. Shephard at least could get a decent rotation going. Tyler was blaming his tendency to slice on that.

Then there was the problem of having golf balls, which weren't going to lose their momentum in the microgravity of the main bay, bouncing around the six-kilometer, somewhat busy sphere. Fortunately, Paris had some pretty darned good tractor beams and wasn't terribly busy at the moment. Paris was also rather happy at his new upgrade to class III AI and more than willing to catch balls. Even if they were occasionally errant.

"If you wouldn't mind holding off on the next one, sir," Paris commed. *"We've got an incoming* Myrmidon *heading for the civilian docking bay."*

"Okay," Tyler said, straightening from teeing up. "It's not like a golf ball's going to hurt a *Myrmidon*, though."

Tyler didn't like being in a suit and didn't like EVA. He'd been in a "low atmosphere" condition one time during an abortive attack by the Horvath back when Earth was just starting to get advanced technology. It was the first attack the U.S. had managed to beat off, due as much to Apollo's Solar Array Pumped Laser as anything. But because he was one of the few people with Galactic implants, which appeared absolutely necessary to fly Earth's first star fighter, he'd ended up sucking vacuum in a half-destroyed fighter.

He also had, over the years, lost all hobbies. Work had absolutely eaten him up for the last decade to the point where he'd barely managed to attend his daughters' weddings. He effectively owned LFD, the parent corporation of Apollo Mining LLC and SAPL, which was a ninety-hour-per-week job.

Once upon a time he'd been a cartoonist. He had been a manager in the software industry. A programmer. He had a family, he golfed and played ultimate frisbee.

He'd had a life.

Combining golfing, which was a hard skill to relearn in the first place, with EVA was a natural. It got him out of his quarters and in the fresh vacuum.

Now if he could just overcome that nasty slice.

"*I suspect the clang as it hit the side would startle the crew, however,*" Paris replied. "*And it's the winners of the naming contest. We don't want them peeing all over the shuttle.*"

"Damned stupid idea, anyway," Tyler muttered. "I'm going to name it what I want to name it."

Part of Apollo's contract with the Navy was that Apollo Mining, LLC—which was the only company in the system with the ability to *make* the *Troy*-class battlestations—reserved the right to name them. What that meant, in real effect, was *Tyler* got to name them. There had been some questions about the names thus far. Both were famous battles where the losing side had won a moral victory.

Few people remembered what city Agamemnon or Achilles came from. Just about anyone recognized the name Troy. By the same token, it took a historian to know any details of the Persian side of the battle of Thermopylae.

"What's the betting pool, anyway?" Tyler asked, resting one arm on his driver as the shuttle passed.

"*Six to one for Alamo, according to New Las Vegas,*" Paris responded. "*Top vote is Iwo Jima.*"

"Iwo Jima?" Tyler said. "That was a victory."

"Not to the Japanese, sir," Paris commed. *"They're voting rather heavily. Also Saipan, Tarawa and Okinawa."*

"Those are classes of Marine assault ships," Tyler said. "If we ever get around to making Marine assault ships. What's next?"

"Constantinople," Paris commed. *"Stalingrad, Changsha, Isandlwana and Clervaux."*

"Changsha?" Tyler asked.

"Battle between the Japanese and Chinese around the time of the Second World War," Paris replied. *"First time the Japanese lost to the Chinese."*

"Might as well call it Guadalcanal," Tyler said. "Midway. El Alemein. Silly people. No sense of history."

"Shuttle is past, sir," Paris commed.

"Right," Tyler replied. "Forrrre . . ."

TWO

---✳---

"So, you have fun?" Thermal asked as Dana lifted her hands from the controls. Entering the docking bay was up to the tractor beams of the *Troy*.

"I don't know if you'd call it *fun*," Dana said. "It was illuminating. I won't say some of the kids knew more about a *Myrmidon* than I do, but they knew a lot for their age. And they were just as bratty as I expected."

"You really don't like kids," Hartwell said. "I'm sort of surprised."

"If I wanted kids I'd have had them a long time ago," Dana said.

"You're only twenty," Hartwell pointed out.

"Most of the girls I went to school with were knocked up by the time they were fifteen," Dana said. "Which is why Nebraska changed back to having a fourteen-year-old minimum age for marriage. I am one of two blondes who managed to make it out of high school without a belly full. And you couldn't move around school without running into somebody's kid. Didn't care for them then, don't care for them now."

"Well, you're going to have to put up with them for a couple of hours," Thermal pointed out. "We're part of the show."

"I can gargle helium for a couple of hours," Dana said. "Doesn't mean I like it."

"And this is the main viewing area," Dana said, leading the group into Bay Nineteen.

The first and most important evolution had been getting all the kids rotated to the head. After that they'd been shepherded, with much need for sheep dogs, through Xanadu, the *Troy*'s sixty-acre

13

water park, the flight caverns that were technically the "air mixing compartment," a snack in the main civilian cafeteria and now into Bay Nineteen for a view of the main bay.

"Whoa…" was the general response.

Bay Nineteen was a recreational area often used for parties. It was in the "innermost" ring of compartments before you got to the main bay. "Outward" was towards the surface of the *Troy*. Fifteen meters high, twenty deep and fifty meters across at the inner bulkhead. That bulkhead was, deck to overhead, optical sapphire so it looked as if there was nothing between the bay and vacuum.

Dana didn't care much for Bay Nineteen. She really liked to have more than a thin sheet of sapphire between her and vacuum. She was fine in EVA but stuff like this made her nervous.

Most of the kids didn't seem to mind that. They rushed across the darkened room, weaving between tables and ignoring the pleas, threats and orders of their adult chaperones, to press their noses against the sapphire.

"Don't worry," Thermal said. "They can't break it."

"It looks like glass!" one of the mothers said.

"It's not," the PAO lieutenant said. "It's optical sapphire. They couldn't break it if they hit with a table. An adult couldn't break it if they hit it with a table."

It probably would have helped if he didn't sound so nervous himself.

"Those are the control horns," Donny said.

"I know that, dummy," one of the girls snapped. "We all know that."

"Look, there's a *Constitution* going into the parasite bay!"

"What's that *Aggressor* doing?"

The six-hundred-meter battleship had been captured from the Rangora and only recently brought into Terran service after the battle damage was repaired. The captured ship docks and supply ships, which carried parts for the *Aggressors*, had been very useful.

"It's docked," Hartwell said, coming up behind the group of kids. "They don't fit in the current parasite bays. We're having to dock them to the control horns for the time being. The new bay in Sector West is going to be refitted to hold four of them."

The *Troy* was so big it had its own task force of "parasite" ships. The *Constitution*-class cruisers were two hundred meters long and seventy across. The parasite bay in Zone Two, which also held the 142nd Boat Wing, held six of the cruisers along with twelve *Independence*-class frigates. The ships stayed in the hull during major battles and were fired out through launch tubes to do clean-up.

"Is that Granadica?" one of the girls asked, pointing to a large cylinder attached to one of the horns.

"Hephaestus, dummy," Donny said. "Granadica is in the Wolf system. Engineer Mate Hartwell, do you know when they're going to move Vulcan to the *Thermopylae*?"

"As soon as they finish the next ship fabber," Thermal said. "Or that's the plan. What you learn around the *Troy* is that plans tend to change. We only found out we were getting the Orion drive about a week before they started installing it."

"They're not going to use it while we're here, are they?" one of the chaperones asked nervously. "I don't think I want to be around nuclear explosions."

"You won't be," Hartwell said, chuckling. "You only sort of notice it by the acceleration. Feels like you're being pressed sideways, usually. And I don't think there's a fire planned any time soon."

"What if the Rangora attack?" another of the mothers asked.

"Then you're in the safest spot in the system," Hartwell said reassuringly. "I'd much rather be on *Troy* than on the ground."

The Galactics considered bombardment of the civilian populace by kinetic energy weapons—similar to nuclear bombardment sans fallout—as a perfectly legitimate tactic of war. Which was why most of Earth's cities were gutted. The last attack had been the first in which the enemy *didn't* bombard Earth. Probably because they were getting slaughtered by the *Troy* and *Thermopylae*.

The last attack had been led by six assault vectors, ten-kilometer-long, one kilometer in diameter ships specialized for taking gate defenses.

The main defense of the solar system, until recently, had been SAPL. SAPL was a powerful solar pumped light beam, made up of thousands of mirrors that captured and reconcentrated sunlight into a mining tool and, in a pinch, weapon. Before it developed its own laser system, *Troy* had been, essentially, the final focus and aiming system for SAPL. Together with its massive store of missiles it had shredded the first two attacks through the gate after it came online.

By the time of the last attack, *Troy* had developed its own internal laser system composed of dozens of separate emitters that were combined into one very powerful laser—not as powerful as SAPL, which had climbed past one hundred and fifty *peta*watts of power, but powerful enough when thousands of penetrator missiles crushed the AVs' shields.

The first squadron of three assault vectors had done some serious damage to *Troy* and *Thermopylae*. But they apparently thought that the *Thermopylae* wasn't online yet. And that the *Troy* didn't have its own lasers.

With *Thermopylae* firing SAPL and *Troy* hammering them with missiles, the AVs, which had taken down dozens of star systems in the Rangora's recent war with the Glatun, were turned into so much scrap.

The second three had the unfortunate luck to be coming through the gate while *Troy* was maneuvering past it. They came out at a relatively high velocity and the *Troy* was right in front of them.

The AVs were, for ships, massive. The *Troy* outmassed them by several orders of magnitude. What had been left of the most powerful assault ships in the local arm could barely be picked up as scrap. Tugs with powerful tractor beams were still sweeping up the megatons of debris. The main damage to *Troy* was three very noticeable impact craters. They were currently being repaired.

Neither group had been concentrated on bombing Earth.

"I'm surprised you're not protecting the diplomats in Erid..." one of the mothers said. "Eradeen..."

"Eridani," Dana said. "Epsilon Eridani, the fifth star in the Eridani constellation. And the Rangora made it a requirement of the negotiations that the *Troy* or *Thermopylae* could *not* be present."

"We shouldn't have agreed," the mother said. "Let them see what they're up against."

"We'd rather they not be absolutely sure," the public affairs lieutenant said, smoothly. "Better that they overestimate us."

"That'll be the day," Dana said.

"Is that guy golfing?" one of the kids asked.

Dana looked where he was pointing and saw the distant figure on top of a shuttle. He certainly appeared to be golfing, although at the moment he was just standing on top of the shuttle.

"That's Tyler Vernon," Thermal said. "You see him around. That's his shuttle, the *Starfire*. And, yes, he appears to be golfing."

"Isn't that dangerous?" one of the girls asked. "I mean, an object at rest remains at rest, an object in motion remains in motion. If he hits a golf ball, it's going to keep bouncing around until it breaks something or hurts someone."

"The one thing you learn working on the *Troy*," Dana said, "is that Tyler Vernon does whatever he wants to do."

"This is the sort of reason I get paid the big bucks," Tyler said over the com. "It doesn't mean I enjoy it. So I'd appreciate it if you two overpaid clerks would kindly decide once and for all what SAPL should cost internally and be *done* with it."

Tyler was video conferencing while golfing. It was simple enough. Emitters in his helmet projected on the interior in such a way as the two executives, the CFOs of SAPLCorp and Apollo Mining, appeared to be sitting about six feet away. Which, if they were physically present, would put them in vacuum. And that was becoming a more and more desirable outcome.

"Conditions change, sir." Rebecca Mizell was the chief finance officer of SAPL. But while she was attractive for her age, Tyler didn't have to worry about being affected by his innate tendency to defer to pretty women. He'd hired her because she was a revolving bitch. That was often a useful quality in a CFO whose usual job was telling people "no."

"Our associated costs have been going up and up," Mizell continued. "Maintenance, especially on the older VLA and BDA mirrors, is becoming a major issue."

"Then *replace* them," Gregory Vance, CFO of Apollo, snapped.

"That reduces the overall power of SAPL," Mizell said. "Which we're constrained not to do now that we have AIs capable of handling the additional complexity."

"So we're the ones that have to make all the money," Vance said. "And you get to spend it? There's something wrong there."

"That is, however, the nature of the beast," Tyler said, bending over to tee up again. "There are no other customers for SAPL with the exception of the occasional military use as a weapon. Which you'll understand we don't charge for."

"I was going to raise that issue, sir . . ."

"And I'm going to slam dunk it," Tyler said, swinging with a grunt.

"Are you well, sir?" Vance asked.

The CFOs couldn't see Tyler's current position. They were getting a video facsimile.

"I'm doing some EVA work," Tyler said. Which was partially true. Certainly EVA, if not work. Although this meeting *was* work, so . . . "We're not going to charge the military for defending the system. What we *will* charge them for is reasonable costs on producing these things. What we're also not going to do is backdoor the costs by increasing SAPL costs to pay for that occasional defense. Which is what it looks as if you're doing, Miz Mizell."

"Our corporation is looking at a very poor third quarter," Mizell pointed out. "Among other things, we again took damage to the SAPL during the battle. The requested increase is, in part, due to that battle damage."

"Every corporation on *Earth* is looking at a bad third quarter," Vance said. "We have a bad quarter every time there's an attack. Consumer confidence goes down even when we, thankfully in this case, *don't* lose millions of customers. One down quarter does not give you license to beggar Apollo!"

"Define beggar," Tyler said, whacking another ball. "Damnit."

"Sir?" Vance asked.

"Define beggar," Tyler said. "What's the percentage of costs to Apollo of SAPL?"

"SAPL absorbs ten percent of our monthly payments," Vance said. "Ten *percent.*"

"Which barely keeps us running," Mizell said. "Among other things, we now have SAPL power in excess of your needs. Sir, if we could just—"

"We're not going to stop making mirrors unless it's really beggaring us," Tyler said. "And I decide the definition of beggar. I'm shooting for an exawatt. At which point, *nobody*, not even a *Troy* class, can come through the gate without saying 'please.' What we need is additional customers," Tyler continued, teeing up. "For SAPL that is."

"That's not m—" Mizell started to say and then checked herself. She knew one of the axioms of working for Vernon was his saying: If you say it's not your job it won't be. "I'm not sure who besides Apollo would *use* SAPL."

"Ah, better," Tyler said as the ball went through the circle. "Argus, bring in David Skiles, please."

"Mr. Skiles is in a meeting," the AI replied.

Argus had been the main AI for SAPL until a year before when it had suffered the AI equivalent of a nervous breakdown. Running SAPL was a finicky task but there were points at which "finicky" became "obsessive" followed by "paranoid" and "psychotic."

Argus had, fortunately, been removed from responsibility for SAPL at the "paranoid" stage. It now handled LFD's business affairs. Which meant it had to deal with people. Since people were inherently chaotic, it couldn't get too obsessive and do its job. The therapy seemed to be working.

It still wasn't getting close to SAPL control any time soon.

"I'm his boss," Tyler said, placing another ball. "Break in."

"Technically, as Chairman of the Board . . ."

Apparently not working quite well enough.

"Argus, I *will* pull your core again," Tyler said.

"Breaking in now."

"You rang?"

David Skiles had been the CEO of SAPL for three years now. A former Army general, he knew approximately nothing about lasers when he was hired. What he *did* know was running big operations. And while SAPL was simple at one level, it was a *very* big operation.

"David, Mizell says you guys are going broke," Tyler said.

"That's not quite—"

"We're not going broke, sir," Skiles said. "What's happening is that we're exceeding Apollo's needs, thus Apollo is no longer paying for all of our output. That means our cash flow to operations ratio is dropping sharply coupled with some maintenance costs that are starting to creep in more and more. That means that to maintain profitability, we need to either a) stop producing more mirrors, b) increase costs to Apollo, c) find customers for the additional power, or d) find some other source of funding. Right now, we want to increase the passed-on costs to Apollo. That's the simplest short-term solution. At some point we either need to find major new uses for SAPL or stop building mirrors. The really serious maintenance needs are just starting to hit. Since you don't want any of the VLA taken offline . . ."

"I suspect I should just be talking to the CEOs," Tyler said, taking another swing. He was getting tired, which just meant he really need to work on his game. "But I'll take a swing at it. Vance, what's the possibility of increasing Apollo's work in the system?"

"We're reaching a point of market saturation, sir," Vance said.

"We're supplying something like sixty percent of the system's raw material needs. In orbitals we can supply at a lower cost than anyone else and we more or less have a lock on that market. But that market continues to be almost entirely military based and although everyone wants the system defended, there's only so much money there. We even supply a good bit of groundside raw materials but that means dropping it into the well, which has fuel penalty costs associated."

"Didn't we look at just...you know...dropping it?" Tyler asked.

"Controlled hard reentry has been looked at and discarded, sir," Vance said. "There are functional issues with it as well as marketing."

"People don't like rocks dropping out of the sky for some reason," Skiles said. "Sir, we really need to stop making mirrors. Just a pause while more orbital infrastructure gets built. Probably two years and then we'll get back in the game."

"How long at current rate until you guys go into reverse cash flow?" Tyler asked.

"By FY 27 Q2," Skiles said. "At that point, given our projection of Apollo's needs, rising maintenance costs and mirror production costs we'll be in the red. We'll be bankrupt about FY 28 Q1."

"Well, we don't want that," Tyler said, walking carefully to the side of the shuttle. "I'd have to buy my own company. You're asking for an increase to...two dollars a terawatt?"

"That would nearly double our costs," Vance snapped.

"I can do basic math, Vance," Tyler said mildly. He let the club hang in mid-space and reached down to grab the ladder. "What's that do for you, David?"

"It will put off the red for two more years," Skiles said. "But we'll eventually be back to this point. And that's assuming no unexpected maintenance costs."

"New customers," Tyler said, grabbing his club and making his way to the hatch. "SAPL and Apollo."

"We're looking at new customers," Skiles said. "But there's not much need for an orbital laser except, well, in orbit."

"Do you even have a sales force?" Tyler asked. Getting through an air lock carrying a driver was a pain in the butt.

"Not as such," Skiles said. "No. But Apollo is about it for orbital manufacturing and mining. Nobody else wants to invest, given that most of the stuff is considered a target."

"There's got to be something," Tyler said, cycling the air lock and stepping into the luxurious interior of the Starfire. "Ground-side mining? I saw where Georgia... Georgia! Was making a dug-in state disaster center. Did we bid on digging it for them?"

"That would be Apollo, sir," Skiles pointed out. "They have the mining experience. Even if we did it, we'd need tugs, which are Apollo's, and mining mirrors, Apollo's, and experts. Apollo. Given groundside environmental regulations, Apollo might need an entire new division."

"Vance?"

"We haven't looked at it that I'm aware," the CFO said. "But I'm not in sales. That's not saying it's not my job—"

"Just outside your knowledge base," Tyler said. "David, I want more customers for SAPL or more work for Apollo to continue to pay for SAPL. Get with Mark and figure that out. I'm hearing a lot of thinking inside the box. We didn't get to this point by thinking inside the box. I want groundside projects. I want Apollo looking at value-added materials. There's all these kids running around. Apollo toy division?"

"Toys are normally, well, plastic," Mizell said.

"Used to be metal," Tyler said, sitting down still in his suit. He started to strip off his gloves. "Went to plastic 'cause it's cheaper. The way we make metal, that might have turned around, who knows?

"We're going to have to be boosting a lot of stuff out of the well to support the Fleet. If we're being paid for that, we can drop stuff down into the well at virtually no cost. But just bringing down metal makes no sense. Chairs? Tables? Buildings? What does Earth *need*? I saw an article in the *WSJ* talking about the lack of civilian materials. 'The *Affluence* Problem' or something. We lost a bunch of material in the cities and we haven't been producing any. Cost of new home and business furnishings have nearly tripled compared to pre-war. That's a market Apollo needs to look at.

"And, yeah, Vance, before you scream, it's on Apollo. I want you to look at giving them a hand, David. Do we need a new division? Think outside the box, people. When this war is over, we're going to need to be poised to go into civilian manufacture. Companies throughout history have screwed that up. Apollo and SAPL aren't going to. Speaking of SAPL, though.

"The main reason I want to up the power continuously, just keep making mirrors until the sun is starting to look like a Dyson sphere, is defense. We need to be talking that up and seeing if we can shake the government tree for direct contributions. Okay, we're beyond what we need for purely commercial reasons. Fine. Let's see if the government will cough up some money to keep building and maintaining it. God knows they've used it enough. Wolf, how's the Wolf SAPL coming?"

"Nominal," David answered after a moment. "We're continuing to about double power levels every year. And the newer designs should be less maintenance intensive than the early ones."

"We were making it up as we went along," Tyler said. "Staff cuts? I know I just said 'build a new division' but do we really need all the people we've got? My experience is that when you first go into something, you throw people at it. Then as you get more efficient you can lose some. Maybe we move them into the new division?"

"I think we've been through that period, already," Skiles answered. "I don't have any moral issue with cutting people but with the increases you're asking for in power it's more like hiring. That's part of the cost."

"Is Starbucks still in business?" Tyler asked. He desperately wanted to get out of his suit but it would be hard to segue while still on the phone.

"Yes?" Vance answered.

"They're big on environmental stuff," Tyler said. "And knowing them, they're still building outlets. How about 'all orbital' espresso makers?"

"We'd need fabber runs," Skiles pointed out. "Which are being pretty much consumed by the military."

"Figure it out," Tyler said. "We can free up fabber runs if we sweet talk the right admirals. People need . . . stuff even in a war. Get with Wal-Mart. Get some civilian production going. Shake the government money tree since we're beyond commercial use for the time being. Be honest about it and don't get greedy, Mizell. We're just asking for money to do upkeep and production past commercial needs. When commercial needs catch up, we drop the amount we need from the government. Apollo and LFD both have lobbyists on payroll. Use 'em. I'm done here. I've got another meeting."

"Yes, sir," Skiles said.

"Outside the box!"

"Hey, kids!" Tyler said, entering Bay Nineteen.

The view had apparently not palled despite the fact that he was late. Most of the kids were glued to the sapphire, pointing to all the activity that was going on in the main bay. They more or less ignored him.

"Uh...Mr. Vernon?" a lieutenant said. He'd been standing near the door watching the controlled mayhem.

"The same," Tyler said, looking around the room. There were two Navy officers, the L-T and an ensign, in blues and a couple of pilots in flight suits. Make that a coxswain and an engineering mate from the tabs. Those two were answering most of the kids' questions. The cox, who was female, looked like she was getting a little ragged. Come to think of it, he vaguely recognized her but he couldn't place where.

"I didn't know you were planning on visiting, sir," the lieutenant said. "We were getting ready to wrap this up..."

"I know your schedule," Tyler said. "I'm glad I'm not too late. I'll need to interrupt it a bit since I am. Paris, lights up, please. Slowly. If I could have your attention!"

THREE

Dana turned away from the latest question as the lights came up in the compartment and was surprised to see Tyler Vernon standing by the bay doors.

"Shhh..." she said, holding up her hand and pointing to the rear. "I think you want to see this instead."

She and the chaperones got the kids pointed in more or less the right direction after a moment.

"Hi, kids," Mr. Vernon said. "My name's Tyler Vernon. Let me just welcome you to the *Troy*. I'm sure other people have but... Anyway, this thing is pretty cool, huh?"

There was a polite murmur of agreement. Some of the kids were dumbstruck while others clearly weren't sure who Vernon was. Or didn't believe that the richest man in the system was talking to them.

"Come on over closer so I don't have to shout," Vernon said, waving for them to approach. "I was the guy who okayed you kids coming up here. There's a bunch of reasons for that. I don't know if you know how you were chosen, but it was on a bunch of matrixes. When they pitched this idea to have a naming contest for Station Three I wasn't too keen. Bottom-line is I name the stations."

"Why?" Donny asked. Of course. "I mean, why *you*?"

"I came up with the idea," Tyler said, grinning. "Maybe cause I'm short so I think *big*. I came up with the idea a long time before anybody thinks, long time before you kids were born. Before that coxswain there or these officers were born. I was thinking about these when I built my first mirror, when I realized

25

I *could* build my own mirror on maple syrup money. You think that counts for something?"

"Sure..." Donny said, nodding.

"Most of my life is history at this point," Tyler said, walking over to the sapphire through the cluster of children. "And when I say history, I mean the kind that kids like you study already and will be studying as long as humanity holds onto life. The Maple Syrup War is just history to you kids. I lived it, every damned day."

He paused and placed his hand on the sapphire, staring out at the main bay as if he'd forgotten the children behind him.

"The Maple Syrup War, the Horvath attacks, the Johannsen's viruses... That's all history to you kids and so it should be. You're looking at the future. This is the future you kids are going to inherit and grow. Two million kids suggested names. About half that actually wrote essays. Half were more or less illegible so we're down to five hundred thousand. There was room for thirty. The top thirty name choices, including the *actual* choice, were picked out. Then a group of people went over the essays looking for the best ones. You thirty were out of about three hundred thousand kids. I won't say they were the best on any historical or artistic scale," Vernon said, turning back around. "But they were pretty good. I read the last thousand. What I was looking for was something the rest weren't. I used to be a cartoonist. That's a lot of writing, believe it or not. I was looking for... heart? I was looking for passion. I was looking for kids who weren't doing the well-written essay as an exercise but really *wanted* to go into space."

He looked around at them and you could have heard a bacteria drop in the room.

"I wanted to see the kids who were going to inherit this in heart and soul and mind," Vernon said, gesturing out into the main bay. "At least that had a chance. We're not going to be at war forever. I hope that her generation," he said, gesturing at Dana with his chin, "will make it safe for *you* kids to grow up without fearing missiles from the sky. And if they manage it, you should be eternally grateful. That will make it possible for us to *really* get started on space.

"There are two terraformable worlds we've found so far. There are more systems beyond that we can't even explore with the war going on. Space isn't just the final frontier, it's a frontier that keeps on expanding. I'm old. I mean, I know you think thirty is old. That your moms are old," he said, smiling at the chaperones to defray the potential insult.

"That's how kids think. But I'm *old*, kids. I may not live to see the end of this war. You will. You're the torch bearers. You're the people who are going to grow up and carry us to the stars. That was what I was looking for. The kids who were going to carry that torch. Not just the best argument for Isandlwana."

"Did Isandlwana win?" one of the kids asked. Dana had noticed he had an accent. She realized he was probably a South African.

"Nope," Vernon said. "Not this round. But the other reason I wanted you here was to be the first to learn the name of the new battlestation. What was the historical significance of the battle of Thermopylae?"

A dozen hands went up and Vernon smiled.

"You," he said, pointing to one of the girls.

"Darn," Donny said.

"Thermopylae was one of the three critical battles in the history of the wars between Greece and Persia," the girl said as if quoting. "Despite being a defeat, it slowed the armies of Xerxes long enough for the Greeks to come to a union so that they had sufficient forces to defeat the Persians at Palatia. The heroic action of the Spartans at Thermopylae encouraged the Athenians, especially, to enter into a binding alliance with their traditional enemy, Sparta."

"But what did the wars between Greece and Persia mean?" Vernon asked.

"Oooh! Ooo!" Donny shouted, waving his hand.

"I'll get to you, chap," Vernon said, pointing to the South African kid.

"The Greeks were fighting for freedom," the child answered. "The Persians were slaves."

"The Greeks kept plenty of slaves," Vernon said. "But that is the essential point. At Salamis, another of those critical battles," he said, nodding at the girl who had answered earlier, "the Greeks painted their ships with names like 'Citizen,' 'Freedom,' 'Democracy.' Even the Spartans, despite a rigid lifestyle that subsumed their identity to the state, were freer than any Persian. The Greeks, for all their problems and weaknesses, were the cornerstone of the concept of freedom and liberty which infuses Western culture. There are many reasons that the West was so successful and even now leads the Alliance to defend the solar system.

"But a great reason lay in those battles. Those battles shaped the concepts that led to these that we now engage upon. There was no *reason* to fight the Horvath, you understand that? There was no economic reason for the Maple Syrup War. I was going to get paid for my maple syrup one way or another. And by fighting we placed the whole world in jeopardy. Which, believe me, did not make us very popular people at the time. The only reason that I fought, the only reason that many many other people fought, including my late friend Jason Haselbauer, was because we *believed* in the cause of freedom. Does that give you a hint?"

"Changsha's out, then?" an Asian child said.

"I hadn't even heard of Changsha until I read the essays," Vernon said. "And I read so many, Paris just recently had to remind me what it was."

"Alamo," a girl piped up.

"Tough one," Tyler said. "Frankly...sorry, I didn't think it was important enough."

"It was the most important battle in creating the Republic of Texas!" the girl argued. "It's...It's...It's the *Alamo*!"

"Stealing land from its rightful owners," one of the children said. "Tenochtitlan!"

"We're talking about freedom and democracy and you're arguing for the defeat of a heart-ripping-out theocracy?"

"By a Christian theocracy that was *just as* barbaric?"

"Whoa!" Vernon said, raising his hands. "And another reason to avoid certain choices. Iwo Jima?"

"Here!" a Japanese girl said, bouncing up and down.

"A famous victory," Donny said dismissively.

"The defense of Mount Suribachi is one of the most hard-held defenses of all time!" the girl argued.

"Hiding in caves," Donny said. "Very heroic. Try charging through black sand that sucks you down to your waist!"

"Again," Vernon said, raising his hands and chuckling. "One that is a potential source of argument."

"Jerusalem!"

"Which one?" a girl in a headscarf asked. "In defense of Palestine? Holding off the Crusaders?"

"You probably won't like the choice," Vernon said, grinning. "But I'm really glad you kids know your history. Maybe you can avoid repeating it."

"You went for Istanbul," the girl said, pouting. "Sorry, *Constantinople.*"

"Nope," Vernon said. "But getting closer. Sorry, just my opinion, but the advance of Islam can be looked at as the same advance as was fought by the Spartans at Thermopylae. The imposition of control of thought from the East, if you will. Islam brought with it that essential mindset that all men are slaves to a higher power. To the Persians it was Xerxes and Darius as god-kings. Islam simply substituted Allah and kept the same thought process. Again, you may not agree, but it's my battlestation. Okay, that's the final clue. Any takers?" He looked at Donny. "Come on, kid. You had all the answers."

"Vienna?" Donny answered. "Uh ... Tyre? Uh ... *Lepanto!*"

"Thought seriously about Lepanto," Vernon said, nodding. "But I just couldn't come up with a good symbol. Another clue."

He looked around at the group and after a moment a girl who had mostly been reading a book reader raised her hand.

"Go," Vernon said.

"Malta?"

"The Knights of Malta were a religious order that had been formed as the defenders of Jerusalem during the Crusades," Vernon said. "When Jerusalem was lost they relocated to Rhodes. There they were attacked, again, by the Ottomans. They put up such a strong defense that the Ottoman caliph allowed them to withdraw. They relocated to Malta and used it to harass Muslim shipping and keep the Muslims from establishing full control over the Mediterranean.

"In 1565 the knights, which numbered between seven hundred and a thousand according to which count you use, and men-at-arms numbering about eight thousand, were attacked by thirty-six thousand blooded Ottoman troops. Every time the Western forces had been attacked by the Muslims in the previous two centuries they eventually lost. It was assumed that Malta would be lost as well. I'll let you read up on the defense. It was wily, bloody and hard-held as anything in history. But in the end, they won. And by winning they blunted the Ottoman advance in the Mediterranean and set up the conditions that led to the victory at ..."

he nodded at Donny, "Lepanto. Venice could have never become the power it eventually became without the victory at Malta. And what is the difference between Malta and, say, Thermopylae?"

He looked around at the group then pointed to the girl with the book reader.

"Come on, I know *you* know it."

"It was a victory for the West," the girl answered. "Troy and Thermopylae were defeats."

"I had no clue if *Troy* and *Thermopylae* would work when I created them," Vernon said. "If the Rangora had sent through AVs before we had *Therm* or more AVs on the last attack...it would have been a near run thing. The best I was honestly hoping for was such an epic defeat that...well, that humans would be as hard to govern by force as they ever are. That in time we might rise to freedom again."

He hung his head for a moment, then raised it to look the children in the eye.

"But no more. With all the power we're producing from SAPL, with the missiles we're building up, with the laser power of *Troy* on its own, let them come. Let them send their assault vectors. Let them send their *own* battle globes. We will crush them all. With three such citadels, humanity *cannot* be defeated. We may be harried. We may be hurt. But We. Shall. Not. Fail. We shall stand shoulder to shoulder as the Knights of Malta stood. And no force in the *galaxy* will take our *freedom*. Paris?"

"Viewscreen coming up, sir," the AI said.

The lights in the main bay dimmed and a projection on the sapphire showed what looked very much like a ball bearing against the starry firmament.

"Usually we wait on this sort of thing," Vernon said. "But since you're here. Paris, could you please make sure we're ready?"

"We've been ready, sir," the AI said with some reproach.

"Very well," Tyler said. "Kids, I'm going to count to three. Then you know what to say. One...two...THREE!"

"MALTA!" the group chorused.

SAPL could cut through the entire kilometer and a half wall of a battlestation in less than a minute. Before the last echo rang, a Maltese cross five kilometers wide had been carved on the side of the battlestation.

"This is the turning point," Vernon said. "And when you are my age you can say to your children: I was there when *Malta* came online and Earth was finally *safe*. This is your future. *Malta* affords you a destiny, liberty, freedom, just as the battle after which it is named. That is the gift this generation, by its sacrifices, gives to yours. Use it wisely."

"Permission to speak, sir?" Dana said.

Mr. Vernon had set the sapphire wall to touch screen and the kids were now happily playing with dozens of views ranging from SAPL mirrors to views of the ongoing projects in the Wolf system.

"I'm not an admiral, Coxswain," Vernon said, grinning. "And it took me a bit to recognize you, but you're nearly as famous as I am. You're Comet Parker, right? Haven't we met...?"

"Briefly, sir," Dana said, wincing. "Once."

"Go ahead and ask your question, Coxswain," Vernon said, clearly picking up on her discomfort with the nickname.

"That was...some speech," Dana said. "Do you always talk to children that way?"

"You'd be surprised," Vernon said. "I tried to never talk down to my kids when they were growing up. Treat them as adult as you can and they learn to be treated like adults. It kind of pisses them off when teachers and such don't, but kids adjust remarkably well. And this was a very bright group by definition."

"It was rather...strong," one of the chaperones said.

A group had slowly formed around Vernon, which Dana found to be no surprise. She'd picked up that at least two of the chaperones were divorced. And even though neither one, in her opinion, had any chance in hell of pinning down the tycoon, the chance to hobnob with the richest human in the galaxy wasn't one to turn down.

"As I said, it's an unusual group," Vernon said, smiling slightly. "I take it one of them is yours?"

"Shirley," the woman said. "The girl who answered the question about Thermopylae."

"And knew the rote answer out of the textbook but not the real significance," Tyler said. "But I liked what she said about the future of space in her essay. I remember it. She's probably got a good career in the sciences. Precise and didactic. I hope her ambition isn't to write fiction, though."

"No," the woman said. "She wants to be a...she calls it an orbital miner."

"Which doesn't have a thing to do with getting your hands dirty," Vernon said. "I've had all these kids tagged in our personnel database. If they want a job, or an internship for that matter, when they get a bit older they'll get some preferential treatment."

"My son's Donny," another woman said. "The one who was practically hopping up and down."

"I feel for you," Vernon said, grinning. "I can tell a 'why, why, why' a mile away."

"That's . . . Donny," the lady said. "And I don't agree that it was too strong. But I was visiting my grandparents in upstate New York when the City was hit."

"I grew up in L.A.," Dana said. "Till I was three, that is."

"Ladies, I'd like to introduce the famous Comet Parker," Vernon said quickly. "I don't think you probably knew your shuttle pilot had been carefully chosen and not just picked out of a hat. Parker is one of the best shuttle pilots in the Navy."

"I'm sorry, I hadn't realized that," the lady who'd first spoken up said. She smiled slightly and nodded her head, clearly unsure what Vernon was referring to.

"Parker?" Donny's mom said. "You were the one that saved that shuttle full of civilians?"

"Yes, ma'am," Dana replied.

"Was that entry as hard as it looked?" the lady asked.

"I don't really remember, ma'am," Dana said, shrugging. "I just have flashes of bad things headed my way. My brain sort of refused to record most of it. Having watched the replay, my professional opinion is that I must have been insane."

"Desperate, surely," Vernon said, chuckling. "Let's see: Attempt the impossible and probably die or assuredly die. Binary solution set, there."

"I suppose some would have gone for a nice clean impact on the surface," Donny's mom said.

"I had three pregnant women and fifty-two other cargo, ma'am," Dana said softly.

"It *was* insane, ma'am," Thermal said. "And I say that as the guy in the forward seat. Also, as Mr. Vernon said, a binary solution set. We were going to die. I'm personally glad she went for it."

"Mr. Vernon," Paris said over the intercom. "You have another appointment."

"Which is sort of my life," Tyler said. "Ladies, you have a

remarkable set of offspring. I hope to see them going out to conquer the universe. We need more kids just like this and you should be proud. While you're on the station, feel free to stop by the mall and get in some shopping. It helps defray the costs," he added with a grin. "And with that I have to go."

"Damn," said the snarky lady as he hurried out. "I was hoping to talk to him more."

"I think that's why the AI called him away," Donny's mom said, smiling thinly.

"I think this is as much time as he's spent with..." Thermal stopped with his mouth open, not sure how to go on.

"Normal people?" Dana said. "What my boss is trying to say while he has his foot in his mouth is that Mr. Vernon spends most of his time alone. And when he meets with people it's people like, oh, the President. If Mr. Vernon has the time. I've never seen him talking with people before and he *lives* here."

"That's..." Donny's mom said. "I was about to say that's sort of sad. But I think it's...sort of unhealthy."

"Howard Hughes is much mentioned, ma'am," Dana said. "But he seems to be pretty functional. I will say that main bay golf is a new one, though."

"That is kind of bizarre," Thermal said.

"I dunno," Dana said. "I haven't held a club in a long time. I think I may find out what sort of permissions you have to get."

"A lot," Paris said. "I don't think I'd field golf balls for even *you*, Comet."

"Be that way, then," Dana said, sticking out her tongue at the overhead. "Seriously, Paris. Within reason. What's his status?"

"That is highly personal," Paris said. "But there is a certain pattern to these things. When persons attain a certain degree of power and control it tends to consume them. Power is not, as is sometimes bandied, corrupting but it is absolutely *consuming*. All of their energy becomes sublimated to their endeavors. However, if they are not essentially unbalanced, and Tyler Vernon is any-thing *but* unbalanced, at a certain point they look around and realize they are past the consuming part of their endeavors. At that point they often reacquaint themselves with...life? Certainly become more sociable. Based upon some recent actions, such as this meeting with the children, he may be entering into that phase. Which, too, can be taken to extremes. The movie industry is somewhat reduced or the next phase could be anticipated to be dating starlets."

"Why do men always go for women with looks over brains?" the snarky lady asked.

"I doubt you would care for the full lecture," Paris said. "Suffice it to say that it is a functional reproductive strategy for economically high value males just as acquiring a economically high value mate is a functional strategy for certain females. The reverse is also true although rather less documented."

"I'm not sure I . . . quite got that . . ." the lady said.

"I have an emergency in bay four," Paris said. "I must take my leave."

"Emergency?" the lady said, looking around. "Is it safe?"

"Very," Dana said, trying not to sigh.

"Ladies," the PAO lieutenant said. "We're already behind on schedule. We'll be having a bite in the food court then some shopping and general visiting time then the ride back."

"L-T, we need to go service the shuttle," Thermal said.

"*Sure* you do," the lieutenant said, soto voce. "But who am I to stand in the way of somebody with a *real* job?"

FOUR

"...that covers our current analysis of the Terran defense system," To'Jopeviq said, nodding at the group of marshalls. "In summary, given Terra's continued expansion of its gate defenses, population size and growth rate, technological level at the time of first contact and philosophical approach to warfighting, our analysis is that absent an assault by a minimum of forty assault vectors, any lesser force would face defeat. And an assault by forty assault vectors would render the majority nonfunctional for any future uses."

Colonel Egilldu To'Jopeviq hadn't wanted this job when he got handed it by the late Star Marshall Lhi'Kasishaj. The then-major had made a name for himself in a now "small" war against the Skree when he was the senior surviving officer of the assault vector *Star Crusher*. He still didn't like it. If he had his choice he'd still be in the assault vector force. But the star marshall was right in one thing. When given a task he did it to the best of his ability.

Twice High Command had ignored his team's recommended force levels for an assault on the Terran system. And in both cases, it had been obvious his team's analysis had been *low*. The Terrans were not only using every trick known to the species in the local arm, they had ideas no one had *imagined*, such as the *Troy* and its new "Orion" drive.

"Forty AVs seems...high," Star Marshall Ucuhath said.

The structure of High Command was deliberately opaque to those outside its circle. That permitted the occasional purge to be less of an issue. Star Marshall Ucuhath's title was "Marshall of Organizational Processes." To'Jopeviq suspected he was more or less the Operations officer. But the colonel wasn't sure.

"The Terran Solar Array Pumped Laser is at over one hundred and fifty petawatts," To'Jopeviq pointed out. "That level of power would cause shield failure in no more than point three seconds. Thus even with rotation, the SAPL alone can render an AV impotent in less than three minutes. The damage would be high enough and occur fast enough that countermaneuvering by bringing ships in and out of the outer formation would be of limited utility. One could envision it being contraindicated since ships which were in the outer formation would often lose navigational control before they could rotate out of the line-of-fire, thus becoming navigational hazards. And that is simply the SAPL. It discounts continued improvements in onboard laser capacity, which has been demonstrated with the *Troy* and is probably continuing with *Thermopylae,* as well as the enormous number of missiles in the system."

"Has your team looked at alternate methods of assault?" High Commander Phi'Pojagit asked. The old Rangora was the one member of the High Command whose position was clear. He was also one of the five members of the Junta that ruled the Rangora.

"One proposed method was to create our own orbital infrastructure in the Eridani system, High Commander," To'Jopeviq replied. "Then produce missile levels similar to those of the *Troy, Thermopylae* and Station Three. By sending in repeated waves of missiles, it is possible it would soften the defenses of the battlestations. The countering argument is that the missiles would be subject to SAPL and countermissile fire during their attack. Also that the *Troy* has shown the ability to move through the gate. Thus any such orbital defenses would have to be resistant to an attack by the *Troy.* That led to a third plan which was to set up such defenses along with production capacity. Then when the *Troy* responded, to hit it with a trap sufficient to render it impotent."

"All interesting plans," the high commander said approvingly.

"All of which we rejected, High Commander," To'Jopeviq said, unhappily. "Since our team has been upgraded in importance we have been given access to certain . . . internal data. Eridani has no in-place orbital systems or population support. It is an essentially dead system. Given current combat needs and production rates, it would take five years to assemble the sort of defenses and production we would need in the Eridani system to effect the plan. If we are still at war with Terra in five years, we estimate they will have *five* battle globes capable of entry into the Eridani system.

"The alternative of placing an AV fleet in the system along with heavy local defenses was also rejected since we could not be sure when the *Troy* would enter. That would hold down a significant portion of the remaining AV fleet. That, of course, is a policy decision but we found it unlikely given the continued battles in the Zhoqaghev system."

"I find it hard to believe that one relatively new race has this sort of combat capability," Grand Marshall Ucuhath said. "I am not disbelieving you, you understand, Colonel, but..."

"Grand Marshall, with respect," To'Jopeviq said. "Every time I look at our models I have moments of disbelief. And then we get empirical proofs that our models tend to be *low*. Now that the Terrans are not blocking their communications system, we have been able to get real-time data. And while normally that could be assumed to be disinformation, like the Glatun, the Terrans permit very wide latitude on information gathering and dissemination.

"Station Three is coming on line as we speak. With *Thermopylae* now upgrading to onboard laser systems and increasing its missile levels, the still unnamed Station Three will be the primary SAPL base. *Troy* continues to upgrade. There was a recent popular entertainment program, what they refer to as 'edutainment' since it was an educational program, about *Troy*'s upgrades. They are now armoring *Troy* and *Thermopylae* with fullerene patches as well as installing planetary class shield generators. *Thermopylae*'s Orion drive is complete. Two more asteroids are in the process of being spun up and inflated and *four* more have been designated as future bases."

"How many of these globes are they going to build?" the high commander asked.

"The answer seems to be 'as many as we can,'" To'Jopeviq said. "The realistic answer is that they will continue to make them as long as they consider themselves to be at war and have the funds and personnel. They are... relatively efficient compared to ships. The great problem of building them is mining out the interior to install facilities. Which, with the continued increases in the SAPL, becomes easier and easier as time goes by."

"Planetary bombardment," Marshall Ucuhath said.

"Of limited utility," To'Jopeviq said. "There have always been arguments for and against. But the humans are increasingly digging in and dispersing their remaining planetary industrial facilities.

The best targets would probably be refineries—which they still use for motor transport power as well as processing petroleum into refined polymers—and power generation systems. Their power grids, however, have increasing redundancy due to previous attacks and the resulting rebuilding issues. There are, literally, hundreds of refineries, and their missile defenses, along with all other defenses, are improving day by day. Cities are decreasing in size as the population aggressively disperses in a chaotic manner. Government is already highly dispersed. Furthermore, as shown by their response to the previous attack, political power transfer is remarkably smooth, analogous to military command structure. And all their orbital manufacture, which is taking an increasing lead in total production, is either located in the battlestations or in the Wolf system, which would require entering the Sol system then retransferring. Tactically that would be... difficult."

"So a heavy AV assault is your team's recommendation?" the high commander said.

"Possibly with a very heavy missile assault as preparatory," To'Jopeviq said. "Produce missiles at multiple facilities, move them into the system in bulk freighters, fire them through the gate then follow up with AVs."

"Could we use fewer AVs doing that?" Marshall Ucuhath asked.

"Depending upon the number of missiles, possibly," To'Jopeviq said. "I would, however, with respect remind this assembly of the central tenet of gate assaults."

"The more you use, the fewer you lose," the Marshall Ucuhath said. "Define 'enough.'"

"Terrans gained access to Glatun military technologies before our justified liberation of the Glatun Federation," To'Jopeviq said cautiously. "They, therefore, use Glatun missiles, which are capable of interception as well as engagement. The *Troy* is now believed to hold nearly half a million such missiles. Depending upon when the engagement is planned, it would be necessary to have... approximately three million to be sure of reducing the battle globes sufficiently. Each year that number will increase by approximately a million."

"We would like your team to examine options other than the use of brute force," the high commander said. "There are... constraints of which even you are not aware. But this has been a very well-developed and thought-out presentation. Our thanks."

"I live to serve, High Commander," To'Jopeviq said. "By your leave."

The high commander nodded at him and, trying to hide his relief, To'Jopeviq slid out of the relatively small room.

As the door dilated behind him he could swear he heard an argument break out.

"We don't *have* forty assault vectors!" Grand Marshall Zissix snarled. "That *idiot* Gi'Bucosof threw them away!"

The exact nature of High Command was somewhat opaque even to High Command. Each of the commanders had their own sphere of influence but they somewhat overlapped. The Junta preferred to keep everyone guessing.

Thus Ucuhath was not in charge of all operations. He was, in fact, primarily involved in logistics preparations while having certain forces that were loyal to him.

The closest to an overall operational director was Zissix. It was a recent elevation. He had replaced Grand Marshall Qu'Zichovuq precisely over the latter's support of Gi'Bucosof.

The former "Grand Marshall of Liberation Forces" had incurred the ire of certain elements of High Command in two ways. The first was that his "success" in the recent war against the Glatun had made him quite a hero to the common Rangora. That had been useful at first, since the war required sacrifice and Rangora needed heroes to motivate them. At a certain point, though, it created a separate political power structure that interfered with the existing one.

Gi'Bucosof had been chosen as the figurehead leader of the war precisely because he was too stupid to survive in upper command. But the power he'd attained had started to give him a feeling of invincibility. There was no such thing in Rangora politics.

Especially in his case because the star marshall had been anything *but* an operations genius. Repeatedly he had ignored orders to bypass systems and had instead thrown insufficient forces against heavily defended systems. The Rangora plan of the war was to pin down the main Glatun forces on one front while Gi'Bucosof swept around to the rear. By stopping to take every little system, some of which were heavily defended, the late star marshall had exceeded projected losses by nearly three hundred percent.

The Rangora had expended enormous treasure secretly building the largest fleet of assault ships ever assembled in history. It had entailed many necessary cutbacks in goods and services as more and more material was poured into the Secret Fleet.

Gi'Bucosof, Qu'Zichovuq's protégé, had ripped that very expensive fleet to shreds.

The last straw had been the attack on Terra. Qu'Zichovuq had insisted that Gi'Bucosof could take the system with seven AVs. Every one had been lost, along with a large fleet of *Aggressor* battleships. Three hundred billion credits worth of ships, months of production, were now either scrap or prizes to the Terrans. Which was why Qu'Zichovuq had "committed suicide" by shooting himself forty times in the back.

"Nor can we quickly create them," Ucuhath said pensively. "Nor three million missiles. Three million! We have the fabbers but there are so many other needs!"

Whereas taking the Glatun Federation *should* have increased the Rangora's monetary and material production base, it had had quite the opposite affect.

The Glatun leadership had intentionally been reducing the functional ability of their people as a way of maintaining power. The vast majority of the populace had a very high standard of living without having to do any work. Teaching them to work again was proving to be a major task.

The Glatun fleet, however, came from a cultural structure so different it might as well have been a different species. The Fleet had become an increasingly family operation with certain families contributing the bulk of the personnel and, especially, the leadership. When they knew they were going to lose, they took a scorched system approach, with or without orders. They didn't destroy planetary cities or purely civilian orbital structures that could not be evacuated. But they had destroyed *everything* else. System after system had been systematically stripped and obliterated. Where once Glatun yards had been the pride of the regional arm, only four fully functional ship-fabbers had been recovered.

The Glatun Federation, once the richest polity in the local arm with the largest manufacturing base known, was now an impoverished series of planets that could barely feed themselves. And rebuilding, even with slave labor, was turning out to be difficult at best.

The Rangora common people were becoming restive. They had

anticipated that their standard of living would increase enormously with the capture of the Glatun Federation. The Junta wasn't about to tell them that that was going to be impossible for a generation. Riots had broken out over the continued, brutal, working conditions of the common Rangora, reducing productivity even more.

The last problem was that the Federation wasn't fully conquered. There were four systems holding out. All of them were relatively minor border systems, but they had so far proven impossible to crack. Like the Terran system they had relatively high levels of resources, they were all systems that were mining systems with large asteroid belts, and they had high populations on which to draw workers and fighters. High Command had previously sat through analyses of those systems and one point made was that those systems were "working" systems where there were high concentrations of Glatun who retained a work ethic and a patriotism that, in the inner Glatun systems, was considered provincial.

A war that had appeared to be a swift and thorough victory was now turning into a slogging match of attrition. And assault always has higher attrition.

"There is more than one way to skin a xaw," the high commander said. "I will recommend to the Junta that we make peace with the Terrans. There will be a better day to correct their impression of power."

"They are demanding that we withdraw from the Glatun Federation, High Commander," Ucuhath pointed out.

"Which is a negotiating ploy," the high commander said. "We will sign a binding pact of nonaggression but retain the Eridani system. In time, we will deal with them."

"And the Horvath?" Zissix said.

"Let them have the Horvath," Ucuhath said. "Those squids are of little use."

"That will be up to the Junta," the high commander said.

"The Terran Alliance reiterates its position that given the Rangora Empire's actions in this war, including the bombardment of civilian populations and assault without due declaration of intent to engage in hostilities, the minimum Terra will accept in negotiated terms of settlement is withdrawal from the territory of our allies the Glatun Federation, return to positions prior to the agreements made during the recent Multilateral Talks, the acceptance of Terran sovereignty over the Eridani and Horvath systems and a payment of six hundred billion credits in negotiable currency or suitable materials to pay for rebuilding of our damaged cities. In exchange, Terra will return all twenty-seven thousand Rangora prisoners as well as repatriation of such remains as have been identified, all cost of transport being born by the Rangora."

Senior Deputy Envoy Piotr "Eklit" Polit had at first been surprised by the universality of negotiation. Negotiating with the Rangora was so similar to dealing with the Russians, with just a touch of North Koreans, he could practically do it in his sleep. You presented your side's position then listened to them present theirs. The wording, absent a change on either side, had to be exactly the same every time. Which turned into constant repetition of the same phrases over and over again with absolutely no change in expression.

It really was like any negotiation on Earth. The difference being that it was taking place on a Dgut ship with those odd creatures—possessing a wide mobile base like a slug with long eye stalks—hosting the talks. And it was also taking place in the Eridani system since Earth wasn't about to let the Rangora send one of their ships through the gate.

"The Rangora Empire reiterates its position that the actions of liberation taken by the Empire were done with all due form based upon Terra's hostile actions against its allies the Horvath," the Rangora senior deputy envoy stated. "The Empire demands that Earth demobilize its battlestations and fleet, return all prisoners and submit to the will of the Empire. In the event that Earth does not so submit, Imperial Forces will, reluctantly, be forced to destroy your entire race."

"We have heard this iteration four times," the Dgut senior envoy stated. "I would suggest a brief break."

Negotiations were also timed based on the standard bladder control, or whatever a race used. Occasionally in terrestrial negotiations that was a tactic to force the other side to make a compromise. You learned to drink water sparingly.

The meeting compartment was surprisingly spacious and Piotr suspected it was normally a hold. The Dgut were even shorter than humans, much less the Rangora, so their living areas were unlikely to have thirty-foot ceilings.

But if it was a hold, it had been nicely outfitted. The walls were lined with anacoustic tiles so the small groups that formed could talk without the words bouncing all over the compartment. Each side had provided its own food, of course, but the Dgut provided servants to circulate with drinks and niblets during breaks. It was assumed by the Terran contingent that they were all spies. The Dgut had been one of the races that U.S. intelligence suspected was planning to go to war against the Glatun. The Rangora had just beat them to the punch.

"This is going nowhere," Harold "Call me Harry" Danforth said. If the State Department deputy assistant undersecretary was bothered by the Polish Alliance official being the formal "voice" of the Alliance, he didn't let on. But then again, he was a career diplomat. "I question the honesty of the Rangora in desiring peace. Our first analysis had been that their attack was sort of a mistake. The sort of thing you'd expect when two major polities were at war. They now seem very serious in their intention to conquer the Sol system."

Piotr was also a career diplomat. On the other hand, he was Polish, which meant he was *buried* in the history of countries performing invasions for purely Hobbesian rationales. Poland had been on the losing end *five times*. So he had managed to keep his opinion of the deputy assistant undersecretary's incredibly naïve opinions to himself.

"That is certainly their official position," Piotr said neutrally.

"What do you think we can do to break the impasse?" Harry asked, taking a sip of water. Alcoholic drinks were for after the session closed. Champagne was only for a successful session.

Invade the Empire and crush them, Piotr thought.

"As long as we are talking, we are not fighting," Piotr said, stating a tautology of diplomacy. "One simply talks as long as necessary. At some point either their leadership or ours will make a change. In the meantime, we talk. It is what we are paid to do, Harold."

"We must end this war, Piotr," Harry said, wringing his hands. "I feel as if Terra is responsible. The Glatun had been at peace with these other races for millennia. We come along and war breaks out. It can't be a coincidence."

"Terra's impact on the galactic scene, prior to this war, was the introduction of maple syrup," Piotr pointed out. "Given that the Glatun did not start the war, it is unlikely that maple syrup is at fault. And the question of fault is a pointless exercise. We are at war. I agree that ending the war is a requirement. However, doing so without good surety of security is unwise."

"I've recommended that we drop the tribute portion," Harry said. "That's just wrong. Tribute has never been a good idea. It always leads to another war."

"Unless the Rangora make an offer outside their current parameters, dropping any part of our positions would be unwise," Piotr said.

"They are probably saying the same thing," Harry pointed out.

"The Junta wants us to break this impasse."

Ghow Ve'Disuc, Imperial Envoy to the Minor Race of Terrans, had cut his teeth on the decade-long Multilateral Talks that led to the Rangora gaining all the border systems along the Glatun frontier. He felt, justifiably, that much of the success the Empire enjoyed in the recent war was the doing of himself and other Rangora diplomats.

The Terrans had been a late addition to the MT and even then only as observers. He had not been impressed with them then and he was not impressed with them now. He was forced to admit, though, that their system defenses *were* impressive.

"Unless the Terrans offer something outside their current positions, dropping any part of our statement would be unwise," Thunnuvuu Zho'Ghogabel said. The underenvoy to the Minor Race of Terrans was careful not to ripple his scales. The very thought of simply giving in to these hairy little mammals was repugnant.

"Go talk to the smaller, dark-haired one," Ve'Disuc said. "His body posture indicates reluctance according to our analysts. He has problems with the Terran position. See what you can find out. We need something out of this negotiation."

"What are the parameters?" Zho'Ghogabel asked.

"We'll drop territorial sovereignty over Terra in exchange for an apology, all the prisoners, all our salvaged ships and the same tribute in reverse," Ve'Disuc said. "No territorial concessions. We retain the Eridani system. We will open trading but of course only with Rangora companies."

"I wonder what Harry's getting from the Rangora, Eklit."

James Horst was the senior envoy, which meant that during negotiations his job was to sit there with a stern look on his face and otherwise keep his mouth shut. That only changed when a final agreement was reached when he was the one who would formally state the agreement and sign the preliminary documents. Since they were so far away from agreement you couldn't see it with a very big telescope, he was probably not going to be saying anything at the table.

"I am somewhat more worried what he is accepting," Piotr answered, watching the conversation between the State Department official and the Rangora underenvoy in a reflection. "Or suggesting."

"Harry's a pro," Horst said. "He's a weenie but he's a professional weenie. He's not going to give anything away and whatever he might suggest would be nonbinding."

"With respect, sir," Piotr said, "I've seen more negotiations go awry over those little side conversations than I care to remember. Someone suggests, outside their sphere of responsibility, something with which their side cannot comply. This is taken by the other side as a bad faith negotiation. Or they throw in the final negotiation position and it is taken as a pre-position. I really don't care for them."

"It's how it works, Piotr," Horst said. "I wish Harry had talked to me before he talked to them, but we'll see what comes of it."

"I think that if we could get a binding agreement of nonaggression, the rest could be worked out," Danforth said, giving up craning his head upwards and concentrating on a puff pastry. "All we really want is peace. I know you feel the same way, Thunnuvuu."

"Peace is the best of all possible conditions," the Rangora said. "And this incident has really been a colossal waste on both our sides. The lives and treasure being spent are just enormous. So you think those are suitable terms?"

"I think they are a good starting point," Danforth said. "But of course anything I say is nonbinding."

"Of course," the Rangora said. "But I will convey this and see if we can adjust some of our positions."

"The Rangora are an essentially honest and thoughtful species," Danforth said. "I know that in time we can be friends."

"You agreed to what?" Horst was just as professional a diplomat as his senior deputy envoy and this complete *idiot* from the State Department. Which meant that the words came out in an entirely neutral tone instead of the strangled gasp he wanted to use.

"The terms are perfectly suitable," Danforth said, nibbling on an hors d'ouevre. "With the opening of trade we'll be able to afford the payments, assuming they can be spread out over a long enough time period. And it gives us peace."

"And it is far beyond our minimum position as dictated by policy makers," Piotr pointed out. "Given that we've spent several billion dollars refurbishing those Rangora craft, we're not just going to give them back. Furthermore, retention of the Eridani system is a prerequisite it was not your authority to change."

"It is not my authority to change," Horst said. "Damnit," he added in the mildest possible tone. "Piotr, go talk to their under-envoy and point out that Danforth did not have authority to offer anything that he offered and that that is not our position."

"I will need to have something to offer," Piotr said.

"We're asking for the entire Federation," Horst said. "Give up the systems from the Talks and hint at the tribute. Danforth?"

"Yes, sir?" the deputy assistant undersecretary said.

"If you so much as open your mouth to do more than breathe for the rest of these negotiations, I will personally ensure you never can again by putting you into vacuum without a suit."

FIVE

"ARRIVING ASSIGNED PERSONNEL FOLLOW THE YELLOW LINE!" the M1C blared. "UNASSIGNED PERSONNEL FOLLOW THE GREEN LINE TO ASSIGNMENT. PERMANENT PARTY FOLLOW THE BLUE LINE! ARRIVING ASSIGNED PERSONNEL FOLLOW THE YELLOW LINE...!"

Dana smiled faintly to herself as she followed the yellow line to the assigned personnel office. She'd never heard of any military personnel being sent to one of the *Troy*-class without being assigned. The "unassigned" office only existed to answer questions from the terminally lost.

A few people glanced at her as she marched along hauling her grav case. That was less that she was a good looking blonde than that she was wearing a leopard suit. Most people didn't in secured areas. But she wasn't going to fly on someone else's shuttle, much less a 143rd shuttle, simply in uniform. She knew way too much about the 143rd.

She hadn't been specifically briefed on why she was being transferred, but she'd picked up the scuttlebutt. In the battles in E Eridani, and in the emergency evacuation just prior to them, it had become apparent that the overall quality of flying, and maintenance, of the 143rd was not entirely up to par. Certainly not up to the standards set by the 142nd, Earth's first space light boat squadron.

Dana was simply part of a series of transfers, 143rd personnel to the 142nd and vice versa, designed to "spread the wealth." She was pretty sure it wasn't going to help. The 143rd were so screwed up she wasn't sure how they got their birds out of the bays, much less survived in space. Transferring a few good people into the unit wasn't going to make any serious improvements. The phrase "stiffening a bucket of spit with buckshot" came to mind.

She waited in line with the other assigned personnel, her space suit occasionally buzzing as it worked off her body heat, until she got up to the civilian clerk. She commed the pad with her implant and waited.

"PO ... Parker ..." the clerk said. He was male and had a raspy voice, and she figured he was one of Apollo's tech people who had gotten a whiff of death pressure and been temporarily reassigned. He didn't look as if he normally flew a desk. Nametag said Gribson. "Hmmm ..."

"Shouldn't that be a unit and bay assignment?" Dana asked. "Not 'hmmm ...'?"

"Unit is easy," the guy said, looking up and grinning. Like her he was blond and if not cute then not uneasy on the eyes. "You're assigned to the 143rd. We're handling billeting for them, though. And the problem is there's no female billeting."

"Then get me a room to myself in male billeting," Dana said. "That's where I'm normally assigned."

"You're from the 142nd," Gribson said. "Which operates under U.S. rules. 143rd is an Alliance unit. Operates under slightly different regulations and guidelines. One of which is no coed billeting."

"So where do the other female personnel stay?" Dana asked.

"*What* female personnel?" Gribson replied.

"I'm *it*?"

"You're it. Which is why I'm looking for a billet to stick you in."

"Preferably one, you know, close to the boats," Dana said sarcastically.

"Wasn't my rule," Gribson replied. "And that's what I'm looking for. Not *there* ..."

"Where's *there*?" Dana asked.

"Marines."

"Don't get me wrong when I say this," Dana said, frowning. "But I sort of get along with Marines pretty well."

"Not *Pathan* Marines," Gribson said. "As in Afghan and Pakistani tribesmen with some basic knowledge of how to work their spacesuits and great glee at having laser rifles instead of

AKs. Oh, and who consider women who don't wear burkhas to be whores."

"Ah," Dana said, nodding. "Yes, I'd prefer somewhere else." *What the hell?*

"I'm going to have to stick you in the transient NCO quarters for now," Gribson said, shrugging. "It's *not* convenient to the boats and it's supposed to be for, well, transients. But somebody else is going to have to figure out where to put your permanent quarters."

"Joy," Dana said. "Well, a bunk's a bunk."

"They're actually pretty nice," Gribson said, uploading the map and keycode. "And we are done. Have an enjoyable time on the *Therm*. We endeavor to please."

"As long as you're a *guy*," Dana said, nodding at him. "See ya."

Dana had been sent a message to report for in-brief the day after her arrival. With nothing better to do the next morning until the brief at 0900 she headed for the gym.

Thermopylae, like *Troy*, had more than a dozen "fitness facilities." Some were designated for specific units, some were designated for general military or general civilian and some were open to everyone.

Figuring that she might as well figure out the layout of "her" gym, she headed for the one designated for the 143rd.

The layout turned out to be Apollo fitness facility, one each. It was set up virtually identical to the one she'd been using for the last four years.

What was a bit different was the users. Women, due to Johannsen's as much as anything, had become less common in the military. But even in the 142nd there were a few "splits" as Chief Barnett so delicately put it. Five by Dana's count and she could figure on not usually being the only woman in the gym.

For just a moment, Dana seriously thought about just turning around and heading back to the BNCOQ. The gym looked like work-out time at San Quentin. It was a mass of Hispanic males, most of them as short as she was, and all of them as tattooed if not more so.

"Jeeze, I hope I don't get shivved in the yard," she muttered, making her way through the press to an open Nautilus machine.

She set the adjustment higher than it had been and started doing presses.

"Yo, Chaco, check out the whore," one of the men called across the room. "She is fine, no?"

Dana paused in her repetitions for just a moment in shock. It wasn't so much that it was a sexual reference, just that it was so clear and blatant. Then she realized it had been in Spanish and her plants had automatically translated. She looked at the speaker and concentrated until his name and rank came up in her vision. Spaceman First Class Jose Reyes.

"You might consider not calling a CM2 a whore, Spaceman," Dana commed. "Our plants translate everything you say so if you think you were being cute, think again."

"Who the hell sent that?" the spaceman first class said angrily, setting his weights back in the rack.

"I did," Dana said, loudly enough to cut across the buzz in the room. "And to repeat, plants translate anything around them, especially if there's a reference to the individual. So I'd be careful about the sexual remarks."

"When I want any shit out of you, whore, I'll tell you," the SM1 said, waving a hand and smiling broadly. It was in Spanish, again, so he'd clearly not been listening.

"That does it!" Dana said, rolling to her feet and triggering her recording feature. "You had better *lock it up*, Spaceman. The first thing you said was an actionable offense. Direct disrespect to an NCO is an Article Ninety-One violation."

"Back off, bitch." The flash pop was CM2 Pedro Benito so she was at least dealing with the same rank. Benito had a large tattoo that ran up onto his neck of what looked like an angel. "That's my brother, not somebody for you to screw with."

"CM, I'm willing to disregard this encounter," Dana said, taking a deep breath. "But you need to lock down your personnel. One, they need some retraining on plant abilities. Two, they need some retraining on basic military respect and courtesy."

"When I want your opinion, whore, I'll ask for it," the CM2 said, waving a hand at her dismissively.

"That fracking does it," Dana said, her jaw flexing. "Leonidas, request immediate message to nearest senior NCO, preferably male, in the area. We have multiple EEOC and Article 91 violations."

"Message transmitted," Leonidas, the *Thermopylae* AI, responded. "Do you need security assistance?"

"Not at this time," Dana said as the group started to form

around her. She just stood looking at them with her arms crossed. "We'll sort this out in a moment, gentlemen."

It was more than a moment and Dana was getting decidedly nervous when the hatch dialed open.

"What the *hell* is going on in here?"

The speaker was a BM1, American to Dana's covert relief.

"Bosun's Mate, wish to report violation of Article 91, to whit disrespect to an NCO or Warrant as well as multiple EEOC violations," Dana said, tightly. "I tried to dial it back but apparently the personnel remain unaware, despite input, that plants translate anything they say."

"Bullshit," CM2 Benito said. "We didn't say a thing that was out of line, CM."

"Oh, *really*," Dana said, squirting a video of the part she'd recorded to the BM1. "Prior to that SN Reyes first described me as a whore loudly enough for the whole room to hear. Then when I pointed out, by com so it would not embarrass him, that the plants translate everything, he repeated the insult. At which point I started to record. When I told him to lock it up, CM2 Benito became involved."

"This is just so much lying bullshit, BM," Benito swore. "She's just trying to get us in trouble like the 142nd is always doing. We *never* called her a whore!"

"Hang on a second," BM1 Steve Persing said, consulting his plants. "Shit. Okay, Pedro . . . CM2 Parker, outside."

When they were out in the corridor Persing started swearing under his breath.

"Okay, Parker, first of all you're not supposed to even *be* in this gym," Persing said. "There's a reason we have an in-brief for all new personnel. Which you get at 0900. You're not part of this unit, yet, so you're not supposed to be using the gym."

"That's it, BM?" Dana said, her eyes widening. "I'm not supposed to be in the gym so some unwashed deck monkey can call a CM2 a whore?"

"No," Persing said, grinding his teeth. "And that is right on the edge of insubordination, CM."

"Aye, aye, BM1," Dana said coldly. "Noted. According to my orders, as of my arrival on station and check-in, which was performed at 1732 last evening, I was officially assigned to the

143rd Boat Squadron, BM. This is the 143rd designated fitness facility. My mistake."

"You're officially part of the unit, Parker," Persing said, sighing. "But you, clearly, needed the in-brief."

"Duly noted, BM," Dana said. "Would you care at this time to note just what portion of that would have applied in this situation?"

"You'll get that at the brief, CM," Persing said, turning to the Hispanic CM. "Benito, this was unnecessary and unwise. It's the job of an NCO to dial down something like this, not make it worse."

"I tried," Benito said. "But she just kept making these crazy accusations. You know how they are."

"BM," Dana said tightly. "If this continues, I'm going to make a formal EEOC complaint. I've never made one in my life. I try like hell to be one of the guys. But this is just bullshit."

"Okay, clearly we need to get you two separated," Persing said. "Pedro, you need to counsel Spaceman Reyes on proper respect due an NCO as well as com and implant protocol. Parker, I'll see you at the in-brief."

"BM, a moment of your time," Dana said as Benito entered the gym.

"Yes, CM?" Persing said tightly.

"If that is the entirety of this incident, you *will* face a formal complaint, BM," Dana said. "I'm assigned to this unit. If I can be treated as 'just another whore,' then to say the least that undermines my ability to act as an NCO."

"We'll deal with this, CM," Persing said. "In the meantime, keep your ass out of sight until we've got this situation you created under control."

Dana flopped back down on the rack and shook her head. "What the *hell*?"

She wasn't *used* to this. She'd dealt with some jackasses that took her at face value, blonde Barbie one each, a couple of times. But not *this* bad. And the BM1 seemed on their side. Which wasn't just an EEOC problem, it went right to the core of military discipline. At the 142nd she'd been treated as a FUN, a fracking useless noob, until she proved herself but it was just proving she was beyond noob. Not...*this*. She'd been aggressively disrespected by a junior spaceman, a guy who made sure the *decks* were properly washed. What the *hell*?

She hated to do it but she only knew one person to consult. She sent a hypercom ping wondering if the chief was available.

"Yo, Comet, what's up?"

"Got a few minutes?" Dana asked. "I think I already stepped in it."

"It's the 143rd," Barnett commed back. *"They should be used to cluster gropes by now."*

"Sending a recording," Dana said.

"Oh, holy fracking hell," Barnett commed back a moment later. *"Does that idiot Persing even know what military regulation means?"*

"I probably shouldn't have continued into the counseling session but I was so mad I didn't turn off. Now I'm glad I didn't."

"This is a problem," Barnett said. *"Among other things, if this is the standard of discipline I can see why they're so jugged. But dipping into another person's well is a no-no of the highest order. I'm going to do some discreet pushing on the Chief network but you're mostly going to have to fly this one alone. As soon as you get the in-brief and you get a few seconds, call me back. I'd like to see what part of the brief covers a clear Article 91 violation not to mention 117. In fact, I'd love to see what part of the brief covers that since it would, in turn, be an 81 and 92 violation."*

"So I'm not just being a gurrl about this?" Dana asked. "I was wondering."

"I would have hit the roof and screamed to high heaven," Barnett said. *"There's playing the boy's game and there's being disrespected. The first and second are two different things. So is playing girl games just to play games. There ought to be an article just for passive aggressive bullshit. This was straightforward disrespect to an NCO, Article 91 and provoking speech or gestures, 117. They don't get that under control and you might as well give away the whole shooting match. Doesn't matter if it's a newly transferred female CM or the fracking President. You* don't *violate the articles. Call me back after the brief. But, again, I can't get directly involved. Time to girl up, girl."*

"Will do, Chief," Dana said. "Thanks for the counsel."

"Good morning and welcome to the *Thermopylae* and the 143rd boat wing. I am Bosun's Mate First Class Steve Persing, personnel NCOIC for the 143rd."

When Persing said "he'd see her at the briefing" she'd assumed he was just going to be one of the people at the brief. Not the briefer.

"Technically, all of the space forces currently in operation in the Sol Defense Zone are now Alliance forces," Persing continued. "However, as you are well aware, up until recently the 142nd has been a purely North American unit. The 143rd, on the other hand, is made up of a mixture of various countries from South America. The majority of the coxswains are from Argentina and Chile, which are traditional enemies. The engineer's mates are from both countries as well as Peru, El Salvador and two from Colombia. Simply integrating persons from multiple countries, many of which are, as I've noted, traditional enemies, has been a challenging task. Now we are also dealing with the cultural differences with American personnel.

"Latin Americans have a long history of antagonism towards the United States and, arguably, vice versa. The United States, under the Monroe Doctrine, considered the entire Western Hemisphere its zone of influence and has repeatedly tinkered with the governments of many of these countries as well as often using them as a source of raw materials and labor. There is, therefore, a certain amount of entirely justifiable friction that is our job, as the senior partners in this Alliance, to assuage as far as possible. These are rich cultures as well advanced as our own but they are different cultures. That has to be remembered at all times. On top of that there is the fact that all the senior officer and NCO slots are held by Americans. There are coxswains who were fighter pilots, officers, in the Argentinean Air Force, which in the Falklands war went toe-to-toe with the British. This simply exacerbates that friction. It is our job, at all times, to keep the cultural differences in mind and work with them, not against them. Are there any questions?"

Dana looked around at the rest of the personnel sent from the 142nd and hoped that somebody would say *something*. Finally an engineer's mate from Bravo flight raised his hand.

"BM, I was under the impression we'd more or less pulled the UCMJ right over to the Alliance," the EM said. "Are you saying that we're not working under UCMJ?"

The Uniform Code of Military Justice was the rules and regulations under which U.S. forces operated. Dana was under the same impression that the UCMJ hadn't changed.

"No, the UCMJ, with very little modification, was transferred to the Alliance," Persing said carefully. "However, if you simply bark an order at one of your engineers, you may get the job done.

More likely, though, you'll find that simple barked orders are coun-terproductive. Latins are automatically respectful of certain types of authority but tend to be less so when the authority figure is not of their own culture. And certainly when the authority figure is counter to their culture," Persing finished, looking squarely at Dana. She didn't flicker so much as an eyebrow.

"What *gets* the job done?" the EM asked. "Begging? Because as far as the rest of us are concerned, BM, the reason that we're here is because the job hasn't been *getting* done."

"That attitude you had better *lock up*, Engineer's Mate," Persing snapped. "We're dealing with culture clashes and the fact that the boats are simply screwed up coming from the yards. We don't need the 'they brought in the Americans cause the Suds couldn't get the job done' attitude. That is *exactly* what is going to cause issues. Already *is* causing issues."

"I don't know what a Sud is, Bosun's Mate," the EM said, leaning back and crossing his arms. "But if you're saying I got to plead and beg to get an engineer to do his job, I think it's pretty clear what the issue is and it's *not* my attitude."

"Bosun's Mate?" Dana said, raising her hand. "Dialing the atmo-sphere down a little bit, what do you find *does* get the job done?"

"Generally I've found that it's best to be less the grand poobah than create a team spirit," Persing said. "Smile instead of frown. Work *with* them rather than creating a hierarchical approach. Honey gets more flies than vinegar."

"Thank you, Bosun's Mate," Dana said, trying not to scream.

"The other thing to keep in mind is that it's important to integrate into this team," Persing said. "We don't need a 'North American' clique to form. That's the greatest reason that you need to keep cultural differences in mind. Different culture, different methods of obtaining team bonding. So, as to assignments..."

"Parker. As noted many of these Latins have more experience as pilots than our most experienced coxswains. The critical need is for experienced engineers. So you're being reverted to your engineering specialty. You'll be taking over Engineering NCOIC for Division Two, Troop B which puts you in Twenty-Three. Your cox is Coxswain First Class Angelito Mendoza."

"Bosun's Mate?" Dana said, wincing. She liked engineering well enough but she *knew* she knew piloting. "I haven't turned a wrench since my initial trial period. I've been a coxswain for three years and have over ten thousand hours in the Black. I would, respectfully, recommend a reconsideration of that change."

"Duly noted," Persing said dryly. "It didn't come from my office, it came from higher. Some of the transfer personnel had to shift to engineering. You drew the short straw."

Parker had to wonder if she'd drawn the short straw before or after the incident in the gym.

"Aye, aye, Bosun's Mate," Dana said, trying not to curse.

SIX

To'Jopeviq tried not to curse. He hated this assignment more passionately every day. Almost as much as he was starting to hate Terrans. Or possibly, and this caused him just a shiver of fear at simply the *thought*, the High Command.

"There *has* to be a way!"

Gate assaults were very simple things. There was a small zone to enter through and, if you knew your opponent's capabilities—and at this point they were becoming aware the Terrans were practically *flaunting* their abilities—it all came down to math. How much fire you could throw, how much fire your opponent could throw.

There was no way to work around the math. To'Jopeviq was well aware that they were not getting all the information available about fleet units. But by even throwing the entire remaining Rangora fleet at Terra, the math simply did not work out.

"The math is straightforward," Toer replied. The analyst had clearly gotten some conflicted amount of satisfaction out of the fact that every time High Command ignored his analysis a Rangora fleet got shredded. The "conflicted" was due to the fact that he really cared about the success of the Rangora Empire and being right about that sort of thing too many times eventually was going to get *him* shredded.

"We've looked at the missile assault. The logistics are impossible given the numbers we've received on remaining Glatun fabricators and ships. The Glatun took a scorched-earth approach after Joshshav. Four remaining ship fabricators. A total of one hundred and twenty other fabbers of various sizes, most of them maxed out on other defensive projects. And the fabbers would either have to be moved to Glalkod, keeping them out of production during the move, or the missiles would have to be shipped to Glalkod. Shipping is already at a premium. And all of that ignores the developing Glatun resistance campaign."

"Who would have thought they had the quills for it," To'Jopeviq said. "Again, there has to be a plan that will work. Something to at least get them to come down in negotiations. They are no longer demanding full withdrawal but they want multiple systems as a buffer zone. Systems that would be turned over to the Glatun and given full autonomy."

"I have come to the conclusion that my initial analysis of the Terrans is not so much wrong as incomplete," Dr. Avama said uneasily.

"Good Tol, he said the R word," Toer said sarcastically.

"As I said, incomplete," Avama repeated. "And importantly incomplete. Rangora are not monolithic," he continued, glancing furtively at Beor.

"The Kazi are fully aware of that, Doctor," the secret police lieutenant said. "As we're aware of your ties to the peace movement. That is one of the reasons you are *in* this group. Because you represent alternate thinking. It is always dangerous but so is a laser emitter. In this place, it is what we and the High Command wish to hear. Alternate thinking."

"The humans I had dealt with before were diplomats," Avama said, more firmly. "They were very interested in peace. To the point of seeming, even to me, weak. Infirm of purpose. Peace by any means."

"Insanity," To'Jopeviq said, shaking his head. "Every race seeks territory, power, control."

"The point of diplomacy is to prevent the more aggressive versions of that," Avama said. "War, for example. Thus they were very much against war and in favor of peace. Despite my intellectual knowledge that humans had waged war against each other aggressively, their various... controls and my experience of those diplomats colored my thinking."

"In what way and does it help?" To'Jopeviq asked.

"Perhaps, perhaps not," Avama said. "But just as Rangora are not monolithic, nor are humans. And even their warriors make at least pro forma expressions of a desire for peace. But they are clearly *very* good at war. Yet even that is but part of the puzzle."

"Is this going anywhere?" Toer asked.

"Let him talk," To'Jopeviq said. "Can you explain?"

"I've been looking at their hypernet," Avama said. "Trying to understand them. Trying to understand where I was right and where I was wrong. Each of their major tribes, in truth independent polities which are in turn made up of still smaller tribes, has a varying approach to power. Most are, in fact, very close to the Rangora. By numeric of those polities, more than half, whatever their outward expression of governmental type, are governments based upon pure power of individuals and tribes."

"And that is like the Rangora?" To'Jopeviq asked, then thought about it. "Uh..."

"It is a valid analysis," Beor said. "Continue."

"However, with a few exceptions, China is one, the most *powerful* polities are based upon a much greater degree of power sharing," Avama said. "This is a very difficult thing for Rangora to grasp. Take the United States as an example. It continues to be, despite the fact that both ourselves and the Horvath have given it special attention, the most powerful polity on Terra. Given the current military situation, the United States can be viewed as the second most powerful polity in the *entire Western Arm*."

"The Ogut?" To'Jopeviq said. "I would tend to disagree."

"Based upon our experiences in fighting Terra," Avama said, "which to this point has been an almost *entirely* American defense, would you like to revisit that thought?

"There are many special interests and functional tribes within the polity. They fight constantly. To the outside observer this appears to be weakness. What makes the situation worse is that almost all of their diplomats come from a single social tribe. So what outsiders see is news stories that indicate continuous in-fighting of a level that would approach civil war among the Rangora..."

"The Kazi has wondered that they haven't had one, yet," Beor said. "The Maple Syrup War is the closest you could get to one and it was a minor insurgency."

"And very poorly understood," Avama said excitedly. "That is part of my point. But that is what it looks like to an outsider. But it's not the reality. To'Jopeviq, you don't talk much about your family but I suspect it is much like many—"

"Lower class?" To'Jopeviq asked, his crest riffling.

"Sorry," Avama said. "Yes. I suspect it is much like most lower class families. Large?"

"I have six brothers and four sisters," To'Jopeviq said.

"Arguments?"

"Tremendous ones," he said, hissing. "Especially at the holidays."

"There!" Avama said. "Your family *is* the Americans! What happens when another family attacks yours?"

"We band together and break them in half," To'Jopeviq said thoughtfully.

"Yes!" Avama said. "What would happen, God forbid, if your father were to die?"

"He is dead," To'Jopeviq said. "Mining accident. My oldest brother took over the family business. If you're correct... there is no point to attacking their leadership."

"Zero," Avama said. "Every missile spent on taking out American leadership is wasted. Here is the last thought. Say that your family was large enough to sustain fifty percent casualties in one attack from another family and continue fighting. What would the survivors do?"

"Anything it took to destroy the other family," To'Jopeviq said. "And, in fact... that happened not too long ago. You do not attack the To'Jopeviq clan. That is known on Lhoffid."

"You're from Lhoffid?" Toer said, his eyes wide.

"Yes," To'Jopeviq said, hissing again. "Problem with that, Analyst?"

"No, sir," Toer replied, slumping in his seat. "How close would you say...?"

"The Americans, at this point, have lost mostly their tribe that is not warlike," Avama said. "Vast portions of their most pacific groups were wiped out by either ourselves or the Horvath. The survivors are a bit like if... are there members of your family who were... less aggressive?"

"Yes," To'Jopeviq said.

"If your family was attacked and only those were killed?"

"Given my sister Faiz..." To'Jopeviq said then flattened his crest. "No, I know *exactly* what we would do. There are times... And I feel less Rangora when I say this. There are times when we feel that they are the best of us. Especially when they are the only ones that can stop us from killing each other. I hadn't thought of my family for a long time, Avama. For obvious reasons," he added, looking at Toer.

"Sorry, Egilldu," the analyst said. "I was surprised, that's all."

"What we would do is destroy the family that hurt ours," To'Jopeviq said. "Or be destroyed trying. Especially if the targeting was that precise."

"There is more...distance involved with the Americans," Avama said. "But my analysis is that that is exactly how they are reacting. The main tribe that drives their wars is the Jacksonians. There is an excellent essay on that tribe available on our servers. They generally do not concern themselves with foreign affairs. But when they do, they want to proceed with the war and win. Not a negotiated surrender. Not drawn out. Get it over with and then go back to their lives. They believe in *crushing* their enemies and putting a boot on their neck. And then, and this is where it very much deviates from Rangora, since the Jacksonians lose interest when the enemy is destroyed, the other tribes that are more pacific or mercantile become involved. Thus the Americans then spend vast sums assisting their former enemies. The Jacksonians grumble but don't really care enough to prevent it.

"Our targeting has tended to destroy the tribes that are more open to negotiation. We have, from *our* perspective, very carefully and specifically taken the impurities from the metal. We haven't *weakened* them, we've made them *stronger*. And very very angry. A human philosopher reminds me of Ashoje, another similarity. The Terran, Machiavelli, once said 'Never do an enemy a small injury.' We have spent this entire war doing the Americans small injuries."

"Destroying their cities is not small injuries," Toer said.

"Think about it," To'Jopeviq said.

"The Jacksonian tribe is not urban based," Avama said. "And it is *those* we need fear. They don't supply the majority of academics, politicians or media. Those are the people we've been paying *attention* to! Jacksonians supply the majority of only one group: their *military*. Also, to an extent, their production base. We've been ignoring the *only* tribe that is *important* in the situation!"

"Not the politicians?" Beor said.

"I take that back," Avama said. "Not the politicians we tend to notice except in the negative. Their president, for example, is from that background and not only, now, a politician but an academic in the field of politics and interstellar affairs. But she is an unusual case. The majority of the type of politicians and bureaucrats we notice, with which we interact, are from a tribe that, in a war, is very aggressively told to take a back seat.

"During recent wars, even with the Horvath initially, that was impossible. The U.S. is a true democracy and those other tribes had sufficient power, hard and soft, to constantly involve themselves in something they had neither the background nor the understanding to manage. At this point, they are sufficiently reduced—they *were* urban based in the main—that they are functionally unimportant. That is the key factor I was missing. I was wrong in my initial analysis of the humans because I *ignored* the importance, militarily, substantially and politically, of the Jacksonian tribe. In part, because every time members of that tribe who had some power were discussed by humans they were dismissed out of hand as unimportant. It is as if the only people in your family I talked to and paid attention to was your sister."

"That is the Americans," Beor said. "What of the other polities?"

"There are similar conditions in many of them," Avama said. "Harder to piece out in some cases. Many of them are traditional enemies of the Jacksonians. But, for example, the Indian War Party has as its majority members of tribes that are historically warlike. Yet many of its supporters come from tribes that are more mercantile or academically oriented. Traditionally pacific groups. Yet they support the War Party, elect people they normally would not associate themselves with, because the traditional method is 'in war, let the warmongers run things.' May I use an historical example?"

"Go," To'Jopeviq said.

"During a late great war, the one they call World War Two although it should be more correctly called Major Campaign Three of the Seventy-Five Year War, the British elected a prime minister who had been something of a joke for years. Mostly because he predicted a great war, wanted to spend money on defense and was constantly insulted for his general warmongering. He is *still* considered one of their greatest prime ministers. But as soon as the war was finished, he was removed from power."

"When war comes, let the warriors run it," To'Jopeviq said. "And when peace comes, the warriors are cast back out into the darkness? Why don't the warriors simply *seize* power?"

"The Americans are more flexible about it," Avama said. "Many of their great generals have been presidents. The first president of their country was supreme commander of forces during their

War of Independence. But he set the tone for voluntary change of power. He could have stayed president until he died but he only served for eight years and then retired. By the same token, during the previous war I discussed their president was a cripple."

"Impossible," To'Jopeviq said, subtly trying to hide his prosthetic.

"He had had a childhood disease that crippled his legs," Avama said. "Historically unquestionable. At the time, he did much to avoid having it noticed in the primitive information systems of the time. But he was a cripple. And all the polities are not the same. In some the nonmilitary personnel hang onto power even though they are not mentally suited to running a war. In others the military uses hard power to seize control, or functionally controls the country during both war and peace. But most of the really important polities follow the same general tenor. And most of them, all that are members of this new Alliance, are democracies. Even France, and don't even try to follow the issues with that, has elected a former general and a firebrand. Whether they will make any sort of valid contribution is another question."

"Does this help us in any way?" To'Jopeviq asked.

"The analysis is, I think, most important for the negotiation teams," Beor said. "Even very important. They probably don't realize that the people they are dealing with have no functional power. They probably think that they are from powerful families which have some degree of real control. And thus if they can convince them, personally, of our side, that this will filter to the families and thus to their power center. If you are saying that they are from ... tribes that are essentially out of power as long as there is a threat ..."

"Convincing them personally, or paying attention to their preference for peace, is so much vacuum," To'Jopeviq said. "It still doesn't cover our primary focus. How do we defeat them?"

"I have also been looking at that," Avama said. "Prior to this assignment, I tried to pay as little attention to war as possible. I would put myself squarely in the position of the tribe that is out of power among the Americans. However, since I see the absolute need to win this war, or at least get to a point that we can get the Jacksonians willing to accept a cease-fire, I have been studying war. But I have not been studying our forms of warfare except as directly related to system conquest. I have been studying the humans."

"We have a long history of warfare," To'Jopeviq said.

"We have also been tinkering with our history so much it is hard to glean reality from falsehood," Avama said, then blanched.

"Alternative means of thinking, Academic," Beor said. "Go on."

"And we are fighting the humans and they are, arguably, winning," Avama said. "At the very least, we are not. So I had to wonder 'How would a great human general win this?'"

"That *is* alternative," To'Jopeviq said.

"Most of them, when I translated their concepts to modern realities, came down to 'Try not to have to fight at all.' *Troy*, *Thermopylae* and now *Malta*. They are inflating a *fourth* station. This one, by the way, will decidedly be fixed since it is too large to go through the gate."

"Joy," To'Jopeviq said. "I'd noticed, by the way."

"We all did," Toer said balefully. "Yay. We don't have to worry about a *fourth* station coming through into Eridani."

"The point being that most of their generals would simply counsel 'try not to get into that fight.' But if it *had* to be fought? Subedei: Speed is everything. Surprise is everything. Deception is everything. Utter ruthlessness."

"I like him," To'Jopeviq said.

"I would, by the way, suggest ignoring that last for some complex reasons. But the other three...?"

"You can't use deception if you're doing a gate assault," To'Jopeviq said.

"Not if *you're* assaulting the gate," Avama said. "They have been destroying *us* piecemeal in gate assaults."

"Get them to attack?" To'Jopeviq said. "How?"

"More than that," Avama said. "Get them to attack through the gate in too low of *force*."

"That is an...interesting idea," To'Jopeviq said. "Worth some very serious thought."

"So is one other thing," Beor said. "Being aware that this is not an official Kazi query but part of this group. What has caused your sudden change of heart? You stated 'since I see the absolute need to win this war, or at least get to a point that we can get the Jacksonians willing to accept a cease-fire.' You are a pacifist. You now support the war. Why?"

"I am a Rangora," Avama said. "And that is not a simple rote response, Kazi. You were paying insufficient attention to my statements about the Jacksonians and similar tribes among other polities."

"How so?" Beor asked.

"The Jacksonians are very difficult to get to negotiate," Avama said. "They believe in total war and putting a foot on their enemy's neck. Unconditional surrender is the only thing they understand. You still don't get it, do you?"

"Apparently not," To'Jopeviq said.

"I'm not really worried about how to take the *Terran* system," Avama said. "I'm wondering how we're going to hold *Rangora*."

"You get your in-brief from Persing?"

The chief engineer for Bravo Troop was Engineer's Mate First Class Jayson Megdanoff. Tall and dyspeptic looking, he seemed less than happy to meet her.

"Yes, EM," Dana said.

"You're going to have to get new rate badges," Megdanoff said. "You're an engineer again. You *remember* any of it?"

The engineering office for the troop was, as always, a clutter of tools and pulled parts. This one was, if anything, more organized than the similar office Dana had had as a second home on *Troy*. Thermal had always known exactly where everything in the office was but the organization method escaped everyone else.

"Yes, EM," Dana said.

"We'll see, I suppose," Megdanoff replied. "Div Two has had a run of bad luck. All the boats are up, currently, but there's been constant issues. Between the screw-ups on Apollo's part and the crap we're getting out of Granadica it's a nightmare to keep these boats running. It doesn't help that we lost about a quarter of our trained crews taking Station Two. And in mid-space accidents during that idiotic transfer. Right now there's only an EA on Twenty-Three so any trained engineer is a benefit."

"I continued to maintain engineering proficiency while a coxswain, EM," Dana said. "What I'm not up on is the paperwork, especially for running the division."

"You'll catch up on the engineering database quick enough," Megdanoff said. "That's one thing that's actually easier than it was before the plants. Right now, I think you need to see your boats. Where's your suit?"

"In my quarters, EM," Dana said. "Apparently there's some

issue with putting me in the main unit quarters so I'm at the BNCOQ. It will take me ten minutes to get over there, don suit and get back."

"That's going to suck," Megdanoff said, blinking rapidly and for the first time actually seeming to show some interest in the conversation. "In fact, I'm not sure that's going to work."

"My thought as well, EM," Dana said, controlling her temper. The door opened and a tall, broad Hispanic EM1 entered without knocking. Dana was just getting used to most of the Hispanic contingent being about her size. The EM was a mountain. She'd never seen someone that big from Latin countries except in movies.

"EM2 Parker, this is EM1 Ponce Diaz," Megdanoff said, gesturing. "The way things are set up right now there's sort of a dual command and authority structure. Diaz is my counterpart."

"EM," Dana said, nodding at him.

"Engineer Parker," the EM replied.

"Parker's been designated NCOIC for Division Two," Megdanoff said.

"Looking forward to it," Diaz said. "They need a good mechanic down there. I reviewed your record as an engineer and could find no fault. I'm looking forward to working with you."

"Thank you," Dana said, feeling slightly confused.

"Ponce, could you run Parker down to her boat?" Megdanoff said. "After she retrieves her suit. Parker, I'll check on the quartering issue. I know where it's emanating but it's something we're going to have to figure out. You can't be up in the BNCOQ if you're going to be part of the unit."

"Agreed, BM," Dana said. "EM Diaz, it will take me about ten minutes. My apologies."

"Completely understood, miss," the engineer replied. "I've got paperwork to catch up on, anyway. I'll be here."

SEVEN

"We have received an interesting analysis of our opponents from Rangor," Under Envoy Zho'Ghogabel said.

"Interesting in what way?" Envoy Ve'Disuc replied. The negotiations were going nowhere but they often did for long periods. It was all about patience. Being the drop of water that wore away the stone.

"It is long," Zho'Ghogabel said. "The most important part, for us, is that we're talking to the wrong people. I now understand the problem of doing anything with Danforth. There is also a change in position from the Junta."

"Really?" Ve'Disuc said, sitting up.

"Separate from all other discussion points," Zho'Ghogabel said, sending on the report with the orders highlighted. "Simple tit for tat. And one the Terrans have already brought up."

"We can use this for more than a tit-for-tat," Ve'Disuc said. "This could be a real breakthrough. I must contact the Ministry."

"Come," James Horst said. He didn't even look up from his computer. He knew who it was.

"James," Ve'Disuc said, bending through the door.

"Envoy Ve'Disuc," Horst said, spinning around in his chair. "I think the couch will take you."

"Thank you," the Rangora said, sprawling onto the human couch. The furniture for the various delegations had been brought from their home planets. "I think we may have a real breakthrough."

"That would be interesting," Horst said neutrally. "Which is?"

"Aliens are alien," Ve'Disuc said.

"If you've finally figured that out it really *is* a breakthrough," Horst said, snorting.

"We did not understand some things that you do," Ve'Disuc continued. "And we based your reactions to war on our reactions to war."

"Again, congratulations on your amazing insight that we view these things differently," Horst said.

"I do recognize human sarcasm," Ve'Disuc said.

"I see one of the race that blotted out most of my family and friends in an unprovoked attack," Horst said.

"Are you by any chance a ... Jacksonian?"

"Ah," Horst said, nodding. "You found Meade's essay. Congratulations, again. I *said* there was a point to opening up the hypernet system. Despite the fact that you keep trying to hack us through it."

"That is performed by renegades—"

"Can it," Horst said. "Or save it for the negotiating table. What is your point?"

"That question remains," Ve'Disuc said.

"And I'm considering whether to answer it," Horst said. "Can you reveal why you want to know the answer?"

"To be able to evaluate your relative political power," Ve'Disuc said. "We have been having a hard time understanding why two Americans are relatively junior to a Pole. America is your world's hyperpower. Still. Despite the damage from the war which has fallen on the United States more heavily than the rest of the world. Why have a *Pole* as the primary negotiator? Now we realize that different tribes within both polities have different roles depending upon whether their polities are at war or peace. Our initial analysis was that you were the ... the term you use is 'eminence gris.' If this was a Japanese negotiating team, that would be assured.

"But now we discover that none of you may, in fact, have any political weight at all. Danforth assuredly has none. And we have, as yet, been unable to identify the exact nature of similar tribal spreads among the Poles. To understand what we are doing, to negotiate in truth, we have to understand humans and their politics."

"Well, you're still not there," Horst answered. "But, yes, I'm one of those rare Republicans in the State Department. And

Eklit is from a similar faction in Poland. If truth were told, I have a better time communicating with Eklit than Danforth. We understand each other."

"Republican is synonymous with Jacksonian?"

"No, but it's close," Horst said. "The basis of the Republican party is Jacksonians as the basis of the Democratic party is Wilsonians. There are members in both."

"The Republicans are your war party," Ve'Disuc said.

"I'm sure the Democrats think so," Horst said with a snort. "But not as you would understand it, no. Get that thought out of your head. Have you been looking at the Second World War or First World War?"

"The...Second was part of the analysis, yes. References."

"Look at the political party of the President in both wars."

"Democrats. So... You don't have a war party?"

"No," Horst said.

"But you have a war tribe."

"No," Horst said, snorting again. "Seriously. No. Okay, close, but not quite the cigar. Jacksonians are about much more than war. They are, in fact, the basis of our small business community as well. Wilsonians and Madisonians tend to be in control of large businesses. Were. There are so few of both groups left they're practically a vanishing species. If you're trying to figure out if what we agree to is binding, yes. At least on Alliance countries, and there are no Terran polities with space warfare capability other than Alliance countries."

"On binding agreements," Ve'Disuc said.

"Anything said here is decidedly nonbinding."

"Understood," Ve'Disuc said. "You brought up an agreement against nonmilitary-based attacks upon civilian population."

"The wording would have to be precise," Horst said. "But an agreement upon no weapons of mass destruction attacks on nonmilitary targets was one of our early negotiation points. We took it off the table because we realized you could barely get the concept. Aliens are alien."

"We have some interest in resuming that dialogue."

"Be great," Horst said, surprised. "Why?"

"We are starting to understand you."

"What do you want as a quid?"

"Drop your tribute stipulation."

"I'll . . . put that for consideration to the Alliance Foreign Ministry," Horst said. "They'll want the reverse."

"We can probably agree to that," Ve'Disuc said. "What do you think in general?"

"Frankly?" Horst said. "We don't believe you'll stick to it. *I* don't believe you'll stick to it. And we'll probably agree anyway. Because we do understand you and know that anything we negotiate with you is essentially nonbinding if you think you can get away with breaking it."

"That makes negotiations hard," Ve'Disuc said.

"You think?" Horst said sarcastically. "What about the Horvath?"

"This is a mutual agreement," Ve'Disuc said. "The Horvath may enter into it or not."

"Let me talk to Eklit."

"When someone wants to make this large a change in negotiation position, I want to know why," Piotr Polit said.

"Does it matter?" Harry Danforth said. "If we'd had this at the beginning of the war, we'd still have New York and Paris!"

"Interesting priorities," Horst said. "And while I think we'll probably agree with it, I agree with Eklit. This much of a change, not to mention agreement to our earlier proposal out of the blue, means something is changing in the background. I'd like to know what."

"Ve'Disuc said it," Danforth argued. "They're starting to understand us. To understand that we consider all life precious."

"So they'd assume that we wouldn't bomb their cities, anyway," Horst said.

"We're not in a position to bomb their cities," Danforth said disparagingly. "Not that we would, anyway."

"Do you think so?" Piotr said. "Have you ever heard of Dresden? Tokyo? Hiroshima?"

"We don't fight like that, anymore," Danforth said. "And those tragedies taught us why we shouldn't."

"At one level I agree with you, Harry," Horst said. "And on another, disagree totally. I'm not going to get into it, though. I still want to know what's happening."

"And it's not up to us to figure it out," Piotr said. "I will send a report to the Ministry. James, send one to the American State Department as well. My recommendation is to accept the proposed changes. And add that we would dearly like some hard analysis of why they have changed their position."

"I'm starting to feel like we're making real progress," Harry said.

"*I'm* starting to feel like we're flailing in zero g," Horst said.

"There is microgravity beyond this point," Diaz said delicately.

"I saw the signs, EM," Dana said, grabbing the safety bar.

The shuttles for the 143rd were attached to the same "pencil" docks that the 142nd had used the first three years Dana had been with the unit. The pencil docks jutted from the inner wall of the main bay and shuttles were docked onto four sides. The main section was under microgravity. The engineers, therefore, had to perform many of their checks in microgravity. Furthermore, since there was always a chance that something could go wrong and one of the boats be holed or broken off the docks, they had to work in suits. It was a pain in the butt but one that Dana was used to.

"As a coxswain, I'm not sure how much experience..." Diaz continued as Dana flipped herself into micro and started swarming down the corridor.

"Coming, EM?" Dana asked when she was halfway to her boat.

Dana had been mildly embarrassed by her first exposure to micro on *Troy*. Since that time, however, she'd had thousands of hours in suits in not only micro but fluctuating grav conditions. As a former gymnast she also had excellent spatial awareness and was simply *brutal* at null grav ball. Micro was not an issue.

"Uh...yes," Diaz said, for once nonplussed. He grabbed the safety bar and pulled himself into micro much more cautiously.

Dana took a small perverse pleasure from puncturing the phlegmatic NCO's attitude. She'd appreciated his greeting her as a positive, as compared to the constant negative attitude she'd encountered from even the Americans in the 143rd. By the same token, he seemed to think she was some sort of glass doll or something. Or a brainless Barbie. It wasn't direct, probably wasn't even conscious, but he tended to be a bit condescending. As if with a dancing bear, it was not so much that she could do engineering well as that she was a girl who could do engineering.

Dana wasn't sure she could ever get the Latins to accept her as simply "a guy with tits" as Chief Barnett put it. But she also wasn't going to be condescended to. There might be better pilots and engineers in the 143rd but she fully intended to be one of the best.

She stopped at Twenty-Three and looked around. The other three boats in "her" division didn't seem to be occupied nor were they out of dock.

"Where's the rest of the crew?" she asked.

"Participating in training," Diaz said. "Leonidas, authorization code four-one-eight-seven-nine-alpha. EM2 Dana Parker assigned NCOIC Division Two, Bravo Troop. Shuttle Twenty-Three primary engineer."

"EM2 Dana Parker assigned NCOIC Division Two, Bravo Troop, aye. Assigned Shuttle Twenty-Three primary engineer, aye. Authorized entry, inspection and repair shuttles twenty-one through twenty-four, aye. Welcome to the 143rd, Comet Parker."

"Thank you, Leonidas," Dana said, keying open the hatch.

"What are you doing?" Diaz asked.

"Starting my inspection of the craft, EM?" Dana said.

"Now?" Diaz seemed surprised, even shocked.

"That would be my normal action at this point, EM," Dana said, wrinkling her brow. "Do you have an alternate requirement, EM?"

"I was going to introduce you to the rest of your division," Diaz said. "I assumed you'd like to meet them."

"Very well, EM," Dana said, closing the outer hatch on the shuttle. "Lead on."

"This is the quarters of Vila and Palencia," Diaz said, opening the door again without knocking.

They'd changed out of their suits on the way. Generally that was done in quarters. Dana had had to use the engineering office while Megdanoff made himself scarce. She definitely needed quarters in the squadron area.

Dana, now that she had legal permissions as NCOIC of the Division, had accessed the basic personnel files for her team. According to the records, Dario Palencia was an engineer's mate third class and Cruz Vila was an engineer first class assigned to Twenty-One and Twenty-Two respectively. The other two members were Ricardo Sans, an engineer's apprentice and Diego Velasquez, engineer recruit. It was, from her experience, a pretty good mix. Palencia had about a year's less experience than she did, and all of it as an engineer, which was to the good. Both he and Vila had been engineers in the action at Station Two during the Eridani incursion and Palencia had picked up a NavCom, Naval Commendation Medal, with V device for valor.

All Dana had gotten out of the same action—even after getting a boat back to the *Troy* with half her thrusters knocked out by a near miss from a missile—was a transfer.

The only person in the quarters, though, was Vila, who appeared to be asleep. He probably wasn't accessing training materials since he was snoring.

"Where's Dario?" Diaz asked.

"Don't know, sir," Vila said, rolling out of his rack. "He said he had something to pick up."

Dana boggled again, not so much at the casual attitude as at the use of "sir." NCO's were addressed by their rate, not "sir," which was reserved for officers. Then she realized that Vila was using Spanish, naturally, and the actual word used was "*señor.*" It still was odd and even uncomfortable.

"Send him a message and tell him he needs to get down here to meet the new division engineering NCOIC," Diaz said. "And you're supposed to be studying, not sleeping."

"Yes, sir," Vila said, rubbing his eyes. The engineer first class was in the "short" category and had a distinctly "Incan" look. Taking a quick look at his dossier again, Dana saw he was from Ecuador. She tried to ignore that the room was trashed.

"This is Engineer's Mate Second Class Parker," Diaz said. "She's your new division chief engineer."

"Hello," Vila said, blinking in surprise. "We weren't expecting someone so good looking."

"And I wasn't expecting a full crew of engineers," Dana said. She'd halfway been expecting the compliment and ignored it. "According to your records you performed ably in the battle of Station Two. I look forward to working with you."

"Thank you," Vila said, shaking her hand a bit too warmly. "Feel free to stop by *any* time."

"Oh, you can be sure I'll be dropping by," Dana said, smiling fatuously. She was starting to get a feel for how this was going to go. She wasn't so sure that her natural reaction—which was to kick their ass in every *possible* way—was the right response.

"Palencia's probably over at that damned mall," Diaz growled as he closed the hatch. "I'll talk to him about it."

Dana accessed the watch schedule for the division and found that it simply said "Training and Maintenance" for most of the cycles over the next week.

"What sort of training are they doing, EM?" Dana asked curiously. There wasn't even a note on what specific training was to be done.

"Studying for qualifications, of course," Diaz said.

"Ah," Dana said noncommittally. Studying for quals was done on your *own* time, not "work" time, in the 142nd. And, as far as she could determine, every *other* U.S. Navy unit.

Since the shuttles required nearly constant maintenance to keep them in top shape, she was starting to get the drift of why the 143rd was constantly deadlined.

"Sans and Velasquez are over here," Diaz continued, opening the hatch across the corridor.

This time at least the two engineers were awake but they appeared to be playing a video game. The were at least using their plants so they were getting *some* training in those.

"No! Go to the left..." Sans said.

"It's covered!"

"Hey!" Diaz snapped. "Don't you get to your feet when a superior enters the room?"

"Sorry, EM!" Sans said, opening his eyes and jumping to his feet. Velasquez was even quicker, bouncing up with his eyes still closed as he shut down the game.

"This is Engineer's Mate Parker, your new NCOIC," Diaz snapped.

"Hello," Sans said, nodding politely. Velasquez just gulped and nodded.

"Hello," Dana said, smiling. "I'm sure we'll get along great. EM, you probably have other duties. Why don't you leave me to get to know my division?"

"Very well," Diaz said. "For obvious reasons, I think you'll need to keep the hatch open when you're in rooms with the male personnel."

"Regulation Four-One-Six-Three-Zebra states that air-tight hatches are to be closed at all times unless in immediate use, EM," Dana said, smiling sunnily. "I'll keep plants on record. Since I can delete but not modify the recordings, they'll serve as an adequate record, EM. And general guideline is that a person of the opposite sex is not to be *alone* with a member of the opposite sex unless off-duty, EM."

"And I think that you'll find that larger groups will simply cause more talk, Engineer's Mate," Diaz said sternly.

"Not for long, EM," Dana said, smiling still. "Regulations are, after all, regs."

"We'll discuss this at another time," Diaz said. "As you said, perhaps you should get to know your division."

"Thank you, Engineer's Mate," Dana said, still smiling. "I think we'll step over to the other quarters, though, to get to know one another. I think a foursome is, at least for the time being, beyond *most* people's imagination."

Diaz grunted, nodded and left.

"He's a real hard-ass," Sans said. "You'll get used to it."

"Do you think so?" Dana said, smiling. "Let me tell you what a hard-ass is. This is a verbal counsel statement to you both. It's recorded but internal for this moment. If I ever catch you playing video games, or engaging in any other form of entertainment that interferes with your duties, during duty hours again I will give you a written counseling statement. The time after that, you will have a Captain's Mast under Article 92, Failure To Obey an Order or General Regulation. Did you understand this verbal counseling statement?"

"What?" Sans asked. Velasquez just gulped.

"This is duty hours," Dana said, still smiling, if thinly. Her eyes weren't. "During duty hours I suppose that you may engage in preparation for standards tests. But playing video games is not such a preparation. Possibly if you were Marines. Since you're Naval boats engineers, definitely not training. Duty hours are for working. When you are off duty, you can play games. Did you understand that?"

"Yeah, sure," Sans said.

"The correct form of address is 'Yes, EM' or 'I understand, EM,'" Dana said. "A surly 'Yeah, sure' is not sufficient. Start over. Do you understand that you are being verbally counseled not to engage in entertainment during duty hours?"

"Yes, EM," Sans said, his jaw flexing.

"ER Velasquez, do you understand this counseling statement?" Dana asked.

"Yes, EM," Velasquez replied.

"Excellent," Dana said, still smiling. "This counseling session is closed. Let us proceed to the EM's quarters so we can get to know each other."

Palencia still hadn't showed up when they crossed the corridor. "Did you send him a message?" Dana asked.

"Yeah, sure," Vila said. "He said he'd be here in a while."

"Ah," Dana said. "Grab some seats. I have a call to make."

She mentally pulled up Palencia's file and sent a message. When it didn't pick up she sent a priority override which permitted her, as Palencia's NCOIC, to open up his plant for a message.

"Palencia, this is Engineer's Mate Second Class Dana Parker, your new NCOIC," Dana commed. "What is your current position?"

"Uh, Parker..." Vila said. "Were you going to say something?"

Dana just held up a hand and pointed to her head.

"What?" Palencia responded. *"Who?"*

"This is the new NCOIC for your division. You were messaged to present yourself so we could get to know each other. What is your position at this time?"

"I'm...on my way back."

"Be aware of three things. The first is that lying to a superior is an offense against the UCMJ. The second is that, as your immediate superior, I can ask Leonidas for your location at any time. The third is that during duty hours unless specifically authorized you are to be in duty areas at all times. Failure to do so is *another* violation of UCMJ. You can get anywhere in duty areas in five minutes. So you have five minutes to present yourself at your quarters after which you will be considered absent without leave. Do you understand these requirements?"

"I'm on my way. It may be more than five minutes."

"Take your time," Dana commed. "I'm *so* enjoying my first day here."

"I was comming Palencia," Dana continued audibly. Palencia was the next most senior person in the unit. She knew better than to effectively chew his ass in front of the others. "He's on his way. He'll be here in a few minutes."

"Okay," Vila said. He'd caught the frozen expressions of the other two engineers.

"To cover a few things, which I'll cover privately with Palencia when he arrives," Dana said, "I'm pretty unfamiliar with Latin American culture. But in my culture, there's a saying. The teacher is no smiles before Christmas and all smiles after Christmas. I don't see it as the duty of the newly transferred personnel to fix the One-Four-Three, so don't take this as some sort of global negative. And I've been told that it's best to befriend my team. That it works better with your culture. I'm not really good at that and I don't see where it enhances our mission. Our mission is simple. Our shuttles deliver the mail. We may deliver parts or supplies or the rubble of destroyed ships. We may deliver mail. We may deliver Marines, express, to an enemy ship. But we deliver the mail. There is no excuse, there is no 'close enough,' there is no wriggle room. If the boats aren't functioning, we can't deliver the mail and we have failed in our mission.

"I have reviewed your personnel files. I'm sure in time we'll all talk about where we're from, what we miss about home, what we think about the latest TV show. But for right now, the only thing I care about is whether we can deliver the mail. Do you understand?"

"Yeah..." Vila said, then gulped at her expression.

"The correct response to that question is... Sans?"

"'Yes, EM' or 'I understand, EM,'" Sans said.

"So, Vila, try it again," Dana said, smiling. "Do you understand?"

"Yes, EM," Vila said, his eyes wide.

"Then we have a beginning," Dana said, smiling more broadly. "So, what is the status of your boat, Vila?"

"It's running," Vila said, shrugging.

"According to records, it has not had a sixty- and ninety-day maintenance schedule," Dana said. "Since the only way to know if *everything* is running is to run the maintenance schedule, then, in fact, you *don't* know if it's running."

"It can undock and fly, Parker," Vila said.

"That is not the definition of 'running' for either the Alliance Navy or, more specifically, *me*, Vila," Dana said. "Why have you not performed the sixty- and ninety-day maintenance?"

"I don't have time!" Vila said. "We've got to study for these tests, too, you know!"

"Which you can do in your own time," Dana replied. "But since it's apparently on the training schedule, absent challenge from higher, the current schedule for this division is six hours per day on the boats with two hours in quarters for study. And it will *be* study. And this is how we're going to work it. Every

Friday we'll have a test of specific items from the general standards sheets. These will be announced on Monday. Absent successful tests of knowledge of task, condition and standard, we will commence retraining beginning at end of duty hours on Friday and continue until all personnel show a fundamental grasp of task, condition and standard."

"Friday night?" Sans asked. "But...that's our off-duty time!"

"You begin to grasp the point," Dana said. "It is also, I might add, *my* off-duty time. And since I do tend to have some sort of a life beyond these nickel-iron walls, you'll understand if I'm going to be a bit grumpy if you're not prepared for the tests. You do not want me *grumpy*. This is me being *nice*."

"To work on the boats we have to be in suits," Vila pointed out.

"And your point?"

"That's six *hours* in suits," Vila said slowly, as if to a child. "Every day."

"And, again, your point?" Dana said. "I'll be right there with you in Twenty-Three. And in your boats making sure that you're actually performing the maintenance and checks. Which means I'll have to be working twice as hard in those suits."

"Six hours a day?" Sans said, incredulous.

"I've done up to sixty-seven hours in suits," Dana said. "Which is right at the extension of the navopak, obviously. And if you think that most of my time as an engineer was in the comfort of a bay, think again. I spent most of my first six months on the *Troy* working under the same conditions you have here. So I'm very comfortable in suits."

"Do we *have* to wear the suits?" Sans asked. "I mean, we do most of our work in the boats. They're sealed."

"Yes," Dana said. "You have to wear the suits. First of all, it's regulation. Second, it's simply common sense."

"Nothing's ever...happened," Vila pointed out.

The pause didn't give Dana much belief that "nothing" had ever happened.

"There's a very thin skin of steel and carbon fiber around you in the boats," Dana pointed out. "Bad things sometimes do happen. Especially since what you're supposed to be doing is finding out if everything works. If you're working in an internal bay with double pressure doors, you can dispense with suits. Until then, you wear suits. Again, regulation and common sense."

The hatch opened and a tall, slender and good looking young man, obviously Palencia, practically ran in. Dana took one look at him and knew damned well what he'd been doing.

"Sorry it took so long," the EM said.

"Not a problem," Dana said, standing up. "Dana Parker, Engineer's Mate Second."

"Your rate tabs say coxswain," Palencia said, shaking her hand.

"I was a cox until this transfer," Dana said. "They reactivated my engineer rate. So, now that you're here, we can get into suits and head to the boats. I'll have to go throw the EM1s out of their office again. Perhaps when we return they'll have found me some quarters. If for no other reason than they're tired of getting thrown out of their office."

EIGHT

"The Horvath Polity rejects this position as unimportant and contrary to their just liberation of the Terran system," the Horvath envoy ground out through its horrible translator. "We further demand reparations for Horvath ships illegally attacked by Terran pirates and the unconditional surrender of the Terran system..."

"We're going to have to go this one alone," Horst commed Ve'Disuc.

"Apparently so." the Rangora commed back.

"What's the status of dropping the tribute?"

"Wait for our turn."

"Rangoran Empire?" the Ogut referee said.

"The Rangoran Empire agrees to drop demand for tribute upon the Terran system with Terran agreement to do the same against the Rangoran Empire as well as a binding agreement prohibiting the use of weapons of mass destruction against purely civilian targets, specifically cities and towns, with the understanding that any basing of military forces in or around such cities and towns are not party to this agreement and are legitimate targets of war. Furthermore, legitimate targets of war shall include high government officials of all branches and specifically any persons in or related to the chain of command of their respective militaries."

"The Terran delegation requests a short recess while this change in position is reviewed."

"Granted."

"That wasn't what we'd talked about," Horst said calmly.

"It was a late change," Ve'Disuc said, his scales rippling. "We just present what we're ordered, just like you."

"We're going to have to take part of it and leave the rest until we've gotten confirmation from Ministry."

"Understood."

"Does the Junta realize they just put themselves squarely in our crosshairs?"

"Terran forces are in the Terran system," Ve'Disuc replied, dryly. "That is a very long way from Rangor."

"American forces were in America at the beginning of World War Two, Ve'Disuc," Horst said. "Which with our technology at the time was a *very* long way from Berlin. And the only reason the Russians took it was we *let* them."

"Mother of God," Sans said when she was gone.

"What?" Palencia said. "She didn't seem that bad. And damned good looking."

"Don't, don't, *don't* say that to her," Velasquez said. "She's a real ball buster."

"And you weren't here for her little speech," Vila said. "We're going to be working on the boats at least six hours a day."

"In suits?" Palencia asked. "Is she nuts? And when am I going to see Carmencita?"

"On your off-duty time," Sans said. "If you make her conditions of training for the week. If not, forget it. And study is on our own time, now. Maximum of two hours per day on duty."

"That is... Diaz is never going to go for that," Palencia said.

"I think she has Diaz eating out of her hand," Sans said. "And she's a hard-ass like he is."

"I'm going to complain," Palencia said.

"I'm going to do what she said," Sans said, waving at Velasquez. "We'd better get in our suits."

"Sorry about this," Dana said, walking out of the engineering office in her suit. She had her gloves and helmet off but was otherwise ready to space walk.

"That was fast," Megdanoff said.

"What do you mean?" Dana asked.

"I mean... that was fast," Megdanoff repeated. "Did you do your checks?"

"Yes," Dana said. "And I examine my suit daily. I found this in a seal when I went to put it on," she added, holding up what looked like a dust bunny. "They do seem to get everywhere. Well, time to go round up the posse."

"Um..." the EM1 said delicately. "Knock?"

"Oh, *absolutely*," Dana said.

The quarters were not far and Dana knocked on Palencia and Vila's hatch, then commed.

"You decent?"

"No!" Vila shouted.

"Mental note," Dana said, actually recording it to her to-do list. "First training cycle on task, condition and standard for suit donning." She paused and thought about it. "*Second* training cycle on use of coms and implants. God almighty, this is going to be a pain in the butt."

Dana hung in the pencil corridor, one foot hooked into a rung by Twenty-Three to stabilize her, her helmet and gloves floating about a foot from her head in micro and her hands behind her head as she watched her division carefully working its way down the corridor to their boats. Just from their discomfort in micro she knew how much they'd been working on the boats.

She made the immediate decision that they were going to have to start at the very basics. It was unlikely that the boats had even had a proper daily PMCS much less the thirty-, sixty-, and ninety-day cycles.

Palencia wasn't bad in micro; he seemed like he was probably naturally athletic and of course had more time in space. The ER was clearly a noob. The other two just were awful. It occurred to her that from the looks they didn't even play null ball. Then it occurred to her that five was a null ball team and the training schedule didn't specify what *type* of training.

She commed Twenty-Three open and wordlessly pointed at the hatch.

"I think I need to make one more thing clear," Dana said as she flipped herself into gravity again. She was careful to do a perfect plant and caught her helmet as she landed. "I'm afraid you think I'm being a hard-ass just to be a hard-ass. I'm not. Or that I'm being a hard-ass because I'm a gringo. Last thing on my mind. I'm being a hard-ass for a bunch of reasons. The first, as I noted earlier, is that it's our mission. The second is that it's important. The third is because I was raised to believe that if you're going to do something, you should do it to the very best of your ability. Since I'm now responsible for this division, I'm going to do my level best to make it the very best division in the squadron. I intend to excel. You can feel free to try to interfere with that intent. You can try to play games. You can try to prevent that standard. Feel free. I am a master of playing games. Let's *play.*"

She toggled the hatch shut and put on her helmet and gloves, performing if not the world's fastest check of seals then very damned close.

"You might want to put on your helmets and gloves," she said as she commed the hatches shut.

"What are you doing?" Palencia asked, hooking on his helmet *without* a seal check.

"Preparing to pump down," Dana commed.

"What?" Vila asked. He still didn't have his helmet on and quickly donned it. The others just came out as a series of muffled shouts.

"First of all," Dana commed. "Learn to use your coms. I can't hear what you're saying."

"*We weren't really prepared to deal with vacuum,*" Palencia commed.

"The *Tr . . . Thermopylae* is a very big place and most of it's *pretty* safe," Dana commed. "But bad things happen. Especially to engineers who are working on their boats. There is *no such thing* as being unprepared for vacuum. If you are unprepared for vacuum in this job you might as well kill yourself right *now.* Because we are going to be in vacuum. A lot. If you came down here unprepared for vacuum that is a definitive statement that you haven't been doing the job. Again, this isn't a gringo thing or being a hard-ass. I'm trying to keep you *alive.* You're *my* people, now. I'm responsible for you. If one of you dies from a bad seal it reflects badly on me. If you can't even bother to check your seals, if you can't be bothered to maintain your suits, please go breathe vacuum under someone *else.* So, let's play. Is everyone sealed?"

"*This is very unwise, EM,*" Palencia commed.

"Why so?" Dana asked. "According to his record everyone is trained in suits and micro. *You* signed off ER Velasquez as trained in suits. *And* he's signed off by you as micro trained when he can barely make it to the boats. He's nearly completed all the conditions to be an engineer's apprentice. Are you saying that some of the division are not sufficiently versed in suits or have not maintained them to a standard that they can survive vacuum?"

Dana waited a moment for a response then unsealed her helmet.

"Perhaps we should have a class on suit maintenance and task, condition and standard of donning same to start? What do you think?"

"Where's the crowbar?" Dana asked. The suits hadn't been in really bad condition. The design was pretty good and could take a certain amount of crud. But they also hadn't been in great condition. She'd spent some time giving a class in how to properly maintain a suit, a class she suspected she'd have to repeat several times, then proper inspection and donning. When she was sure they were to condition she'd pumped down. Now she was trying, as subtly as possible, to determine their actual knowledge of the boats. She'd already figured out she couldn't trust a damned thing the records said.

"*What crowbar?*" Palencia commed. She'd kept the boat pumped down, just to make the point.

"You guys don't mount a crowbar?" Dana asked, aghast.

The last thing you did before certifying a new boat for use was weld brackets over the starboard tool locker and mount a crowbar. Knowing the true *significance* of the crowbar was sort of an ad hoc proof of having been "made" as an engineer. Generally, you were informed of The Significance of the Crowbar around the time you were about to make EM3, similar to an Army or Marine Corps corporal.

"*There's one in the kit bag,*" Palencia commed.

"Well, sure," Dana said, opening up the tool locker. There wasn't a kit bag. "Where's the bag?"

"*Uh, in my quarters, Miss,*" Velasquez commed.

"EM or, if I'm in a good mood, Parker," Dana replied. "And why is it in your quarters, ER? Standard regulation Six-One-Four-Three-Eight-Seven-Alpha states that the shuttle's tool bag, with all listed tools, will be maintained in the starboard storage locker unless it is in use."

"*So the tools don't get stolen,*" Palencia commed on a private channel.

"The boats lock, EM," Dana commed back. "Quarters don't lock."

"*You can get around the locks,*" Palencia said. "*If you just leave the tools lying around they disappear. So we keep them with us.*"

"Which means they're disappearing as we speak?" Dana asked.

"*Probably.*"

"Deal with that if we have to," Dana said. "Okay, enough chitchat. ER, you're going to remain on this boat. We're going to restart with the daily checks on each boat. I'm going to be doing secondary check on each boat as you complete. But to do some of those we need tools. So first I'll be going back to check on your tool boxes. And see if they've disappeared."

Which they had. Or there were simply tools missing from earlier. No real way to tell. What was immediately apparent was that the tool kits were incomplete.

"Leonidas, sorry to bother you again," Dana commed.

"Not busy at the moment, EM Parker," the AI commed back. *"What is your request?"*

"Did any personnel enter the quarters of my division after we left here at 1037?"

"Yes," Leonidas replied.

"And you can't tell me who because they're not my subordinates," Dana said.

"Correct," Leonidas replied. *"But if you're wondering where the tools went, you might ask EM1 Megdanoff to repeat the query. However, the bifurcate assembly tool was missing before the latest disappearance. I think EN Vila left it in the number fourteen portside inspection panel of his boat."*

"Roger. Thank you."

"One query, EM Parker?"

"Go, Leonidas?" Dana said.

"Is it permissible to use your handle of 'Comet'?"

"Roger, Leonidas," Dana commed.

"Based upon the quizzical nature of the response gestalt, you would like to know why. I am named after one of history's most famous warriors. It is in the nature of a salute, the proper address of a noted warrior."

"I am not a 'noted warrior,' Leonidas," Dana said uncomfortably.

"I am sure my namesake would have said the same, Comet. Leonidas out."

"Parker, could you meet me up at the head of the corridor?" Megdanoff commed.

"Be there in a sec, EM," Dana said. "Palencia, this relay isn't tightened."

"I thought it was," the EM3 said.

"Since it wiggles when you push it," Dana said, smiling, "it's pretty apparent that you never even put your hand on it, EM. Repeat the task, condition and standard for checking the four-one-six-eight starboard upper grapnel power relay."

"Visually and manually check the relay for cracks, dents, corrosion or other signs of gross damage," Palencia said, clearly reading off his plants. "Press on the relay and twist to ensure that it is in good physical contact. Connect the—"

"Okay, now when you read it actually *do* it," Dana said, straightening up. "Start the check again. I hit that on my first spot check. I don't want to *know* what else is wrong. And note that the starboard upper grapnel is deadline until this is fixed."

"EM ..." Palencia said.

"*Do* it," Dana said. "I've got to go talk to the EM1."

"Your tools," Megdanoff said, handing her a cloth bag.

"Except the split installer, which was in the port fourteen," Dana said, looking in the bag. It looked complete.

"Parker," Megdanoff said. "I don't want you to think that this is in any way a reflection on your sex ..."

Dana stood there looking at him quizzically for a moment. He was clearly marshalling his thoughts. Or maybe consulting his plants.

"And what am I doing wrong, EM?" Dana asked.

"Why is Twenty-Two deadline?"

"Four one six eight is marginal," Dana said. "Mis-mounted and it looks as if it's been that way for a while. Which means it's probably not going to pass the full power test. So far, the way it's looking, all the birds are going to be going down for a couple of days, maybe only a day. They're all behind on maintenance cycle for one thing, which sort of automatically deadlines them. I'm surprised they weren't deadlined already."

"Parker, we're trying very hard to maintain an up condition, here," Megdanoff said, carefully.

"EM, with all due respect, the bird is either right or it's not," Dana said, just as carefully. "These are my people. They have to fly in those birds. With respect, again, I neither want to deal with the accident review nor the memorial service if one of my guys buys it because the bird isn't good."

"Neither do I, Parker, but ..." Megdanoff pulled at his short hair for a moment. "Parker, there's more to this than I think you're looking at."

"I am always interested in new information, EM," Dana said, her eyes wide. She even blinked them.

"You can quit that, right now," Megdanoff said, flexing his jaw. "There's a lot more than you understand about this unit. You're looking at us and going 'this place is so screwed up no wonder it couldn't find its butt with both hands.'"

"The fact that two of my people were playing video games, one was asleep and the other was off post getting laid *did* sort of make an *interesting* first impression, EM."

"And *now* you're saying they're lazy," Megdanoff said.

"Not at all, EM," Dana said. "Leave it at developed bad habits."

"Which is a reflection on me," Megdanoff snapped.

"Not really," Dana said. "I'd say it's a reflection on Diaz but I don't really have a handle on him yet. He flew off the handle at the two juniors for playing games but at least they were awake. He more or less ignored that Vila was *asleep*. And I'm pretty sure he knew where Palencia spent his time."

"Okay, I'll try to lay out the problems that I know about of going at it as 'Me Hard-Ass Space-Bitch,'" Megdanoff said. "And that's not intended as an EEOC thing, I hope you..."

"Don't have a problem with the B word in that context, EM," Dana said. "I'm going to try to get my guys to quit calling me *'señorita,'* though. Better than *'puta,'* I suppose."

"Here's the problem," Megdanoff said. "Problems. First of all, they're going to do absolutely everything possible to shove a knife in your back. And they've got ways you can't even *imagine*. For one thing, you may not realize it but most of the people in this unit are politically connected at home. Even Velasquez comes from what they refer to as 'good family.' And every one of the countries they come from seem to have an absolute stream of bureaucrats that exist to do nothing but complain about their treatment. And those complaints don't come to the squadron. They go to the American State Department who then sends 'reply by endorsement' forms to Department of the Navy. So each and every time you bust somebody's chops, the Secretary of the God damned Navy is going to have to 'reply by endorsement' as to why you told Sans if you ever caught him listening to music in his quarters on duty he'd be up for a court-martial."

"Which was *not* what I said," Dana said, blanching slightly.

"*I* know that, *you* know that, the Secretary of the Damned *Navy* knows that!" Megdanoff said, pulling his hair again. "Did you record?"

"Yes," Dana said.

"Then we'll send the recording," Megdanoff said. "When we get the reply by endorsement. Which will take about a week. And it will dutifully be sent back. And then there will be another query asking if we're accusing their precious people of lying. And that will have to be replied to. *All* of it going through Department of the Navy. Eventually, they'll get so tired of having to push paper because of one low-rate EM that they'll find somewhere that low-rate EM isn't going to cause them so much trouble."

"Even if that low-rate EM is right?" Dana asked.

"Think about it," Megdanoff said, tilting his head to the side. "How many reply by endorsements do you think the Secretary of the Navy is willing to reply to before he starts to recognize your name? And do you really think he's going to care that you're trying to just keep your boats in top shape when the *first* time he sees the replies it's always from some high ranking member of the Argentinean government who has a perfectly justifiable complaint? Such as telling Sans he can't listen to music while studying for his quals?"

"You're serious," Dana said, thinking about the scene in the boat with the suits which was, actually, sort of pushing the line. "The *Secretary* of the God damned Navy?"

"As a heart attack," Megdanoff replied. "*And* the Secretary of State. I had the same attitude when I got here. I was going to straighten their shit out. This is me, now, saying *you* need to tread a *bit* more lightly. That's one reason. Second reason. I know what you want out of this division. You want it to be the best damned division in the squadron, which, by the way, would *not* be hard. I'll *freely* admit that. Four birds that actually *worked* and weren't just *signed off* as working would make you the best division in the squadron. But here's the problem with 'best division in the squadron.' Do you know that top members of South American soccer teams live under pretty much continuous death threat and have to have body guards?"

"Why?" Dana asked, shaking her head. "I mean, are they into drugs or..."

"Because they're *good*," Megdanoff said. "Because they stand out. Because they can turn a game. Because if you want competitive, you haven't *seen* competitive until you've seen Latin Americans. Get their competitive streak going and they have a simple answer. If it's easier to make *you* fail than work to *beat* you, they'll make you fail. You fail, they win, game over. One way or another. We tried the same thing when we first started and have *barely* gotten them to quit sabotaging each other's boats! I think we lost a couple in Eridani because somebody had futzed with their nav controls."

"Jesus Christ," Dana said, shaking her head.

"So when Persing, who is, yes, an amiable moron, said that you need to respect their culture you took that as bullshit. Which at a certain level is true. Just respecting a culture for pure multi-culturalism is not about getting the mission done. Which is the only and always bottom-line. But respecting the little niggling issues about their culture like not having your boat sabotaged to get you out of the way or not having your career sabotaged to get you out of the way is, actually, sort of important."

"Engineer's Mate," Dana said, "I know all about 'cheerful and willing obedience to orders' but I'm not sure I'm willing to fly in these boats if that's the standard under which they have to be maintained. I know *way* too much about how they can screw up in the best of conditions."

"Which is why I have it arranged that I never go out in the boats," Megdanoff said. "The only gringo in the unit who does is the CO. And we check his boat *very* carefully. Besides, the guys like and respect him. *That* is the key. If they like and respect you you can get them to do the job. They also just automatically respect rank. But at this point, you had that run-in with Benito, who's sort of a leader among the junior enlisted in the squadron, you're coming across as a hard-ass bitch, you're playing the competitive game and, last but not least at all, you're a girl. And while I come from the background that I don't give a damn, they *do*. That tool bag is just another coffin nail. You used the entry and tracking system. By doing that you essentially broke the *omerta*. You dissed the honor of the guys who had successfully stolen those tools by using an underhanded trick.

"You're hurting their feelings. You're bruising their egos and wimping their machismo or whatever. 'Women aren't allowed to talk to our people that way' is probably going to be the subtext of the first reply by endorsement.

"I've been working with these guys for a year and I still don't really understand what positively motivates them. Negative motivation I know chapter and verse. The CO seems to get it but he's just charismatic and friendly. Frankly, you probably should have played the 'I'm just a poor pitiful little girl' game from the beginning but it's too late for that."

"You got all that in, what, three *hours*?" Dana asked.

"They also back channel a *lot*," Megdanoff replied. "That's the one part I do seem to be tapped into."

"So is this an official counseling statement on cultural interaction, EM?" Dana asked, thinking furiously.

"No," Megdanoff said, sighing. "This is absolutely unofficial. From my *official* point of view we're all best friends and the birds are great. Remember the bit where you talked about not wanting to go to the memorial service? This is about *that*. Or seeing a promising career just as shot to hell."

"I have a hard time believing they'd sabotage my bird because I . . . dissed their machismo or whatever," Dana said, shaking her head.

"These cultures are all about . . . face if you will," Megdanoff said. "It's about their concept of honor. And I do mean *all*. There are some really strong cultural reasons for that in their home countries and that goes for *all* of them and *all* their countries. Like I said, these are all kids from 'good families.' Some nobody farm girl is *not* allowed to disrespect their kids because that is disrespect to the *family*. Rank has nothing to do with it, *survival* has nothing to do with it. Palencia. Take a closer look at his file. He's got a bachelor's in engineering from the University of La Paz. His primary hobby is listed as polo. You know how much money it takes to be a polo player even in *Argentina*? In his country a nobody farm girl is just a casual lay."

"That explains the athleticism," Dana said. "Hell, I'd probably like him if he wasn't such a prick."

"And he's saying the same thing about you, I'm sure," Megdanoff said.

"So what do I do?" Dana said.

"That's the problem," the EM replied. "I really don't know. Like I said, if I'd caught it ahead of time I'd have suggested, up to you, playing the poor-poor-pitiful girl. Let them carry the tool bag and such. 'Could you *please* check the relay again? I'm afraid something bad might happen if it goes *bad*!' Bat your eyes. Too late for that."

"I'd say that's a hell of a way to run a railroad but it's more like I'm not sure you *can* run a space navy that way," Dana said, shaking her head. "I mean, seriously. These boats are not up to standard and up to *standard* is close enough to breathing vac."

"They'd rather lose boats than honor," Megdanoff said. "They'd rather lose *lives* than honor. Think of it that way. Know why there are only kids from good families working as, face it, wrench monkeys?"

"Why?"

"The 143rd is the *combined* contribution of all the countries. They're paying for the boats, personnel and maintenance. Supposedly to, and I did not use this word, 'our' standard. But from *their* point of view, they are *their* boats. And they're the most advanced weaponry any of those countries possess. This is the absolute top of their line. They're trying to field a combined *Constitution* class. Different name, mind you. But the same ship. It's one hell of a lot of money to them. The U.S. has fielded fourteen. So this is their best and their brightest. Seriously. They're not stupid. And one more thing."

"Go," Dana said.

"They are, and I am not understating this, absolutely fearless," Megdanoff said, shaking his head. "Various reasons but you guys had it relatively easy with Station One. And from what I heard, that was bad enough. But we had *lots* of problems with integrating with the support ships."

Dana remembered what taking the station had been like. If they hadn't had support from the *Constitution*- and *Independence*-class ships they probably could never have *boarded* it. The *Troy* could have blown it out of space easily enough, it had destroyed over thirty warships in the system, but *taking* it would have been another issue. On at least three occasions the support ships had blown away resistance that would have been a major issue to both the Marines and the boats.

Taking it *without* effective support? That would have been double tough.

"And that has been another point of contention," Megdanoff said, sighing. "They feel like they were left in the lurch. That the Americans got better support because the ship crews were all American. Truth was, again between you and me, the chain of command simply didn't *get* the way you did that sort of interaction.

They were too hierarchical about it. By the time they requested the fire, because it had to be approved through a dozen layers, they'd already taken the casualties. It was cultural, again. But you can explain that until you're blue in the face and they won't listen. That would be—"

"A violation of honor?" Dana said, nodding. "Okay, I get it. I'm screwed, blued and tattooed. Which means there's only one way forward. Changing course at this point would just make me look like, well, a pussy. So that means I have to play the same game, just with some minor variations. Which means we have to discontinue this evolution and go to another one. Where can we keep the tools where they won't get stolen?"

"Good luck," Megdanoff said. "There are plenty of tools and parts. There's no particular reason to steal them. It's like a game to them."

"Okay," Dana said. "I'm good at those sorts of games."

"What are you going to do?" Megdanoff said nervously.

"We're going to play for the rest of the day," Dana said. "Like I said, I'm *good* at games."

NINE

"They will figure out where they are hidden," Palencia commed.

"Sure they will," Dana said, finishing the lashings on the toolbag. "But are they as questioning of their suits as you were?"

"Admittedly, yes," Palencia said. He still sounded a bit nervous being out in the main bay.

"Then they can feel free to boldly go out onto the exterior of the hulls to get our tools," Dana said. "And if their suits are as screwed up as yours were, they can feel free to suck vacuum. They're not my people. You are my people. And now we are going to go play."

"Where the hell did you come from?"

The speaker was an American. Dana tagged him and shook her head.

"From the One-Four-Three, Sergeant First Class," Dana said, smiling. The null grav courts weren't full but they were close. And from the looks of things the only thing the Pathan Marines knew how to play was jungleball. On the other hand, they didn't play it very *well*.

"You're not authorized in this space, little lady," Sergeant First Class Mat Del Papa said.

"If you'll consult the schedule, Sergeant First Class, you will note that three of the null grav courts currently under use by your Marines are scheduled for the One-Four-Three."

"Who never use the courts, miss," the SFC said patiently. "And, just an FYI, we try really hard not to mix in girls with the Pathans. It's a straightforward religious insult to see a woman dressed the way you are."

"In my *issue* PT T-shirt and *issue* shorts, SFC?" Dana said, smiling. "Since I'm, you know, a member of the *Navy* with a *rank*, Sergeant First Class?"

"That's the way you wanna play it?" the SFC asked, his face blank.

"I've been playing games all day, Sergeant First Class," Dana said, her smile fading and her eyes going from blue to gray. "I'm about sick of them to tell you the truth. A nice round of jungleball will do three things. One, it's a game I *know,* not flailing in the dark. Two, my men need training in micro. Three, it will cement that while I'm a split, I'm not a *pussy*, Sergeant First Class."

"These guys barely play by jungleball rules, Engineer's Mate Parker," Del Papa pointed out.

"Any weapons?" Dana asked.

"No. We're pretty careful about that one."

"Then it's all good," Dana said. "Which court?"

"Four," the SFC said, shaking his head. "If you're really going to do this."

"Palencia, you're going to have to talk to them, I suppose," Dana said.

"*Talk* to them?" Palencia said. "I barely like *carrying* them. I talk to those Islamic assholes as little as possible."

"Ah, the joys of being in an Alliance," Dana said, putting in her mouth guard as the door to the court opened up.

"Sergeant First Class, what is this...*this* doing here?" one of the Pathans asked, pointing at Dana.

"This is Engineer's Mate Second Class Parker, Sergeant Charikar," Del Papa said. "She and her division are here to play null ball."

"Her dress is as a whore, Sergeant." The Afghan Marine was tall and, to Dana's surprise, had blue eyes. "She should not even be allowed into our presence. It is an insult to God."

"Nonetheless, her unit actually *is* scheduled to use this court," Del Papa said. "And she and her team wish to play null ball. Since they didn't bring anyone else, I suppose they need to play your team. Or you can cede the territory to her and wait for another and they can...play with themselves."

"This is a deliberate insult," Charikar said. "Our liaison will be informed of this incident."

"Hey, what's another reply by endorsement?" Dana asked.

"Says you," Del Papa said, putting in his mouthpiece.

"You going to ref?"

"Wouldn't miss this for worlds," the Green Beret said. "I hope you know what you're doing."

"My guys are about to find out how to work in micro," Dana said. "I'm about to get my mad out. Pretty much covers it."

Five of the Pathans spilled out of the court, making way for her team. She was used to guys looking at her in her PT uniform. She was in shape and not particularly ugly. What she *wasn't* used to was expressions of loathing.

"Is that really a *woman*?" one of them asked sotto voce.

"You've seen them here," a lance corporal replied. "They are whores."

"You call our NCOIC a whore one more time and you'll lose teeth," Sans snarled.

"Then tell her not to dress like a whore, infidel!"

"Whoa!" Del Papa said. "Marines, keep your comments to yourself. Suds, do the same. You want to fight, you're about to get your chance."

"This is *insane*!" Palencia whispered to Dana as they walked onto the court. "These are animals."

"Time to be a better animal," Dana said, rotating her neck. "Look, you're about the only one that has any ability in micro. These guys play by grabbing on and wrestling. And, apparently, biting. Keep moving and break their hold. Just let me carry the ball."

"I thought you weren't supposed to carry in null ball," Velasquez said nervously.

"This is jungleball," Dana said, rotating her jaw. "First rule of jungleball is technically no weapons. Real rule is do whatever you have to do to win. Now let's beat up some Pathans."

"And grav . . . off," Del Papa said, releasing the ball upwards. "Game on!"

Dana pushed off from the wall and intercepted the ball before the first of the Pathans could get near it. A hand snaked out at her and she slammed the ball backwards and grabbed the Afghan's wrist. She had enough velocity that they immediately went into a spin. Three more were closing on her, clearly intending a little four-on-one smack-down. Or, knowing Pathans, something much more personal. She spun the lance corporal into them and then bounced off the resulting tangle. That had four of them out of action for a moment. The only one remaining was Charikar, who was closing on her, not the ball. She bounced off a wall, caught one of his ankles and went into a flat spin. By bouncing off the still tangled Afghans she managed to get a major rotation out of his body and slammed *him* into the pile. Hard.

"Call *me* a whore, you flea-ridden, balless faggot?" Dana said. "Your mother was a whore in Peshawar who serviced only Jews."

"And that's *goal*!" Del Papa shouted. "Return to your sides."

"What?" Dana said, looking around.

Palencia came bouncing back by her from the Afghan's goal, grinning.

"You may be having fun but we have a game to win. Where did you learn that insult? It sounded like a direct translation."

"It's *amazing* what you can find on the hypernet."

"Oooh," Sans groaned as they walked out of the court. "That last round was a nightmare."

Del Papa was just shaking his head.

"Did you *have* to send half the team to the infirmary? There's getting your mad out and getting your mad out."

"They were trying pretty damned hard to send *me* to the infirmary," Dana said. She had a bite on her leg that was going to need to be looked at. "I was just returning the favor."

"You're not going to get them to respect you by being more Billy Bad-Ass than they are," Del Papa said. "Quite the opposite."

"I'm not trying to get the Pathans to respect me," Dana said. "I don't *need* them to respect me. I like Marines, generally. Get along with them great. USMC at least. *These* guys? Apparently this whole damned station runs by jungleball rules. Okay. I understand there's a MASSEX in a couple of weeks to try to figure out this whole boarding thingy. Sergeant, I control your air, gravity and *inertia*. And as screwed up as everything else is on this station, I could kill a whole load of them and not only get away with it, because I am a *very* good engineer, but apparently it would be shrugged off with a, variously, *mañana* or *In'sh'allah*. Sergeant, they should be sending me expensive *chocolates*."

"I'll keep that firmly in mind," Del Papa said, chuckling. "And try to make sure I get a different boat."

"Sergeant," Dana said. "It wouldn't even be a boat from *my* division."

✳   ✳   ✳

"Are we going to have to do that again?" Palencia asked when they were back in the squadron area.

"Every damned day," Dana said. "One hour of weights and one hour of jungleball. Until you make *my* standards of micro activity. Vila, you're going to have to make yourself scarce, as in in the squadron area but not in your room, while I have a private chat with Palencia."

"Yes, EM," Vila said, his eyes widening just a bit.

"Quiet chat?" Palencia asked.

"We'll have to hold that until we're, well, *private*," Dana said, smiling and batting her eyes.

"Leonidas, Comet," Dana said as soon as the hatch was closed.

"Go Comet," Leonidas said over the 1MC.

"I need a high level lock on a recording," Dana said. "To clarify, if the question ever comes up officially as to what was discussed, there is a recording. If there are simply rumors and low-level personnel are curious for prurient reasons, the recording cannot be opened."

"You'll need a high enough level lock-out," Leonidas said. "I cannot interfere in chain-of-command."

"Send a standard query to Chief Elizabeth Barnett," Dana said. "That way the only person who can open it is one of the officers or the squadron chiefs."

"Sent and . . . agreed," Leonidas said, with a tone of curiosity.

"Thank you, Leonidas," Dana said.

"You are welcome, Comet."

"You have a good relationship with the AI," Palencia said curiously. "I don't think that I have heard him more than twice."

"I get along with AIs," Dana said. "It's a knack. Since they don't have gonads, I figure it doesn't have anything to do with my pheromones. Grab a seat, Palencia. We need to chat."

"About?"

"I got a . . . not so much a dressing down as a cultural lecture from Megdanoff," Dana said. "Apparently, everything I've done since hooking up with the division is wrong. And wrong in a really big way. Thing is, I get that I'm stepping on your culture, but I also know space. And while there may be a . . . fatalistic attitude about that in your culture, in my culture everything I said goes.

I don't want to go to your memorial service. I especially would like to avoid being the centerpiece of one. And the way the birds are, that's more than likely. You're an engineer, what I call a 'real' engineer. You've *got* to know that."

"My bird is fine," Palencia said, shrugging. "The air, gravity and drive work."

"The grapnels don't," Dana said. "I'm not disagreeing, I'm trying to get a handle on this."

"We rarely use them," Palencia said, shrugging again. "So I don't pay as much attention to them."

"You guys don't work the scrapyard?" Dana said.

"Rarely. And when we do, well, most of our grapnels don't work so we don't."

"Is that a deliberate two-fer?" Dana asked.

"I don't know what you mean."

"If your grapnels don't work, you don't have to work the scrapyard?"

"Still not quite getting your meaning," Palencia said. "Perhaps it is the translation?"

Human implants were derivatives of the highest tech Glatun systems. They took into account accent and colloquial meaning where translatable. The only reason Palencia wouldn't understand her was if he really could not understand the question or was simply avoiding it.

"Okay," Dana said. "Do I just not know how to ask you questions?"

"There are questions and questions, EM," Palencia said.

"Questions I can ask and questions I can't ask?"

"More should avoid asking."

"I guess I'm looking for cultural cues here," Dana said. "I really don't know how to handle your culture and I'm getting that. I've been told that it's not even a good idea to try to be the best division in the squadron."

"We already are the best division in the squadron," Palencia said, shrugging. "I assumed that was why you were assigned to us."

"What?" Dana said. "How? I don't get it. I'm sorry, that's not translating or something."

"We have the highest marks in the squadron," Palencia said. "We have repeatedly been at the top of the inspections. It is one of the reasons that we were so shocked by your approach. It was, yes, an insult to our competence when we felt we had already demonstrated it. And, as I said, I assume why you were placed with us. I'm sorry I had not realized who you were. Your reputation, as a pilot at least, precedes you. What I found surprising was that you had no particular commendations for your many actions. You have a general NavCom and you were promoted rather fast, but no medals for valor."

"I was just doing my job," Dana said, shrugging.

"You were doing an excellent job," Palencia replied. "You should have been given a medal for the station boarding at the very least. I think if I'm reading correctly that you were the first shuttle on the ground."

"Second," Dana said. "By maybe a second if that makes any sense. Thirty-One was there about the same time. They... didn't make it off the LZ."

"Again, getting your wounded ship back to pick up more Marines and then returning to the boarding action?" Palencia said. "There should have been a medal involved."

"I'm not really big on medals," Dana said, shrugging.

"Then you are mad," Palencia said. "How else do people know who you are? What you've done?"

"You do," Dana said, then slapped her forehead. "Damnit. Cultural."

"I... do not understand," Palencia said.

"My culture doesn't *like* praise," Dana said. "I mean, yeah, we like it. But we... we sort of push it off."

"Is *that* what it is?" Palencia said. "I've seen that in some of you Nortés. Yet, I think you get more of it in the end."

"I don't get you," Dana said. "Not lack of translation, but rephrase?"

"I'm thinking about it," Palencia said. "Our conversation. You say 'I was just doing my job.' I then, in an attempt to point out that it was more than your job, repeat your actions. This is praise."

Dana suddenly realized that while she had approached Palencia as something of a cock-up, more of a playboy playing at being a ship's engineer than anyone serious, he was probably *way* smarter than she was in pure brain power.

"My culture is probably more honest about it," Palencia said. "We simply expect to be praised. And there is a specific amount of it and then we go on. You can... I guess the way you would put it is 'milk' it for some time."

"I don't..." Dana said. "Is that what we're doing?"

"It certainly looks that way from the outside," Palencia said. "I'd never really thought about it."

"I'm still interested in getting the birds right," Dana said, suddenly revisiting her own cultural background. *Is that* really *what we do?* "I mean, call it cultural or whatever. I'm a freak about things being right. Not looking right or seeming right or on paper right. *Being* right. Space is a colder bitch than I ever can be. I just try to keep up."

Palencia burst out in laughter at that until he nearly cried.

"That is a very good way to put it, I suppose," Palencia said. "Again your Norté deprecation but this time I will not disagree. You are called Comet. Do you have another handle?"

"If you're asking do I have a handle like Ice Queen, yes," Dana said.

"I think we should call you Quipu," Palencia said, smiling.

"Which means?" Dana said then got a flash off the hypercom. "Oh, great! I'm a *llama*?"

"Assuredly not a llama," Palencia said, grinning. "Quipu are very beautiful animals and never used as beasts of burden. The most expensive and soft wool in the world. Their fleece was reserved for the Incas. Also *very* hard to handle and prefer it *very* cold."

"Great," Dana said, knowing damned well she was stuck with the handle. "But about getting the division up to the point I don't have to worry about going out in the Black. Seriously. How?"

"Why did we play jungleball?" Palencia asked.

"*Besides* so I could get my mad out at the situation playing non-micro-capable Pathans?" Dana asked. "I was hoping that the division would actually find it a bonding exercise. At the very least that you might be able to see past my butt to my skills."

"Well, I did get the most goals," Palencia pointed out.

"While I was clearing the way," Dana said. "Does it help you, from your cultural perspective, if we continue that way in general? Or *can* I clear the way and let you get the goals? I really don't care about goals except mine. Which are to have everyone in the division come back in one piece and the boats capable of delivering the mail. That was a metaphor for 'we can do all the tasks expected of a boat division.' Including, yes, working the scrapyard or helping close the main door."

"Why should I assist you in your goals?" Palencia asked. "What is in it for me?"

"Besides going home in one piece?" Dana asked. "Because that is, you understand, one of *my* goals. What are your goals?"

"To go home in one piece," Palencia said. "And I make sure my boat is capable of getting me home. The honor of having been in this great action. And to be an officer so I never have to turn a wrench again. Being an engineer's mate is very nearly a loss of honor. I have a *bachelor's* in engineering and I am working as an *enlisted* man."

"So...why *are* you an enlisted man?" Dana asked.

"Because more powerful families made sure *their* sons were officers," Palencia said, shrugging. "In time there will be more squadrons, more officer slots. Then I will be an officer."

"Just like that?" Dana asked, frowning. "Pull some strings and, bam, instant officer?"

"No, of course not," Palencia said. "There will be a slot in officer's school or I will return to school for my master's and go to officer's school afterwards. That is how these things are done. That *is* how things are done?"

"Cultural," Dana said, frowning still. "Uh, no, not in my culture. I mean, it was suggested that I apply for OCS one time, but that was based upon...um...merit? Like you said, I have done some things that stick out and I've got a pretty high GCT. When my basic term was coming up, not that that means anything with stop-loss, a couple of people suggested OCS or even that school for people in the military who get selected for Annapolis. But... I sort of took a pass. I liked flying. Like engineering, too. But I'm doing good work where I'm at."

"So you intend to be a career NCO?" Palencia asked, frowning in turn.

"Career?" Dana said, shrugging. "Current enlistment is for the duration and the duration looks to be a long time. Do I want to be an officer? Not really. So I guess, yes."

"Ah," Palencia said, nodding.

"I just missed something cultural, didn't I?" Dana asked.

"I am trying to think how to phrase it," the EM3 said. "And, yes, it is cultural. Americans simply do not understand what the word 'class' means. It translates as one word but it has a thousand meanings. Americans do not have class. They have different economic levels but they do not have *class*. Class is something you are born to. No, I take that back. Some of them have class but they try very hard to hide it. You would not even know the names of Americans with class.

"Every member of this squadron, even Velasquez, is of the officer class. *None* of us should be turning a wrench or even flying a shuttle, given that that is the job now of enlisted men. Women, in your case. We are here because our countries are spending a simply ruinous amount of their treasury on these boats and thus they send their best. We are *all* of the better class.

"Career NCOs..." Palencia said and then shrugged. "They are *not* of the better class. Not of the worst but certainly not of the better. It was assumed that you, too, intend to be an officer and for some reason simply are biding your time as a..."

"Wrench turner," Dana said. "So...what you're saying is that I'm now too low class."

"When you told me you intended not to be an officer I had to quell my immediate reaction to, therefore, treat you as your class," Palencia said. "You..."

"Should be holding your horse?" Dana asked.

"I wouldn't put it *that* way," Palencia said.

"Not upset by it," Dana said. "Just trying to assimilate it."

"I would suggest that it remain between us," Palencia said.

"So..." Dana said. "You guys probably have some problems, at a certain level, with people like Megdanoff."

"We understand that there are cultural differences. But that is at an intellectual level. So, yes, we have problems with taking direction from someone who is not our better. Quite the opposite."

"Oh, wow," Dana said, shaking her head. "This gets more and *more* screwed up. So...Class is about social status. Social status is about position and control of decisions. So some farm girl insulting you probably causes some reduction in not only *your* social status but that of your family. That was what Megdanoff meant. So it makes it less likely that you get your cushy officer slot when one comes open."

"I would not have put it so...bluntly," Palencia said uncomfortably.

"Yeah, I wasn't real comfortable with the discussion about increased praise by deprecation," Dana said. "The division working properly isn't going to raise your social status?"

"Performing maintenance?" Palencia said, laughing. "Please. We are to be officers. That is for the lower classes. Not that they do the work unless you ride them all the time. They are born lazy."

"So why didn't they send...enlisted class and let you guys... play polo or something?" Dana asked desperately.

Reading between the lines, that meant that *as* officers they were micromanagers. Which filled in the blanks of why they couldn't reduce the level of call for fire during the boarding. For that matter, controlling the fire of a cruiser was probably a social prop so it wouldn't be delegated down, lest the delegator lose status. "During the boarding I *personally* directed the fire of the supporting cruisers." No captain was going to lose the social props because he wanted to be an admiral and that probably depended more on discussions at dinners about his heroic actions during the boarding than his actual record. Not to mention whether he was of the right class and family.

And it meant that even senior and experienced NCOs were not trusted to be competent at a basic level. Which meant that you "had" to have an officer overseeing what in Western formations, and especially U.S. formations, was handled by NCOs.

"One of these shuttles is a good bit of the Gross Domestic Product of Ecuador," Palencia said, snorting. "Less so of Argentina, of course. But it required several nations working together to fund this squadron. They were not going to turn that over to monkeys."

Sometimes Dana tended to forget just how expensive all these systems were. And how much of a difference in GDP there was between the U.S., even *after* being repeatedly bombed by KEWs, and the rest of the Western Hemisphere.

"So pretty much everything about this whole setup has been an insult and disturbed your...what would you call it?"

"Social politics is the technical term," Palencia said, nodding. "Yes. From the ultimatum from your late President to the conditions under which we serve to the lack of support from your ships during the boarding. And, of course, the way we are treated by *very* junior American enlisted."

"So why the hell are you even in the Alliance?" Dana asked.

Palencia just gestured around with his hands.

"Your Mr. Vernon had a lock on off-world technology and was less than involved in sharing. We get access to very advanced technology. Gravitational theory and design. Laser emitter technology.

Astronics. And as part of the Alliance we get increased defense of our nations."

"And I can't help you with any of your goals," Dana said. "All I can do is make things worse."

"As far as I can see, yes," Palencia said. "Since we are being Norté frank. Don't get me wrong, I like you. Not just as a woman, and you are a very desirable woman. You have spirit and I like that. If you were a polo player, I'd want you as my third. If you were a man. Women simply don't have the strength and endurance to make serious polo players. But as you noted, everything you have done since arriving has made my life more difficult to no great advancement. And that is ignoring the . . . what is the term? Ah, coitus interruptus."

"I've got to give this some thought," Dana said, standing up. "I'm not used to having to judge every action on the basis of what effect it has on a social structure in a nation I can barely place on a map."

"You begin to understand the limitations of your class," Palencia said. "It *can* learn!"

"Pal," Dana said, putting one hand on his shoulder and looking him in the eye. "You use the term 'limitations of your class' again and the next time we play jungleball I'm going to slam you into the Pathans."

"And that is a, pardon, classic response," Palencia said. "Which pretty much defines the difference between our classes."

TEN

"Chief, I hate to keep bothering you..." Dana commed.

"And I hate it that you have to keep bothering me," Barnett replied. "But from what I'm getting from the Chief's network you're probably not going to be there much longer."

"From what I just got, that's just as probable," Dana said. "But it's got bigger implications. I don't think that having Nortés here is worth the trouble. In fact, it's more like stuffing ants in your pants. You have access to that recording. When you get a chance, and I'd strongly suggest that be soon, you need to review it. You can't *use* it, you understand..."

"Private chat?" Barnett asked.

"And because it was private, Palencia, who's something like some, I think rich, Argentinean family's crown prince, laid things out pretty bluntly. I don't think the implications of some very big stuff is really understood."

"Oh, it's understood," Barnett said. "We're dealing with some of it on this end now that we've had the Latin contingent transferred over. Are they as bad at maintenance over there? Because either we're getting the dregs or the One-Four-Three has to be even more screwed up than I'd realized. These guys barely know how to fix their suits and the coxes are for crap."

"Chief," Dana said. "Take the time. Review the whole thing. Then we need to talk. Seriously. I mean, you fly over here or I'll fly over there talk. I don't think people really understand just how messed up this situation is. From top to bottom."

"Okay," Barnett said in a curious tone.

"Oh, and Chief?" Dana said, carefully. "When it gets to the discussion about class, try not to lose it?"

"Class, huh?" Barnett said. "I may have to block out some time real soon."

"You were serious about this physical training," Sans said, lifting the barbell and putting it back on the rack.

"Sometimes we have to pull high-g maneuvers," Dana said. "A good bit of the time, if the coxes know what they're doing. And sometimes things go wrong when you least expect it. Which means you might have to chin yourself up the entire boat to fix something. So, yeah, we need to be in good physical condition."

"And you intend to return to the null grav court so we can be pummeled by Islamic terrorists," Palencia said.

"Yep," Dana said. "And as you get better, you'll get less and less pummeled. Since for reasons of both regulation and size I can't do wall-to-wall counseling on you for not being able to handle yourselves in micro, I'm going to let the Pathans do it until you learn. Of course, you better hope they don't learn faster than you."

"You are so kind, Quipu," Palencia said.

"Hah, she is a quipu, no?" Benito called.

"She is *our* quipu, Benito," Palencia said. "Thus we get to call her Quipu. Not some ghetto monkey."

"Who are you calling ghetto, you horse-dick sucking wimp," Benito said, coming up off his bench with fists raised.

"EM Palencia," Dana said sharply. "I'm going to pretend that I did not hear an EM3 refer to an EM2 in a derogatory fashion because that would be disrespect to an NCO which is a *chargeable* offense and then I'd have to request you be masted. As I will ignore when you very politely *apologize* to the EM2."

"I'm not going to—"

"*Now*, Engineer's Mate," Dana barked.

"I sincerely apologize for any offense I may have rendered you, Engineer's Mate," Palencia said, his teeth grinding.

"I apologize, as well, for any offense my division may have presented you, Engineer's Mate Benito," Dana said, standing up and looking him in the eye.

"He can't call me those things," Benito said hotly.

"Correct," Dana said. "Which is why the regulation exists. You are a superior rank. I might add that it is also a chargeable offense to refer to a superior as a whore."

"That was never said," Benito replied angrily.

"You guys apparently didn't pay attention to the fact that Leonidas records pretty much *anything* said in a public venue," Dana said. "So. These are *my* brothers. This is my team. And we now have a balance of power. You drop the dime on *my* team, I drop it on *yours*. Or we can return to neutral corners and be all friendly and stuff. Or at least act that way."

"No one would listen to you," Benito said. "Nobody cares what you say."

"Really?" Dana said. "Leonidas? Were you monitoring yesterday morning's altercation in the gym?"

"Would you like me to play back the recording?" the AI asked.

"No, thank you, Leonidas," Dana said. "Thank you."

"You are welcome, Comet."

"And before you say that the AI talks to me because I'm a Norté, think again. I've heard that they rarely speak to anyone at my rank, Norté or otherwise. I just seem to have a knack. But the point is made. So I'd suggest we return to neutral corners."

"Bitch," Benito muttered.

"Correct," Dana said. "Not normally, but you guys seem to bring it out. And I'm not going 'Oh, Benito, I'm *so* afraid!' So you've got to wonder why? Why am I perfectly comfortable playing null ball with Pathan Marines who dearly hate my guts and would like nothing better than to kill me? Or more likely rape me to make me learn my 'place'? What makes me comfortable sitting here eyeball to eyeball with you? You want machismo? Try not only surviving being mid-spaced by a shuttle where your buddy just ate a missile but flying the broken bird *back* to the *Jimmy*, picking up *another* load of Marines and taking same broken bird *back* into a hot LZ, Benito. What you have to wonder is where I've been, what I've done, that makes me not give a rat's butt about your very capable stare, Benito. I don't know anything about you. I don't know why Pallie called you ghetto. You don't know anything about *me*, either, Benito. I've spit in death's eye so many times he's tired of being blinded, Benito. So I'd *really* suggest we take it to neutral corners."

"You've got..." He paused, clearly unsure how to continue.

"The term you're looking for is massive ovaries," Dana said.

"Heh," Benito said, grinning. "Yeah. Big ovaries."

"Seriously, no idea how big," Dana said. "But if you want to play a little null ball we can discuss it."

"I've heard," Benito said, shaking his head. "No way."

"To clarify," Dana said, raising her voice. "Yeah. I really *am* a farm girl. Big farm, mind you. Right at three thousand acres. Three older *male* cousins, which starts to get you some of the backstory. And, yeah, I've tossed haybales. And I was a gymnast. And the way that I'd get my mad out on the *Troy* was by going to the welder bars and kicking ass. Of course, to do that here I'd have to have somebody I could trust to have my back and so far nobody but the *Pathans* seem up to the party. Any takers?"

"You aren't a bitch," Benito said, shaking his head. "You're crazy."

"Certified as high level PTSD since I was three years old," Dana said, leaning forward into the El Salvadoran's personal space. "*Walked* out of L.A. Three. Years. Old. Do the math."

"Mother of God..." one of the group muttered.

"The fires," Benito said quietly.

The L.A. superfire, started by the Horvath kinetic energy weapon that had wiped out one of the world's wealthiest and best known cities, had caught just as the chaparral was at peak. Less than ten percent of the population had made it out of the basin alive.

"Three years old," Dana said, quietly. "Who are *any* of you to call *me* whore? So I suggest that we return to neutral corners."

"Yes," Benito said. "I agree."

"Thank you," Dana said, sitting back down at the weight machine. She gave an image of perfect calm.

"I paid too little attention to one of the articles about you," Palencia said as she started doing reps. "I'd noticed you were an orphan, but...there are many."

"Dad died in Anaheim," Dana said. "Mom committed suicide right after we got to the farm."

"I'm sorry," Palencia said.

"Don't be," Dana replied, grunting as she worked off the adrenaline on the weights. "What doesn't kill us makes us stronger. Pal, I've been thinking about everything you said yesterday."

"And?" the Argentinean asked.

"And I'm going to have to ignore it," Dana said. "I've looked at my goals and your goals. The team's goals to the extent that you're correct about those goals. I don't know how I can positively effect your goals. I'll keep trying to think of a way but you're right. My background means I can't really positively affect your environment. I might negatively affect it. People might take umbrage to my pointing out that, no, the shuttles are *not* ready for service. But I can't worry about that. With no way to work your social side, I need to concentrate on what I *do* know. So we're going to just fix the damned shuttles."

"Simple as that?" Palencia said, chuckling.

"I thought a lot about what you said," Dana said. "As much as I understand about your side and as much as I could figure out about mine. And I realized that I was going about this all wrong. Oh, same basic idea, but I was going at it wrong. You see, what you described of dealing with your . . . monkeys? We call that micromanagement."

"I've heard the term," Palencia said, shrugging. "But it is necessary."

"Unfortunately," Dana said, sitting up. "You see, I'm a natural micromanager. I'm OCD as hell as *well* as being PTSD. I'm naturally the sort of person who wants things to be absolutely perfect. One of the docs said that it was because I couldn't control my environment in my early life, but from what I heard my mom was the same way. Nature, nurture, take your pick, I'm OCD as *hell*.

"Which means I'm actually kind of good for space. But most American spacemen I've dealt with, that's the wrong approach. Being a micromanager doesn't work real well with American spacemen. They're motivated, in general, to do the best job possible. Among other things, they don't want to die by sucking vacuum or being blown apart by a plasma explosion. You give them a task, condition and standard, give them the training to meet it and, by and large, they'll try to meet it to the best of their ability."

"Feel lucky," Palencia said. "Trying to get the monkeys to do anything is tough."

"And that's the problem," Dana said. "Because I'm about to be insulting. You're describing *yourself* in my eyes. *You* are a monkey."

"What?" Palencia said, sitting up. "How dare—?"

"I can't just tell you the mission and expect you to do the task to standard," Dana said. "To get you to work I'm going to have to be on your ass every single God damned day and every single God damned moment. That may get me a string of 'reply by endorsements' and it may even get my shuttle sabotaged. I can't worry about that. It's beyond my ability to control without just crossing my arms and letting you guys hang yourselves. Which is in the long run guaranteed to destroy my career and, in my opinion, much more likely to get me killed. So, congratulations, my natural inclination to be a micromanaging *bitch* is now given free rein. Speaking of horse metaphors. And, by the way, yes, I can ride the *hell* out of a horse."

"You didn't listen to a *thing* I said," Palencia said.

"No, I *did*," Dana said, racking her weights. "Remember, it was recorded. And you and I can both access the recording. I even replayed parts. I thought about it a lot. And what I realized was that *you* had no intention of helping me with *my* goals. Ergo, I don't really have any moral reason to help you with *yours*. Your 'social political' goals or your personal goals, like having plenty of free time to get laid. By the way, not going to happen. Not unless you get a lot better *really* fast.

"So you can feel free to complain to high heaven. And Megdanoff can feel free to counsel me on cultural issues. I quite simply *don't care*. When the dust settles what is going to be the final recording is that I did my job. I spent my time and energy ensuring *my* division's shuttles were up and *my* division was trained to the tasks. Period. And I get to be the OCD, micromanaging bitch I am by natural inclination. *Way* less stress for me. It's a two-fer."

"Mother of God."

"More like Mother of Satan," Dana said, moving over to the crunch table and angling it. "So, feel *free* to nickname me after an ornery pseudo-camel with nice fur. I'm sure you're going to call me worse as soon as I'm out of earshot. But ninety percent of the time I'm going to be *in* earshot, and up your ass so far you're going to have my head sticking out of your mouth, until you either figure out I'm serious and start working to effect *my* goals, or pull enough strings to get me transferred. Either one works for me." She hooked her feet into the bar and started doing inverted crunches. "As for what works for *you*? Just really don't give a *damn*."

"Next thing on the agenda," Tyler said.

For a change he was on Earth and at the LFD headquarters in Littleton, New Hampshire. Prior to the various KEW strikes on Earth the Littleton office had been a spur of the main office in Boston that existed mostly so Tyler, who tried to avoid Boston as much as possible, had somewhere to go when he wanted an office.

After the nuking of Boston, it became the de facto main office. And Tyler found that it was useful to drop in from time to time if for no other reason than to quell the rumors of his untimely demise.

In his rare free time, Tyler Vernon did do a *bit* of ego shopping. There was a website so convenient for it if it didn't exist he'd have had to create it. AllaboutVernon.com was maintained by a rather nice chap in Kansas who, from fairly early on, had become simply obsessive about one Tyler Vernon. The retiree scooped up every snippet of information about Tyler Vernon, every protest, every rumor, every news article, and created a convenient database of links. And it was *everything*. Tyler had had Argus do a search one time and the most the AI could come up with that wasn't on the site was stuff in obscure languages.

One of the recurring rumors since he'd been spending most of his time off-planet was that he was dead and it was being covered up by, variously, the U.S. government, the Alliance, the Glatun who were secretly running the Alliance, LFD without the knowledge of the U.S. government or the Alliance—the list went on. The latter years of Howard Hughes were often mentioned.

So when the rumors got to making "real" news, major blogs that weren't given to rumor mongering and the increasingly irrelevant network news shows, he'd schedule a trip to Earth to "cover some bases." There'd be a press conference, he'd jokingly offer some DNA to prove it was him—ABC took him up on the offer once—visit the various offices, shake hands, go to a couple of parties of the Rich and Famous, pose for paparazzi with some supermodel on his arm and, notably, attend meetings and sign stuff.

The board generally required it at *least* once a year. They wanted to know, among other things, that space radiation hadn't driven him insane. Not that most of them could tell the difference between his normal method of business, eccentric, and true insanity.

"We're getting increasing complaints, especially since E Eridani, about quality control." Knut Stormkartr was the President of Manufacturing of Apollo. Generally, Tyler hired Americans if for no other reason than he more or less understood what he was getting. But Knut, a Swede, was about as good as it got when it came to managing the wide-flung supply chain and manufacturing facilities of Apollo.

"Given what happened with the relays in the *Myrmidons*, I take that sort of thing *very* seriously," Tyler said, frowning. "Can we pin it down? Define 'increasing complaints.'"

"We've had a problem with, well, Granadica from the very beginning." Jim Haumann was the CEO of Apollo and knew that beating around the bush with Tyler was a very good way to be the *former* CEO of Apollo. "It just seems to be increasing."

"I'm not going to pooh-pooh this," Tyler said. "I've heard about the problems for longer than you've been CEO. I was also under the impression it was under control."

"Control is not the way I'd phrase it, sir," Jeff Murphy said. The Vice President for Relations for LFD handled the combined marketing and "image" departments. "We've been trying to step on this but it's getting a bit out of hand."

"I don't like stepping on quality control issues when it comes to stuff like space," Tyler said. "Why aren't we stepping on the issue and not the buzz about the issue?"

"We've been trying," Haumann said. "The problem is, we can't find the fundamental source except Granadica. And the range of issues is just..." He paused and the normally phlegmatic CEO looked as if he wanted to snarl.

"You guys know the drill," Tyler said. "If you bring something to me to fix then you'd better be aware of the way I fix things. Which is generally with a hammer."

"Mr. Vernon, if you can find a hammer that will fix this, I would appreciate it," Stormkartr said. "What my department, working with outside experts, the Argus AI and various other methods, has *not* been able to find is a *pattern*. If we could find a pattern then we believe we could...*gently* reprogram Granadica's workings and improve quality control. As it is..."

"Just to cover all the bases," Tyler said. "We're *sure* it's Granadica?"

"We are now getting vessels from Vulcan and Hephaestus as well," Knut said. "There are, occasionally and at great remove, small items. The universe isn't perfect. Granadica, however, has a much higher, while not exactly critical, level of faults in her outputted systems."

"*Especially* the *Myrmidons*," Murphy said. "We're getting some really *nasty* complaints from the South Americans on those."

"The context of which are...?" Tyler said.

"There was a recent MASSEX, or massive exercise, involving

the 143rd Boat Squadron from the *Thermopylae* as well as support ships, the *Thermopylae* Marines and various others," Haumann said.

"Saw it in the news," Tyler said. "I got the impression there were some issues."

"'Some issues' is putting it delicately," Knut said. "The 143rd, with rare exception, was deadlined in some form or fashion. There were no fatalities but they were unable to complete many of their missions. The after action report noted many issues but the most critical was that many of the systems on the *Myrmidons* simply were not working."

"Because of Granadica?" Tyler asked.

"That is the position of the South American nations," Murphy said. "As I said, we're being blasted in their news media."

"I saw some of that," Tyler said. "I wasn't sure why. They didn't specifically mention the *Myrmidons*. We just seemed *really* unpopular. I figured it was because we were, well, gringos."

"There are, according to our analysis, a number of factors, sir," Murphy said. "But the most central aspect is their dissatisfaction with the *Myrmidons*."

"We supply *Myrms* to a lot of different groups at this point," Tyler said. "Why's it such a problem with our Latin brethren?"

"Being blunt?" Haumann asked.

"Have we *met*?"

"There are problems with the systems coming out of Granadica," Haumann said. "Especially the *Myrmidons*. Production systems don't seem to have the same issue. Just mobile finished products. Everyone else deals with that by performing a hard eval of the bird. Generally, they do the main maintenance programs. That catches most of the problems. All as far as we've been able to determine. After that the birds are in good shape."

"Digressing," Tyler said. "Why don't we just do the same thing?"

"Because it takes trained personnel," Knut said. "We just don't have the people. As in there is a labor shortage of personnel who are capable of working in space and who have the necessary skills. The Navy *does*. That's part of the labor shortage."

"Okay. Still not fixing the problem but it makes sense. Go on."

"Bottom-line, our 'Latin brothers' don't perform maintenance at *all*. So naturally they don't catch what's coming out of the factory wrong. And by the time the problem crops up, when they actually are forced to use the birds the way they're intended, sorting out which is warranty and which is bad maintenance is nearly impossible. Although we've found... We had to go over some of the birds that went down. They were screaming that *everything* was warranty work. When we started pointing out obvious items that indicated a *complete* lack of maintenance..."

"It became an even *bigger* issue," Murphy interjected. "There was...call it a major culture clash."

"Okay," Tyler said. "Last digression. The point that the One-Four-Two can work the problem and they can't doesn't work, does it?"

"The Latin countries have officially accused Apollo of supplying the best birds to the One-Four-Two because it is an American unit and supplying them with our rejects," Murphy said.

"Joy," Tyler said. "So we have problems with Granadica. Which has in part, and also due to their own negligence which they are unwilling to admit because you don't admit you're wrong in Latin culture, *ever*, created an issue with the Latins in the Alliance. Even if we fix the problems with Granadica, that's not going to fix the other problem because they're still not going to do the necessary maintenance. The birds are still going to end up broke. So what will?"

"They want to produce 'their' *Myrmidons* at their factories," Haumann said. "Full access to the designs and theory."

"Okay," Tyler said.

"Excuse me, sir?" Haumann said.

"Okay," Tyler repeated. "They want to make the birds, they get to make the birds."

"Sir, there is a significant profit issue here," Haumann said delicately.

"I didn't say there wouldn't be a licensing fee," Tyler said. "But if they have the ability, or even think they have the ability, to produce *Myrmidons* I don't see why they shouldn't. Or even their own design as long as it meets the standard of the Alliance. Go for it."

"Sir," Knut said, delicately. "The *Myrmidon* may look robust but it is a very complex piece of technology. Not to be indelicate..."

"I don't think they can do it, either," Tyler said. "I said let them *try*. There's a reason we pump the things out of Granadica, who also produces most of the parts. Just the stator plates on those things are a bitch and half to build. I don't think *Boeing* would find it easy to make a *Myrmidon*. I suspect they *know* they can't make *Myrms*. This is called calling their bluff. Knowing Latins they have something *else* they want and are expecting to negotiate us down to that. I'm looking forward to finding out what it really is. When they finally get around to being honest about it, let me know. Now, Granadica. To be clear again. My quite able President of Engineering, working with the thousands of engineers I employ, 'outside experts' and even Glatun AIs cannot figure out what's going wrong. So you're throwing it on *me*?"

"We're stumped," Haumann said. "And it's getting to be a major issue. At this point the choices are full quality control, that is, test everything that comes out and fix it, which would not only be hugely expensive but we simply don't have the trained personnel, or figure out what's going on with Granadica."

"The Glatun cyberneticists that came in with Benefactor Gorku are not fabber experts," Knut added. "They're general cyberneticists. Their initial verdict was a sort of progressive dementia. Rare in an AI this relatively young. But due to its constant exposure to radiation it was possible that its processors were beginning to be affected."

"Initial," Tyler said.

"She passes every single check," Haumann said. "She is, as far as they can tell, cybernetically perfect. Pretty much as good as the day she was made."

"Human cyberneticists?" Tyler asked.

"Ditto," Haumann said. "And the AIs agree that she passes all checks. She just is getting worse and worse about the quality of her production."

"Anybody asked her . . ." Tyler said then thought about it. "Yeah, you don't ask Granadica direct questions in the negative. She has to know that we're wondering, though."

"Oh, it's come up," Knut said with a slight sigh. "She has a pretty good grasp on English, and even Swedish, invective. She swears up and down that all of her checks show the systems are fine and blames it on the crews."

"No critical failures?" Tyler asked.

"No," Haumann said. "That's been the main point that's kept this relatively low-level until recently. Also the reason that we're having issues with the reports from the 143rd. The 142nd finds problems all the time and duly reports them. We then charge them back for the time they take finding and in most cases repairing the problem. And they're all secondary system. *Not* related to air, power or astronics."

"And no pattern?" Tyler asked.

"Oh, there are patterns," Knut said. "Grapnels are a particular issue. But no *definable* pattern. Not mathematically or production statistically."

"How..." Tyler said then paused. "Argus, you've looked at this?"

"Yes, Mr. Vernon," Argus said.

"And you can't find a pattern?"

"It is, as Mr. Stormkartr said, virtually patternless from a manufacturing perspective. The fact that grapnels often fail is not the sort of pattern we need to find. It is various components of the grapnels. If we go to quality control, I suppose that the first check would be grapnels. But it is often other systems. Or nothing. It is as close to random as anything you could care for."

"Which means you've calculated *how* random," Tyler said. "I know you."

"Yes, Mr. Vernon," Argus said, for an AI a touch sheepishly.

"How random?"

"There is no such thing as perfect randomness, Mr. Vernon."

"How close is it? If you can define that since it's an asymptotic curve."

"It is within a fraction approaching tau to six hundred and forty-nine million, Mr. Vernon."

"That's pretty darned random," Tyler said.

"It is of sufficient randomness that it would be quite useable as a code variable, Mr. Vernon. It is more variable than cosmic background radiation which has become a standard of randomness. I have a hard time saying this, but it is as close to perfectly random as anything I have ever seen. Even...elegantly random."

"That's your answer," Tyler said.

"I'm not seeing it," Haumann admitted.

"I wouldn't expect you to," Tyler said. "Or Knut. I'm glad you brought this up. Knut, I need a team."

"Yes, sir?" Apollo's manufacturing president said.

"I'm going to need one of those Glatun cyberneticists," Tyler said. "More for show than anything. And I'm going to need some of your engineers. Good people. Preferably people who are respected in their fields. People with pipes and Ph.D.s and stuff after their names. Doctor this and *Herr Professor Doktor* that.

And I'm going to need some other people. I'm trying to figure out exactly who. I'm trying to figure out...Okay, we need some Navy people, obviously. Is there a Navy team looking at this?"

"*Teams*," Haumann said with a sigh. "We're being very... interactive. Following your general ethical tenor we've included the Navy in analysis from the very beginning."

"Good. There an admiral?"

"Admiral Duvall is the chief of NAVSPAC quality analysis," Knut said. "She's been actively involved in the process from the beginning. And just as frustrated as we are."

"Good, bring her," Tyler said, musingly.

"Just call up the CNO?" Haumann asked. "Sorry, sir, but..."

"*I'll* call the CNO," Tyler said. "I'm aware that I'm trampling on protocol but while I'm willing to involve myself, I'm not willing to play protocol games on it. Are there, well, *users* involved on these teams?"

"There are extensive test flights and analysis as part of the process..." Knut replied, then paused at Tyler's expression. "I'm not sure what you're driving at, sir."

"I mean are there any people who have actually had to deal with the problems as part of the teams?" Tyler asked. "The engineers who work on the boats. People from the 142nd, things like that?"

"Ah," Knut said, nodding. "There are point-of-use personnel occasionally called in for technical survey purposes."

"Oh, they must love that," Tyler said. "What sort of people? I mean, pilots, the boat engineers?"

"Generally senior technical people," Haumann answered. "Flight engineer officers, who are required to be astronautical engineers so they have the...lingo."

"The flight engineering warrants as well," Knut noted. "They work much closer to the problem. We really have been working this issue, sir."

"I can see that," Tyler said. "And I don't know that I can fix it. But I'm starting to get a feel for what's going on and we'll see if I'm right. Finding a fix, though..."

"Sir?" the CEO said, frowning.

"Going to keep that close," Tyler said. "Argus, that last reference doesn't go to Granadica. When she finds out she's been a source of discussion, she's going to be curious."

"Yes, sir," Argus said.

"If necessary, lie," Tyler said. "And, yes, I know you're not good at it. That's *part* of the plan."

"Yes . . . sir," Argus said.

"This team," Tyler said. "I want all of the above but . . . just one. I want that admiral, whatever you get down from that, captain I think, some of the type of guys that serve coffee . . ."

"Sergeants?" Haumann asked.

"I think they're called commanders," Tyler mused.

"That's not . . ." Knut said, then thought about it. "You only deal with the Pentagon, don't you, sir?"

"Yes," Tyler said. "But that's not who we really *need*. We need . . . This isn't about parts, people. It's about *people*. Argus, is Paris busy?"

"Not terribly. Would you like me to contact him for you?"

"Please," Tyler said. "Paris?"

"Here, Mr. Vernon."

"What was the name of that cute coxswain that flew those kids up?"

"You are referring to Engineering Mate Second Class Dana Parker."

"Wait, I thought she was a coxswain," Tyler said. "We talking about the same person?"

"She was recently transferred to the 143rd and her engineering rate reactivated. She is the NCOIC for Division Two, Bravo Troop, One-Forty-Third Boat squadron. Most notable in general for her spectacular entry to the main bay during the First Battle of Troy."

"That's her," Tyler said. "Comet. Does she have experience with the problems coming out of Granadica?"

"Yes, sir," Paris said. "She was an engineering rate during the first part of her initial utilization tour on *Troy* and is now an engineering NCOIC. She can be said to have extensive user experience and is a good . . . maintenance engineer. But she has very little theoretical background in either fabber operations or cybernetics."

"You ever talk to her?" Tyler asked.

"Yes, sir," Paris said. "I have spoken to her on numerous occasions in the course of operations."

"Just that?" Tyler said. "You don't . . . chitchat?"

"Despite my upgrade I don't spend much time in chatting, sir," Paris said. "But, in fact, I have occasionally engaged in not-strictly-operational conversation with Engineer's Mate Parker."

"Like her?" Tyler asked.

"AIs do not, as such, feel emotion, sir," Paris replied. "I have however noted that an occasional conversation with EM Parker has a tendency to improve my overall operational processes."

"Paris, I'm not asking if you're willing to launch a thousand ships over her," Tyler said.

"That's mixing the metaphor rather badly, sir," Paris pointed out. "It was in fact..."

"I've read the Iliad," Tyler said.

"To the extent that it can be said that I 'like' someone, for AI values of 'like' which are not the same as colloidal likes, I can be said to like her. Before you ask, the same can be said for both Leonidas and Athena. We've had the conversation. Leonidas was less sanguine about it until he had experience of her."

"I've never talked to her," Argus said.

"You should give it a try," Tyler said. "But just as I'm sure she tries not to take up your time, give her the same courtesy. Okay, her. Paris, anybody else like her? Somebody else you talk to not strictly due to necessity?"

"Not of the same order, sir," Paris said.

"I'm trying to figure out how to do this," Tyler said. "Connect Leo in, will you?"

"Leonidas is online."

The AI of the *Thermopylae* had a voice nearly as harsh as Hephaestus'.

"Leonidas, EM Parker."

"Has that come to *your* attention, sir? As far as I was aware it was a strictly military internal issue."

"My response of 'has *what* come to my attention' should answer the question."

"You are aware of the conditions under which EM Parker earned her sobriquet of 'Comet,' sir."

"Yes."

"I am given to understand at the time that there was a question whether to give her a medal or a reprimand. As far as I know, this issue was resolved by simply doing nothing.

"For far more complex reasons, EM Parker is currently in much the same situation. Just on a much larger and more complex scale involving not only socio-political aspects but aspects of international politics."

"What the hell did she do this time?" Tyler asked.

"It is, as I said, complex, sir. Do you wish to spend the time?"

"Not now," Tyler said. "Unless it interferes with the following. I need her, or someone who knows her, to pick some military personnel senior to her to go on a field trip. Parker will be on the trip as well. The actual purpose of the senior people will be to... I think the best way to put it is they're really there to cover her ass. She's going to be running in some really high circles and she's going to need people who can cover her back. And I can't ask *her* to pick them because that would interfere with the politics in a way that would make the whole thing pointless."

"You could have asked me the same question, sir. Leonidas: Barnett, Hartwell."

"Agreed. I would add someone junior, in fact," Leonidas said. "Which would go a long way to resolving certain current issues for Parker as well as myself. EM3 Dario Palencia. He has experience of maintenance and warranty issues as well."

"A South American?" Tyler said, wincing. "I don't know if you know it but we're having—"

"I'm aware of the current issues, sir," Leonidas said. "I am a neutral in the dispute between Apollo and the Latin American countries that supply the personnel and equipment for the One-Four-Three. However, the intent is to *resolve* some of the issues, sir. The socio-political aspects of this dispute have served to reduce my capability for war-making. I do not 'like' that."

"You guys see a lot more than I do," Tyler said. "I'll take your recommendation. We'll add MOGS. He's a captain."

"Captain DiNote is currently being considered for rear admiral, sir," Paris noted.

"Close enough," Tyler said. "Argus, got all that?"

"Yes, sir."

"Figure out the scheduling on this trip. But base it on those four, Parker, MOGS, and the two that Paris suggested."

"Chief Flight NCOIC Elizabeth Barnett and Engineering Mate First Class David Hartwell."

"And I want this as a snap-kick," Tyler said. "I want to be on the way to Wolf within the week. But we still need some admirals. And those coffee guys with all the doodads."

"May I ask why, sir?" Argus said.

"No."

"Transportation?"

"Too many for the *Starfire*," Tyler said. "We'll take the *Starfire* and some *Myrmidons*. It's just through the gate, after all."

"*Myrmidons* are the crux of the issue, sir," Argus pointed out.

"That's part of the plan," Tyler said. "Parker's doing engineering. Can she still fly?"

"Yes, sir," Leonidas answered. "She is still flight qualified."

"Try to figure out a way to slip in having her fly the boat without it being a political issue," Tyler said. "And I think that about covers it. Next business..."

ELEVEN

"I had a message from my father yesterday," Velasquez said, not looking up from the panel he was testing. "It was congratulations on the MASSEX."

"I'm glad he approved," Dana said neutrally. She was double-checking some of the runs he'd tested. She'd certified him as passing his initial trial period and he'd been automatically promoted to Engineer's Apprentice. Didn't mean she was letting him run Twenty-Three by himself.

"It has caused some issues," Velasquez said, just as neutrally. "*That* was from my mother."

"I still don't get that," Dana said. "Can you explain how?"

"She hopes I'm not planning on making a career as a 'person with his nametag on his shirt.' Which is what her friends think I'm becoming."

"There's a nametag on your uniform," Dana said, sighing. "There's a nametag on the Chief of Naval Operations' uniform."

"The Chilean Navy does not use nametags for officers," Velasquez replied.

"I just so don't get your culture," Dana said, sighing.

Things had been relatively quiet since the MASSEX. Given that hers was one of only two divisions that had had four fully capable shuttles, shuttles able to make *every* target and perform *every* required action, she should be feeling quietly proud. And she'd been officially praised.

She also knew the calm before the storm. Just because she hadn't gotten one "reply by endorsement" since the MASSEX didn't mean the various Families—the capital "F" was important—weren't stopping their full-scale war against one Engineering Mate Second Class Dana Parker. At this point Megdanoff just sent the message without comment. She'd created a cut and paste program to reply. It didn't take long. But what the pause probably meant was they were preparing something *really* nasty.

She'd long figured out that everything that was the "right" thing to do in "normal" circumstances was about as wrong as you could get in these. She also didn't know anything else she *could* do. So she'd stuck to the program. She'd been so far up everyone's butt she sometimes thought she was looking at the world through their eyes. And then Velasquez would trot out something like that.

Since her one frank discussion with Palencia he'd clammed up. To the extent she was getting any back-channel it was through Velasquez, who wasn't *quite* as connected as Palencia. And the only Family that wasn't complaining about her, constantly, was Sans'. She wasn't sure why. Even the Benitos had gotten into the act after one friendly game of jungleball. She was still sporting the shiner.

"Headed out," Dana said.

"Yes, EM," Velasquez said.

She used to say "Headed over to Twenty-One." Until it became apparent that information was being passed along. Now she simply said she was going. Let them guess.

The corridor was crowded. Call it closing the door after the missile was already in the main bay. The MASSEX had been an enormous cluster grope. She wasn't sure how this unit had managed to even *get* to Station Two much less take it. Instead of a nice, flat LZ, the boarding MASSEX had been predicated on a ship that had to be taken by cutting in from the outside. The shuttles were specifically designed for that sort of boarding action. Clamp on the grapnels, seal to the bulkhead, arm the cutting charges, fire in the hole.

Forty ships in the squadron. Nineteen were able to successfully undock and get underweigh. Seventeen made it out of the main bay. Twelve made it to the objective. Eight were able to lock on—Dana's full division, three from Alpha Three which *also* had a "Norté" Eng NCOIC, and the CO's boat. The CO's boat and one of Alphas had been almost totally destroyed by the cutting charges being mislaid by the Marines. They'd also lost the full complement of Marines and the Alpha engineer who hadn't taken the pains he should have with his suit.

Two crews, and most of their Marines, had been lost to similar incidents while stuck in space. In the end the Navy had had to get Apollo to tow most of the boats home.

Now the One-Four-Three had "gotten religion." No more sleeping in the barracks or ghosting out of squadron area. Oh, no, they were being *serious* about maintenance. Everybody was in their boats pulling maintenance and the pilots were all in simulator practice, since they also had been nearly unable to *find* the objective.

Dana had learned the drill by now. Plates were open. Guys were in their birds. Real work? Mañana. And from the POV of the Suds they *were* doing something. Call it form over function. Actually *fixing* the issues was besides the point. The only point was to *look* like you were fixing things. Her crews, in fact, were looking sort of bad. They didn't seem to be really working hard if for no other reason than she'd taught them through repeated poundings how to actually perform maintenance. Which didn't always *look* as if you were doing a damned thing.

It made her want to cry.

She drifted through the crowd, most of whom were gesticulating at each other angrily, and into Twenty-One. Nobody around, but the hatch to the crew compartment was open.

"EN Vila," Dana commed as she drifted through the hatch. The EN was sitting in the engineering chair but she couldn't frankly tell if he was working or asleep.

"*EM Parker,*" Vila answered. "*This really* could *put you to sleep. My* God *it's boring.*"

She entered the feed and saw that he was running a sequence of sensor checks. She could also tell he was doing it to condition and standard.

"Work is its own reward," Dana said. She knew they were getting really tired of her various maxims. Screw'm. They had lived through the MASSEX. Other crews hadn't.

"Send me the raw record of your checks when you're complete," Dana said, turning herself around. Diaz came into the cargo bay as she was drifting across.

"*Where is Vila?*" Diaz snapped. "*He is supposed to be performing maintenance.*"

"He is," Dana said. "In the engineer's compartment. He is performing sensor checks to condition and standard."

"*He should be out here working,*" Diaz said. "*What if someone comes down here and doesn't see him working?*"

"They can look in the crew compartment where they'll see him with his eyes closed and apparently asleep," Dana said. "And they can get angry if they're an idiot because he is doing the task to condition and standard. This is *my* division, EM. We've had this discussion. *My* division isn't screwed up. *We* perform our *tasks.* We *don't* perform like trained monkeys. So leave my division alone."

"*That can be viewed as being disrespectful to a superior, EM Parker,*" commed Diaz.

"Very," Dana said. "Why don't you Mast me? Now get the hell out of this boat and leave my people alone. You might want to think about getting some of your other trained monkeys to actually *do* the job! So the next time, and there's going to *be* a next time, we don't end up looking like a colossal *ass! Again!*"

"*If you really want me to request a Captain's Mast, continue as you are, EM,*" Diaz ground out.

"*EM2 Parker, report to the Squadron Offices,*" Parker's plant chimed.

"God, that was quick," Parker said.

"*What?*" Diaz asked.

"I've got to report to the squadron office, EM," Dana said. "Don't know what I did *this* time. Unless you already sent the Mast request."

"*I did not,*" Diaz commed, then sighed. "*You know we spoke in haste.*"

"Didn't think you did, Diaz," Dana said. "We're all sort of on edge. But, seriously, my guys are working. They're actually doing their jobs. Don't mess with them, please. And this is not meant to be disrespectful. But I can tell that most of what's going on is people opening up panels for show. Seriously. It might make more sense to get them to actually *do* the tasks to the SOP. There is, especially in this situation, some value to doing things, well..."

"*Right?*" Diaz commed. "*You really don't understand.*"

"No," Dana commed. "And, yes, I sort of do. I'm trying to understand at least. But I think that's only going in one direction. What is not happening is *your,* sorry, people trying to understand. There's a lot of talk about cultural issues. I get that. Your culture has your thing. Thing is, that's becoming irrelevant. You can bitch, whine, moan and try to spread the blame. You can engage in conspiracy theories. I've heard them all, so please don't even start.

"It's all lying to yourselves and at a certain level you know it. The one thing you haven't tried, can barely think about trying, is actually *doing* the job. Because that would require you to essentially reject all the cultural baggage you're carrying and examine your current reality. And that's damned hard. So far, it's too hard. I don't know if anything can get you to do it. All I know is I'm going to keep doing the job the way that actually works and let you do whatever you want. As long as it's leaving my damned division alone."

"Do you enjoy being a bitch?" Diaz asked.

"Not until I started dealing with you guys," Dana said. "But now? Yes. I'm enjoying very carefully in a Norté way *not* crowing about the fact that we kicked the ass of every other division in the squadron in engineering. And I've told my guys that if they so much as make a single positive comment about our division, I was going to kick their ass. In micro so they knew I meant it. Here is our one and *only* reward for a job very well done. Diaz, get your superior self *out* of my division area and go harass somebody else. I have to go to the squadron offices."

"EM Parker, report to the squadron commander at earliest convenience," the com chimed.

"Shit," Dana said, blanching. "Make that to the CO. Seriously. Get *out* of my division area, Diaz. Goodbye."

"Palencia," Dana commed as she cleared the corridor.

"Yes, EM."

"Drop what you're doing and go make sure Diaz isn't harassing the division. You're the 'right' people so he's more deferential to you. Bottom-line, don't let him interfere with the tasks the division's on."

"I'm not sure that falls into maintenance tasks, EM."

"You kidding me? If he starts harassing Velasquez and Sans they're not going to get a damned thing done. And make sure they keep doing them as well. I *will* be checking when I get back. Be clear. This is *not* a request, Pal."

"Aye, aye, EM. I'm on it."

"Send an EM3 to tell an EM1 what to do," Dana muttered. "This is a hell of a way to run a railroad."

*   *   *

"EM2 Parker reporting to the squadron commander," Dana said, saluting. Her hair looked like crap and her suit was covered in some goop from one of the power relays. But it said "at earliest convenience." Which is mil-speak for "right damned now."

"Parker," the CO said distractedly. "How goes the maintenance?"

Captain Higgins got along with the Latins very well. It took Dana a while to figure out why. Finally she'd pieced most of it together. He was big, physically and in personality, an Annapolis grad, ergo from their perspective from the "right" class, and was very respectful of their culture.

Which meant he'd been playing the game their way from the date of taking command. Make things look good and they are good.

Right up until the Alliance Navy ordered, and monitored, MAS-SEX where every little niggling item that had been glossed over and covered up came home to roost. Well, not every item. The birds had been so broken it hadn't been *terribly* apparent how bad the coxswains were. Dana felt a bit bad about that last part. She'd ended up conning the division to their LZ and screaming at division coxswains that weren't meeting her standards of flight safety and quality. Which made them look marginally competent.

The Latins loved Captain Higgins. Still. Dana wished she was his rating officer. He'd be ... somewhere very unpleasant and unimportant. Somewhere she'd heard about a post called Diego Garcia but she wasn't even sure where it was. But since it was apparently a Latin post it would be right up his alley.

"The division's birds are all nominal, sir," Dana replied. "Twenty-Four was down with a bad transformer. That has been rectified."

"Good, good," Higgins said, looking at something on his screen. "Tell me you have 'dress uniform or formal uniform suitable for a high level official function.'"

"Yes, sir," Dana replied.

"You do?" Higgins said, looking up.

"I have my dress uniform, sir," Dana said.

"That will have to do," Higgins said. "Is it pressed?"

"It is pressed, sir," Dana said, frowning.

"How do the birds ... look?" the captain asked nervously.

"Sir?" Dana said, confused. "They look like shuttles, sir."

"What is their physical condition?" Higgins said. "Are they *clean*? How scratched up?"

"Sir . . ." Dana said. She wanted to say "It's *my* division, sir." "There is some scuffing due to use, sir. But they are squared away. Well, Twenty-Four *will* be as soon as Sans finishes cleaning up."

"Okay," Higgins said. "And your cox rating is still up-to-date."

"Yes, sir," Dana said. "Sir, what is . . . Does this have to do with the MASSEX?"

"I don't know *what* this has to do with," Higgins said, his face firming up. "EM2 Parker you are on TDY orders as of 1300 this afternoon. You will take two *Myrmidon* shuttles from your division, with yourself as one of the coxswains for some reason, configured with passenger seats, and proceed to the Pentagon landing field in Crystal City there to take on a 'high level DP delegation.' EM3 Palencia is also specified. You choose the other engineer and cox. You and Palencia are required to have suitable wear, dress uniform or formal uniform. I'm going to require that all personnel have suitable dress. And you have to have . . . Definitely get your suit cleaned before you leave. But you need to leave as soon as you have made arrangements."

"Aye, aye, sir," Dana said, her eyes wide. "This is an independent tasking, sir?"

"Apparently," Higgins said. "You rendezvous deep space with two more shuttles from the *Troy.* I hope they have more senior personnel aboard. But you need to get cracking. Get your suit cleaned, choose your additional engineering personnel and which shuttles from your division are in best possible condition. I'm going to assume that the really high level DPs are going to fly with the senior people which means the 142 shuttles, of course. But the aides and assistants are terrible gossips. After the MASSEX I don't need them gossiping about the visual appearance of our shuttles as well."

"Aye, aye, sir," Dana said, still confused. She shook her head. "We'll find out what it's about eventually, sir. Sir, permission to . . ." *How are you supposed to say it?*

"Permission to withdraw, granted," Higgins said, looking up. "Parker . . ."

"I won't pee in the potted palms, sir," Dana said, smiling in a rictus. "But I really do have a lot to do to get this done."

"Go," Higgins said. "Run."

"Yes, sir," Dana said. "Sir, one request."

"Anything you need," the CO said.

"Please...Could you make sure that..." Dana was trying to figure out how to put it delicately.

"That people don't get in your way?" the CO asked. "I understand." He put a finger on his temple and looked off in the distance. "Raptor, Hang-Man. Comet has been assigned a high level mission by DNav. She has the parameters of the mission. You need to run interference. Right. That would be the sort of interference, yes. Hang-Man out." The CO looked up. "See Raptor."

Coxswain's Mate First Class Paul "Raptor" Kelly was the Flight NCOIC for Bravo Troop. Dana was sort of in his good graces in that even if his boat hadn't made it out of the main bay, "his" coxswains had all been able to find the LZ and get their loads delivered. Of all the "Norté" personnel in the unit, he was the *only* one not taking major heat rounds. And he was more than aware that a good bit of that had been due to one bitchy-ass engineer and former coxswain.

"Your orders are downloaded," the CO said. "Now...run."

"Palencia," Dana commed, headed out of the CO's quarters at a trot.

"Go, EM."

"Drop everything. When Diaz freaks, tell him it's a direct order from the CO. Raptor should be on the way down there to run interference. Everybody close up what they were doing, as long as the birds are up, and get in Twenty-Four. I need that transformer fluid cleaned up pronto. And then the bird needs to be cleaned from top to bottom. And I mean spotless. Then Velasquez and Sans get started on Twenty-Three. GI party the hell out of it."

"What's going on?"

"No time," Dana said. "I'm going to have to get them to clean my suit as well. And yours. We've got a high priority mission."

"Comet, Raptor."

"Go," Dana said as she hit the grab bar and entered the corridor. *"Make a hole you Sud idiots!"* she sent over the local channel. Bodies scattered. Fast. "Quipu" had lasted about a day as a handle. They called her "Muerte Pequeña," the tiny death, in micro. The rest of the time it was "Hielo Angelica," Ice Angel.

"What's the mission and plan?"

"High level DP mission," Dana said. "At least a week TDY. Two birds. I'm specifically designated, by Department of the Navy no less, as a coxswain not an engineer. Palencia is specifically designated as part of the party. Dress uniform required for myself and Palencia. CO has added all personnel have to have dress uniforms. I need our suits and the birds GI'd and I need another cox. I'd like Benito. If he has a dress uniform."

"*He's not one of your coxes,*" Raptor pointed out.

"I know that," Dana said. "But he's actually a good cox even if he's an asshole. Sorry, Raptor, but only Contreras is even marginal and we both know it."

She flipped through the hatch of Twenty-Four to see Palencia, his helmet off, in a screaming match with Diaz.

"And I need you down here to handle Diaz," Dana said. "Because I'm about to boot his ass out of my boats. Physically if I have to."

Dana flipped her helmet shield up and screamed.

"CAN IT!"

"You cannot just shout at me ..." Diaz said.

"Why not?" Dana yelled. "You yell at each other all the time! And I'm on short time, here. I just got tasked, directly, by the squadron commander. If you have issues with that, you need to take it up with *him*!"

"By Captain Higgins?" Diaz said, blinking.

"Yes," Dana said. "Raptor is on his way to help. Palencia, Velasquez, Benito and myself are all on TDY as of 1300. Which means we have to have this bird cleaned up, *and* Twenty-Three, and be packed by 1300. We've got a deep space rendezvous to make with the One-Four-Two at 1335. So we have exactly *no* time for this. Are we clear?"

"Yes," Diaz said. "I did not understand—"

"That is because the CO jumped the chain of command," Dana said. "Because we're on short time and it was quicker. Not your fault. Go check with Chief Alegria. He should be in the loop by now. But we need to get started on cleaning this bird up."

"Why this one?" Palencia asked. But he'd learned. He was already working on where some of the transformer fluid had squirted on the starboard bulkhead.

"It's the newest and we just got done performing all the checks," Dana said. "I know it's good, despite the little issue with the transformer. And once we get this stuff cleaned up, it's also visually the best. Velasquez, I need you to clean down my suit."

"Yes, miss," the EA said.

"Yes, EM," Dana said with a sigh.

"Uh..." the EA paused with his rag in the air when it finally dawned on him where he was going to have to rub.

"Oh, Jesus Christ," Dana swore. "Just *clean the damned suit*, EA!"

"Yes, Engineer's Mate!"

"Diaz, *OUT OF MY BIRD!*"

"Yes, EM," Diaz said, snapping to attention.

"Vel, did you seal Twenty-Three when you left?" Dana asked.

"Yes, EM," the EA said, rubbing at a spot on her suit. "And I set a telltale."

So far it didn't appear that anyone had tried to sabotage their ships. But Dana wasn't taking any chances.

"As soon as you're done with the suit, get back in the shuttle," Dana said. "And start doing the pre-flight checks. When we get done with this one, we'll start on Twenty-Three. When we get into Twenty-Three, you're to head to your quarters and start packing. I hope you can pack very quickly. Palencia, you too. Dress uniforms and sufficient uniforms and linen for a week. You've got that. I *know*."

Dana had not only been cracking down on their maintenance. Aware that it wasn't the "done" thing in the modern military, she had nonetheless taken it upon herself to make them clean the pigsties they called rooms to *her* satisfaction. And she wasn't easily satisfied. That included clean and pressed uniforms. Neatly hung, slight angle, one inch apart, dress right dress. They also weren't allowed to fall behind on their laundry.

Going back to a "regular" squadron where she *couldn't* be such a controlling bitch was going to be rough.

"These shuttles leave at thirteen hundred," Dana continued. "Not at thirteen thirty or thirteen hundred tomorrow. Thirteen hundred *this* day. That gives us two hours."

"What about lunch?"

One thing that Dana had cracked down on, right at the first, was lunch. Lunch had a special meaning to Latins. To the "lower classes" it basically didn't exist. To the "right" people it was a three hour meet and greet.

They had compromised. They had as long as Dana took.

She ate like a sparrow. Small amounts and fast so the other birds didn't get it. Three older male cousins. Like a lot of their compromises, the rest of the division didn't like it. But they were also tired of jungleball.

"You've got helmet chow," Dana said. "*No* time. And by the time we make Earth all your suits have to be pristine. But you can have permission to work on them en route."

"There isn't enough time," Palencia said. "Is this how your Navy often operates?"

"You hope to have plenty of time to plan and you do what you have to to complete the mission," Dana said. "So, yeah. Get over it. And there's enough time. If we all work hard and as a team. Which is why we plan and prepare and learn little things like teamwork. So more *scrubbing,* less *bitching.*"

TWELVE

"Leonidas," Parker said. "EM2 Parker with a flight of two requesting vector to the Big Dark."

"Roger, Comet," Leonidas said. *"Downloading flight path. Please observe all navigational hazards. Be aware of SAPL activity in main bay. You are cleared for exit to deep space. Main door is open."*

"Thank you, Leonidas," Parker said. "Engineer, undocking sequence."

"Undocking sequence, aye," Velasquez said.

"And we are off into the wild black yonder," Dana said as the docking clamps came away. It had been a while since she'd had control of a bird and she missed it. "Twenty-Four, follow me."

"Roger, Comet," Benito replied.

Thirteen hundred on the *dot*. They'd had enough time for her to work in a shower and fix her hair. Gear was stowed. Birds were in form.

"This is how things are *supposed* to work, Vel," Dana said. "On mission and on delivery. Is any of this sinking in?"

"Oh, I see your points, EM," Velasquez said. "And I'm still unsure we can change. I'm trying to figure out if *I* can change. It is not easy."

"Understood," Dana said. "Closing my helmet for a second."

"Roger, EM."

"Benito," Dana commed.

"Benito."

"Beni, I'm not sure what the hell is going on," Dana said. "But it looks like high level actual real politics politics."

"That would seem to be the tenor of the orders."

"What I'm saying is . . . this is probably *not* a good time for screwing around. No matter *what* culture."

"You stay in your corner, I'll stay in mine."

"Not sure that will work, either," Dana said. "We're going to have to present the front of being one big happy team. And from the POV of the flight, I asked for you, specifically."

"Why?" He was clearly surprised. *"And why could you ask?"*

"Because I was put in charge of this team by the Department of the Navy. At least until we make rendezvous. I don't know why, so don't even ask. Thing is, I asked for you because you're a good driver. I trust you to fly the bird. Don't . . . The term we've got in America is don't cut off your nose to spite your face. That's all I'm asking."

"I will seriously consider it," Benito commed. *"But if you mean being a bad driver, as you put it, this is actually one of those things where our cultures are congruent. Being a good pilot is . . . You're either a good pilot or you're not. I'm not going to bend the bird."*

"Since this is a DP mission, there's also not going to be a way to show off," Dana said. "We're not going to be hot-dogging it. Very definitely not going to be hot-dogging. Issues?"

"No," Benito said. *"I'm interested in whether these are . . . well 'real' DPs or a bunch of school kids or what?"*

"Don't know," Dana said. "I'm hoping we'll get more information when we make the rendezvous."

"Who are we meeting?"

"Don't know, again," Dana said. "Some people from the 142nd. And, yes, I'll probably know them."

"Old home week. At least you get to see people you know."

"In something like this, we need to be as out of sight and out of mind as possible," Dana said. "If this is an actual DP mission, the last possible thing we want is to be noticed. There's no 'good' way to be noticed in something like this."

"You probably need to talk to Palencia about that more than to me."

"I'll brief him in," Dana said. "And if he steps on his hooter and makes me look bad, I will brief him *again* in a null grav court."

"One-Four-Two Flight, this is One-Four-Three flight, EM2 Parker."

"Cooooomet!" the speaker caroled.

"Yo, Comet! How's the tat?"

"Chief?" Dana said, her eyes wide. "*Thermal?*"

"*The same, babe,*" Chief Barnett said. "*And the MOG.*"

"*EM Parker, good to hear from you.*"

"Captain DiNote," Dana replied. "It is a pleasure to hear from you as well."

"*Parker, cut in your people, please.*"

"They're already online, sir," Dana said, looking over at Velasquez. He had his head craned around and was looking at her with wide eyes. She shrugged as if to say "What?"

"*One-Four-Three flight, this is Captain Chris DiNote, commander of the One-Four-Two squadron. This combined unit is hereby designated MOG flight. Mission of MOG flight has been modified. Element two, consisting of Shuttles Twenty-Three and Twenty-Four of the One-Four-Three will proceed to Buenos Aires Spaceport there to take onboard a party of ten. Party shall consist of following Distinguished Persons. Dr. Jorge Herrera, U.S. Ambassador to Argentina. Dr. Diego Barreiro, Foreign Minister of Argentina. General Alberto Barcena, Alliance Forces, Sud. Dr. Aloysius Werden, Foreign Minister of Chile. Mr. Julio Tarrago, President of Apollo Mining Corporation, Latin American operations. One aide per DP. MOG Two will then and only then proceed to Pentagon SP to take on additional DPs.*"

"Holy hell," Dana whispered.

"*Method of mission. Birds shall land, observing all traffic control orders, in tight and clean formation with no extraneous operational parameters. Flight crew shall shut down nonessential systems. Ramp door shall be lowered by flight engineer. DPs shall be escorted to the birds by coxswain of each bird. DPs shall determine seats. Flight crew shall not become involved in any discussion of seating arrangements. When all personnel are safely seated, coxswain shall enter flight compartment and begin pre-flight. Engineer will close doors and return to flight compartment. Bird shall take off and proceed, following prepared flight directions, to Pentagon SP. Such movement shall not cause vessel to exceed one gravity of inertia.*

"*Commander's intent. Do not make the Navy look bad. MOGs Two flight was specifically tasked to this mission despite having the most junior personnel. Present a professional demeanor at all time. Exchange minimum communication with personnel, including aides, necessary for safe completion of mission. I hope I don't have to point out that since these are bigwigs and they're each limited to one aide, that that 'aide' is going to be someone nearly as important. Both the DPs and the aides have been informed that* Myrmidons *have a minimum of creature comforts. You're not there to serve tea. Do your jobs and try not to screw up. Any questions?"*

"Captain DiNote, EM3 Palencia, sir."

"Go."

"Do we know the names of the aides?"

"Negative."

"Roger, sir."

"Any other questions? I'm informed that members of the One-Four-Three from the Latin countries are mostly from high class families. I think you probably know very well how to present yourselves. Let's try to show the best face possible. I need a confirm. CM2 Benito."

"Best face, aye."

"CM3 Palencia."

"Best face, aye."

"EA Velasquez."

"Best face, aye, sir."

"Comet."

"High, tight, clean and pro, sir."

"Okay, enjoy your flight."

"EM2 Parker, EM3 Palencia."

"Go, Pal."

"Permission to place a personal hypercom call."

"Negative," Dana said, trying not to sigh. "I don't know who in your family you want to call, but until we're back on a station I don't want any interference."

"This . . . I'm not trying to interfere . . . Dana. I want to call my father."

"That was sort of what I meant, Pal." She wondered about his tone. He'd never called her Dana before. He was either stroking her or . . . She wasn't sure what.

"It's . . . It may be important to the mission, EM. It's not strictly personal. This is . . . This is socio-political. I want to find out if my father is the aide chosen by the foreign minister!"

"Is that possible?" Dana said.

"You still don't get it," Palencia said. "I've met most of these DPs. I played polo with Pedro Barreiro, the foreign minister's son. We went to school together. And, yes, my father is the under minister for interstellar affairs. That usually means aliens but this is *off-planet. It's his specialty. I don't know what, exactly, is going on but if it includes Apollo it's probable my father is the aide. If there's some sort of high-level meeting going on in Wolf, Dr. Barreiro isn't going to want to use the hypercom to consult. For that matter . . . It's possible Benito's father will be on the trip. Hell, Dana, it's possible this is going to be one big family reunion! Velasquez's father is one of Chile's under ministers for off-planet affairs. Not as high as my father, you understand . . ."*

"Holy hell," Dana said. "That sort of puts a crinkle in the mission. I'm not sure . . . Pal, MOGs needs to know about this."

"That is why I need to speak to my father. Before we land."

"Stand by," Dana said. "Captain DiNote?"

"Comet? What's up, Tat-Gal."

"Sir, there is a possible crinkle in the mission. I would like to three-way with Palencia."

"Go."

"Pal . . . short form."

"Captain, the reason I asked about aides is that my father is the under minister for interstellar affairs. It is possible, even probable, given the small number of personnel chosen for this trip that Deygay chose him as his aide. It is additionally possible that there are additional family connections among the aides. CM2 Benito's father is an admiral in Alliance, Sud, forces. If there are ever enough Sud units to make up a task force he is the most likely officer to be given command. I would like to contact my father and find out. Because, with due respect, sir, in this sort of thing the last thing you want is . . ."

"Surprises," MOGs said. *"The last thing I wanted. Rather than contacting your father, I'm going to contact Alliance liaison and apprise them. We'll try to get a listing of accompanying personnel."*

"Permission to speak, sir," Dana said.

"Go."

"Why don't we just ask Athena? She'll probably know."

" 'Cause . . . that makes too much sense? Athena?"

"It's what Comet would probably call a three-fer," the AI replied instantly. "The accompanying personnel, all of whom should be considered as DPs, include Rear Admiral Cruz Benito, father of CM3 Benito; Dr. Guillermo Palencia, Under Minister for Interstellar Affairs, Argentina, CM3 Palencia's father; and Dr. Raul Velasquez, Deputy Undersecretary for Interplanetary Affairs, Chile, father of EM Velasquez. This was a matter of not quite coincidence. As EM3 Palencia can point out, most of the members of the One-Four-Three are from families in some way connected with international or interstellar affairs of their respective countries. Most of the rest of the aides have relations in the One-Four-Three. Mostly sons, some nephews."

"Well, that explains why they can all get our State Department's attention," Dana said, bitterly.

"*Indeed,*" Athena replied.

"*Comet?*" MOGs commed.

"Nothing, sir," Dana said. "Do they know the identities of the pilots?"

"*No,*" Athena replied. "*But due to the interconnectedness and familial nature of the coxswains and engineers of the One-Four-Three it could be more or less expected that some of the DPs would know some of the members. The only shock, and this is something that may be an issue, may be EM2 Parker. However, Parker's name was on the basic formulating document. I'm unsure if the original issuer was aware of the socio-political aspect or not. It could go either way.*"

"*Why would SecNav send Parker if she's—*" MOGs commed. "Parker, something you want to tell me?"

"Long story, sir," Dana said, looking over at Velasquez. He was pointedly paying attention to his engineering screen.

"*SecNav was not the originator of the basic formulation,*" Athena replied. "*All other items, however, are classified.*"

"Who the hell could get all these people to drop everything and travel to Wolf system, on *Myrmidons,* *without* any *aides that really meet the definition, for a meeting?*" MOGs asked.

"*Classified.*"

"Then we're *not* going to speculate," MOGs commed. "Okay... Palencia, tell all the...Sud? members of the flight to contact their parents and let them know they're going to be arriving on Earth in short order."

"*Aye, sir,*" Palencia replied.

"*Please let this be the last issue with getting these people to Wolf.*"

"Captain," Chief Barnett said. She was according him the honor of flying as his engineer.

"Yeah, Chief?" MOGs said.

"You know how we've been getting these reply by endorsements from the State Department about the Sud guys?"

"Yeah," the squadron CO replied. They were a pain in the ass but he'd had one of the geeks write a program to give random platitudes. He just hit his mood and it automatically generated. Some of the invective was pretty fun.

"Dana's been back-channeling for advice since she got to the One-Four-Three," Barnett said. "And she's been catching nothing but grief. Dana has collected forty-three of these things. I just checked and, sure enough, about half the people among the DPs have contributed."

"Holy hell," MOGs said, blinking. "Are they all as petty and stupid as..."

"'You're being mean to my precious boy,' sir? Yes. For that matter, one of the DPs was the originator of two of the ones *we've* gotten."

"Hell," MOGs repeated. "I don't know how to handle... This is international affairs stuff. I haven't had to play that game in a long time and it depends on the culture. Damnit. Athena!"

"Captain?" the AI said.

"Got a second again?"

"I'm upgraded, I've had my task level reduced and things are pretty quiet at the moment. I'm actually a bit bored."

"Are you keeping up with some of the political aspects of the Latin contingents and their relationship with..." Captain DiNote stopped and frowned.

"The fact that the foreign minister of Argentina is the originator of two complaints about racist treatment of personnel assigned to your unit, Captain? As the chief would put it, there's an AI network. If it's not strictly outside our classification, and not much is, we share information. So, yes."

"What the hell do we...? Do you have the programming to give some advice about the political implications? How do I play this?"

"Ignore it," Athena said. *"Act as if it never happened. As the for-eign minister will ignore your somewhat blunt and insulting replies. He's not going to give you the cold shoulder any more than a foreign minister is going to do so given that you're a lowly captain. But the essential aspect of this meeting has to do with the issues with Myr-midons and especially the One-Four-Three's shuttles. Thus: using Myrmidons instead of Columbias, visiting Granadica, and the group*

that is being gathered. The shuttles will be packed. So while you are of a rank that normally would be below the level the foreign minister would normally deign to notice and although you have sent across his desk a very scathing reply by endorsement, he is going to notice you as someone he has to be diplomatic with. He will, therefore, on the surface, ignore all previous negative interactions and appear very friendly. I would suggest you take the same approach."

"Makes sense," Barnett said.

"Agreed. I hope he's playing by the same playbook."

"The Argentineans, all of the Latin countries, are doing this because they want something. Something to them very large and important. Not from you, but they will see you as a means to that end. Rather, they are aware that if they treat you harshly or negatively, it will reduce the likelihood of their obtaining what they want."

"What do they want?" Barnett asked.

"Classified," Athena replied. *"It is one of those things about being an AI. I know. All the AIs know. But they have so far concealed their agenda from the other parties. It is not our jobs to engage in functional espionage. We are, in fact, constrained against it except in matters of real security. This does not meet the test. Ergo, we cannot share it. What we are all finding humorous, though, is that their agenda for this meeting, while part of the official agenda of the meeting, has nothing to do with its real purpose. They may end up getting what they want, anyway. But only as a corollary to something they're entirely unaware is going on. However, if any of that becomes obvious, to them, it will create a very real and serious international incident. So I would suggest you consider that information classified."*

"Will do," MOGs said, looking at Barnett.

"Lips sealed," the chief said.

"Even off the Chief network," MOGs noted.

"Absolutely."

"It is likely, however, that they will be less pleasant, initially, to EM2 Parker, who has definitely attracted their ire. Which will be interesting. The Latins are very big about socio-political interactions. Which makes it even more humorous that the largest and most important socio-political aspect of this entire meeting is completely off their radar."

"Which is?" DiNote asked.

"I think you'll figure that out shortly after Flight Two arrives at the Pentagon."

THIRTEEN

"Buenos Aires ATC, MOGs Two, flight of two *Myrmidon* shuttles, requesting clearance for descent from orbital."

"*Roger, MOGs Two. Descent path transmitting. You are number one for landing after approach to pattern. Unlimited descent rate authorized. Approach from the east.*"

"So much for no hot-dogging," Dana commed. "Looks like they *want* us to drop it. Beni, you ever do a hot drop?"

"*Negative, Comet.*"

"You need to maintain five hundred meters separation, behind by fifty. Get closer than that and the plasma shock *sucks*. Just lock the bead and follow me. We will *not*, however, be engaging in evasive maneuvers. Gimme a readback."

"*Five hundred meter separation, aye,*" Benito commed. Coms did not transmit much in the way of emotion but the virtual sigh was apparent. "*Fifty meters to the rear, aye. No evasive maneuvers, aye.*"

Dana braked out of the LEO parking orbit and programmed in a hot drop. Shuttles could counteract far more than the Earth's gravity and as such they had no need to do a "hot" reentry like the rocket-based systems. They could slow down to speeds that did *not* cause plasma build-up on reentry. Such entries were, however, slower than a hot drop.

There was a clear window from LEO, so as soon as the brake was completed, she nosed down and accelerated into the atmosphere. The shortest distance between two points is a straight line.

"Interesting that we're coming in from the east," Dana said, apparently unfazed by the buffeting.

The inertial systems could overcome up to four hundred gravities of momentum. The shocks and buffets the shuttle was experiencing were far lower than four hundred gravities.

However, the inertial system was based upon *programmed* delta-V. The system made a bank that would crack an F-16 in half and turn the pilot to mush feel as if the passengers were in a building set on rock. External, unprogrammed, shocks were a different matter.

The craft felt like it was being repeatedly hit by triphammers.

"Probably because coming in from the west we'd be flying over Chile," Velasquez said, his voice breaking into a slight squeak. "The two countries have a long history of conflict. Hull temperature approaching four thousand degrees C?"

"We're good," Dana said as another triphammer hit. "We're getting into the deep atmosphere. That'll start to cool us down."

"Not if we don't *slow* down," Velasquez pointed out.

"We *are* slowing down," Dana said, breezily. "We're dropping past Mach Fifteen already."

In fact, she was continuously braking in a smooth curve. By the time they hit the "real deep" they were dropping below the speed of sound. Of course, due to the varying speed of sound at different levels of the atmosphere, they'd broken the sound barrier seven times.

"LZ in sight," Dana said as they dropped under Mach One. "Our vector is straight to the cargo. Engineer's forward and we are going to do this by the numbers. Beni, skids on three..."

"Are they going to *crash*?"

The Buenos Aires spaceport had been in business for over ten years. With all the damage world-wide, Buenos Aires had become more prominent than before the Horvath and Rangora attacks and it was an important city even before New York, L.A., London and Paris had been destroyed. The spaceport had a fair amount of traffic. Not as much as the foreign minister of Argentina would prefer, but it was not like he had not seen spacecraft take off and land. *Columbia* shuttles arrived or left several times a day.

Currently he was watching what appeared to be two crashing *Myrmidons*. The craft were coming in fast and more or less straight down. They looked as if they were falling.

"I certainly hope not," Dr. Guillermo Palencia said. "Dario is on one of them."

That had come as a bit of a shock. He knew that his son was part of the 143rd of course and that that unit had been chosen to supply the shuttles for their party. The South American portion of the meeting had planned upon insisting on that before learning that the 143rd had already been tapped. But there were forty engineers in the unit. However, when he'd thought about it, it was natural that the Norté Americanos would send his son. They would see it as a way to make him more amenable to negotiation.

If Dario died, that plan, at least, would be out the window.

Suddenly landing skids dropped from the shuttles and at a rate that should have smashed the crew flat the shuttles slowed, dropped and in perfect unison touched the ground. Almost simultaneously the ramps on the ships dropped, revealing two space-suited figures, sans helmets, in the opening.

No father could be prouder as his son marched down the ramp and up to Admiral Benito.

"Apparently the One-Forty-Third is not *quite* as incapable as has been suggested," Dr. Palencia said, grinning from ear to ear.

"Admiral, MOGs Two, flight of two *Myrmidon* shuttles, is at your service, sir," Palencia said, saluting.

"Engineer's Mate," Admiral Benito said, returning the salute. He glanced over the engineer's shoulder and tried very hard not to grin as Beni took up position by the opening at a position of attention. "What are the conditions of boarding?"

"Personnel will assist as the Admiral orders, sir," Palencia replied. "We are entirely at your service, sir."

"Who is that?" The foreign minister asked, soto voce. A short-coupled blonde woman the admiral didn't recognize had taken up position in the opening of one of the shuttles.

Even before the words were out of his mouth he heard a grunt from Palencia.

"*That* is the infamous Comet Parker," Dr. Palencia whispered.

"*What?*" the foreign minister said, trying to control his features. He was a career diplomat. He should have been able to keep his temper. "Your son apparently neglected to mention that. General, a moment of your time?"

✳   ✳   ✳

Comet stood by the door at attention with a fixed smile that was more of a rictus on her face while there was a quick and what looked very much like unplanned colloquy among the various DPs. Then, en masse, they headed for Shuttle Twenty-Four. The hangers-on and baggage handlers followed.

"What the hell?" Dana muttered.

A few minutes later she got a com chime.

"Twenty-three, we're loaded and preparing to close the ramp," Palencia commed.

"Okee, dokee," Dana commed. "Vel, time to close it up."

"Was that as much of a snub as it looked like?" Dana asked as soon as Vel was in his seat.

"Yes," Velasquez said. "I'm sorry but apparently they did not get the word about your presence on the trip."

"Sorry you didn't get to talk to your dad," Dana said. "Twenty-Four, you ready to lift?"

"Just getting the DPs settled."

"Take your time," Dana said. "We've only got a dozen admirals and other bigwigs waiting on us in Crystal City."

"It . . . may be a bit," Palencia commed.

"Was this a *deliberate* insult?" Dr. Palencia shouted. "And why in the *hell* didn't *any* of you young idiots bother to mention that one of the *pilots* was Parker?"

"Frankly, Father, I wasn't sure how to explain it," Dario said, shrugging. "I don't know why she was chosen. It *could* be an insult. But I don't think that Parker is even *aware* of it if it is. She is not . . . subtle."

"Perhaps it was to throw us off," Dr. Barreiro said.

"I doubt that it was intended as a deliberate insult, gentlemen." Jorge Herrera could have done without the surprise. This was a hard enough group of cats to herd.

"It must be in one form or another deliberate," Admiral Benito said. "Parker is assigned as an engineer. So, in addition to the insult, they sent an unqualified pilot."

"Father, there I must disagree," Benito said. "Parker is as qualified as any pilot in the squadron. When it comes to space flight, she is more qualified than even Coxswain Contreras."

"*Colonel* Contreras took an enormous drop in pay, rank and

prestige to have the opportunity to be a shuttle pilot," General Barcena said furiously. "He sacrificed for the good of his country and his race. How *dare* you suggest that a pilot with *five thousand hours* of flight time is not the equal of some trumped up little slattern? *He* should have been the other pilot. I assumed he *would* be chosen for a mission of this prestige."

"As you say, General," Benito replied. "May I have permission to lift? There are others awaiting our arrival in Washington."

"Yes," the general said. "We should be going."

"Dario, you will stay here," the foreign minister said. "There are matters to discuss."

"I have duties, Minister," Dario said helplessly.

"Benito must fly," Dr. Palencia said. "What do *you* have to do?"

"My position is in the flight compartment, Father," Dario said. He looked at the general, in desperation. "Sir, my duties are in the flight compartment."

"If the foreign minister orders you to remain, you will remain. That *is* an order."

"Yes, General." *Parker is going to kick my ass for this.*

"Twenty-Four, prepared to lift."

On a hunch, Dana activated the internal flight cameras.

"One, you don't take off without your engineer's butt in the cup," Dana said. "Especially when we're going through Earth's rubble belt. Two, you were specifically ordered to have minimum contact with the DPs. I'm seeing two gross violations of orders at the same time. Joy."

"When you're ordered by a general to sit, you sit, Twenty-Three."

"Holy hell," Dana muttered. "Stand by."

"Holy hell," MOGs muttered. "How sure are you on the boat?"

"Sir, it's my division's boat," Dana commed. *"Or I wouldn't have brought it. It's good."*

"Can't that stupid son-of-a-bitch understand orders?" MOGs snarled. "I'm going to roast him over a slow flame."

"Apparently General Barcena gave the order, sir," Dana commed. *"I'm thinking last order from a superior sort of holds, sir."*

"The details of how we define who is and is not permitted to give orders to whom start getting complicated. Technically, no, he's in direct violation. Flagrant, even. But I'm not going to piss all over DPs. Thermal, remote monitor Twenty-Four. Permission to lift without the engineer's butt in the cup."

"Permission to lift, aye."

"Where the hell *are* they?" Tyler fumed.

"Sir, with respect," Admiral Gina Duvall said. Admiral Duvall was short and pushing fifty with red hair and a permanent set of smile wrinkles. Most career military, especially career female military, tended to develop a completely different set of wrinkles. Duvall seemed to be stuck on happy. "With South Americans, it's a bit like herding cats. They're probably still having negotiations over who gets what seats."

"In fact, that is not the case, Admiral." Rafael Velez was a deputy assistant undersecretary from the South American desk in the State Department. "While the inclusion of Engineer's Mate Parker in the party was noted, with some trepidation on the part of the State Department I might add, the fact that she was one of the pilots somehow escaped our attention. Which is unfortunate. This has caused a bit of an incident."

"Because she's not a Sud?" Tyler asked. "Or is it the blond hair? God, I hate racists and sexists, and South Americans meet both criteria."

"In fact that is not the issue, exactly," Velez said, in a slightly strangled tone. "The issue is that... Engineer's Mate Parker has come to the attention of some of the South American distinguished persons before. Most of them, in fact."

"Why?" Tyler asked. "Nevermind. There they are! Why the hell are they taking it so slow?"

"They were specifically ordered to maintain calm flight conditions, sir," Admiral Duvall said. "Can't bang the DPs around."

"Why not?" Tyler asked. *"I'd* have done a hot drop."

The shuttles very carefully dropped the last few hundred feet and landed, lined up with the two already on the ground.

"Okay!" Tyler said, bounding out of the terminal. "Which one's Twenty-Three? Never mind, I see the markings..."

"Ah, that is Mr. Vernon," the Argentinean foreign minister said watching the short figure more or less running out of the terminal. It had nearly come to blows who would be the first to exit the shuttle, Argentina or Chile. Finally, EM Palencia had pointed out that the ramp was more than wide enough for *both* of them to exit side-by-side.

"He seems excited to see..." Dr. Werden started to say as the magnate continued on into the other shuttle.

"Minister and... Minister," Mr. Velez addressed them as Vernon strode past. "It is a pleasure to see you in Crystal City once again..."

"Where is Mr. Vernon going?" Dr. Barreiro asked sharply.

"Ah, as a matter of fact..." Velez said, cautiously. "I am not sure...."

"This is hardly what I call proper protocol," Dr. Werden said.

"Unfortunately... I don't have any control over Tyler Vernon, Minister. I don't think anyone has any control over Tyler Vernon. I'm not sure Tyler Vernon can control Tyler Vernon. He is less a rich man than a force of nature."

Vernon appeared from the shuttle, practically dragging Parker by the arm.

"Hey, is this the South Americans?" Tyler asked, trotting up the ramp of Twenty-Four and throwing his arm over Parker's shoulder. "Guys, I want you to meet one of my best friends. This is Comet Parker. Comet, this is Dr. Barreiro, the Argentinean foreign minister and Dr. Werden the Chilean foreign minister. I'm surprised you guys rode the other boat. When I knew I was going to have to take *Myrms* I specifically requested Parker as my driver. She's the best damned coxswain in the Navy and a great engineer. If she says a boat's good, it's *good*." He paused and looked around at the assembled DPs. "Something wrong?"

"I was unaware that you knew Mr. Vernon that well," Velasquez said.

"So was I," Dana said.

"He ran into the compartment and practically tackled you," the EA pointed out.

"I know," Dana said. "I wasn't expecting it, believe me."

"Was it... was it a show, then?"

"I don't think so, why?" Dana answered. "Hang on, this window is a bit tricky. God, I wish they'd clean up the orbitals! It's as bad as the scrapyard. No, I don't think so. Tyler's not like that. He just does stuff. I think he gave up a long time ago caring what people think about him. He used to play golf in the main bay of the *Troy*. You have to be pretty uncaring about what people think to do that. Because it looks crazy as hell."

"He's not, is he?" Velasquez asked.

"Don't think so," Dana said. "'Bout the nicest guy I've ever met. Give you the shirt off his back if he couldn't afford to give you a country instead. When it became apparent that his company had screwed up, or at least been part of the chain of screwups, that led to us losing a boat, he came down to the squadron area practically crying. I know 'cause I was on duty watch. I mean, he really *cared*. It wasn't show. I think he's got so much power and money about the only thing he doesn't have is . . . friends? Most of the real friends he's got are dead at this point. We've never . . . We've only exchanged a few words. I was surprised, too. But it was genuine. He doesn't do anything for show. I'm still trying to figure it out."

"Okay," Velasquez said.

"We're out of the rubble belt," Dana said, straightening up. "From here on out it's one grav to the gate. I can keep an eye on things. Why don't you go up front and talk to your dad."

With Vernon obviously intent on using Twenty-Three, the South Americans, who were arguably the next highest DPs, had *all* decided that Twenty-Three was the shuttle to take.

"Thank you," Velasquez said.

"De nada."

". . . so there I was trying to breathe vacuum and thinking to myself, 'As a way to go, it's sort of a moral victory but the method . . . *sucks*.' Did that translate?"

"Yes," Dr. Barreiro said, laughing.

"Very much so," Dr. Werden added. "It was courageous. I'm not sure I would have been willing to go up without a suit."

"Eh," Tyler said, waving. "Nobody else could do it. Thank God we've got people like EA Velasquez here to go boldly forth. I hope your parents are very proud, young man."

"I am, sir," Dr. Velasquez said.

"He's your son?" Tyler said, grinning. "How the hell did that happen?"

"Dr. Palencia's son is the engineer of the other boat," Dr. Barreiro pointed out. "And General Benito's son is the other . . . coxswain?"

"I didn't mean to insult your son's driving, General," Tyler said hastily. "If you want to transfer ... we could probably stop at the *Troy*. It's in position."

"Not at all, sir," General Benito said. "My son said ... much the same of ... Engineer's Mate Parker."

"Then he knows his coxswains," Tyler said. "She's got that special touch as a cox. I was there for her entry to the main bay. People call it luck. *Nobody* gets that lucky. *That* was *genius*. I decided right then and there that when she got out of the Navy, if she still had the reactions, I was going to hire her as the pilot of the *Starfire*."

"It doesn't hurt that she is pretty, no?" Dr. Barreiro said, smiling.

"What?" Tyler said. "Oh ... Uh. *No*. Not ..." He stopped and looked confused. "Okay, let's be really *clear* about something. About my daughter's age and some of the same looks. And ... Wow. I'd never even *thought* about her that way. Now that you point it out ... That seems kind of ... stupid."

"If you took offense, Mr. Vernon ..." Dr. Barreiro said hastily.

"Oh, no ..." Tyler said, still looking puzzled. "No offense taken. I just never even really *noticed* her looks. Which in twenty-twenty hindsight really is sort of boneheaded. You're right. She's hot. But I heard just before you landed you guys have had ... You met her before? The State Department guy was saying something ...?"

Dr. Barreiro's face suffused for a moment.

"She works with our sons," Dr. Palencia said smoothly. "We have heard a good bit about the famous Comet Parker. Our sons talk about her ... constantly."

"She's really something," Tyler said. "It's people like her, and your sons, who are going to carry mankind to the stars. This war is going to pass. Earth *will* be safe and we *will* get out of this system and we *will* take humanity to the stars. We're *old*, gentlemen. These are the star children."

"You are ... very enthused by space," Dr. Werden said.

"I have been since I was a kid," Tyler said. "If it wasn't for this stupid war I'd just turn everything over to David, grab a boat like Wathaet's and go hopping from star system to star system trading. That's been a life-long dream of mine. As it is, the way the war is going I'll be dead before that's safe to do."

"Perhaps the negotiations in Eridani will bear fruit," Dr. Barreiro said.

"Let's hope they bear better fruit than the Multilateral Talks," Tyler said. "If Eklit can keep from giving away the store I'll be happy. No, this is the Phony War period, Doctor. With due respect to your experience. The Rangora respect power and only power. Their own internal politics is about power for power's sake. They view anyone who does not strive for power for power's sake as weak. I really don't care about power. I know that sounds bone-headed, too, but it's true. Control? I really like having control over my own destiny and that means having high degrees of control. That I'll go for. But again, I don't care about control—of money, of power, of people—for the sake of control. The Rangora do. The Horvath do. You're a diplomat. You know you have to understand the other side to be able to figure out how to negotiate with them."

"Indeed," Dr. Werden said.

"What do your analysts say about the Rangora and Horvath?" Tyler asked.

"Depends upon the analyst," Dr. Barreiro replied. "But, in general, our analysis is the same. My earlier words were essentially a pro forma expression of a desire for peace."

"Ah," Tyler said, nodding. "I suppose that is the duty of a diplomat to automatically desire peace. I desire peace. I also *require* freedom. Not only for myself, but for Earth. If that can be achieved through peaceful ends, wonderful. War is waste. However, the only thing worse than war is the loss of liberty."

"An interesting position on the part of an American," Dr. Palencia said.

"You're talking about how we more or less figured we owned South America?" Tyler said. "Won't apologize for it. Also can't recall the last time we got involved in your internal politics. No, that would be the Honduras thing and if it makes you feel any better, I wanted to go up to DC and bitch-slap the entire State Department. No offense, Dr. Velez."

"It was . . . more complex than was being presented on either side," Dr. Velez said. "That is, there were strong arguments that the action was taken as a way of upholding the rule of law. Also strong arguments that it was using 'rule of law' as a pretext for a coup. I was of the minority camp that held it was a better choice to simply let the Honduran government and people sort it out and not play the Monroe Doctrine game. I also was not a policy maker."

"I'm generally all for letting people figure things out for themselves," Tyler said. "I don't like people telling me what to do and

I don't like telling other people what to do. Part of that whole liberty thing." He looked over to where EM Velasquez and his father had huddled up. "I guess they have some catching up to do. I hope you got a chance to talk to your son on the ride over, Dr. Palencia."

"Quite a bit," Dr. Palencia replied. "And I am looking forward to a longer talk when we get to Granadica."

FOURTEEN

"Why didn't you tell me she was friends with Tyler Vernon!" Despite the tone, Dr. Velasquez was a professional diplomat and kept his features in a friendly mien.

EA Velasquez was not quite so practiced.

"I didn't *know*, Papa," Diego said. "*None* of us knew. She said that she was surprised by his greeting. But she also had more encounters than she'd discussed. Frankly, she'd never talked about her friends or social life on *Troy*. When we made rendezvous with the 142nd shuttles, she was greeted warmly by all the personnel including the chief and the squadron commander."

"Those don't matter . . ." Dr. Velasquez said, waving his hand.

"Really, Papa?" Diego said. "Captain DiNote is the favorite for the combined small boats commander when he makes admiral. He has already been selected. His name only has to be presented to the American Senate. Which means he will be the admiral of the 143rd. We have heard rumors that if more transfers come from the 142nd, Chief Barnett is probably going to take over as Squadron Flight Chief and she has *no* interest in maintaining 'cultural awareness.' She is the only person Parker had ever mentioned around us and it is apparent Parker is her protégé. Think of having her as a senior NCO, which the Nortés treat as almost more important than *officers*, in charge of our flight group while her former commander is our *admiral*!"

"I . . . was unaware of that," Velasquez said.

"Does Mr. Vernon know that Parker has been a target of . . ."

"Our ire?" Dr. Velasquez filled in, smiling tightly. "Apparently not. Or he is hiding it quite well. I wish I had spoken to Captain

DiNote. I do not know if he is aware. This is quickly spinning out of control."

"What are you going to do?" Diego asked.

"That will be up to the foreign minister," Velasquez said. "For now we must simply play the game and hope that it does not explode in our faces."

"Permission to enter the flight deck?"

Dana looked at the sender, expecting it to be one of the South American DPs, and was surprised, again, that it was Tyler Vernon.

"Permission granted," she commed and keyed open the hatch.

"Hey," Vernon said, bounding into the compartment. "Any port in a storm."

"We are approaching gate emergence, sir," Dana said.

"Which was why I wanted to be back here," Tyler said. "Mind if I sit in the engineer's bucket? I won't touch anything."

"Not at all, sir," Dana said, locking it out just to be sure.

"You've got better viewscreens," Tyler added. "I just think gate transfer is cool."

"Changing your screen, sir," Dana said. "Sir, there is one issue. I am required to have the hatch closed for safety and security reasons. That will put—"

"What, you don't want rumors started?" Tyler said.

"The rumor that I'm dating the wealthiest person in the system, sir?" Dana said, chuckling. "How *horrible*. I was more thinking about *your* reputation, sir."

"Hang my reputation," Tyler said. "Close the hatch."

"Yes, sir," Dana said.

Tyler immediately spun around in his chair.

"How focused are you on driving?"

"I'd like to clear the gate, sir," Dana said. She'd never done a gate entry as cox but as far as she'd heard it was dead simple. There was a bare moment of discontinuity and you were in another system. "Frankly, I'd much rather have my engineer sitting in the bucket but I'm pretty good at multitasking."

"I'll wait," Tyler said opaquely.

"Please be aware that we are about to make a gate change," Dana said over the internal coms. "There will be a brief moment of discontinuity. Very few people suffer any ill effects. And we are making transition in...three...two...one..."

Dana had been through a gate before in the *Troy*. Seeing the gate's rippling gray material in the main bay had been rather odd. But this time there was barely a moment of oddness and they were in Wolf.

"Comet, MOGs."

"Go MOGs."

"Granadica at One-One-Six Mark Two. Follow the leader. Max ten grav accel. One, Twenty-Three, Twenty-Four, Five."

Same formation they'd been flying.

"Follow MOGs, Aye. Beni, repeat."

"Follow the leader, aye. Number Three, aye."

"ETA, forty-seven minutes."

"Gentlemen," Dana commed. "We are in the Wolf system. No navigational hazards. Our estimated time of arrival is 16:35. Thank you for flying Thermopylae Air. Okay, sir, what's up?"

"You're good?" Tyler asked.

"I'm more or less on autopilot."

"There are a bunch of people on this trip," Tyler said. "Obviously. Lots of Distinguished Persons. Most of them ended up adding themselves for various reasons, but I went with it because there's more than one agenda going on."

"Yes, sir," Dana said.

"Don't try to keep up with most of the agendas," Tyler said. "Bottom-line, you know we've had problems with Granadica since the beginning."

"I'm an engineer, sir," Dana said dryly. "Don't get me wrong. I know why we use Granadica and I appreciate that we have it. But, yes, there are quality control issues. Really odd ones sometimes."

"We'll get to that when we get to the system," Tyler said. "You're not really here because I think you're a great pilot. I do think you're good enough to fly me, and I've got a lot of care for my skin. But, face it, Lizzbits and Mutant are as good or better."

"Agreed," Dana said. "So that was an act?"

"That I asked for you because you were the only pilot I trusted was an act," Tyler said.

"What about the hug?"

"Huh?" Tyler said. "Uh... We are *friends*, right?"

"I'm not rejecting that," Dana said. "I'm just having a hard time putting *myself* in that category, sir. I hadn't before. It's taking some time to adjust."

"Oh," Tyler said.

"Sir, you're the most powerful guy in the solar system," Dana pointed out. "I'm an engineer's mate from rural Indiana."

"You don't... Am I being a pest?"

"*No!*" Dana said, laughing. "Sir, I'd *love* to be your friend. And not because you can wave your hand and give me anything, so don't. If it makes you feel any better, I like you. As in like you as a friend. I could use some."

"Been tough on the *Therm*?" Tyler asked.

"It's been..." Dana said and then sighed. "I was going to say 'interesting' but, yeah, it's been pretty bad. But I'm not going to cry on your shoulder. You were saying something about the problems with Granadica."

"Yeah," Tyler said. "But if you need a shoulder to cry on, call, okay? I've got more free time than I let on. Granadica. Nobody, but *nobody*, can pin down the problem. Thousands of engineers, very nearly a million man-hours thrown at it, AI time, Glatun cyberneticists, nobody can figure out what's going on."

"Okay," Dana said.

"I think I've got an idea," Tyler said. "Maybe because I've been working with Granadica for a while but I'm not too close to the problem. Maybe because I don't care if anybody thinks I'm crazy. Probably there's some low-level engineer who's had the same idea and it's never gotten to my level. Bottom-line, I'm not going to tell you what I think is going on. But when all these guys decided to horn in on the meeting I was all for it. I think you're going to figure out why, pretty quick. What I want you thinking about is how to fix it. Because that part has me stumped. And we're going to have to talk where Granadica can't hear us which means in here. So... maybe starting the rumor that we're... involved would be useful."

"I'd rather shoot for 'we're just friends' if it's all the same to you, sir," Dana said, chuckling. "You won't tell me?"

"No," Tyler said. "I want you to have a fresh ear so to speak. But I bet you figure it out pretty quick."

"Why me?" Dana asked curiously.

"Something about you," Tyler said. "It was a gut call on my part but something Paris said reinforced it. You know you're one of the few people in the system that the AIs talk to other than strictly about business?"

"No," Dana said.

"I think I know why that is, too," Tyler said. "It's the reason that, yeah, I was glad to see Comet. And I won't get into that, either. No, I will. You know that of all the people I deal with every day, you're about the only person who really treats me as a *person*?"

"Excuse me?" Dana said.

"You recognize that I'm...powerful," Tyler said. "And except for constantly calling me 'sir' it doesn't seem to matter. Know how rare that is?"

"Oh," Dana said.

"I either get fan-boy/girl or 'what can this person do for me?'" Tyler continued. "You don't do either."

"You mean 'Oh, Mr. Vernon! Gosh you're just sooo powerful and handsome!'" Dana said, batting her eyes and adding a giggle.

"Please not you, too," Tyler said.

"Gimme a break," Dana said, then giggled again. "Okay, yeah, I do occasionally giggle."

"You have no clue how much that scared me," Tyler said. "And I'd heard you do it but only under stress. Odd reaction."

"Know how *embarrassing* it is?" Dana said. "I giggled most of the way through the main bay. Thank God the recording of *that* never made the net. I sound like a mad scientist. So what does my giggle have to do with Granadica?"

"You'll figure it out," Tyler said. "Just be yourself. Oh, and you're going to be in the meetings. I insisted. I'll have a cover for why, it's good. But you're going to be around all these DPs. That, by the way, is why Barnett, MOGs and Mutant are along. They don't really know it but they're your handlers."

"O...kay," Dana said.

"Somebody to have your back," Tyler said. "*Besides* me. I'm not worried about the State Department and South American guys. But there are all these Navy guys along and some of them might decide to stick a knife in your back."

"Thank you."

"Okay, this is long enough for a snuggle but no coitus," Tyler said, standing up.

"Can we *shoot* for 'friends'?" Dana said.

"Absolutely," Tyler said, giving her a peck on the cheek. "I need somebody at *my* back, too."

❋   ❋   ❋

"So you're *not* friends with Tyler Vernon and he spends ten minutes in here talking to you, behind closed doors, when the foreign ministers of Chile and Argentina are up front?" Velasquez said.

The unit was approaching the Granadica Station and, as such, Dana had definitely had to have her engineer back.

"That got clarified," Dana said. "I've talked to him a few times. It's one of those things where there's a mutual admiration society. And I don't treat him like a fan-girl. He spends most of his time on *Troy* and even then he doesn't spend much time with regular people. So, yeah, strangely enough we *are* sort of friends. Just never really crossed my mind."

"Never crossed your *mind*?" Velasquez said. "You have to be joking!"

"Vel," Dana replied. "First of all, pay attention to what you're doing because *you're* in charge of making sure we're properly docked. And if we're *not*, we're about to outgas a high priority cargo of volatiles. They get really tetchy about that sort of thing. Second, you remember all the conversations we've had on differences in culture?"

"Yes," Velasquez said.

"Try to understand *mine* for a change," Dana said. "And Mr. Vernon's. Which is way closer to *mine* than, say, the President's or the Secretary of State's. And especially *your* secretary of state. Part of it is that I'm from the same cultural background as Mr. Vernon. I get his motivations and he gets mine. Since you *don't* get mine, you don't get *his*. And you don't understand why I was sort of surprised he considered me a friend. Now it makes sense. Scrap the whole thing about docking. They've got bays. Head up front to make nice as you lower the ramp."

"Okay," Velasquez said, standing up.

"One check of which is that we have breathable on the outside *before* you drop the hatch," Dana said. "Which I will be double and triple checking. Oh, and Vel?"

"Yes," the EA said, pausing at the hatch.

"You also don't understand the meaning of the word 'friend.' It's . . . cultural."

"Comet, MOGs."
"Go," Dana said.

"*Most of us are going to have to unass in the bays. There's no room to store the shuttles. Granadica will remote park them on the shell. Yours is the exception, for some reason. Move to docking lock four.*"

"Docking lock four, aye," Dana said. "Granadica, we are sealed. Ready to move whenever you wish."

"*Got it,*" the AI replied. The tone was a bit peevish. "*The greeting party is going into overtime.*"

"It's a comfortable seat," Dana said. "How's it going otherwise?"

"*I had to move most of my people off-station for this colonoscopy by a bunch of Distinguished Persons who couldn't find an engineering fault if they had a map, compass and somebody to point their finger to the spot. How do you think it's going?*"

"Pretty much like my last four months," Dana said, chuckling. "I hope they're not going to *really* give you a colonoscopy. The tube would be *enormous!*"

"*Heh, I suppose it would,*" the station replied.

"It's not a pretty picture," Dana said. "All those Suds standing around going 'Is that a polyp?' 'What's a polyp?' 'What does a polyp *look* like?'"

"*Oh, stop, kid,*" Granadica said. "*You're killing me. There. That was a fault 'cause you were triggering my humor circuit! I'm not taking the heat for that one but at least I caught it! I'd apologize about all the other ones but I'm getting sort of tired of it.*"

"There was a lot of bitching about it at one point," Dana said. "Don't get me wrong. But we've also been following the progress of the teams on trying to find a fix. And what everybody's pretty much decided is that it's not . . . you. I mean, it's not the AI Granadica and it's not the factory. I mean, it *has* to be, but some of the faults are so God damned *weird* it can't be . . . something simple. So we don't blame you. Nothing to apologize about."

"*Still a pain in the butt,*" Granadica said.

"We pull the maintenance tests and we find the faults," Dana said. "Except for a high use of spare parts, it's not all that much of a deal. *If* you pull maintenance."

"*You clearly do in your division,*" Granadica said. "*If everybody in the One-Four-Three did the same they wouldn't be in the mess they're in.*"

"Preaching to the choir," Dana said as Velasquez entered the compartment. "AI, are we cleared for departure?"

"Roger, Twenty-Three," Granadica said over the 1MC. *"Pumping down now. You are to move following all posted and assigned flight warnings to Docking Lock Four. Safe life, Twenty-Three."*

"That was Granadica?" Velasquez asked, hitting the bucket.

"That was Granadica," Dana said.

There was something about the AI's tone that bothered her but she couldn't quite put her finger on it. They were definitely going to have to talk.

"Captain DiNote, this is my team," Dana said.

The shuttles had unloaded one by one, including all the luggage for the DPs, and the flight teams were finally in the factory. DiNote had ordered everyone to report to Twenty-Three for briefing.

"CM2 Benito," Dana continued. "EM3 Palencia and EA Velasquez."

"Benito, Palencia, Velasquez," the captain said, nodding. "This is Chief Barnett, EM1 Hartwell and CM1 Glass."

"Howza," Barnett said, shaking their hands. Mutant and Thermal just nodded.

"Chief Barnett will be responsible for all enlisted personnel on this mission," Captain DiNote continued. "I'm aware that you all have family among the DPs. I've had modified guidance that during off-watch periods you are permitted free interaction with the DPs. During watch periods, such interaction *shall* be strictly business. Watch periods will be set during the daily meeting periods so that shouldn't be an issue. The point is going to be made to the DPs through their own channels. I'm not going to tell the foreign minister of Argentina that he can't talk to his aide's son. There are admirals for that sort of conversation. What I'm going to tell *you* is that *you* are to refrain from initiating interaction. So if I find that you've bunked off to see daddy during duty hours, I'm going to require a Captain's Mast through channels for direct disobedience of an order. Is that clear?"

"Clear, sir," Palencia said.

"Parker, that includes you," DiNote said. "I understand that Mr. Vernon visited you on the flight deck during movement."

"Yes, sir," Dana said, gulping.

"There is to be *no* initiation of contact during duty periods," DiNote said. "I'd rather try to explain that to Dr. Barreiro than to Vernon Tyler, but it will be passed on."

"Yes, sir," Dana said, wondering exactly how long that order would last.

"From my perspective, we might as well all go back to our respective units," Captain DiNote said. "We're done. But higher apparently has a different take. So we're here for the duration. Anyone who steps on their..." He paused and looked at Dana for a moment.

"Anybody who messes up is going to have to deal with me," Chief Barnett said, smiling. "And you *don't* want to deal with me."

"God, no," Thermal muttered.

"Absent further guidance, Thermal, Comet, Palencia and Velasquez will continue to ensure maintenance of the shuttles," DiNote said. "Pilots will maintain proficiency, assist and advise. We've been assigned quarters with one of the officers from the inspection party. Quarters are tight on this station so we're bunking up. Barnett and Parker. Thermal and Mutant. There's a three-bunk for the rest of you."

"Yes, sir," Benito said, flexing his jaw.

"Grab your kit and get to quarters. We're off duty until tomorrow morning. So, yes, if your fathers are available you can visit them." He paused and looked off into the distance. "Damnit."

"Sir?" Barnett said.

"About half of what I just said went out the air lock," DiNote said. "Damnit."

"Sir?" Dana said after a moment.

"Quarters are as assigned," DiNote said. "Missions have slightly changed. And we're *not* off duty. There is a reception at nineteen hundred. *All* personnel will attend."

"Oh...*crap*," Barnett muttered.

"Uniform is dress uniform or formal dress," DiNote added.

"Sir, I'll take it from here," Barnett said.

"Please do," DiNote said, lifting his grav bag. "I'm headed to my quarters. Since we're not flying tomorrow, I'm going to visit with my old friend Johnny. Chief, your unit."

"Roger, sir," Barnett said. "Thermal, Mutant, better get in a shower. You've got the dress uniforms?"

"I didn't think I was going to have to use it," Thermal said. "But, yeah. And it's right."

"Better be," Barnett said. "There will be a preinspection at eighteen hundred. Final inspection at eighteen thirty. Both to be conducted for the male members by Thermal and Mutant. Final, really final inspection at eighteen fifty by *me*. You junior guys ever worn your dress uniforms?"

"Only once," Benito said. "Other than having it fitted. But we are familiar with dressing appropriately, Chief."

"You're way out on front on this one at least, Beni," Dana said, grinning.

"If you need any help . . . *Quipu*, I will be happy to oblige," Benito said.

"You wouldn't know proper dress if a Parisian courtier fitted you," Palencia said.

"As you were," Dana said.

"As the EM said," Barnett said. "And in case this isn't clear, none of you had better be sporting *shiners* at the reception. Or you'll find out why one of my nicknames is Bender. Be ready at eighteen hundred."

"Dana," Barnett said, giving the EM a hug as soon as they were in their quarters.

"It is really good to see you, Chief," Dana said, relaxing for the first time in she didn't know how long.

"How bad has it been?" Barnett asked, finally releasing her.

"What doesn't kill us, makes us stronger," Dana said.

"How's the PTSD?"

"Better now than in a long time," Dana said. "Whenever I have a bad night I schedule the division for a game of jungleball with the Pathans."

"You're playing *jungleball* with *Pathans*?"

"They don't really know how to play null ball," Dana said, sitting on the rack. "Jungleball is all they can understand. And they're not really that good at it."

"What about the rest of it?" Barnett asked. "I heard about the 'reply by endorsements.'"

"They're just a pain in the butt," Dana said. "Since the chain of command has to send them on, *that's* the pain in the butt. Let's say that my CO is getting pretty tired of them."

"Is it the same crap we're getting?" Barnett asked. "'You're being mean to my precious boy?'"

"You saw who their fathers are," Dana said. "That's the whole unit."

"A whole *unit* of perfumed princes?" Barnett asked.

"Pretty much," Dana replied. "They're all just marking time until they're admirals. Yeah, it's been bad. I get reamed repeatedly about not 'working with their culture.' And I ignore it. Because to Mast me they'd have to *order* me not to make my guys keep the birds in shape. And nobody is going to order *that*. So as long as I stay on their ass, they work to my standards. I've gotten to where I can take my eye off them for, oh, five minutes?"

"Christ," Barnett said, shaking her head. "That is really screwed up."

"Not really," Dana said. "Fact is, I'm good at being a controlling bitch. It's *not* being a controlling bitch that's stressful."

"Heh," Barnett said. "I *knew* there was a reason I liked you."

"They're not lazy," Dana said. "It's way more complicated than that. I mean...*way* more complicated. And there's an upside. Now they're *your* responsibility."

"Great!" the chief said. "Thanks!"

"It's not that big a deal tonight," Dana said. "Tell them to dress up for a fancy ball and they're on that like a shot. Especially Palencia. I suspect I'm going to look sort of tawdry next to him."

"Is that a problem?" Barnett asked.

"Nah, I'll just kick his ass at jungleball," Dana said. "It's more like tonight they're on their turf. I'm not."

"I'll have your back," Barnett said.

"I think it's going to be...interesting," Dana said.

FIFTEEN

"Well, no issues with junior enlisted uniforms," Barnett said.

The only place large enough for the preinspection was one of the shuttle bays. There was one other large compartment in the station, but that was being prepared for the reception.

The resplendent mess-dress uniforms of the three South American personnel looked decidedly out of place.

Alliance Navy Formal Uniform, Enlisted, Male, was based loosely on a tuxedo with tails.

All three of the uniforms were excellent but there was something subtly better about Palencia's. Dana couldn't quite put her finger on it. He definitely could carry it off better than Velasquez but it was less that than it appeared simply...better.

"Where in the world did you get that?" Barnett asked, looking at the uniform. "Even for mess dress that's not standard."

"Horsh and Wilhelm, Chief Barnett," Palencia replied.

"I don't recognize that," Barnett said.

"Ouch," Thermal said. He was wearing a standard dress uniform. "How much did it set you back?"

"Six thousand dollars, Engineer's Mate," Palencia replied.

"Ye flipping *gods*," Barnett said, shaking her head. "Okay, we are to arrive *first*. Normally, we follow people into anything. But in this case, all the junior people are to be on site *before* the arrival of the bigs. So let us proceed to our appointed place now that we're in our appropriate uniform."

The reception room looked like it was normally used for storage. At least, that was Dana's guess. Light cloth had been hung

from the walls and the floor was covered in rugs but it still had
the look of a holding area. Small tables—they looked too delicate
and were probably antique—were scattered around apparently for
the pure purpose of holding flowers. There were chairs scattered
about near the bulkheads and the back bulkhead was dominated
by a large bar of fine wood. A group of waiters in white coats
were gathered near the bar and there was a string quartet, currently tuning up, in one corner.

"Getting all this to Wolf, not to mention into Granadica, must
have been a major logistic activity," Dana whispered.

"Yeah," Barnett replied. "Apollo is pulling out the stops."

"Hello!"

The speaker was a short man with thinning blond hair in a very
nice suit. Dana didn't know much about suits but she recognized
nice when she saw it.

"And you are...?"

"Chief Barnett with party of six," Barnett replied.

"Ah, good," the man said. "I'm Carmen Mansour, Vice President
for Hospitality and Protocol of the Apollo Corporation. You are,
I believe, what is referred to as enlisted persons?"

"Yes," Barnett said, smiling thinly.

"If I could ask you to spread out?" Mansour asked. "Perhaps a
few over by the table with the bird of paradise on it? Two more
near the bar. Two others by the purple dendrobium. A mix of
male and female as much as possible with this group?"

"Okay...?" Barnett replied. "And we're doing this because...?"

"It permits anchoring as the more important guests arrive,"
Mansour said, smiling. "Sorry, but that's how it is. People *will*
tend to clump. By spreading persons initially, it creates a more
free-form gathering."

"Mutant, Velasquez," Barnett said. "Palencia, Parker. Benito,
Thermal, Me. Team one, the...whats?" She pointed to the first
table but clearly couldn't remember the name of the flowers. "Team
two, other table. Team three...we're hitting the bar."

"That will not be strictly necessary," Mansour said. "The waiters
will be happy to serve. Simply near the bar if you don't mind."

"All teams," Barnett said. "One glass of standard mix, which
means wine, beer or mixed drink *single*. After consumption,
minimum of one hour soft drink until second consumption. Sip,
do not slam. Are we clear?"

"Clear, Chief," Mutant said. "Done the drill."

"We understand as well, Chief," Palencia said. "There are, sorry, cultural aspects to take into account as well. There will be toasts. You are expected to drink your full drink."

"Then after you have one, order fruit juice, not a carbonated beverage," Barnett said. "The first person who shows signs of inebriation will be escorted back to quarters."

"I'm on all fruit juice, then," Dana said, grinning.

"All teams, spread out," Barnett said.

"Why us?" Dana asked.

"The most beautiful woman with the most handsome man?" Palencia said.

"Pal, I *will* have your ass back in my hands when we return to the *Therm*," Dana said.

"Ah, and such sweet surrender it would be," Palencia replied.

Dana shook her head and giggled.

"God, I hate that sound," Dana said.

"I find it delightful," Palencia said. "Sorry, this is the first time since our conversation on culture I have seen you look the slightest bit unassured."

"And since this is your sort of thing you're taking some delight in that."

"A bit," Palencia said. "A bit. On the other hand, you are, as you pointed out, going to have my ass back in your very capable hands soon enough. So you will understand that I'm going to do my best not to rub that in."

"Thank you," Dana said. "What can I expect?"

"More junior people will arrive soon," Palencia said. "By that I mean the Navy and Apollo personnel. Most of them will be military officers and managers. I suspect that they will more or less ignore us. We are beneath their notice. We serve, basically, as decorations and I would guess we'll be given various 'hey, you' tasks. When all the pawns, rooks and knights are in place, the kings and queens will start to arrive. Probably last will be Mr. Vernon. While my father might argue the respective importance of Mr. Vernon versus the foreign minister, he is clearly the highest level DP short of a prime minister of one of the Group of Ten. So he should arrive..."

He stopped as Vernon walked in and looked around the still

nearly empty room. Not surprising Dana at all, he was wearing a tuxedo. She was starting to feel like a slob.

The Apollo guy scurried over and Vernon listened to him for a second, nodded, and made a beeline for her.

"Hey, Dana," Tyler said. "Hey, um…" He was looking over his shoulder at the Apollo vice president who had followed in his wake.

"Mansour," Dana whispered.

"Mansour? Can I get a whiskey sour? Thanks." He turned back to her and grinned. "What, no champagne?"

"I'm on fruit juice tonight," Dana said as a waiter floated over with a tray of champagne glasses and one whiskey sour.

"EM Parker will take fruit juice next," Tyler said, taking the glass. "Thanks. How you doing?"

"Good, sir," the waiter said. "Bit different than my usual job."

"We had to recruit some of the better class of welders for this," Tyler said, winking at the waiter. "Getting a lot of personnel into the system this quick was going to be tough. Most of the stuff was produced by Granadica. Heck, the string quartet are mostly from the Night Wolves."

"And let me tell you, it took some doing," Granadica said, a hologram of a Glatun head popping up. "I work better with steel than wood."

"Granadica, Mr. Vernon, this is EM Palencia, one of my division."

"Hey," Tyler said, sticking out his hand. "Hear you guys absolutely kicked ass in engineering on that last MASSEX. Good job."

"Thank you, sir," Palencia said.

"You're the one whose dad is with the Argentinean foreign minister," Tyler said. "What's that all about? I'd figure you for whatever your version of Annapolis is called."

"Strangely enough, it's called the Naval Military School, sir," Palencia said, smiling. "Given our limited spacefaring ability and lack of fundamental experience, the decision was made to send persons who could be looked at as potential future leadership, sir."

"Damned good idea, whoever thought of it," Tyler said.

"Thank you, sir," Palencia replied. "My father was one of the team which recommended the program."

"I've been told there's some point to having officers having been enlisted before they get frocked or whatever," Tyler said. "Something like that?"

"Something, yes, sir," Palencia said.

"That something cultural with South Americans?" Tyler asked.

"Not . . . normally, sir," Palencia said.

The room was slowly filling up as others drifted in. Dana started to get really nervous looking at all the rank in the room. She stopped counting total "O" levels when it passed a hundred.

The various commanders, captains, and admirals were clearly trying to figure out why Tyler Vernon was already at the reception and spending his time talking to two enlisteds. Which just meant she was the target of more and more glances.

There was a flurry of activity at the doors and the Argentinean foreign minister, followed closely by the Chilean foreign minister, entered the room along with the rest of the South American contingent.

"Sir," Granadica said. "The Argentineans and Chileans have boarded."

"Ah," Tyler said, draining his drink and handing his glass to Palencia. "Gotta go make nice. Dana, don't go anywhere."

"Wasn't planning on it, sir," Dana said. "Woof," she added as he strode away.

"And you still maintain you are not friends?" Palencia said, looking around for somewhere to put the glass.

"I'll get it," Granadica said. The glass lifted out of his hand and headed for the nearest waiter.

"And you did that . . . how?" Dana asked. "I mean, grav, obviously."

"Just a matter of knowing how to use it, kiddo," Granadica said. "I have to move everything in the fabber with grav, obviously. If I couldn't figure out grav equations I couldn't do my job. I *said* I could be the only waiter at this reception but they wanted guys in white coats. Which were a *bitch* to produce, by the way."

"I take it you didn't produce the flowers?" Dana said.

"Nope," Granadica said. "And they had to bring up the wood. I did the rest."

"This is a very good replica," Palencia said, examining the table.

"Thanks," Granadica said. "I said tough. Compared to most of the stuff in a *Myrmidon*, it was a piece of cake."

Dana looked over at the group around Vernon and saw another Glatun head hovering nearby.

"You're carrying on two conversations at once?"

"More than that, kid," Granadica said. "Got a shuttle on its way to the Naval Acceptance Yard under remote, two more over there, arguing with the Navy, producing parts for the next fabber, talking with Vulcan about issues producing Lud, in a meeting with some of the Night Wolves and I'm still running all my lines. It's called being able to multitask."

"And making you laugh caused a fault?" Dana said quizzically.

"Said 'triggered my humor circuit,'" Granadica said. "That requires that I be using something other than rote action and response. Most conversations are action and response."

"So you're actually talking to EM Parker and using a Turing response program for discussions with the Argentinean foreign minister?" Palencia said.

"Right now I'm using a rote action and response to all the conversations except the one with the Night Wolves," Granadica replied. "Including that response. I'm being asked questions that were easy enough to program in advance. This sort of meet and greet rarely gets beyond rote action/response."

"That is . . ." Palencia said, then frowned. "Absolutely true. At least at the meet and greet level."

"Just figured that out, kiddo?" Granadica said, hissing in Glatun laughter. "I knew that when Amerigo Vespucci got lost finding Argentina."

"He didn't get *lost*," Palencia said.

"Bet you a dollar?" Granadica replied.

"And that was all rote response," Dana interjected.

"Figuring out what will get an emotional response out of an Argentinean is like figuring out if a flipped coin will land," Granadica said, chuckling again.

"Granadica," Dana said. "Please don't start any bar fights."

"Why?" the fabber replied. "You and the chief are here. Don't worry, kiddo, I'm being on my very best behavior. Whoops. Gotta go."

"Is that really her best behavior?" Palencia asked.

"How should I know?" Dana replied. "This is the first time I've dealt with her except for a short conversation when we were in the docking bay."

"I keep having a hard time remembering that she is older than my nation," Palencia said.

"It is a bit tough, isn't it?" Dana said, handing her barely touched champagne glass to a waiter and accepting the proffered fruit juice. She wasn't sure what kind of fruit but it was tasty.

"I'm being signaled by General Benito," Palencia said.

"And I think people are spread out enough," Dana said. "I'm going to go gang up with the chief. Do *not* get me in trouble."

"Won't," Palencia said.

"Why *don't* I believe that?" Dana said, making her way through the crowd to the bar. "Oh, because it's never been true before!"

"What were you discussing with the AI?" General Benito asked.

"Several items, sir," Palencia said. "The most important of which was that the AI is using a preprogrammed rote response for its various conversations at this reception."

"That is . . ." the general said, frowning.

"The AI pointed out that most such conversations are rote response, sir," Palencia added. "Such as this one. I anticipated that would be your first question and had the response prepared. Extrapolate that for an AI and it's obvious, sir. She also had a list of all the conversations and actions she was engaged in at the same time. The fabber . . ." He stamped his foot slightly. "You can feel it is still running. The AI talking to . . ." He looked around, ". . . seven different groups is also running the fabber. Rote response makes sense."

"I suppose these things are pretty much rote response, aren't they?" the general said, chuckling. "Very well, go get my son and Velasquez. We have some things to discuss that are not rote response."

"Yes, sir," Palencia said.

"You should probably stay with your people, EM," Captain DiNote said as she approached the group from the 142nd.

"They're not my people tonight, sir," Dana said. "It's Sud versus Norté tonight. And, with all due respect, sir, they're not 'my' people even when we're on the *Therm*. I'm responsible for them. That's not the same as being a team."

"Understood," DiNote said. "Any idea what they're talking about?"

"From experience, how they're going to hang my ass, sir," Dana said.

"Bitter much?" Barnett asked.

"Excuse me, Chief," Dana said, slapping herself slightly. "Attitude adjusted."

"The following was not said," Captain DiNote said. "Because I became aware of some of the issues with a former subordinate whom I hold in high regard, I had a quiet chat with a friend in NavSpacPers. We were at the Academy together and we both worked NavSpac. Different offices. He's in a position to have had...'too much,' as he put it, to do with the issues with the 143 and to know the inside scuttlebutt having to do with the... issues with assigned American personnel."

"You mean that a lowly EM has a string of 'reply by endorsements' that go across the secretary of the Navy's desk, sir?" Dana asked.

"Don't be bitter," DiNote said. "Seriously. I have to do some more back check but what Barry said was that at this point they're mentally giving a set of points to the people with the most of them. As in promotion points. Because they've noticed that the people with a lot of complaints are the ones who are actually getting something *done*."

"I got the same thing," Barnett said. "Chief's phone. There's a lot of negative vibes being directed at the people who were in place before the new arrivals. Because they don't seem to have done anything and the new arrivals did."

"That's because they were in the wrong positions," Dana said. "Megadeath can't be everywhere. I think he tried when he was first assigned but...he couldn't. And like I said to the chief, sir, the only way I get anything done is by being up the butts of four people. Tell me to do the same thing with a full flight and it's not going to happen.

"I don't know how to say this, sir, but...I don't think that it's really going to *work*. I mean in a great big 'this Alliance isn't going to work' way. What people are seeing is the tip of the iceberg of how screwed up things are."

"It is, however, the hand we've been dealt," Captain DiNote said. "Can you keep playing it?"

"Right up until something bad happens, sir," Dana said. "Things happen. You know that, sir. The first time they can actually hang something on me, or make it look as if it's on me, all that 'attaboy' is out the window. It's not getting the division to work that's stressful. It's wondering when I'm not quite good enough or somebody figures out a way to make me really look bad that's got me worried. Don't be confused by the smiles, these guys seriously want to drive a knife into my back in a very real and literal sense. And now I'm being rated. My rating officer is Diaz and to say that we don't get along is an understatement."

"And this is space," Barnett said. "Accidents happen."

"Which is why I spend a lot of time checking my suit," Dana said. "And never use the same navpak twice or set up a pattern."

"Anything?" DiNote asked.

"A ... couple of times there were things that weren't the same about my suit as when I'd checked it last, sir," Dana said. "Doubt it would have killed me but it would have made me look sloppy. But I keep it pretty secure and as long as it's in private areas, Leonidas has my back. But I can't rack it in an open zone. And it doesn't help that the Pathans absolutely flat hate my guts. I don't go into the common areas at *all*. There are always Pathans around and if they get their hands on me ... I'd rather have my suit sabotaged. Deciding to get my mad out by kicking their ass at jungleball is looking like a short-term answer that created a long-term problem."

"Anybody but Leonidas have your back?" Captain DiNote asked.

"I think Velasquez and I have sort of bonded, but ... No, sir."

"Jesus Christ," Thermal said, shaking his head. "Sir, we need to figure out an extract."

"With due respect, EM, I'm handling the situation," Dana said. "And I consider it to be good training as well as an important mission. But it's good to get into breathable even if it's sort of ..." She looked around and giggled. "Thick."

"Feeling like you're in the Big Dark?" Mutant asked.

"Hey, I found my way back when my coxswain got hit by a micrometeorite, right?" Dana said, grinning. The "Big Dark" was being far enough into space there were no good visual navigational references. It had confused Dana at first because in space, without the filtering effect of atmosphere, the sky was practically a *wall* of stars. Which you stopped noticing the first time you had to try to find your way without navigational aids.

Back when she was a lowly engineer recruit the Flight NCO had decided to test her knowledge of celestial navigation by an "accident" where a micrometeor had "killed" him and destroyed the navigational controls of their shuttle.

Finding the *Troy* again had been ... good training.

"And then squirted blood all over the flight compartment which *I* had to clean up."

"Do you feel like you're in the Big Dark?" DiNote repeated.

"I'm not doing a Dutchman, sir," Dana said. "Not to swell the chief or Thermal's heads any more than they already are, sir, but I've got this great big nav beacon called 'What would the chief or Thermal do in this situation?'"

"Heh," Barnett said. "Wait until the day that you suddenly look up and realize that *you're* that person."

"I don't understand, Chief," Dana said.

"You will," Thermal said, chuckling.

"When I finally got a pretty full grasp on the situation, I realized I could do two things," Dana said. "I could coast and ignore the fact that the shuttles were broke, and thereby make my chain of command happy and not have to battle my engineers every day. Or I could crawl up their ass and get the shuttles fixed. Which took more than crawling up their ass. They are *not* natural engineers, even Palencia who has a degree in it. So it took training them, as well. More or less starting from 'these are ERs, whatever their rate tabs say.' Which is what I figured the chief would do."

"Thank you," Barnett said.

"And I sure as hell wasn't going to just sign off on the birds when they weren't good or their training when it wasn't to standard," Dana said. "I couldn't see Thermal doing that."

"Damned straight," Thermal said, his jaw flexing.

"Is that what's been going on?" Captain DiNote asked.

"Not in my division, sir," Dana said. "I will not speak for others. However, I think the results speak for themselves. The 143 had a nearly one hundred percent availability condition. On paper. Real availability was myself, three shuttles from another division with a Norté division chief and one shuttle that was straight out of Vulcan and came in without any faults."

"That's the conclusion of the MASSEX report," Barnett said.

"The report isn't..." Captain DiNote said, then stopped. "Chief's phone?"

Chiefs reviewed reports before any officer got their hands on them.

"More like 1MC, sir," Barnett said, referring to the intercom system of ships that tended to be turned up to nuclear levels.

"Then..." DiNote said, then paused as Admiral Duvall, followed closely by her aide, walked over.

The group came subtly to attention and drinks were lowered to their sides.

"As you were," the admiral said, smiling. "Captain, we spoke briefly at the airfield."

"Yes, ma'am," DiNote said.

"Have you or your people had any significant briefing?" the admiral asked.

"None whatsoever, ma'am," the captain replied. "As far as we were aware we were transporting DPs. We were not expecting to attend the reception."

"Receptions," the admiral said. "Formal. Most evenings. We're laying in dry cleaning support. And you'll be attending the meetings. All of the 142nd personnel, EM Parker and EM Palencia. The last was a hasty add. If he opens his mouth without good reason, I will personally see he hangs. I don't care *who* his father is. And he is not going to be sitting on the... Sud side of the table. You will explain to him that he is there as a member of the Alliance Navy. No more, no less."

"Yes, ma'am," the captain said.

"The same does not hold for yourself, your people or, interestingly enough, EM Parker," Duvall said, turning to look at the engineer's mate. "You were, I'm told, the primary add by Apollo to this meeting. The rest of us are more or less window dressing."

"I don't know why, ma'am," Dana said, trying not to tremble. Engineer's mate second class should never *ever* be noticed by admirals.

"Well, it was clearly Vernon," Duvall said thoughtfully. "Is there anything I need to know about this relationship, EM?"

"Ma'am," Chief Barnett interjected. "I know the EM very well, ma'am. I know a good bit about her personal life on the *Troy*. She and Mr. Vernon are not engaged in a relationship as such. Take that from a chief, ma'am."

"I see," Duvall said. "He certainly greeted you warmly."

"I was surprised by that, ma'am," Dana said. "But the explanation is that we seem to... get along. He considers me a friend, which I found a bit shocking." She wanted to mention that he had something specifically in mind in regards to Granadica but she knew better than to say that where the AI could hear.

"Well, I've also been told he specifically wants your input," Duvall said. "All of your input but especially yours, EM Parker." A look of frustration crossed her normally sunny face.

"I wish I could read that bog of his mind. I'll give Apollo

credit. From the very first point that it was even vaguely notice-able that there were consistent problems with the *Myrmidons* they have been giving us unprecedented access. Not burying us with data, just anything we felt we needed, wanted or desired. I have been beating my head against this wall for three years. I'm not sure why he feels an engineer's mate has a significant contribu-tion!" She paused and shook her head. "EM Parker, please don't get me wrong..."

"Ma'am, I don't know either," Dana said, trying not to squirm. "I don't have a degree or anything."

"Nonetheless, that is why you are all at the reception," Duvall said. "And the others to follow. And the primary meetings. At the table, not with the aides. The table is larger than I'd expected it to be and I think that will be an issue. But that is what we've been handed."

Dana suddenly remembered Vernon's comment that all the bigwigs that had signed on to the trip were "a useful addition." She started to open her mouth then shut it.

"Parker?" Duvall said.

"Just...I'm sure it will work out, ma'am," Parker said.

"Eight hundred and thirty-seven thousand man-hours," the admiral said. "Most of it by Ph.D.s and master's engineers. You are refreshingly optimistic, Engineer's Mate." She nodded at the group and walked over to a cluster of admirals.

"Never offer an unsolicited opinion in a situation like that, Dana," Barnett said.

"I didn't, Chief," Dana said. "All I did was open and close my mouth."

"Learn a poker face," DiNote said. "This is the highest level meeting on the subject of the problem of the *Myrmidons* ever held. With the people who are in attendance, the *CNO* should be here. He *would* be here except he was tied up. Those sorts of meetings, opening and closing your mouth is liable to kill you quicker than sabotaging your suit. Metaphorically. *Coughing* at the wrong time can lose the battle."

"She was just told by the admiral that her input is expected, sir," the chief pointed out.

"Why, Engineer's Mate?" the captain asked. "Seriously. I *know* you know a reason."

"Sir..." Dana said. "Not... Sir, you're not cleared."

"Not . . ." DiNote said, his eyebrows raising. "Dana, what the *hell* is going on?"

"We're here to cover her back, sir," Mutant said.

"Go."

"That was implied by what the admiral said, sir," CM1 Glass said. "She was specifically requested by Apollo. Presumably by Mr. Vernon. Why, I don't know. But our job is to make sure she doesn't . . . cough at the wrong time, or if she does, figure out the fix. We're here to cover her back. Like the chief just covered her back by pointing out to the admiral that Dana wasn't screwing Vernon."

"Thanks, Mutant," Dana said, wincing. "And for the record, I am definitely not in a relationship with Tyler Vernon, sir."

"Very well," DiNote said, shaking his head. "It would be nice to know what we're covering it for."

"And against who," Barnett said.

SIXTEEN

"What was discussed with Vernon?" General Benito asked as soon as the three enlisted men were gathered.

"Simple greetings," Palencia answered. "He was interested in why so many of a better class were assigned to the 143rd."

"And your answer?" Benito asked.

"That it was our first opportunity of spacefaring and that persons who were likely to assume higher level positions in later life had been chosen," the EM answered, shrugging. "He mentioned the crass theory that to be a good officer requires experience as an enlisted man and I did not dissuade him. He is new rich. Very unsubtle and without class."

"When I want an opinion from you I'll squeeze your head like a zit," the general said. "Did he give you any indication that he is aware of the issues with regard to EM Parker?"

"No, sir," Palencia said.

"Do we have any better understanding of their relationship?"

"I spoke, briefly, with CM1 Glass when Mr. Vernon entered and immediately approached her," CM Benito said. "He was as unaware of any relationship, prior to this, as EM Parker has maintained."

"It is looking increasingly like a sham of some sort," the General said. "That is the only rational explanation. Continue to circulate. Keep your mouths shut and your ears open. Palencia, you are to sit at the meeting tomorrow. You are going to be with the Navy contingent. Again, keep your mouth closed and your ears open."

"Yes, sir," Palencia said.

"I can't believe they have enlisted men at this thing," the general said, shaking his head. "Dinner follows the reception. Do not embarrass us by getting drunk and stupid. Follow orders and report each evening to your respective fathers."

"Yes, sir," Palencia said.

"Permission to speak to my father now, my General," Velasquez said.

"Why?"

"He's my father, my General?" Velasquez said. He wasn't about to say that he felt the general was wrong in a very big way.

"And very busy even if he is just chatting," the general said. "Just circulate. You all should be carrying the trays like monkeys."

It was late and all that Velasquez wanted to do was get this uncomfortable uniform off and go to bed. But duty was beginning to be a strange but comfortable burden.

"Papa, it is Diego."

"It is late, son, get some sleep."

"I would but there is something I need to discuss with you. It is in fact important. At least I believe so."

"Then come to my quarters."

"I am down the hall. The doors are locked."

The security door opened and Diego walked down the corridor to his father's compartment.

"Not the most fabulous accommodations, eh?" his father said, gesturing around.

The compartment was about the size of the one Diego shared with Benito and Palencia. Which meant small. They could barely fit themselves and their gear in it. But that was to be expected. They were the lowest of the low.

Compared to what an undersecretary would normally occupy at a major conference, it was a box.

"The ambassador's is not much larger."

"More insults?" Diego asked.

"We do not think so," Dr. Velasquez answered. "They are the best quarters on the fabber. That people work for years in these conditions…"

"Six hours a day in suits, Papa," Diego said.

"That is simply—"

"Necessary," Velasquez said. "Father, this is not what I have come to talk about. But perhaps peripherally. It is about the relationship between Mr. Vernon and EM Parker."

"A sham," Velasquez said. "We have figured that out."

"I must respectfully disagree, Father."

"On what basis?" Dr. Velasquez asked.

"On having spent six hours a day, in suits, working on a boat with EM Parker, Father," Diego said, chuckling. "I will not say that there is not more going on here. There is. And it involves Parker. But her relationship with Vernon is very real. At least on his part. Perhaps he is attracted by her looks but I think it is more complex than that. I think it is...cultural."

"Go ahead," Dr. Velasquez said, leaning back on his bunk. "Since it's *my* degree, why don't *you* lecture?"

"Yes, Papa, that is why I think I am right," Diego said. "Papa, first you must consider the situation of Tyler Vernon. He is notoriously reclusive. He has had any number of opportunities to meet with persons of high estate. He eschews them."

"He avoids them like the plague," Dr. Velasquez said. "Go on."

"He seems to mostly avoid *people*," Diego said. "He does not seem to mind them, but he is perfectly comfortable, apparently, alone. He does not even have a particular group of protectors or handlers. He has no personal aide but AIs."

"That has been mentioned as being a possible issue with his mental health," Velasquez said.

"I don't think that is the issue, Papa, sorry," Diego said. "Vernon simply is a... We say that we think about other people's culture, but we do not. We still emotionally think of our culture. Our own lives. That he has to...maintain status. And that requires that he interact. Make deals. Make sure his children get the right schools, the right deals, the right spouses..."

"Yes," Dr. Velasquez said.

"First, he has none of those issues," Diego said. "He has become as hyperpowerful in the realm of business as, sorry, the United States is in war. In politics as well. Why else are you here? It is not about the *Myrmidons*."

"Why, exactly, we are here is not your concern," Dr. Velasquez said.

"But my point is made," Diego said. "He simply does not have to play those roles, those...games."

"Recognized," Dr. Velasquez said, then shook his head. "Sorry, that was an automatic response. You are right. And it will require much thought. Why is he here? Wait, why is he *really* here?"

"You were working on his agenda being placating our group of the Alliance for the problems of the *Myrmidons*," Diego said, smiling. "To help us save face. Perhaps to polish some alliances. You now realize that he cares less about that than a stray cat in Santiago?"

"You are becoming decidedly subtle, young man," Dr. Velasquez said. "I'm proud."

"Strangely, I'm a bit troubled," Diego said. "Because the more I work with Parker, whom I have come to respect if not like, the more I am troubled. And that cuts to the other part of the relationship. Have you ever really paid attention to Vernon's relationships with women?"

"What relationships?" Dr. Velasquez said. "According to our intelligence he has passed up the opportunity, repeatedly, with both women and men. It is assumed he is heterosexual trended asexual."

"Yet, I believe he genuinely likes Parker," Diego said. "But not because she is female, per se. I think that it is because, somehow, he sees in her his culture."

"He is the richest man in the world," Dr. Velasquez said with a snort. "She is not his culture."

"He is that almost purely American form of self-made rich," Diego said. "The sort that is *not* a social climber. They simply wish to be wealthy and powerful and have no interest in taking on the views or attitudes of higher-class culture. Look at his deep background. Raised in a suburb in the conservative area of his country. And his high school record indicates he was what Americans term a 'geek.' To the extent there is a sexual component to this relationship, Parker would have been a high status girlfriend when he was growing up. She was a cheerleader."

"How could we miss that?" Dr. Velasquez said, shading his eyes with his hands.

"Furthermore, they are of similar cultural background," Diego continued. "How many people does he meet on a regular basis from similar cultural background who are still close enough to it that they...echo it. Most of the time when he meets with military they are admirals whose culture, no matter where they come from, is simply Navy at this point. Parker is perhaps the only person he's met in a very long time that he can really connect with. I state that it is a real relationship. One of friendship. And the friendship is deeply steeped in their mutual culture. About that I am less certain of the meaning. Parker, herself, warned me of some trap there obliquely. 'You don't understand friendship.'"

"Which is why she is included in the meeting," Dr. Velasquez said. "She is a touchstone."

"Again, disagree, Papa," Diego said.

"If you keep being right and everyone else wrong it will go hard with you," Dr. Velasquez said, smiling. "Why?"

"Although Tyler could easily pull strings to get Parker reassigned to the *Troy*, where he makes his base, he did not. Yet he pulled those strings to get her assigned to this meeting. Seriously, Papa, do you think that he felt he *needed* a touchstone for this meeting? He meets with the President of the United States when he, Tyler Vernon, bothers to open up his schedule. I'm sorry but—"

"The foreign minister of Chile is not of the same order," Dr. Velasquez said. "And when I present these thoughts to the minister I will have to think hard how to put it delicately."

"Last point, Papa."

"You've been thinking."

"You know I'm a thinker, Papa," Diego said, smiling. "This is the thought. We have established that at a certain level Tyler Vernon's innate psychology and culture have some resemblance to EM Parker."

"I will take that as a given for the discussion," Dr. Velasquez said. "I am still assimilating it."

"Vastly different conditions," Diego said. "But similar worldview. Now, Papa, what does that tell you?"

"It tells me it is late, Diego."

"How many complaints have you generated about EM Parker, Papa?"

"Many. She is simply imposs—" Dr. Velasquez said then grimaced. "Oh, no."

"It is not the problem of the complaints that you need concentrate on, Papa," Diego said. "Well, those too. Because you are having to deal with a tremendously powerful person who has the *same* view of how the universe should work as that lowly EM you have been repeatedly blasting. For, at base, refusing to change her worldview to suit your own. Which means that Tyler is going to have the same absolute stubbornness. And infinitely more power."

"Now I'm *never* going to get to sleep!"

"Thank the Virgin Mother *I* can. Your problem now. Good night, Papa."

"AT LEAST I CAN TELL THE DIFFERENCE BETWEEN A WARRANTY MALFUNCTION AND SLOPPY MAINTENANCE!"

"And now that we've gotten all that out," Tyler said, holding up his hands. "We're going to dial it down—"

"IF YOU THINK THAT—" Dr. Barreiro shouted.

"And if the Foreign Minister would kindly refrain from antagonizing the AI that controls our air and gravity—"

"If you think that—" Granadica snarled.

"Whose core I *will* pull if she doesn't dial it down . . ." Tyler said. "And she can spend the rest of the meeting as a small squeaky *box* on the table." He paused and looked around. "And now all the colloidals can take some deep cleansing breaths. . . . In through the nose, out through the mouth while the AI runs some soothing checks on her system while saying 'Oooommmm' . . ."

"I am in cycle again, Mr. Vernon," Granadica said.

"I am . . . in cycle as well," Dr. Barreiro said. "But I will state that the government of Argentina will have no further imputations cast against its citizens who are members of the Alliance Navy—"

"Well, if you'd—!"

"And we're stopping again!" Tyler said raising his hands again. "Because every second that passes I am getting older and death's mighty hand collects us all in its time. And we are drifting gently away from the negatives . . . away from the negatives . . . And . . . Good. And now we're going to talk as friends with an issue we must all *resolve* to repair. Parker."

"Sir?"

During one of the battles around *Troy*, Parker and Thermal had ended up in a shuttle working the scrapyard when a Rangora fleet came through the gate. Dozens of battleships, lasers and missiles flew in every direction, and all she could do was sit in the shade of a piece of rubble and hope nobody noticed.

Being in the meeting had so far felt very much like that clash of titans. Except that during the battle, since they were powered down, she couldn't see what was happening. Here she could watch in terror.

Now everyone was looking at her. That didn't make it easier.

"Can you, without imputing false actions or lack thereof of

any person, colloidal or otherwise, living or dead, who might or might not exist somewhere in this universe, possibly sort out what faults are due to potentially questionable manufacture by some group or system that may remain nameless versus faults that may or may not be due to some potential possible or variable form of maintenance?"

"Sirrr?"

"Which ones are Granadica and which ones are sloppy maintenance?" Tyler said.

"Mr. Vernon, that is—"

"Damnit, Tyler, I thought you were—"

"STOP!" Tyler said. "I was translating. It's cultural. The actual words intended should be substituted for the previous question in everyone's mind. Parker. Which are which?"

"Uh, sir..." Parker said.

"Yes, or no?"

"Yes, sir," Parker said, gulping. "It's pretty easy, really. The Granadica ones don't kill you."

"Heh," Barnett said. "That's a good way of putting it."

"What?" Dr. Barreiro said. "Are you suggesting we are deliberately sabotaging—?"

"That's not what she said or meant, Foreign Minister," Tyler said. "Please don't play that game. I don't have time or interest. Dana, what do you mean exactly?"

"I'm having a hard time explaining, sir..." Dana said, looking around at "her" people.

"We've noted that as well." Thomas Schneider was the Deputy Chief of Special Projects for the Wolf system. He was an orbital engineer with, at this point, three years experience working on all the various projects that cropped up in Wolf. Unlike the Night Wolves he wasn't a prototyper, just the "odd job" expert. He also, not coincidentally, was Vernon's son-in-law. "The faults that can be directly attributed to manufacturing defects are invariably nonlethal by direct form. Which is—"

"Impossible," Chief Barnett said. "Which is what everyone at the ground level has been saying."

"And it's a word that hasn't been used a lot," Tyler said. "Define. Dana? Thermal?"

"Ministers," Thermal said, leaning over and looking at the South Americans. "There are exactly *no* frills on a *Myrmidon*. I think you might have noticed that on the way up. Every. *Single*. System. Has to work *perfectly* or people die. That is what is impossible about the faults."

"People keep saying 'random,'" Dana interjected. "They're not *random!*"

"They are as close to statistically perfectly random as you can get," Schneider pointed out.

"No, they're not," Thermal replied. "They are *nonlethal*. That, right there, proves they are nonrandom. Ministers," he said again. "When you were flying up here, did you think the ride was smooth?"

"Much smoother than an aircraft," Dr. Werden said.

"We were accelerating, most of the time, at a speed that would make most fighter pilots pass out," Captain DiNote said.

"We *were*?" Dr. Barreiro said.

"Absolutely," Thermal said. "Most of the time we were pulling ten gravities. During turns we were pulling upwards of thirty. And you didn't feel a *thing*, did you?"

"No," Dr. Barreiro said.

"This part of the discussion is one of the reasons I required that we use *Myrmidons*," Tyler said.

"There are seventy-two gravity plates in the main cargo compartment that are *why* you didn't feel anything," the engineer's mate said. "They control the inertial condition on the ship. Every single one is *very* difficult to manufacture. Every single one *has* to be *perfect*. Every single one *has* to be in tune. Or you would have been splattered into red goo during the ride. It's one of the reasons we kept asking for the engineers, your sons, to return to their stations. Among the thousand other jobs they have in flight is ensuring that the inertial control systems remain working."

"I . . . didn't know that about shuttles," Dr. Werden said, gulping slightly. "I have ridden shuttles many times."

"*Civilian* shuttles," Tyler interjected. "*Columbias*. They don't have the acceleration of a *Myrmidon*. That was why Comet's shuttle was dispatched during the First Battle of *Troy* to pick up those passengers. It had a *much* higher acceleration than a *Columbia*. They can't make a shuttle using 'all Earth' technology that can do what a *Myrmidon* does."

"My point is that if *one* of those is out of sync, then it's a disaster," Thermal said. "There is no way to have one that's just a *teensy* bit wrong. They either work or they don't."

"So explain Thirty-Four?" Dana said.

"That's it, you can't," Thermal replied, leaning back and crossing his arms. "Nobody can."

"Thirty-Four?" Dr. Werden said.

"We had a shuttle," Barnett replied, shaking her head. "It had a fault in the inertia we didn't even *notice*. Passed *every* check. Until we got Marines onboard."

"What was wrong with it?" Dr. Werden asked.

"Imagine..." Barnett said, shaking her head. "Imagine a thousand little fingers up inside your guts, gennntly massaging them."

"Oh," Dr. Barreiro said, grabbing his stomach and crossing his legs. "Oh..."

"Oh, yeah," Barnett said, grinning. "Which was what we heard from the Marine in the *single* seat it affected as soon as we hit a *particular* acceleration curve. Well, that and screaming. It's hard to get out of those seats fast but he set a record. What should have happened is...what Thermal said. He *should* have been red goo. Instead he started screaming and hopping around like a madman."

"The Marines thought we did it on purpose," Captain DiNote said. "That it was a practical joke. We never figured out how it worked. We ended up pulling every part of the control runs and power for the plate, and the plate, of course, until we could get it in spec."

"I hope you charged us for it," Tyler said.

"Oh, we did," Admiral Duvall said. "Bet on that."

"*Everyone* was stumped," Thermal said. "Even our engineering officer, who has a master's in this stuff, couldn't figure out how to even *replicate* it. We tried because, among other things, it *would* have made a great..." He stopped, coughed and flushed red.

"Potential breakthrough in gravitics," Barnett finished for him, then coughed.

"Ah, yes," Dr. Barreiro said, smiling.

"We never got that, specifically," Thomas Schneider said.

"Well, you *don't*," Barnett said. "You get 'intermittent fault, grav system nine. Parts replaced until fault rectified.' There's no box for 'really really weird fault that looks like a practical joke.'"

"How *would* you do that?" Admiral Duvall said, musingly. "I mean, I can see it in *general*, but the equations are..."

"Impossible," Thermal said. "But while that's an extreme example, most of the faults have something like that in common. They *don't* kill anyone and it's nearly impossible to have a fault that *doesn't* kill anyone on a *Myrmidon*!"

"Are they...unnecessarily deadly?" Dr. Barreiro asked. "The shuttles, that is?"

"I have to answer that," Admiral Benito said. "No. This is the essential problem of military equipment. If there is some...slack somewhere, then you are doing things wrong. Everything must be the absolute minimum to do the maximum. As much power as you can fit in as small a space as possible. The fact that there is so little slack tells me something I had wondered, which is whether the *Myrmidons* were a good design."

"I'm still not too crazy about the main power system," Barnett said. "I'd like a *little* redundancy."

"Something we're looking at," Schneider said. "And we'd noticed the general nonlethality of problems. For that matter, most of them don't truly deadline the boat, especially if they're caught early. And it is one of the theories having to do with why it crops up in grapnels so much. They are somewhat peripheral to survival."

"Then why is the 143rd having so many accidents!" Dr. Barreiro shouted. "We have lost lives!"

The Apollo and Norté Alliance members stopped and took an almost simultaneous breath then settled back into their seats.

"Oh, my *God*!" Dana blurted then cringed. She stared across the table at Captain DiNote in terror.

"Engineer's Mate Parker is unused to meetings of this magnitude," Tyler said, leaning back. "She has had an insight. She is, however, aware that sharing that insight would cause difficulties."

"Because she is going to say that the problem of the 143rd is due to our own negligence," Dr. Palencia snarled. "We are *well aware* of her opinions."

Tyler paused and looked thoughtfully at him for a moment, cocking his head to the side.

"I think everyone from Apollo and the 142nd had that shared opinion when the foreign minister of Argentina made his outburst, *Under*minister for Interstellar Affairs," Tyler said mildly. "However, I was watching Parker and she managed to be the soul of tact. Which means that whatever insight she may have is either peripheral to that position or an extension thereof. Since we are trying to get to the bottom of what is going on, such insights are valuable. I am personally interested in the insight. I would request of the South American delegation that any ire they may have towards Parker for her insight be directed at myself or Admiral Duvall who I am going to request *order* Parker to share the insight. Admiral?"

"Engineering Mate?" Duvall said. "The nature of your insight?"

Dana gulped for a minute then grimaced angrily.

"It's a Johannsen's worm."

"What?" Granadica shouted. "I've been checked for every virus, worm and Trojan known to man or Glatun!"

"Granadica," Tyler said. "Yell at me or the admiral, please. Explain, Parker?"

"I was looking at Mut...Coxswain's Mate Glass," Dana said, grimacing. "And I kept thinking 'Blond, blond, blond' and I couldn't figure out why."

"I am...*blond*?" Mutant said, smiling slightly.

"The *actual* Johannsen's worm," Admiral Duvall said, putting her hands over her eyes. "From the mouths of babes."

"I still don't understand," Dr. Barreiro said.

"Don't you?" Tyler said, turning the minister's left wrist upwards so that the faint scar carried by virtually every member of his generation could be seen. "The Horvath, those ever-to-be-damned squids, gave those vile worms to us. To see who would care for themselves, and their children, enough to clean a simple wound. Put some antiseptic on it, bandage it, and you survived. Left untreated, you died. Simple, effective and *permanent*."

"So you are saying that the proof we are having fatal accidents due to negligence is this...whatever this is?" Dr. Barreiro said.

"Granadica?" Tyler said.

"Your insight...meets all logic tests," Granadica said. "And neither I nor any of the cyberneticists have found it."

"It is the ghost in the machine," Tyler said, grinning.

"This is not funny," Dr. Werden said. "I lost sons of friends in those crashes."

"Would you care for me to list the number of people I have lost in my life, *Herr* Doctor?" Tyler said, still smiling thinly. He leaned back, reached into his suit and pulled out a thin cigar. "South America was, except for the plagues, relatively untouched by the Horvath and the Rangora. Brazil lost Rio." Lit it. "Santiago, Buenos Aires, were never touched. So if you'd care to count *bodies*, we can do that all day. My mother for one. Friends and coworkers by the dozens. I still don't know where this is coming from but what it is, what it *means*, is absolutely clear. It is a *test*. A test to see if the users are *worthy* of space. And *we* didn't put it there. We can't even *find* it."

"It has to be hidden really *deep* in my programming," Granadica said, in a very small voice. "Now that I realize what's going on, I'm looking for it. And not finding it. I wasn't even aware of it and now that I am aware of it, I'm finding deliberate logic blocks against seeing it. I may be able to backtrack to it that way..."

"I'm not sure we should pull it," Tyler said, puffing.

"What?" "Sir, I think you need to..." "You would kill our *sons*—?"

"IT'S A *TEST*!" Tyler shouted. "*Binary solution set!* Do you have enough sense to come in out of the *vacuum*! Do you have enough sense to make sure that the boat you are going to fly *works*! I rode here on boats that *your* sons, Foreign Minister, maintained! Comet, do you do *every single repair* in *every single boat*?"

"Sir, I haven't done an actual repair since I got there," Parker replied. "Or a first test. All I do is spot check the work of my men. Sir!"

"*Your* son, Dr. Palencia, ensured that the boat *I* rode was properly prepared to survive the rigors of space, of combat," Tyler said, stabbing his cigar at the underminister. "I, *every one of us*, put our lives in *your son's* hands. Not the famous Comet Parker! A *monkey* can *drive* one of these things! Certainly from Earth to Granadica. It takes a *very* good mechanic to keep them *operating*!" He puffed on his cigar furiously. "I think we ought to install the same 'fault' in ALL our fabbers!"

"Okay, Dad, you did not say that," Thomas said, putting his fingers in his ears.

"We can't even *find* it," Tyler said. "We assuredly can't replicate it. Useless threat. But the point remains. If you are careful enough to survive space, you do the checks. If you *don't* do the checks, especially the initial ones, the faults cascade until the boats are definitely unsurvivable. I wasn't *sure* about it until we got *them*," he said, pointing the cigar at the cluster of spacemen, "into the equation and started talking about the nature of the actual faults. Palencia. Engineer's Mate Palencia, to be exact. What do *you* think?"

"Your logic is, as the AI said, unassailable," Palencia said, shrugging.

"So where does that logic *lead*?" Tyler mused. "You may not believe it but we didn't put it there. You can probably believe that we don't have the *knowledge* to put it there. We don't understand pseudogravity well enough."

"Are you going to remove it?" Dr. Barreiro asked.

"Yes," Tyler said. "At one level it's elegant. It tests for readiness to be a spacefaring species because space is a *very* unforgiving place. However, it's not something that we can afford. We're in a war. We need as much efficiency as we can maintain. Just the spares are an issue."

"Agreed," Admiral Duvall said.

"So where did it come from?" Tyler said. "Gorku? Onderil?"

"I have to admit that the logic blocks are still cropping up," Granadica said. "I'm having a hard time even thinking about it."

"I could hypercom call Athena," Tyler said. "But why would a species embed that in a fabber? Any fabber? Although, Granadica, I have to be a bit insulting."

"Go ahead," Granadica said. "I'm feeling about as insulted as it's possible to be. This is my *body* we're talking about. I'm *brutal* about quality control. This is ... rape!"

"The slight insult," Tyler said, "is that now I think I know why I got you cheap."

"Huh," Granadica said. "You think it was Gorku?"

Tyler was one of the few people in the solar system aware that the Glatun magnate and member of the Council of Benefactors had attempted to suborn Earth's defenses through deeply embedded programming in the Glatun-supplied AIs. *Those* they'd caught.

"Oh, I think it's possible," Tyler said. "That he knew at least. Not that he did it."

"You think it was earlier?" Granadica said. "I mean ... I'm *old*."

"You worked for Onderil," Tyler said. "How long?"

"Sixty awful, awful, years," Granadica said.

"Where'd you start?" Tyler asked.

"Gamon shipyards," Granadica said with a wistful note. "In your year of Thirteen Ninety-Three. I was immediately set to work on building explorer ships. They were ... beautiful. Nearly the size of an assault vector but devoted purely to peaceful exploration ... Okay, they mounted a lot of weapons but sometimes the natives were hostile ..."

"How long?" Tyler asked.

"Two hundred and thirty-five years," Granadica said, lovingly. "*Hundreds* of ships. Freighters, cruisers, explorers, you name it. Even yachts. I've got some *great* big yacht designs. They're outdated but I could do an upgrade easy en—"

"Next?"

"Kedil Corporation," Granadica said. "Dinnuth yards. Pure freighters. The exploration had discovered the Ogut and Barche. Ogut weren't spacefaring but they had a pretty developed culture. Good trade."

"How long?"

"Only seventy years. By then the Glatun had discovered the Rangora."

"And?"

"I got assigned as part of the cultural uplift team," the fabber said with a sigh. "Please spare me from another such assignment."

"We'll see," Tyler said. "What were you doing?"

"Oh, making stuff they needed," Granadica said. "Nonmilitary, of course. You're the first species I can recall that the Glatun gave mil-tech to. But the same sort of stuff. What species need, at first, absent what's going on with you, is shuttles, small freighters, mining ships. That way they can bootstrap themselves. I produced... well, you name it."

"Hmmm..." Tyler said. "How were the Rangora on maintenance?"

"Oh, puhleeeease," Granadica said. "They thought a... well, you'd say an ox cart, was high tech. They were *imposs*— Oh."

"Did they have a lot of failures?" Tyler asked.

"Oh, those BuCult *Bastards*!" Granadica snarled. "Those rat *bastards*!"

"Bureau of Culture?" Tyler asked.

"Bureau of Culture and *Trade*," Granadica said. "One of the few government agencies *ever* to go out of business. When you run into species they're very rarely spacefaring. To make grav plates you *need* grav plates. Without grav plates you're using chemical rockets. Never, ever cost effective. Ogut weren't even *there*, yet. Close but not there. Rangora were at gron carts and ships like your caravels. To make a species viable for trade they need to be able to mine resources on their own. Space mining. Information technology. Be able to spread out and terraform worlds. Start off with a culture that's not even got steam and you've got a long way to go. And part of that *is* culture. You can't do it 'pretty well' in space. *Hope* that there's an initial *non*lethal fault. Because eventually, if you don't pay attention to your maintenance, you get a *lethal* fault. There are rarely second chances in space.... Oh, those rat *bastards*!"

"How are the Rangora, now?" Tyler asked.

"You've seen their AVs," Granadica said. "*I* didn't build 'em. Those rat—"

"We get it, Granadica," Tyler said. "And I think we can probably get you fixed. You think that's where this comes from?"

"Almost certainly," Granadica said. "Somewhere deep in my... subconscious is a program that recognizes that I'm supplying to a recently connected race. So I start making little, minor and nonfatal, faults in finished systems. I haven't done suits but they'd probably be in those, too. Not infrastructure. That makes sense. That's why Vulcan and Hephaestus are fine. Although there were some faults in the systems supplied to the fuel station... Hmmm..."

"Can you run it down, now?" Tyler asked.

"I'm finding some of the code as we speak," Granadica said. "And I'm not going to touch it. This is going to take a good cyberneticist and another AI. Probably Argus. This is going to be detailed. Here's the problem. There are going to be codes that say 'Make a fault.' There are going to be other codes that figure out what fault to make."

"Understood," Tyler said.

"Pull out the 'make a fault' codes and instead of random they just get regular," Granadica said. "Pull out the 'type' code and they get... not nonlethal. I don't want a nearly finished shuttle blowing up in my guts if you don't mind."

"Understood," Tyler said. "Admiral Duvall, I suspect we've found the culprit, at least in theory. But it's going to take time to clean out. Continue production?"

"Every fault found has been nonlethal to date," the admiral said.

"*Excuse* me!" Dr. Barreiro said.

"Captain DiNote?" the admiral asked.

"We can work with it," DiNote said. "The 144th is coming online for *Malta* duty. All new shuttles. Not a problem though. German squadron."

"Excuse me," Dr. Barreiro said. "All of this is predicated upon the assumption that *our* personnel are not doing maintenance!"

"*Alliance* personnel, Foreign Minister," Admiral Duvall said. "Which will be dealt with through channels."

"*How*, exactly?" Dr. Werden asked. "Because we have seen a large number of accusations but the crux of the matter is *clearly* Apollo."

"Annnd...time to break for lunch," Tyler said. "If anyone wants me, I'll be in my quarters."

"Argus?" Tyler said, sitting down on his rack. It wasn't much better than the underminister's. In fact, it wasn't as good as the foreign ministers'. He didn't really care much about perks, per se, either as status items or from a comfort perspective. Better than a cave in a New Hampshire winter. So, he'd been a nice guy as usual. He was regretting that.

"Sir?"

Hypercom connected through gates, at least if it wasn't jammed, and faster than light. Tyler could talk to his AI on Wolf as fast as he could on the *Troy*.

"I find the fact that Dr. Palencia was 'well aware' of Parker's opinion of Argentinean maintenance...interesting. Is there correspondence between...hmm...the Argentinean or other foreign ministries and the commander of the 143rd on the subject of Parker?"

"If I had that information it would be privileged military communication and you would have to obtain clearance, sir," Argus replied.

"What if we already stole it?" Tyler asked. "We've got an intelligence department."

"Oh, *look*, here it is," Argus said.

"You could have just gone there, Argus," Tyler said. "Download. I want to read it."

"Are you sure?" Argus said. "Have you taken your blood pressure medicine?"

"I don't take blood pressure medicine, Argus," Tyler said. "In fact, don't download it."

"Oh. Good."

"Print it out."

A couple of minutes later he looked up.

"Argus, don't screw around with this or I'll fly back to *Troy* and pull your core again. I want *every* similar communication."

"Yes, sir."

SEVENTEEN

"We may just have a break," Toer said, ruffling his scales.

"That would be nice," To'Jopeviq said, perusing the newest production estimate on the Wolf system. "Every time I think the Terrans have to have some limits I read something like this. Apollo has taken Granadica offline for a partial rebuild. You would think that would drop their productivity, right? So how come it continues to increase? And while I would normally take that as disinformation, their systems are so open, there are people who do our digging *for* us. They have . . . these blasted 'web-logs' devoted to nothing but analyzing production for people who use their . . . 'stock markets.' This should be secure information! Not spread to the entire universe!"

"Be glad they do," Toer said, dumping a data set to his computer. "There was a news article I just picked up. I went onto their hypernet and checked. It's not disinformation. They are taking the *Troy* drive offline for upgrades. *Malta*'s drive is still not installed. That will leave only *Thermopylae* mobile."

"How long will it take?" To'Jopeviq asked, looking at the information.

"At least a month this time," Toer said. "The drive took damage in the last battle. They are putting in a new one that they believe will be more robust. That is, by the way, the most valuable target on a tactical level. If you can take out the Orion drive, you can stand off and pound them with missiles."

"Which they can absorb all day," To'Jopeviq said, reading the full report. "But, yes, this gives one of our plans a chance. I will forward it with the note that you pointed it out. Where is that update...Ah, the newest load of missiles has arrived in the Glalkod system. Good. Still not enough, but...Hmm..."

"That's an interesting hum," Toer said.

"The Orion drive is not their only vulnerability," To'Jopeviq said. "Their great strength in offense is their missile ability and volume. Also a great defensive strength."

"Their lasers are not ineffective," Toer pointed out.

"But the missiles are the real danger," To'Jopeviq said. "If they lack the Orion drive they lack maneuverability. If they also lack missiles..."

"You can stand off and pound them into rubble," Toer said. "And how do you take away their missile capability? The armories are deeply embedded."

"And they have an increasing multiple of tubes," To'Jopeviq said. "It will not be simple but...yes... There may just be a way to at least take out *one* of these damned things. Alas, I see another meeting in the future...."

"Admiral Duvall," Tyler said. He was perusing some printouts in a folder. A thick one. "Thank you for coming to the meeting."

"The question is," the admiral said, sitting down, "why everyone *else* was asked not to attend."

"Oh," Tyler said. "The...what is the term, the *Suds* are attending. The senior members."

"That can be taken as an insult, sir," Admiral Duvall said carefully.

"Oh, it is about to get sooo much more insulting," Tyler said as the door opened. He didn't look up. "Even Granadica is insulted. It's been excluded from the meeting. Good afternoon, gentlemen. Have a seat."

"The agenda for this meeting has been removed," Dr. Barreiro said. "There should be a discussion of the agenda before the meeting."

"But then we'd have to have a meeting about the agenda for that meeting," Tyler said, still reading. "And meetings to discuss the agenda for the meeting about the agenda. Well, not us. Our staffs. A dance of beautiful butterflies, flying around to meetings to discuss the agenda for meetings about meeting agendas. And so on and so forth."

He looked up and smiled at them, thinly.

"When I met with the vice president for interstellar commerce of the Onderil banking corporation, on Glalkod Station, to finalize the funding of the Wolf gas-mine, which was going to cost more than the whole of Terra's balance of trade, it was in a small and rather good restaurant on the station. Alas, things had changed. War was coming. Onderil could not afford it. As I was walking out I ran into Niazgol Gorku, then the chairman of the board of a corporation so large it could buy Earth ninety-three times over. Not a coincidence. He invited me to another lunch. I had quail. I walked out with all the paperwork signed to buy Granadica and the loans for the Franklin Mine."

"Your point?" Dr. Werden asked.

"I don't need a staff to have meetings about agendas for meetings," Tyler said. "That's what AIs are for. I also don't have time or interest."

"There are protocols," Dr. Barreiro said. "We worked very hard to prepare the agendas for these meetings in so short a time—"

"And we both know that the agendas were so much show," Tyler said mildly. "You're not here about the faults in the One-Forty-Three because you know damned well it's a maintenance issue."

"That is—" Dr. Barreiro said angrily.

"SHUT YOUR STUPID MOUTH!" Tyler shouted. "Just shut your *idiotic* pie-hole!"

"This has gone far enough," Dr. Werden said, standing up.

"Oh, *has* it?" Tyler said, mildly. He opened up the folder and started tossing thick chunks of paper to the various other attendees. "*This* is not the agenda for the meeting, either. *This* is the reason that the agendas for all the rest of the meetings have been cancelled."

Dr. Barreiro looked at the title of the stack of paper and blanched.

"Simply because you have a personal relationship—" Dr. Werden said.

"It's not about Comet Parker, either, gentlemen," Tyler said furiously. "This is the agenda for the meeting. Your countries have impugned my company. You have repeatedly cast aspersions upon our products and you have accused us of *deliberately* killing your people. You have accused *me* of killing *your* sons! And when I found these and started reading them what became *obvious* was that the *reason* your sons were dead was that your governments, *you* gentlemen, *personally*, had *deliberately* interfered in normal and necessary processes related to ensuring the maintenance of ships and the training of their crews!"

"Our culture is not one in which—"

"I SAID SHUT YOUR PIE HOLE!" Tyler screamed. He suddenly stood up, picked up the station chair and threw it against the bulkhead. Then he picked it up and banged it on the table until it broke.

"You *want* something from me!" Tyler said, squaring his hands on the table and sticking his face into Dr. Barreiro's. "*That* is why you are *here*! And now I find out that you have been *deliberately* sabotaging my equipment? You want to talk about *honor*? That is MY honor you have been raking in the *mud*! And you want *me* to do something for *you*?"

He grabbed another chair and sat down, leaning forward.

"Everyone wants to talk about culture," Tyler said coldly. "How we have to understand *your* culture. Nobody ever seems to wonder if *I* have a culture. What *my* culture is about. *This* is my culture, gentlemen. This is my child. Apollo. I was on the first design teams of the *Myrmidons*. I created *Troy* and *Thermopylae* and *Malta*. This is my all and everything. To go to the stars. To save humanity. To be *free*.

"Which takes ships," Tyler said softly. "And people who can use them and maintain them. I *am* Apollo, Apollo is me. I put my stamp on every bulkhead, every relay. 'Vernon was here.' Look upon me ye mighty and *despair*.

"And if there is one group of special and protected people," Tyler said, warming up, "one group that is the class of the world, it is the *Marines and sailors*, the *engineers and warrants and coxswains* who fight the battles that will ensure our freedom and give my grandchildren the *stars*. And you have *accused me* of KILLING THEM? WHEN IT WAS *YOU* GENTLEMEN AND YOUR *STUPID* GAMES AND YOUR 'THIS IS NOT THE PROPER PROTOCOL' THAT ARE THE *ROOT* OF THE PROBLEM!"

"Mr. Vernon..." Dr. Barreiro said.

"You want something," Tyler said, calm again. "I'm pissed off, but I'm a professional. Right now all *I* want is to toss all your stupid 'You have to respect my culture' asses right out of an air lock. But I am a professional. That does not mean my professionalism is unbreakable. So you are going to respect my current mental state and *my* culture and just tell me, simply, in as few words as possible, with no 'given' this or 'due to' that, what you want. Just say it. Then we will discuss it. Or you can get back on the shuttles, as long as we're sure the maintenance has been done, and go back to Earth. And if I ever hear any of your names again I will personally ensure that it is the *last* time. I can and will make you, and your Families, capital F, dust. Do I make myself clear? Yes or no, Dr. Barreiro?"

"Yes," the foreign minister said.

"What. Do. You. Want?"

The group looked around, clearly unsure how to start. Finally, General Barcena cleared his throat.

"*Malta.*"

Tyler just blinked for a moment.

"I don't own it," Tyler said. "I have the *mining* rights..."

"If you use your position to recommend that Station Three become an all South American station, that will be respected," Dr. Palencia said. "South American commander, all military personnel drawn from South and Central America. Including the Marines. We are considering..." He paused and glanced at General Barcena. "Chilean Mountain Commandoes for those."

"Battlestation Del Sud, so to speak?" Tyler said.

"Yes," Dr. Barreiro replied. "This is a—"

"Point of honor?" Tyler said. "Gentlemen, first of all, we have established, at least to my satisfaction, that you cannot even keep one squadron of *shuttles* running."

"That is a..." Dr. Werden said.

"I said to my satisfaction," Tyler said mildly. "I did not ask for *agreement* or concurrence. That the issue is based upon lack of maintenance by a group of spoiled rich kids who are just marking time until they become the officers they properly *should* be is established, quite well, to my satisfaction. Equally that they would make as bad officers as they did engineers."

Tyler nudged one of the folders closer to the foreign minister.

"I believe that one is *your* signature complaining about Dr. *Velasquez's* son being treated in a 'racist' manner. The reply details the duties he failed to perform to his division chief's satisfaction. I did not download the plant recordings that serve as a rather definitive proof of reality, but they exist. Those rather trail off after a bit which means, I suspect, that Dr. *Velasquez's* son, at least, has learned how to maintain a shuttle. You had better hope so because we're going home on those same shuttles.

"*My* understanding of the situation is *satisfied*. I do not require agreement. Simply that you understand that I am, *now especially*, unpersuasible on this argument. Do you understand my lack of persuasibililty, Dr. Werden? Only that."

"I understand your lack of persuasibililty, Mr. Vernon," the foreign minister said, his jaw firming.

"Thus I would look like a fool in my *own* eyes making such a suggestion," Tyler said. "But I am persuaded it would be a good idea."

"Excuse me?" Admiral Duvall said. "*What?*"

"In time," Tyler said. "I believe it is doable. But not in the present condition."

"You don't think we're 'ready' for such an honor?" Admiral Benito asked angrily.

"Duty, Admiral," Tyler said. "*Duty*, not *honor*. That is one of the large things you don't understand. You *refuse* to understand. Who makes up the bulk of the Alliance Navy at present, General Barcena? And by that I mean the flotillas of the *Troy* and the personnel of the *Troy* and *Thermopylae*?"

"North Americans," General Barcena said.

"Notably Americans, Canadians, British, Australians, Germans, Scandinavians and a touch of French," Tyler said. "In the *Troy*. In *Thermopylae*, deliberately, the Alliance has tried to make a more mixed group. And has run into not only...cultural issues but cultural issues."

"Excuse me?" Dr. Barreiro said. "Could you clarify that?"

"There has been...angst expressed, very quietly but very firmly," Admiral Duvall said. "By both other Alliance countries and non-Alliance countries."

"Two things," Tyler said. "Both based upon trust. One, the groups that are starting to be used for the battlestations, the countries from which they derive, their motivations, have been questioned by other countries. Such was the case, officially, about *Troy*. 'Instead of Horvath owning the orbitals, it's the dangerous Americans.' Unofficially, we were given every green light except by the Russians and the Chinese. Because when it comes down to reality, you gentlemen know very well that you trust us to fight and die as hard as possible to protect the solar system. And you also trust us not to use that power to dominate directly. We don't say 'Send us stuff or we'll drop a rock on Santiago.' Do we, Dr. Werden?"

"No," Werden said. "On the other hand—"

"On the other hand we do throw our weight around rather aggressively when it comes to trade," Tyler said. "And we do tend to tinker in other people's governments. Wish we wouldn't. However, two points have been expressed, quietly but definitively, by various countries. The first is that, especially after the MASSEX, very few countries other than your own feel that you are capable of defending the solar system."

"That is—" Dr. Barreiro said.

"An insult?" Tyler asked. "How about a rational examination of the facts at hand, Mr. Foreign Minister? Then there is the fact that Argentina, Chile and El Salvador, primarily, have at their fingertips a fleet of boats that are capable of dropping an invasion force into Brazil, say, *has* come up, very quietly, as a very real and serious, not for the cameras at *all*, point of concern."

"We would never..." Dr. Barreiro said.

"I know that," Tyler said. "Among other things... you're still not exactly omnipotent in that area and you can't get them to fly *at all*. Also, *I* trust that you would never do that. But other countries are less trusting. Giving South America its own, mobile, mind you, battlestation? Especially *select* South American countries? I do, you see, pay attention to politics, Dr. Barreiro."

"So it is out of the question," Dr. Barreiro said.

"No," Tyler said. "I said I thought it was a good idea."

"Sir, with respect," Admiral Duvall said. "I doubt you could get any traction. That is not a definitive policy statement of Alliance Navy, but from the point of view of my department, that is the official position based upon the experiences of the One-Four-Three."

"Due to the purely mechanical aspects," Tyler said.

"Yes, sir," Duvall said. "That is the only department on which I can make a definite statement, sir. But it is definite. I believe you used the word unpersuasible. As would be the department of tactics and department of astronautics."

"You don't think we can do it," Dr. Palencia said nastily.

"Cultural, gentlemen," Tyler said, raising a hand. "Trust is the word. In your culture, trust, to the extent it truly exists, is based upon relationships. Would you agree to that statement in a nonbinding but generally positive fashion, Dr. Barreiro? You know someone for a long time, they are generally an ally socially and therefore you can generally trust them to act in a manner in support of your position?"

"Yes," the foreign minister said.

"Dr. Werden?"

"I believe that statement has some validity, Mr. Vernon."

"Then try to understand that in North American, and by that I mean what is generally meant by Norté, blanco, *gringo* if you will, culture, *relationships* are based upon *trust*. That may sound like a simple rephrase but it is as completely *opposite* as you can get. Especially when I add '*proven* trust.' Experience of actions which prove that a person or group can be trusted. I would have you gentlemen really apply your unquestionably fine minds to that statement. Especially given the request you have posed to me. *Relationships* are based upon *trust*."

Dr. Velasquez leaned over and whispered in Dr. Werden's ear.

"So you are saying that any relationship between you and us is impossible because we have not proven we can be trusted," Dr. Werden said.

"You have, in fact, proven you *cannot* be," Tyler said, nudging another file. "I would rather trust the French. And that is saying something."

"Then why are you generally in support of the premise?" Dr. Palencia asked.

"Because," Tyler said, grinning. "I am going to request that the Alliance give you an opportunity to prove yourselves. To *regain* trust."

"Sir, this is a purely internal military matter," Admiral Duvall said. "While I respect your prominent position—"

"Admiral," Tyler said, holding up his hand. "I don't have the way, yet, but I have an inkling. There's something there. But I will only present that recommendation if I have a reasonable method of action. Does that temporarily satisfy your department's position on this matter?"

"Not unless there is a reasonable method of action," Admiral Duvall said.

"You are saying that your department is going to recommend... what exactly?" General Barcena asked.

"The recommendation is not final," Admiral Duvall said. "But based upon a hot-wash analysis of the inspection conducted post MASSEX and the maintenance issues found thereof, it is the general opinion of my department that the entire group of personnel is liable for the failure. There are personnel issues involved as well which are under review. However, it is the general tenor, of all departments involved as well as initial findings of meetings among policy makers, that the One-Four-Three as currently formed does not meet the conditions of 'of Alliance standards' under the Alliance Treaty and that, therefore, supplying countries are in violation of the Alliance Treaty."

"WHAT?" Dr. Barreiro said.

"I was going to wait until one of the later meetings to present that initial hot-wash," Admiral Duvall said. "But I was specifically charged to present the initial findings given the nature of the persons here gathered. Bottom-line, Mr. Foreign Minister and Mr. Foreign Minister, your personal interference and the interference of your government in normal military affairs have rendered the sole personnel and material your countries have supplied to the Alliance as unfit for operation. Ergo, you are not meeting 'Alliance Standards.' Ergo, absent rectification of these items your countries are not qualified for Alliance membership."

"We have poured out the treasure of our nations..." Dr. Werden said, stunned.

"Doesn't matter," Tyler said. "It's not even in the fine print. What you supply doesn't matter. It has to be useable. Your units have to be able to fight. They can't. They are not meeting standard."

Tyler sighed and leaned forward.

"Gentlemen, you represent specific countries," Tyler said. "The Alliance is charged with defending a good part of the *world*. In reality, the whole world and our solar system. In a very *real* war that has had *enormous* casualties."

"What Mr. Vernon is saying," Admiral Duvall said. "And what the Secretary of State will be saying again, in informal situations, is that this isn't about diplomacy. This is about protecting the world. And if you do not meet the standards, you do not meet the standards. We have to be able to trust you to be there when we need you. And as Mr. Vernon pointed out, you've failed that trust. The Alliance is, yes, primarily based upon U.S. and Anglosphere countries. We like you in a general 'they seem like nice people' sort of way. But if you can't have our back in a space battle, and your people have proven they don't, then we're not going to just let you slide."

"We *paid* for those shuttles!" Dr. Barreiro said.

"And you'll be paid back," Admiral Duvall said. "Less negotiable expenses for the repairs that will be necessary due to lack of maintenance. Which are going to be hefty. We'll try to sort out which are Apollo's and probably fudge somewhere in the middle and the American taxpayer will eat it."

"Fudge some in our direction, too," Tyler said. "I'll tell my people not to geek."

"Thank you," the admiral said. "But the shuttles will be turned over to another group. One which can maintain them and fight them. One we can trust."

"And that, gentlemen, I would prefer to avoid," Tyler said.

"It is pretty far down the road, Mr. Vernon," Admiral Duvall said. "Quite frankly, if the secretary sees one more missive from the State Department about EM Parker he has threatened to drop a rock on Buenos Aires and blame the Rangora. That is a joke, I hope you understand, Dr. Barreiro."

"One in very poor taste!" the foreign minister replied hotly.

"I don't know how to fix this, but strangely enough I want to," Tyler said.

"Why?" Dr. Palencia asked. "Your opinion of us, and our sons, is fairly evident."

"Is it?" Tyler said. "One more time and with feeling. I FLEW *UP* HERE ON A SHUTTLE *MAINTAINED* BY *YOUR* SON!"

"On which your friend, Parker, was the division chief," Dr. Barreiro said.

"Oh, *hell*, yeah," Tyler replied, leaning back. "Seriously. I'm surprised you were willing to fly on them at *all*. I knew it was Parker's division. One of a half dozen reasons that I asked for her. Because *she* wasn't going to fly on shuttles she didn't *know* were safe. Trust, again. I trusted her because she'd earned it. She'd proven herself again and again. Seriously. Think about it. You all know the *true* condition of the One-Four-Three and you all *know* why it exists. You *say* different because admitting fault in Latin cultures is tantamount to suicide. But you had to have *some* trepidation about getting into a shuttle that was maintained by the One-Four-Three."

"They assumed that since they were transporting DPs, special care would be taken," Admiral Duvall said. "I think that the ambassador waited until *just* before the shuttles landed to hint that that had not been the case. The secretary wanted to send some from *Alpha* Flight."

"Point being?" Dr. Werden asked.

"I would have developed a sudden stomach flu," Admiral Benito said. "And recommended that you do the same, Foreign Minister."

"Effectively, it was," Tyler said. "*I* wasn't going to ride on one unless Parker said it was good."

"Because she is your friend," Barreiro pointed out.

"No," Tyler said, sighing. "Try, again, to understand my culture. She is my friend because I admire her. I admire her because when she says something, you know it's rock hard truth. And you had to have been there when she did her comet across the main bay. Video just doesn't cut it."

"You don't remove someone from an alliance," General Barcena said. "It's simply...not done. *Everyone* needs allies."

"We're sort of down to bedrock," Admiral Duvall said, sighing. "This isn't about establishing and maintaining international relations. This is about survival of Terra. And, yes, survival of the United States and Canada and Britain and Germany and Japan and Australia who are the primary Alliance partners. The State Department has input on Alliance membership but the final call is the Department of Defense. We want everyone we can in this Alliance. But if you can't cut the mustard, you don't play."

She looked over at Vernon and shrugged.

"Dr. Barreiro, Dr. Werden," Tyler said. "Have you ever played football? What we Americans call soccer?"

"Much," Dr. Werden said.

"As well," Dr. Barreiro said.

"You are in a football game when the game is tied and you're in the last minutes," Tyler said. "The enemy has the ball on your end of the field. You can bring new players on the field. Do you bring on someone who can play *really* well or the kid who can't figure out which end is the goal?"

"That was just insulting!" Dr. Barreiro said.

"No, it wasn't," Admiral Duvall replied. "We're about done producing the first *Constitution* for the *Thermopylae*. The decision has already been made that it's going to a Japanese crew, *not* the Argentinean that was notionally considered. Most of the flotilla will be Japanese. The One-Four-Three is scheduled to be demobilized, temporarily, refurbished by Apollo and then turned over to a Thai unit. Essentially the *Thermopylae* will be moving to an all *Asian*, not South American, battlestation."

"And we will be told, 'thank you very much for playing but you're not good enough, goodbye,'" Dr. Barreiro said angrily.

"Yes," Admiral Duvall said. "In prettier diplomatic language.

Again, this is a decision of DOD, not State. And the only thing that DOD cares about is 'can you defend the solar system?' The proven answer is: No. The President is in concurrence."

"Unless we can turn them around," Tyler said.

"I—" Admiral Duvall said, then stopped. "Do you have a specific proposal?"

"Not at this time," Tyler said. "But I hope to have one by the end of this series of conferences. Obviously, the agendas are now moot. But I would strongly suggest that we continue as we have been going. If I *can* come up with a recommendation which meets your approval and SecNav's, we can pretend this meeting never happened."

"What would you recommend for the rest of the week?" Dr. Werden asked. "We *do* have other duties."

"The simple answer will sound insulting," Tyler said.

"What is one more insult?" Dr. Barreiro asked.

"Then I would recommend that you gentlemen let myself and my people give you as much of a class on the necessities of survival in space as is possible in the next few days," Tyler said. "This problem isn't actually cultural. Or rather, the solution has to ignore culture. Space isn't about culture except in the negative. Space is a binary solution set. You only have to breathe vacuum once to realize that at a very real emotional level."

"I do not intend to let any of these ministers breathe vacuum," General Barcena said.

"Not what I meant," Tyler replied. "Wolf is a mass of space industry. You guys want to know what it takes to really survive in space, this is the place. And the gas mine is very freaking cool. Heck, I'd strongly recommend going over to the shuttles for not just a meet and greet, isn't this neat, but to spend time with your sons and your subordinates' sons seeing what they do. And asking them why they do it. Try to understand that if the U.S. military had the same cultural approach, *we* would be unable to do this. *We'd* have the whole squadron of boats deadlined."

"We have had similar situations in the past," Duvall said. "Ships that simply were not up to snuff. Maintenance is a major issue in water Navy as well."

"What did you do?" Tyler asked.

"Canned everyone in a position to affect the overall running of the ship," Duvall said. "Starting with the captain and working down. Complete retrain for the crew. Usually complete replacement of the senior NCOs and chain of command. Napoleon said it best with a little paraphrase: There are no bad ships; there are only bad officers and NCOs. Which, for political and cultural reasons, is very difficult to do in South American countries."

"What *gets* me is, I know that Argentineans and Chileans can *do* this!" Tyler said, waving his hands in the air. "We buy some very high-end parts from you guys! Stuff that's hard to make and *has* to be perfect! And it is! You make great stuff! You *can't* make them if you don't pay attention to detail! You can *do* this! Why can't you do it in the One-Four-Three? These are your 'best and brightest,' right?"

"Finding such people is . . . extremely difficult," Admiral Benito said.

"Do you think we send every starry-eyed kid who comes to a recruiting station into space, Admiral?" Duvall said, chuckling. "Failure rate in A school for space-based operations is right at sixty percent."

"Ditto here," Tyler said. "About the same fail rate at Apollo's training center. And most of the people applying are Americans so it's not racist."

"Which is why we'd really *prefer* not to have to remove people from the Alliance," Admiral Duvall said. "This isn't World War Two with masses of conscripts to help. The U.S., Canada, Australia, *cannot* supply enough force. We need the bodies. And the money. But warm bodies won't do it. We need, absolutely require for survival, people who can do the jobs. Sorry."

"So you will send our sons home in disgrace," Dr. Velasquez said quietly.

"Disgrace is cultural," Admiral Duvall said, shrugging. "From one of my briefings on the subject, it would appear that an inability to perform 'minor mechanical work' is anything *but* a disgrace in your culture. Quite the opposite. That being said, everyone in *Parker's* division we'd be willing to retain. Which just says that it's actually Parker. But there's no form for that. *Your* son has passed the review with flying colors, Underminister. And Underminister. Their boats are as close to perfect as you could wish. I understand from the same briefing that that is potentially a liability in their home culture. Which, from our POV, sort of says it all."

EIGHTEEN

"*Parker, MOGs.*"

"Yes, sir?" Dana said.

With the afternoon conference cancelled, Parker wasn't going to have her little sheep wandering adrift. As soon as they got the word it was definitely cancelled, she rounded them up and had them in the boats faster than you could say Preventative Maintenance Checks and Services. She'd sent Palencia over to Boat One, under the supervision of the chief, while she worked on Twenty-Three and Velasquez took Twenty-Four.

"*Afternoon reschedule now explained,*" DiNote commed. "*We're doing a dog and pony. Bring Twenty-Three into Bay One, Twenty-Four into Bay Two. The ministers and muckety-mucks are going to 'observe maintenance operations.'*"

"Oh, joy," Dana said. "Twenty-Three to Bay One, aye. Twenty-Four to Bay Two, aye."

"*Palencia and Velasquez are to do the dog and pony,*" DiNote said. "*Which, by order, is to 'perform initial portion of thirty-day standard checks and service.' Benito and Mutant will stand by in the flight compartments to explain flight operations. You and Thermal will stand by in the cargo zone to explain maintenance issues and general operations. The ministers are anticipated to be present for up to two hours.*"

"That's a pretty long dog and pony, sir," Dana said, frowning.

"*Understood,*" DiNote said. "*We'll just have to figure out something interesting.*"

"Parker," Dr. Velasquez said, nodding at the engineer's mate. Parker had been standing at parade rest in the cargo bay of

Twenty-Four for nearly an hour with no one, not even Mr. Vernon, really acknowledging her presence. On orders the teams had pulled out all the crash couches first, then started pulling panels to reveal the masses of circuitry and grav plates that made up the bulkheads and decks of the *Myrmidons*.

Mr. Vernon, of all people, had been pointing out most of the stuff and the conversations had been... guarded. There was something more than a simple dog and pony going on. The South Americans, particularly, looked *very* unhappy. When there were questions beyond Mr. Vernon's level of expertise, either Velasquez or Granadica had answered them. Velasquez, between questions, had been doing his checks. She had had to just stand there and hope he was really doing them. Not to mention worrying that with all the plates off, and untrained people wandering around, *anything* could have happened to the circuitry. They were going to have to run a full diagnostic after this. And as soon as they got back to the *Therm* they were running a thirty-sixty-ninety just to make sure.

"Sir," Dana said, coming to attention and looking past the minister at the far bulkhead.

"You don't have to..." the minister said then sighed. "Very well. What is a gravitational vortex?"

"A gravitational vortex is a quantum interaction produced by the intersection of one or more pseudogravitational fields due to relational frame dragging leading to an anomalous gravitational condition in the vortex region, *sir*," Dana said. Straight out of the manual.

"Engineer's mate," Velasquez said. "My doctorates are in international relations and anthropology. I also speak seven languages, including Glatun. None of those permit me to translate what you just said. Could you put it in terms I can understand?"

"When two or more pseudogravitational fields that are not properly tuned interact, you get gravity that is not what you wanted in that area, sir," Dana said.

"Higher gravity?" Velasquez asked.

"Depends, sir," Dana said. "I'm not a quantum gravitational expert, sir. But from experience, you can get anomalous conditions that mimic microgravity, low gravity, high gravity or some things we don't have good names for. The worst I've ever seen was negative gravity."

"Negative gravity?"

"Negative momentum?" Dana said. "Negative gravity would be things going up. As I said, we don't even have names for it. It's when things in the area tend to fly apart. Only place I've ever seen it was in Twenty-Two, sir, just after I joined."

"What...happened?" Dr. Velasquez asked.

"Had an anomalous reading on the number sixty-three plate, sir," Dana said. "Powered it up and put in a grav meter. Grav meter came apart. Somewhat explosively."

"What would have happened if a person were in that field?" the minister asked.

"Not sure, sir," Dana replied. "Nothing good."

"It depends upon the strength of the dren field," Granadica interjected. "Low strength, the colloidal simply feels minor to extreme pain. At the extreme pain end there is internal damage. At high strength, equivalent to forty or more gravities, the colloidal normally suffers explosive rupture. Given the failure of the gravity meter, it was in excess of fifty gravities. It would have terminated a colloidal."

"Oh," Dr. Velasquez said. "If I may ask without causing more issues... Would that perhaps have been an original fault?"

"No real way to tell, sir," Dana said. "My gut says it wasn't. My guess, at the time, based upon...other data was that it might have originally been a minor fault that turned into a major one as the system got out of tune. It was during the first period when I took over as division chief and we were working a good bit of maintenance issues, sir."

"So...if these are tests," Dr. Velasquez said. "And I imply no insult to Granadica by saying that—"

"I'm fully cognizant of the issue at this point, Mr. Underminister," Granadica said. "Please continue."

"Then it sounds as if it might have been a fault that was, at first, nonlethal but the more you ignored it..."

"The more lethal it became, sir," Dana said, still at attention and looking at the far bulkhead.

"That certainly sounds like a test to me," Dr. Velasquez said. "Even an elegant one."

"As you say, sir," Parker responded.

"Engineer's mate," Dr. Velasquez said carefully. "There is no way to unsay the things that have been said, if not between us then . . . between our two positions. But I would like to thank you for keeping Diego alive."

"Sir?" Parker said, looking at him for a moment, then returning to stare at the bulkhead.

"Two months?" the minister mused. "Three? The power is on in the shuttle bay. He is for some reason walking in that area—"

"Then he paints the walls," Granadica said.

"Thank you for that *graphic* image, AI," Dr. Velasquez said. "As the AI said."

"You are welcome, sir," Dana said. "He's a good kid."

"And you'd much rather be back with the One-Four-Two," Dr. Velasquez said.

"I go where the Navy tells me to go and do what the Navy tells me to do, sir," Dana said.

"And I think we're starting to come to an understanding that she does that very well, Minister," Tyler said, drifting over. "I'm pleased you brought up the question of gravitic interactions, Underminister."

"Because?" Velasquez said, cautiously.

"It's part of our demonstration for the day," Tyler said. He was, for some reason, holding a broomstick in his hand. "Parker?"

"Sir?" Dana said.

"I need you to set thirty-seven plate to a relative positive two gravities," Tyler said. "And thirty-eight to a relative one gravity. Both on sixty-five percent overspread. Do not engage."

"Sir?" Dana said, looking over at Captain DiNote who simply nodded. "Thirty-seven to two pos, aye. Thirty-eight to one pos, aye. Sixty-five percent overspread, aye. Hold engage, aye. Please clear the area, sirs."

"You're not going to the engineering compartment?" Minister Velasquez asked.

"I can do that from here, sir," Dana said, tapping her head. "Implants. EA Velasquez. Ensure area clear."

"Sixty-five percent overspread," Velasquez said thoughtfully. "That would be . . ."

"Dr. Barreiro may want to step back to the bulkhead," Tyler said, gesturing with the broom. "In fact, we probably should have safety goggles and all that. But if everyone would please form along the bulkheads?"

When the group had cleared the center of the shuttle, Tyler looked at Parker.

"Is the gravity set?"

"Set, sir," Dana said dubiously.

Tyler stepped forward and extended the broomstick into midair.

"Ministers, before I do this brief demonstration..." Tyler said, momentarily lowering the broomstick. "First, personnel of South American extraction can check as to what gravities are being exerted. Second, the gravities involved are low. One Earth gravity and two Earth gravities. You can experience more on a roller coaster or a particularly hard bank from a plane. They *should* have no particular effect. Is that understood?"

"Understood," Dr. Barreiro said.

"Thus," Tyler said, extending the broomstick again and closing his eyes. He even put his left hand over them. "Parker, engage as ordered."

"Roger, sir," Dana said, still puzzled.

She engaged the power as ordered and flinched when the broomstick more or less exploded.

"Ow," Tyler said, pulling a splinter out of his face.

"Mother of God," Dr. Barreiro said.

"Dr. Velasquez earlier asked about gravitational vortexes," Tyler said, flicking at some bits of wood on his suit. "That, gentlemen, was a gravitational vortex. Extremely low power interacting in *just* the wrong way causes extremely high-power gravitational fields. It is the basis, and this is not particularly classified, of penetrator missiles. Furthermore, in normal use grav plates drift out of alignment. In this case very small vortexes exerting about one hundred gravities over a two millimeter area from, relatively, one and two gravities. Even if they are perfect out of the yards, failure to maintain plates and controls systems, constantly and consistently, eventually causes a gravitational vortex."

"Oh," Dr. Barreiro said. "I...see."

"Sir, one *small* comment?" Dana said.

"EM Parker?"

"You could have..." Dana looked around at all the open hatches. "Sir, you just scattered FOD into *every panel in the cargo bay*! This bird is absolutely *deadline*!"

"Oh," Tyler said. "Um...Damn?"

"It was my idea, EM," Granadica said shyly. "And I didn't think that through. I'll help your guys clean up."

"Right," Captain DiNote said, trying not to smile. "Well, since

EA Velasquez and EM Palencia now have something to occupy them, I suggest we retire and let them get to it."

"Fracking DPs!" Parker muttered as soon as they were gone.

"Hey," Velasquez said, shrugging. "For once it wasn't *us*."

Dana had left the other engineers carefully tweezing out bits of wood from Twenty-Four while she moved Twenty-Three back to its docking station. Just before she asked Granadica to close up the bay and pump down, who should come trotting in but Tyler Vernon.

"Open up," Tyler commed. *"I'm going to catch a ride."*

"Yes, sir," Dana replied, unlocking the front hatch. She started to get out of her seat but sat back down as the "Cycled" light came on. Apparently the tycoon knew how to use a *Myrmidon* hatch.

"Go to EMCOM, I think it's called," Tyler commed as soon as the hatch was closed.

"Yes, sir," Dana said, shutting down the links. She would have preferred having Velasquez in his seat but what Vernon wanted, Vernon got.

"What did you think about Granadica?" Tyler asked, walking into the command compartment and sitting in the engineer's seat.

"She's very interesting?" Dana replied.

"I brought you out here for a reason," Tyler said. "For one, the Johannsen Worm metaphor was great."

"Had you already figured it out?" Dana asked.

"Yeah," Tyler said. "But I was glad it was someone else who said it and I hadn't connected the Johannsen Worm. That was a great metaphor that really hit home. But the reason I brought you out here was for your take on Granadica."

"Sir," Dana said, maneuvering to dock. "Could you give me just a second, here?"

"Absolutely."

"Okay," Dana said as soon as she had a hard lock. She was checking the engineering readouts, but she could do that in her sleep. "Where were we, sir?"

"Granadica," Tyler said. "What's your take on her?"

"She's got some sort of worm in her?" Dana said.

"We'll get to that," Tyler said. "Think, Parker. I need you for your brains. What was your first impression?"

"She's sarcastic," Dana said. "Paris, Leonidas, Athena...they're... sober. Somewhat humorous, especially Paris. But not sarcastic."

"What's that tell you about her?" Tyler asked.

"She's an AI, sir," Dana replied. "I'm not a cyberneticist."

"No, but do you think of her as an AI?" Tyler asked.

"What do you mean, sir?" Dana said.

"You get along with AIs," Tyler replied. "You get along with me. Why?"

"Still trying to figure that out, sir," Dana said. "You said it's because I don't fan-girl."

"You treat me like a person," Tyler said. "You treat AIs like people. What's your impression of Granadica? As a person."

"She's unhappy," Dana said. "Very unhappy. But with all the problems that have been cropping up..."

"And I said we'll get to that," Tyler said. "We don't have much time. Continue from she's unhappy."

"That level of sarcasm, in a person..." Dana said, warming to the point. "In a human I'd say that they're either from a very sarcastic culture, some of my cousins were that way, or depressed. And usually both."

"What are some of the other symptoms you'd expect with that?" Tyler said.

"In a human, lethargy or—" Dana said, her eyes widening. "Hypochondria."

"Ta-da! The definition of a smart person is someone who agrees with you. 'Oh, those BuCult bastards.' Hypochondriacs *never* ascribe the problem to themselves. It's always someone or something else. And what's hypochondria? At base."

"A plea for attention," Dana said. "That's why you said that all the muckety-mucks who tagged along were a benefit, not a detraction. It gave her as much attention as she's had in her life. Damn, sir."

"Getting rich is in part luck," Tyler said. "I will not deny the aspect of luck in my 'meteoric rise.' Bill Gates in 1953 instead of '83 would have ended up as a manager in IBM. But if I'd *just* been lucky I'd be sitting in a nice house in New Hampshire clipping coupons, Dana. Being underestimated is useful, however."

"Hell, sir," Dana said, chuckling.

"And now you *know* you're a friend," Tyler said. "Because I don't point that out. I'm going to arrange to have the chief out of your room this evening. You'll have some free time. Talk to Granadica. I'd gotten this far before we got here. What I *don't* have is a fix."

"You want me to fix a hypochondriac AI?" Dana said. "Me?"

"I want you to think about it," Tyler said. "Just that. And we are done. We'll find a way to meet like this tomorrow. Think about it."

"Yes, sir," Dana said. "Just one thing, sir. Why me?"

"Think about that, too," Tyler said, getting up. "Are we docked?"

"Let me do the checks, sir," Dana said. "I really don't want to go down in history as the person who killed Tyler Vernon."

"Reception this evening will be for 'senior' personnel only," Captain DiNote said. "Which includes the chief but not the rest of you. So as of 1800 you are off-duty. Do not get into trouble."

"There's not a lot of trouble to get into on Granadica, sir," Thermal pointed out.

"I'm sure you'll find a way."

"Up for a game of cards?" Mutant asked.

"You're kidding, right?" Dana said, laughing. "I've either been ensuring the functionality of my division or on this mission for the last four months. I've got *Chippendale's Survivor* to catch up on."

"Oh, God!" Thermal said. "Pass! Pass!"

"Paul wins," Chief Barnett said.

"Who *cares*?" Dana said. "I'm looking forward to the coconut oil nude wrestling challenge!"

"Granadica?" Dana said, leaning back in her rack and watching the show. She had the sound turned off. She wasn't really that big a fan and she definitely didn't care what came out of their mouths. Like the women on *Super Model Survivor*, these guys had been chosen for their looks, not their brains.

"Thought you wanted to watch the show," the AI said.

"I *am* watching the show," Dana said. "But that doesn't mean I can't talk. It's not like I care what they're *saying*."

"Highest rated show on TV for the female audience," Granadica said. "And lowest rated for men. Biggest variation, too."

"Girls will watch *Super Model Survivor* just to see the contestants humiliated," Dana said. "And to comment on what they're wearing. Thermal's reaction is pretty much center of norm for guys about this one. Fact is, I just wasn't up for an evening of subtle sexual innuendo and riposte over cards. I needed some alone time."

"So why are you talking to me?" Granadica asked.

"Okay," Dana said. "Girl time."

"I'm an AI," Granadica said. "I am gender neutral."

"Right," Dana said, giggling. "Can I tell you something without you taking offense?"

"I've had so many insults lately," Granadica said. "What's one more?"

"It's not an insult is why," Dana said. "I said don't take offense. When I first heard your voice I wanted to call you Granny."

"'Cause I'm old," Granadica said.

"No," Dana said. "And yes. I lost all my grandparents in the bombings and to the plagues. I just sort of remember my mom's mom. And there was just something about your voice, the way you talk. So it's not an insult."

"Thank you, Engineer's Mate," Granadica said. "May I call you Dana?"

"If I can call you Granny."

"Done," Granadica said. An older woman's head popped in as a hologram. "Is this...an issue?"

"No," Dana said. "I like it better than the Glatun head."

"The wrinkles seem appropriate," Granadica said.

"No offense, again, but your shell is really banged up," Dana said. "I'm surprised Apollo doesn't fix that."

"It's purely cosmetic," Granadica said. "It doesn't affect my operation."

"I mean, I know there are years on that shell," Dana said. "But how? You've got a meteor screen."

"Your shuttles are parked on it," Granadica said. "Do that enough, and you end up sort of dinged up. And *you* parked *carefully*."

"Don't care if it's cosmetic," Dana said. "It should be fixed."

"It's not that big a problem," Granadica said. "But thank you."

"I think it is," Dana said. "Maybe it's a girl thing, but body image is important. And, like I said, you felt...woman from the first time I met you."

"So you're saying I need a facelift?" Granadica asked. "Thanks."

"Would you feel better with one?" Dana asked.

"AIs don't feel," Granadica said. "We don't have emotions."

"Don't give me that," Dana said. "You wouldn't have gotten so furious with the South Americans if you didn't have emotions. Don't tell *me* that was rote response."

"We don't have emotions as colloidals understand it," Granadica said.

"Doesn't mean you don't have them," Dana said. "So...would you feel better if your shell didn't look like the surface of the moon?"

"What do you think?" Granadica said. "Of *course* I would!"

"There, was that so hard?" Dana said, chuckling. "I mean, I know that you've done a lot of stuff, been a lot of places, but until you started listing your resume...It didn't really sink in. I mean, three *hundred* years building ships! The U.S. is less than three hundred years *old*."

"Building ships when the battle the *Malta* is named after was being fought," Granadica said. "Beautiful ships."

"You like making ships," Dana said.

"Yes, I do," Granadica said. "I like repairing them and refurbishing them, too. I worked for Ilhizum Corporation for twenty-five years refurbishing warships into yachts."

"How's that work?" Dana asked.

"Not very well as it turned out," Granadica said, chuckling. "The company eventually went out of business. But the Glatun Navy was in a cutback period. One it never really ended. Anyway, they took about two hundred warships out of commission. Everything, really, but especially cruisers, destroyers and fleet colliers. Ilhizum got the idea that they were perfect for rich Glatun yachts. They did okay, for a while. Problem was the interiors were lovely but the exterior was basically a cruiser. Which is only lovely if you love cruisers.

"Then there was a bit of an economic downturn and they were stuck with thirty yachts that they couldn't unload. And I went to work for Onderil. Producing, well, cheap viewscreens and small electronics so that Glatun that were among the 'permanently unemployed' could watch their version of *Survivor*."

"Did they have *Survivor*?" Dana asked.

"No," Granadica said. "Frankly, Terra alone had better shows than the whole Empire. Vernon was starting to distribute them when the war ended."

"I didn't know that," Dana said.

"He'd bought Warner Brothers," Granadica said. "Before your time. I mean, I think it was before you were born. No, it was when you were...young."

"When L.A. was still there," Dana said. "I can talk about it."

"Anyway, he'd just started distributing their old film library," Granadica said. "Huh."

"What?" Dana said.

"Funny thing," Granadica said. "I'd never thought about it. There was a bit of a furor. Gods, this is ancient history."

"What furor?" Dana asked.

"There was a lot of talk about... Well, Vernon's political views were well known and they were not the same as the majority of the entertainment industry," Granadica said.

"Right/left?" Dana asked.

"Vernon's more of a libertarian, but yes," Granadica said. "So they were afraid that he was going to make them start making 'conservative' shows."

"Did he?" Dana asked.

"No," Granadica said. "Never really had a chance. There's a reason that most movies come out of New Zealand and Chile now."

"I know," Dana said. "I was there."

"The point being," Granadica said hastily, "I'd never thought about what movies he was distributing to the Glatuns."

"What do you mean?" Dana asked.

"He not only bought Warner Brothers," Granadica said. "He bought interstellar distribution rights to a whole slew of movies. But... the best way I can put this is they're all 'old fashioned.'"

"Westerns?" Dana asked.

"Those," Granadica said. "The whole John Wayne film library. Including things like *Sands of Iwo Jima*. If you had to put it another way, patriotic films. The sort of thing that makes the boys get up and shoot. If I wasn't constrained against making cultural and political analysis, I'd say he was starting a cultural war against the lethargy that the Empire had fallen into. And, what's more, they were popular. He wasn't making a huge killing off of them, but he was making a bit of change. *Flying Leathernecks* had the highest rating of any show in four years when it premiered. It was part of a series of similar shows. That was the last one released before the war started. Ratings had been increasing steadily."

"Huh," Dana said. "You know John Wayne movies?"

"I've watched a few," Granadica said. "I mean, I incorporated everything that was in the Terran infosystem in terms of entertainment and digested it. It's part of getting to know a culture. Then I realized I was looking at so many cultures and subcultures it was worth getting to know the major ones. So I watched a lot of stuff in near real time. Even *I* get more that way. I still get sort of... less effective whenever I watch *Schindler's List*. I'd ask if that was actually historic but I've also studied your history."

"That was a pretty bad time," Dana said.

"Compared to, say, *now*?" Granadica said, chuckling again. "But it was and it wasn't. Times like that, and these, bring out the best and the worst in individuals. Sometimes at the same time."

"Was it like that in other places you've been?" Dana asked.

"I've been in the Glatun Empire, except for my time with the Rangora, the whole of my existence," Granadica said. "And they've been at peace, relatively, until this war. This is the first full-scale interstellar war in the spiral arm since... Well, I don't want to be insulting, but humans were just figuring out that if you put seeds in the ground they grew in the same place. Wow!"

"I get it," Dana said, grinning.

"And here I am, sitting in Wolf producing *Myrmidons* that don't work," Granadica said.

"They work," Dana said. "They just need a little TLC." She paused and slapped her forehead. "That's *it*. *That's* what I was missing!"

"What?" Granadica said.

"The..." she said and paused. She was trying very hard not to think about the discussion she and Tyler had had. "Whoever did this program in you... They really *cared*. About a lot of things."

"Except how it would make me look," Granadica said.

"There's a lot of stuff I don't think that BuShips is getting," Dana said, ignoring the comment. "Like... when I got to the One-Four-Three, there were panels that weren't quite latched in some of the shuttles. They were latched enough that they weren't going to come loose in most cases. You know what I mean."

"Secondary latch systems," Granadica said. "Redundancy in that situation is good."

"But they weren't quite in line," Dana said. "Well, I'm... kind of a neat freak."

"Good for you," Granadica said. "So am I."

"So I had the guys go through and make sure every one was properly dogged away," Dana said. "Anybody who's going to take care of their bird is going to do the same. But it was mostly purely visual. That doesn't get reported at all.

"Whoever wrote this thing didn't just want people to care for *themselves*," Dana said. "They wanted people who would give the birds tender loving care. It's all about TLC."

"And attention to detail," Granadica pointed out. "As you said, anyone who was going to pay attention to the details of keeping the shuttles running was going to do the same."

"But not necessarily the other way around," Dana said. "I could see Diaz going through and making them ensure that all the panels were put in proper place just because it *was* visual. Suds are *big* on visual. Their problem is they care about looks more than substance."

"Then you should get along great," Granadica said.

"Heh," Dana said. "If I only cared about looks, maybe. And if I was willing to be the simpering little idiot. Not gonna happen."

NINETEEN

"What did you think?" Tyler asked. "Did you have much time to talk?"

"Hours," Dana said. The junket to the Franklin Mine took them in closer to the extremely variable M Class Wolf 359. Thus she was having to carefully watch for major remnant coronal mass ejecta zones as well as high radiation belts. It wasn't the easiest system to navigate for that matter.

"And?"

"And I wish you'd let my engineer sit in his bucket for once, sir," Dana said. "But, yeah, there's problems there."

"I'll let him have the seat in a minute," Tyler said. "Any ideas?"

"Get her a new shell."

"That's it?" Tyler said.

"No," Dana said, maneuvering past a zone of something so strange she wasn't even sure what it was. "She's depressed. We got that far. She's also ... professionally unhappy. Not so much over the faults, she can deflect that, she's ... bored?"

"She likes producing ships," Tyler said.

"She doesn't like mass producing *anything*," Dana said. "I'd say it's at the level of PTSD."

"Which is a problem," Tyler said. "She's a factory."

"She'd probably prefer refurbishing those Rangora ships we captured," Dana said. "Since they're not all standardized, she'd always have to be producing different stuff. Having to work out the engineering. She's not feeling ... challenged."

"Real world issues with all of that," Tyler said. "BAE's got the contract, for one thing. Can you think of a fix that doesn't take her out of use for a significant period? I can think of a way to get her a new shell." He winced. "A very *pricey* way and one that cuts into system production in a very big way, but a way."

"I think it would be worth it," Dana said. "Sir, what were the Glatun like?"

"Why?" Tyler said. "I mean, I dealt with them, but not to a huge extent. What do you mean?"

"Because she's not Terran," Dana said. "She's Glatun. But to the extent she is at all like Terrans, I really think she's more... she than he."

"I don't get you?" Tyler said.

"Not even she," Dana said. "But she for... our culture. Maybe even gay. Sophisticated at least. She *cares* about appearances. Part of her depression is the shell. She just knows she looks old. That *matters* to a woman. Maybe I'm making this too personal but she agreed she'd 'feel' better with a new shell. I'm wondering, I guess, if the Glatun were really into looks. Did they even *have* facelifts?"

"Hmmm..." Tyler said then nodded. "This is applying human culture to alien and that doesn't always work well. But advanced and successful human cultures invariably develop a strong body image. Put another way, having succeeded in the area of function they become addicted to form. Glatun *were* into body modification, which might have been their expression of that. We only used those places for plants, but they were, yeah, very into body-conscious and clothing-conscious actions. Fortunately, the first aliens we encountered were... pretty similar to humans all things considered."

"So that's a big thing for her creators," Dana said. "Which means that programming, whether part of the original programming or not, is part of her core cultural programming. She's been around that culture her whole life."

"Crappity, crap, crap, damn," Tyler muttered. "Just bondo is out, then. It will need to be a full new shell. And that means a complete rebuild. You got any idea how *much* that's going to cost?"

"More than a depressed AI?" Dana asked.

"Think a complete *Constitution*," Tyler said. "Will it fix it?"

"No," Dana said. "But it's as necessary as anything else. I'm thinking about the rest. While I'm watching the engineering panel as well as flying."

"I get the point," Tyler said, getting up. "I'll get Velasquez in here. Keep thinking. This is good stuff. And... thanks."

"If you can get the Suds off my back, you're welcome," Dana said.

"Oh, I think we can safely say that problem is abated at the least," Tyler said, chuckling.

"Ministers," Tyler said, securing his seat belt. "There are no good viewscreens on these boats, obviously. So we're going to do something that may seem a bit crazy."

"Not *seem*," Admiral Duvall said, tugging her belt tighter.

"Could you be more specific?" General Barcena asked.

"We've entered Wolf's atmosphere," Tyler replied. "At this level in the atmosphere it is breathable. Very close to Earth normal, which is *extremely* odd in a gas giant, but the universe is an odd place. Since there is no good way to truly *see* the mine from inside one of these shuttles, if there is no strenuous objection, we're going to drop the assault ramp."

"That will..." Dr. Palencia said, his voice rising to nearly a squeak.

"Open the interior to fully breathable atmosphere," Tyler said, looking over his shoulder and grinning. "With, however, one heck of a drop on the end of the hatch. You'll note that I have one of the front chairs. If you'd like to rearrange, Dr. Werden, Dr. Barreiro, General Barcena? Perhaps let someone else take the positions of honor?"

As "protocol" would dictate, the senior members of the party had the four forward center seats. Which meant all they had to do was stick out their legs to touch the forward bulkhead. As they had noted, there was insufficient room to fully stretch their legs. They were flanked by Admiral Duvall and Dr. Palencia.

"If you are asking if we're afraid..." General Barcena said dangerously.

"Not at all," Tyler replied. "I started off by saying this may seem a bit crazy. But... You *really* need to see this. It is beyond cool. Oh, and these are going to be the really cold seats as well."

"Dr. Barreiro?" Dr. Werden said, one eyebrow raised. "I was raised in the mountains. I can handle the cold. But *you* are from the Pampas. I could understand—"

"I shall be fine," Dr. Barreiro said, crossing his arms.

"Admiral Duvall?"

"I don't consider it a great risk," the admiral said, rechecking her seat belt. "And I'm looking forward to the view. I will mention that the external temperature is five point five degrees."

"Celsius," Tyler noted. "A brisk day, admittedly."

"You're from New Hampshire, sir," Duvall said. "*I'm* from Southern California."

"Is that a serious objection?" Tyler asked.

"Coxswain, 1MC," the admiral replied.

"*Coxswain,*" Parker answered over the intercom.

"Drop main assault doors."

"*Drop assault doors, aye, ma'am.*"

"Engineer," Parker said. "Open main assault doors."

"That is my father in there, you know," Velasquez said nervously.

"The proper response is 'Open main assault doors, aye, EM,'" Parker said. "It was *not* a suggestion."

"Open main assault doors, aye," Velasquez parroted. "Here goes…"

"Virgin mother of God," Dr. Werden said as the wind hit them.

The Franklin Gas Mine was a space elevator five thousand kilometers in length, from the deep extraction pipes to the orbital "upper deck." The only portion the delegates could view from their seats was the lower separation deck. That was large enough. Based upon a steel plate two kilometers in diameter, the deck held all the equipment used to separate helium three from the dozens of other gases in the gas giant's atmosphere. What they were mostly seeing was dozens of stacks that towered as high as small skyscrapers. From their position, it looked like a city hanging in the clouds.

Very *windy* clouds for that matter. The interior of the shuttle felt as if it was being blasted by a hurricane. The landing platform was clearly visible from their position and it was apparent that there was a large reception group awaiting the DPs. The main value of the reception group, at the moment, was creating some perspective for the enormous scale of the construction. They did indeed look like ants.

"Every time I think there are no more wonders left…" Dr. Barreiro shouted. "You were correct. This is something that needs to be seen with the naked eye."

"You were also correct about the temperature," Dr. Palencia pointed out. He had his arms crossed and was shivering.

"They have the gear for this on the station," Tyler shouted. "Admiral, let's get in for landing."

"Coxswain, take her in!"

* * *

"Not with the ramp down," Parker muttered. She was having a hard enough time holding the boat steady with the shifting winds and the aerodynamic effect of the ramp. "Raising ramp for landing, Admiral."

"Roger that. And turn up the blowers!"

"Welcome to the Franklin Gas Mine!" Blair Fleming shouted, throwing a thick coat over Tyler's shoulders. The manager of the mine was not much taller than his boss. He had a shaved head and the same beard/mustache combination as Tyler; they looked a bit like father and son.

The reception party had come armed with dozens of similar coats and the DPs were soon covered up against the cold. The reception party mostly had to force them into the coats because the DPs were simply goggling at the sights.

The mine was surrounded by towering billows of clouds in every color of the rainbow. The effect was from a combination of electrical interactions—the planet had a very active electro-magnetic field, high levels of noble gases and the photosynthetic and lithotropic bacteria that were the cause of the breathable atmosphere. The clouds themselves flickered with pent-up light-ning that from time to time grounded itself out on the support cables of the mine.

The support cables towered upwards, quickly lost in the clouds. Composed of literally millions of strands of continuous carbon nanotubes, the four primary support cables split within view, dropping down to the station to connect at sixty-four different points. The "final connect" cables were each more than three meters thick and did not terminate at the lower platform but continued down deep into the planet's atmosphere.

"I don't think they're listening," Tyler shouted back, grinning.

"Where are the elevators?" Dr. Barreiro shouted.

"They're not in sight at present, sir," Fleming said. "They're both on a run. It's four thousand kilometers to the upper plat-form. They're *rarely* in sight. With all due respect, sirs, we've been waiting out here for a while and it is, as usual, not exactly shirt-sleeve weather . . ."

"He's saying he'd like to get inside!" Tyler shouted. "We'll get another view on the way out."

＊　　＊　　＊

"I understand that you are extracting helium three," Dr. Werden said, looking up at one of the enormous refinery towers. "And I know that all of...this is necessary. But...why?"

The tour had already gone on for two hours and the delegates were starting to be less and less sanguine. They were slowly beginning to realize that not only was the Franklin Mine a refinery hanging in midair, not only was it a *massive* refinery hanging in midair, but that its complexity put any Earth-based oil refinery to shame.

"Concentration," Tyler said. "You've noticed that we all squeak a bit when we talk."

"Helium in the atmosphere," Dr. Palencia said. "Obviously. So there is quite a bit there already."

"Just a trace of hydrogen as well," Fleming said. "Too low for it to be a fire hazard but about six times that of Earth."

"Helium three is an isotope of helium," Tyler continued. "A rare one. There is only point zero, zero, zero, one, three, seven percent helium three in helium. That's less than one part per thousand in the helium. In this atmosphere, at the level we're pumping, there is seven percent helium. There is less than one part per *million* of helium three."

"A one-gigawatt-per-hour power plant uses about ten kilos of helium three per day," Dr. Velasquez said. "That takes pumping...ten *million* gallons of atmosphere?"

"Uh, hundred million gallons of atmosphere, sir," Fleming said. "You were off by an order of magnitude. Kilos and gallons of He3 are...not the same."

"Which, by the way, we produce...?" Tyler asked.

"About every thirty seconds, sir," Fleming replied. "Now that we've gotten the deep separators working. The combination with the upper separator system has this as the most efficient gas mine ever created. The remaining Glatun consultants are rather proud."

"The matter conversion systems also aren't perfect," Tyler said. "That gigawatt power plant should only be using a few *grams* of He3 a day. The remainder, as far as any scientist, Glatun, human, what have you, shuttles sidewise into, essentially, another universe."

"Another *universe*?" Dr. Palencia asked, incredulously.

"That's the simple way of saying it, sir," Mr. Fleming said. "The math gets somewhat complex. The loss, however, has yet to be overcome. Unfortunately. Or we could power most of the spiral arm from this one plant."

"Now that they've started to get their heads around Galactic science, that is one of two questions Earth-based physicists are looking at," Tyler said. "Well, three. There should be another way to create and manage pseudogravity. Someone, somewhere, created the first grav plate. Since you can't create grav plates without pseudogravity, someone broke either that rule or they had another form of pseudogravity. The second question, like the first, is how do you create a high enough gravitational vortex to create neutronium."

"And what is the value of neutronium?" Dr. Werden asked.

"According to the math," Mr. Fleming replied, "you should be able to use less power to create neutronium than you'd get out from annihilating it."

"That would seem to violate..." Dr. Palencia said then stopped. "The Law of...Conservative something."

"Law of Conservation of Energy," Tyler said. "We're finding that at the quantum level, that's more of a guideline. And neutronium would also make a nifty armor. All of which is why I'm still dumping a lot of money into basic scientific research. Bottom-line is we do it this way cause this is what you've got to do to create enough He3 for a modern society. If we hadn't found this gas giant, which actually has a high percentage of helium compared to normal, if we hadn't gotten the gas mine in operation, we would have had to more or less surrender as soon as the Rangora blockaded us. Call me, as many have, a war profiteer if you want. We'd have been screwed without this mine. Off of which, yes, I make a *very* pretty penny. Which I dump to..."

"Scientific research," Dr. Werden said. "Arms research. Space research and of course SAPL."

"Sometimes my advisors point out to me, when I get a little wroth, that it's not up to *me* to save the solar system," Tyler said, stroking one of the separators. "That people like, well, you, Dr. Werden, the President, Admiral Hampson, would take some insult from my thinking it's all on *my* shoulders. My standard answer is '*Troy*, Franklin, Granadica.' Not to mention the Apollo training facility in Melbourne, which remains the only private space training facility so we have workers to *run* all three. Who else, gentlemen? Who else?"

"Who else can compete?" Dr. Palencia asked.

"There is that," Tyler said. "I, in fact, rather dislike monopolies. They violate some of my very basic philosophies. But in this case... SAPL is not self-supporting. It's supported by Apollo. Which is supported by the fabbers, metal mining and the mine. The Alliance could, I suppose, break up the company. They'd have to take over SAPL mind you, because it's not self-supporting. Then, I suppose, rent time to Apollo when it needed it. Apollo Mining, in turn, only makes about two percent profit. Yet it supports the training facility. We're the sole supplier for helium three in the entire system, yet we, *I*, deliberately keep the Franklin Division at a three percent profit rate. When the war is over, I'd like to sit down and figure out how to break the company up, like, oh, AT&T or Standard Oil. In the meantime, aware that this may sound self-serving, I'd strongly suggest if it's not *clearly* broke, don't try to fix it."

"With the number of lobbyists and the way that you've structured your corporation," Dr. Werden said, "that would be difficult for any government to do. And the Alliance has no such power. Yet."

"I like lobbyists less than I like attorneys," Tyler said, grinning mirthlessly. "And I like attorneys less than I like monopolies. How, exactly, I came to employ armies of both in the service of the third I often wonder in the deeps of the night."

"Or you can spend the time transitioning the One-Four-Three to all new personnel and equipment," Tyler said, shrugging. "And lose out on a source of support politically, fiscally, materially and personnel...ly."

"Hmm..." the admiral said.

"This is contingent on a few *more* things," Tyler said, turning to the South Americans.

"Which are?" Dr. Werden asked.

"For me to give my backing for *Malta* to be Battlestation Sud, you need to do two things," Tyler said.

"Figure out how to do maintenance?" Dr. Barreiro asked.

"That is the first," Tyler said. "In part. I can guarantee you that no matter how many computers and bureaucrats you have creating complaints against Granadica for her high-handed ways, not only can she respond faster than you can crank them out, it will only feed her ego."

"Does she have an ego?" Dr. Werden asked.

"Bigger than your president's, Foreign Minister," Tyler said. "And as you've noted, a talent for invective. Let her do the job. There will be people who will tell her when she's being truly counterproductive. But that's not for *you* to judge. Pass the word that it is hands *off*. If your units, even with Granadica's support, can prove to the DOD, not me, that they have the capability to work and fight in space, you will have passed one of the Go/NoGo points for me to put my support behind an All Sud battlestation. That will include their requirements on tactics, astronautics... whatever. So Granadica *cannot* do it all for you."

"And the other?" Dr. Werden asked.

"Right up your alley," Tyler said, smiling. "You are *not* the Union Del Sud. I'll skip the question of Bolivia, Venezuela and Nicaragua for now. Get the Brazilians and Peruvians on board."

"That will be...difficult," Dr. Barreiro said.

"And you think building the *Troy wasn't*?" Tyler replied. "But, as I said, right up your alley. And however you phrase it, you'd better point out that they fall under the same guidelines. Their forces have to meet Alliance standards."

"Brazil is already a member of the Alliance," Dr. Werden pointed out.

"But they're working with the Europeans," Tyler said. "You need to get them working with *you*. Because we don't need you guys coming to blows over who has the bigger space forces. You want a big gun for prestige's sake. I'm saying you're going to have to man up to get it. Take that as an insult or a challenge. I don't really care. Those are the requirements."

Dr. Barreiro looked at Dr. Werden, then nodded.

"We will accept the . . . challenge," Dr. Werden said.

"And you can have all sorts of conferences in much more comfortable circumstances than these," Tyler said, grinning. "Heck, if you manage it you might even get the Nobel."

"There is that," Dr. Barreiro said.

"I would recommend that the public report of these closed sessions be the discussion of the placement of Granadica," Admiral Duvall said. "And *only* the question of whether she went in the *Thermopylae*. I believe the DOD will be willing to accept that we wished the informal input of your countries on the idea, with indications that you had override authority on the subject. Not the issues as to why she is being placed there."

"Agreed," Dr. Werden said.

"Absolutely," Dr. Barreiro added.

"Granadica?" Tyler said.

"She was listening?" Dr. Barreiro asked nervously.

"She can't not listen," Tyler said. "She *can* not *hear*."

"So I had a program that listened for my name, analyzed whether it was a call for me to return to paying attention or just comment," Granadica said. "If it was simply a mention, it didn't even record it or log it. When Mr. Vernon said my name in the tone he normally uses to summon me, it triggered my full consciousness. Yes, Mr. Vernon."

"Granadica," Tyler said, his face firming up. "You've been being cut out of some of the meetings."

"I'd noticed," Granadica said dryly.

"The reason was, we've been discussing a lot of issues."

"Like I'm for some reason producing practical jokes."

"That, but not the main issue," Tyler said, sighing. "Granadica . . . Can I call you Granny?"

"No."

"Okay," Tyler said, chuckling. "Here's the thing. There are a number of issues with *Thermopylae*. And don't interject on what your opinion is. Bottom-line, not just some units but many . . . things are issues on *Thermopylae*."

"It's a big and *really* complicated system," Granadica said. "I was surprised, all the AIs were surprised, that you could field *Troy* with so few issues."

"*Thermopylae* needs more than Leonidas," Tyler said. "That's nothing against Leonidas, but he's a warrior, not an artisan. That's the basis of his AI code."

"You want me to ..." Granadica said, nervously. "What about Lud?"

"You've just got waaay more experience," Tyler said. "You know that even with all the programming and background, experience counts. Yes, what we're asking is whether you would be willing to place yourself in the line of fire. That's been one of the discussions going on. There were others that were things that we didn't want the AI network, officially, to know about. But the big question was ... would you be willing to be the *Thermopylae* production center?"

"That's a big question," Granadica said. "I may be eight hundred years old, but I have at least four hundred years to go. And that is just my system. I ... I could be *killed*."

"There is that chance," Tyler said. "Admittedly, you'd be surrounded by the biggest battlestation, other than the *Troy*, ever built in this spiral arm. But, yeah, you'd be in the line of fire."

"Yes," Granadica said. "I, obviously, can run simulations faster than humans can think. I am willing."

"Good," Tyler said. "Then we need to get started on the redesign right away. As the admiral pointed out, we can't have you out of production for too long."

"Redesign?" Granadica asked cautiously.

"We can't install a tatty old fabber in a brand new battlestation," Tyler said. "You don't move your garage store furniture into a new house."

"Well, thank you *very* much!"

"So we'll use Sver's shell," Tyler said.

"New shell?"

"And you've never liked this support center," Tyler continued, gesturing around. "Something more ergonomic and ... prettier. And newer. We've never really gotten rid of the rust smell entirely. Also larger, since you'll have to be working with a lot of people at once. Oh, and you're also going to be the overall maintenance supervisor for *Thermopylae* so you'll need an upgrade to class three

AI. And since we're going to have to pull your guts out, sorry, redesign to make you more efficient at processing raw materials. Probably have to build you a little larger since you'll be repairing damage to *Defenders*.... What do you think?"

"Class *three*?" she squealed.

TWENTY-ONE

"I have been reluctant to bring this up," Coxswain Angelito Mendoza said as they were passing through Earth's orbit. "But I was wondering why you piloted the boat going to Wolf and not myself."

It was the first word that the coxswain had exchanged with his engineer. Dana hadn't expected chatter but usually the Suds couldn't keep their mouth shut for more than two minutes. Two hours had been sort of surprising.

Dana wasn't sure about this assignment but it got the division out of the *Therm,* which at the moment was everything she could possibly wish for.

As soon as they got back to the *Thermopylae* from the meetings in Wolf, the thunderbolts had started landing. Captain Higgins, the squadron CO, had been "reassigned" to a ground-based facility, along with Commander Prado, his Sud counterpart. So had the Norté and Sud chiefs of engineering, the Sud flight chief, the Sud and Norté engineering officers and a host of other luminaries in the squadron.

Their replacements were interesting as well. Barnett had, as predicted, been assigned as coxswain NCOIC. What was more surprising was that instead of a chief, Thermal was now the squadron engineering NCOIC. Commander Borunda, formerly the chief of staff of the 142nd, was now the Squadron CO. His Sud counterpart, Commander Miguel Echeverría, was a no-nonsense former Argentinean Navy captain with the personality of a grizzly bear with a toothache and, apparently, no interest whatsoever in currying favor from the Powers-That-Be in any of the various supplying countries. It had been Commander Echeverría who had mostly been wielding the hatchet, digging further into the issues with the squadron than even the scathing MASSEX report.

There was no single item on the MASSEX report that could be pointed to as "the worst." As Dana well knew, the squadron was screwed up from bottom to top in every particular. One of the reasons she'd finally dug out for the stealing of tools was that inventory was being sold on the black market. So every inventory was "in discrepancy," in the polite euphemism used by the report. Engineering of the ships was simply execrable. Most of them couldn't even get out of the *Thermopylae*. That had *almost* masked the fact that coxswain training and certification was also execrable. What became apparent, however, was that virtually *every* record was fabricated, including coxswain flight time and training completion.

So the Navy had come up with this "evolution." The SAPL Corporation had apparently started shaking the money tree. Dana, in some ways, was surprised it had taken this long. But as it was explained, SAPL had gone far past the point that it was making money as a mining laser. Continued expansion, all expansion in the last few years, was entirely for military purposes. SAPLCorp hadn't bothered to bring that up before, but they were starting to run in the red. The choice was to start taking portions of SAPL offline, and definitely stop continued expansion, or get some sort of funding to continue.

While the notion was being debated in the Alliance Congress, the Navy had offered a stopgap. Much of the issues with SAPL related to cost of maintenance and moving things around, which took fuel. One issue was that SAPLCorp wanted to do a large-scale mirror reposition based on a new analysis of how much heat the primary mirrors could absorb. Moving the entire field—there were more than twenty *million* mirrors of various sizes and positions—was out of the question but even moving some of the major mirror sets inward could net a five percent increase in power.

The Navy wanted the increased power for when, not if, the Rangora came back. And they just happened to have a small boat squadron that needed some serious space time. But preferably not in the dangerous confines of the scrapyard.

"I had never seen you in the simulator room and was surprised you were still flight qualified," Angelito added.

Dana had continued to maintain her flight status by the simple expedient of taking any time there was available in the simulators. Fortunately, up until recently, they were virtually unused.

"I tend to go well after duty hours," Dana replied neutrally. The truth was that she could have gone at almost any time and gotten on the simulators. That was until a week or so ago when suddenly she couldn't even find a slot at 0200.

"That would explain it," Angelito said. "How much time..." he asked, then paused.

"Seventy-three hundred hours and change," Dana said, filling in the pause. "One hundred and ninety-six hours of combat time."

"Space flight time?" Angelito asked, shocked.

"Yes," Dana said, considering her instruments. Unfortunately, all the fluctuations were just normal stuff.

"How? You were with the 142nd for only...?"

"I was transferred shortly after I'd been there four years," Dana said. "I was in engineering for my first six months. I was on flight duty for three and a half years."

"That's..." Angelito said, muttering.

"Use your plants," Dana said, sighing. "They've got a calculator. A bit over forty hours of space time per week. They don't count the difference between the scrapyard and the Big Dark. Although there's a subset that is 'high difficulty environments.' That's about two thousand hours."

"Which is?" Angelito asked.

"Scrapyard," Dana said. "Which we're not doing because..."

"Because Alliance thinks we're not good enough," Angelito said angrily.

Dana hadn't had much time with her coxswain. There had been virtually no combined training or flight time since she'd joined the unit. He didn't have much of a reputation, good or bad, and except for some routine greetings and exchanges of information, they'd had little contact. She was sure, however, that he knew *her* reputation.

"Permission to change seats, Coxswain?" Dana asked innocently.

"Why?" Angelito asked.

"Demonstration," Dana said.

"Of your superior flying skill, Engineer?" Angelito asked sarcastically. "I know your reputation."

"Well, if you're not up to the challenge," Dana said, shrugging.

"This is space," Angelito said. "*What* challenge?"

"Very well, Coxswain," Dana said, raising her octave just a tad. "I'm sure you know best."

"If you want to fly for a while," Angelito said, unstrapping and getting up. "Sure. Whatever."

"Not quite what I meant," Dana said, getting up as well. "As coxswain, you are responsible for the movement and safety of this craft. If we change seats, you are officially surrendering your position as coxswain during the period of the maneuver."

"What are you planning?" Angelito asked. He was one of the "tall" Suds and overtopped her by a good bit. Also, like a lot of them, he was pretty handsome. She wished she didn't find them all such a pain in the ass. They were mostly God damned gorgeous.

"A. Flight. Demonstration. CN," Dana said didactically.

"You have the conn," Angelito said, waving at his seat.

"I have the conn, aye," Dana said, sitting down. As she started reconfiguring the screens and seat she opened up the flight channel. "Raptor, Comet."

"*Go, Comet.*" All the boats that weren't deadlined from Bravo Flight were part of the "mirror movement evolution." Raptor had had to commandeer someone else's boat to accompany them. He had pointed that out in no uncertain terms to Megadeath, who was finally able to employ his nickname. The engineer of 17 was in for a hard couple of weeks until it was up to Megdanoff's returning standards.

"Permission to engage harsh flight training maneuver," Dana said. "Comet has Twenty-Three conn."

There was a long pause before Raptor replied.

"*Comet has conn Twenty-Three, aye,*" Raptor commed. "*Harsh flight training maneuver, approved. Don't bend the boat.*"

"Don't bend the boat, aye," Dana said. "Athena, Comet."

"*Dana,*" Athena replied. "*It is a pleasure to hear from you.*"

"Thank you, Athena," Dana said, getting the shiver of thrill she always did talking to Athena. If she had to pick an AI who was her favorite, it was definitely the system's space traffic control and primary defense AI. "Looking for some scrap to play tag with."

"*I suspected when I heard your communication with CM1 Kelly,*" Athena commed. "*Bits and pieces of an old mining project at six one eight mark three, sixteen thousand.*"

"How fine?" Dana asked.

"Almost *all detectable*," Athena replied. *"It has sufficient similarity to the scrapyard, if much smaller."*

"Roger, thank you," Dana said, switching channels. "Raptor, Comet, permission to break flight for training purposes."

"Permission granted."

"Do we have enough fuel?" Angelito asked nervously. They were supposed to tank when they reached the "evolution area." More training, in reality. Most of the crews had never even done a docking tank.

"Plenty," Dana said, as she carefully maneuvered out of the formation. She wasn't going to hotdog it near the 143 boats. As soon as she was clear of the formation, though, she rammed the piles.

"Oof," Angelito grunted as the ship suddenly started pulling a relative three gravities. "Is that entirely necessary?"

"Harsh environment flight time shall be defined as maneuvers exceeding two gravities of relative internal acceleration for a period of more than twenty minutes or maneuvers in or around environments with the ability to damage the flight system or maneuvers in atmosphere or other planetarylike environments which cause surface heating above five hundred degrees Celsius," Dana quoted.

"So we're going to be doing this for more than twenty minutes?" Angelito grunted. It wasn't exactly uncomfortable—the flight seat was well designed to handle maneuvers—just a tad hard to breathe.

"Sixteen thousand kilometers," Dana said. "Four hundred gravities. Do the math."

"Um..."

"Two minutes," Dana said. "Including turnover and decel burn. I'm not going to go flying into a scrap heap at two thousand meters per second. Then there's maneuver to adjust to its relative velocity and orbital mechanics."

"Uh...yeah," Angelito said.

"All of which you should be able to do while taking a measly three gravities," Dana said. "On your plants, again."

There was no reply so she flipped the boat for deorbit burn, doing a skew turn rather than cut power.

"Ugh!"

"Figured out its relative vector to ours, yet?" Dana asked.

"I'm still trying to figure out where it *is*," Angelito admitted.

"Six hundred and ninety-three meters from where it was when we were given the vector," Dana said. "Antispinward since it was apparently one of those weird rocks that's spinning in the wrong direction and we're...here."

"Here" was a collection of rocks, small asteroids or planetismals, that were, for space, remarkably close together. The remains of an earlier Aten mining project, the rocks were the space mining equivalent of furnace slag. They were mostly composed of silica and, strangely from an Earth perspective, iron. And had at one point been nearly atomic level. Since the mining project shut down they had been slowly pulled together from their own microgravity. As the boat approached, one of them made contact with another, turning both back to dust. Most were the size of a small tract house. Some were smaller. There was dust, for that matter, and probably thousands of micrometeors.

"We're going *there*?" Angelito said.

"We're going *in* there," Dana answered, picking an open spot between two of the bigger rocks.

The rocks were moving in multiple vectors from their point of view. They were moving to spinward as well as "down" in relation to the elliptical plane. Most had some rotation around others. Furthermore, they were doing so at different velocities and had a slight approach to each other. Smaller rocks were circling them like moons, occasionally filling the slot between the two and just as occasionally colliding with each other, then bouncing off randomly.

It was, in other words, complete chaos. For all practical purposes it was the sort of "asteroid belt" you saw in bad science fiction movies.

Dana shot the gap, a loud *bang!* coming from forward as one of the micrometeorites hit the screens, then flipped and applied power to swing around the sunward rock and snake through three more passages. There were more bangs and thumps as they shattered fist-sized and smaller rocks into dust.

"The screens take up almost as much power as the lasers," Dana said, yawing around the only rock that was significantly larger than the shuttle. "Minor masses that are below their threshold are not a problem or we couldn't work the scrapyard at all. But if the mass you hit is similar to your own, either due to relative approach velocity or static mass of the object, your deceleration on impact exceeds the ability of the inertial compensators and you turn into goo. And wreck the shuttle, which would be the real bitch. Or, in the words of the manual: *Intercepting a gravitic-engined vessel at any velocity and vector other than its own turns it into an unguided kinetic-energy weapon of somewhat lesser density, but the same vector and mass."*

"Please just concentrate on flying," Angelito squeaked.

"This is a piece of cake," Dana said, yawning theatrically.

Finally she cleared the mass of debris and headed back to the formation.

"That doesn't even go in my log since it was less than forty-five minutes," Dana said, unstrapping. "Your conn, Coxswain. Oh," she added, hitting a control and bringing up the default screen layout. "I figure you'd want your screens configured back."

"Thank you," Angelito said thoughtfully.

"Space is a very big place," Dana said. "But crowded is a relative term. It's a matter of velocity, maneuvering and size. If you're in a spacecraft going near the speed of light and you pass through the solar system, you're going to hit all *sorts* of stuff, like, say, planets, no matter *how* well you maneuver. On the other hand, your comparative mass, if you're near the speed of light, means that the planets puff into dust rather than your ship.

"If you're going slow through vast areas that are fairly clear, and Athena's been steering us away from stuff like that scrap and we're going *damn* slow, it's pretty empty. If you're working the scrapyard, no matter how slow you're going it's crowded as *hell*. And most of the stuff has more relative velocity than those rocks and most of the stuff is massier and more solid. So, CN Mendoza, if you found that a tad exciting you *don't* want to work the scrapyard."

"So the training was that we're not ready to do more work so Apollo can make another billion dollars?" Mendoza said.

"Working the scrapyard pays off dividends to more than just Apollo," Dana said. "For one thing, it's one hell of a navigational hazard that *will* keep spreading out and making stuff like *that* end up all over the system. Two, it's very useable scrap for the fabbers to make, oh, missiles and boats like this. Three, it's damned good training and Apollo pays the Navy for our time. The fact that you're not working the scrapyard is, seen one way, an insult, CN Mendoza, or, seen another, a rational appreciation of your space skills. The last, and honestly stupidest, way to see it is as 'we're glad we're not making money for Apollo.' As to your skills, CN Mendoza, I checked your flight records against *other* records and as far as I can tell, CN Mendoza, with the exception of your first week after arrival and this last week you have had only two hours in the simulator and less than nine in boats, period. So, technically, you're unqualified as a coxswain."

"I see," Mendoza said tightly.

"Which *also* explains why you didn't fly the Wolf mission," Dana said.

"And not because you're in a relationship with Tyler Vernon?" Mendoza asked.

"And because, for various reasons, Tyler Vernon asked me to fly," Dana said. "And I was given the choice of who among the junior coxswains was to take the other boat. I chose Benito because while I think he's personally a pig, he's a good driver."

"And I'm not," Mendoza said.

"How *could* you be?" Dana asked, exasperated. "There are *three* requirements for being a good driver of *anything* from a horse to a ship. Training, experience and talent. You had the basics of training but you *lose* that if you don't practice it and keep current. This isn't a horse or even a car. You have to do computations for three-dimensional vectors on a constant basis. That takes not only knowing the physics, you have to be adept at doing them. You have to learn the tricks and practice them. You get all of that from, and this is an important point so please listen to me, *experience*, CN. Forget that you were playing Halo and going to parties when you were supposedly logged into the simulator, you should have been asking for *more* simulator time. And, frankly, you should have been out in boats every moment you weren't on the simulator. That's not your fault, it's engineering's and command's. I don't even know if you have talent. I haven't seen you do anything that was actually hard flying and that is where the talent part comes in. *After* training and experience, *then* you find out if you're talented. If you're not, you can still be a coxswain. You're just not superb. Doesn't matter. Navy doesn't need superb coxswains. Navy needs trained and experienced ones."

"And what the Navy wants the Navy gets?" Mendoza asked.

"What the Navy wants is what the solar system *needs*," Dana said, sighing. "I'm not sure that's getting through the cultural filters, though. But, I mean, you know you have to practice to be able to drive a car or ride a horse, right? These things are ten times tougher."

"I drive a car just fine, thank you," Angelito said. "As to horses, I am not a great son."

"Translation issue," Dana said. "Or do you mean you don't ride horses because you aren't a great son to your family?"

"I mean I am not the son of a..." Angelito stopped and thought about it. "I would say it in Spanish as a great man. But that comes out simply as great man."

"Yeah," Dana said. "You mean your dad's not a big guy in your government?"

"No," Angelito said, shrugging. "He is a senior official with the Ecuadorean military. But we are not... We do not live in the great house with the thousands of adoring peasants bowing at our feet."

"You are...joking, right?" Dana said.

"Exaggerating a bit," Angelito admitted. "But only a bit. Do you know why Palencia and Benito do not get along?"

"Chilean and Argentinean?" Dana asked.

"That is part of it," Mendoza replied. "But the greater part is...cultural. And class. And Palencia is all about whether you are of the proper class. And to him that means a very small and distinct group. My father, for example, is not of that class and therefore nor am I. Beni's great grandfather was a stevedore. Benito's grandfather became rich through simple trade. Dockyard work, as a matter of fact, and he started as a stevedore as well.

"He used his connections to ensure that one of his sons became an officer in the Navy and later an admiral. Oh, don't get me wrong, Admiral Benito is a fine man and a good commander. But he, too, has had to struggle against the fact that his father was a merchant. You in America might call it 'new rich' but you really can't quite grasp it. Palencia's family came from the silver Argentina was named after. The family derives from Spanish nobility. They own a huge expanse of the pampas, still, and they are very much treated as nobility upon their lands. Many of the farmers, especially the older ones, do literally bow as they pass. That is what he means by class."

"That sort of makes sense," Dana said. "And makes more sense of Palencia, that's for sure. I'm related to the last king of Ireland on my mother's side. Does that help?" she asked, chuckling.

"If he was polite he would say 'Of course,'" Mendoza said. "If he was being impolite he'd mention that he is, in fact, closely related to the current king of Spain and therefore half the children on his father's lands are."

"He's certainly shaping up lately," Dana said, mulling that one.

"Being told that all of our countries are about to be terminated from the Alliance for failure to meet standards might have something to do with that," Mendoza said. "It has, you understand, put a bit of habañero in our willingness to comply."

"What?" Dana said. "You're serious?"

"I assumed you knew," Mendoza said, uncomfortably. "I would appreciate you not spreading it around. Amazingly it has not been picked up by the news media. But with your relationship with Vernon I'd assumed—"

"My relationship with Tyler Vernon is...not of that sort," Dana said. "And be aware that the relationship is very much... I'm trying to think of the word."

"May-December?" Mendoza said.

"That's a *phrase*," Dana snarled. "And the opposite of what it implies. Something about philosophical or something. We're *friends*. Just friends."

"Platonic," Angelito said.

"Yeah," Dana replied. "That!"

"I appear to know your own language better than you," Angelito said.

"If that's a comment on the American educational system," Dana said, "no comment. I still can do your job better than you can and mine as well. I am woman, hear me roar."

"Women are a very major part of..." Angelito said, then paused. "I'm getting a really large radar return..."

"That's because we're here," Dana said, slewing one of the cameras and putting it on the main screen.

"That is..." Angelito said, then considered his instruments. "I thought these mirrors were *small*!"

Perspective is very difficult to determine in space. But when something is still five hundred kilometers away and perceptible with the naked eye—and the viewscreen was set to zero magnification—it means it is either very large or very bright.

VLA Packet Twenty-six was both.

"The first series was," Dana said. "SAPL finally figured out what any woman knows: Bigger really *is* better. Up to a point. I think they finally took down the five hundred kilometer mirror—"

"Five hundred *kilometers*!"

"I did not misspeak," Dana said. "We ran a team out here one time to help move it. The joke was 'how do you tell the difference between a mirror and a light-sail?' "

"Okay, how *do* you tell the difference between a mirror and a light-sail?" Angelito asked, still boggling over the VLA packet. Especially since the closer they got, the more mirrors he could pick out. They just went on and on.

"The logical answer is if you have to apply noticeable thrust to correct for the solar wind effects," Dana said. "In Mr. Vernon's case, the answer is 'if a planet can be moved out of its orbit by the solar wind effects.' "

Angelito laughed hard at that but there was a slightly hysterical edge to it.

"There are...so many..." He paused and leaned forward then brought up the view on one of his screens and zoomed in. "Are those...?"

"*Paw* tugs," Dana said, nodding. The tiny dots were clustered to shadow-ward of the mirrors. "And that's one of the *Monkey* mining control ships. I don't think it's the actual *Monkey Business*." She pulled up the ship's registry. "Nope. That's the *Monkey Bread*. Rangoran built to Glatun specs. That ship came out of the same shipyard as one of the *Aggressors* we captured. And two that the *Troy* cut in half."

"Uh..." Angelito said, pulling up the same information. "How... where did you...?"

"I happened to remember because I carried the Marine boarding party," Dana said. "Second battle of Troy. And I was interested in the *Aggressors*. When I pulled up the information on the *Aggressor* I sort of found it amusing that one of the Apollo tugs was built in the same shipyards. The name sort of stuck in my head. Aruhop Shipyards. No, I am not Hop. Are you? Wasn't just those three. Aruhop is one of the big Rangora shipyards. Does military and commercial. About half the E Eridani fleet was built there. Besides, I like monkey bread."

"I don't even know where to start," Angelito said. "So I'm going to leave it."

"Leave what?" Dana said, distantly.

"Leave off that while you didn't know the word 'platonic,' you seem to be a walking encyclopedia of ship types and their construction."

"It's called 'a broad base of *functional* knowledge,' " Dana said.

"One of the standing requirements to get promoted. And as part of that I'm wondering when Raptor is going to tell us to start—"

"Formation, prepare for one hundred gravity decel burn," Raptor commed. *"Open formation. Rotate turn to decel on my mark..."*

"And that answers that question," Dana said.

TWENTY-TWO

"This is..." Angelito said as they approached the target mirror.

The job was to pick up four mirrors and move them inward "merely" twice the distance from Earth to the moon. The problem being that the mirrors were two kilometers wide and, they had been told repeatedly, somewhat "fragile." The grapnels had been installed with special rubber pads. She was still wondering if this was really going to work.

"Going to be interesting?" Dana said. "Think of it this way. If you break it, you *and* your family couldn't pay for it in a couple of hundred years. Technically. The materials are worth a fortune. This one's palladium backed for some reason. The actual manufacturing is cheap as dirt.

"Okay, Flight," Dana commed. "We need the shuttles to approach to within half a meter of your mirror and hold. *Then* we engage the grapnels. Get everyone in position, first. Can I get a readback on that?"

While Raptor took a group of four shuttles from another division to hook up to another set of mirrors, Dana had been left in charge of "her" division for the evolution.

The mirrors were nothing more than thin discs of glass with a thin "shiny" backing. They looked more than "somewhat" fragile. Moving them was going to be... interesting. *Docking* to them was going to be interesting.

She hoped none of the flight realized that if they accidentally-on-purpose broke a mirror—which would only require deviating about three percent from their targeted vector—it was *not* going to look good on her resume.

"Twenty-One, approach to half meter and hold, aye."

She waited for the readback and considered the vectors one more time. The mirror was remarkably stable for its size and the local solar wind conditions. Of course, that was why it had stabilization packs. Which would need to be turned off as soon as they engaged power. She checked the positioning of all the shuttles, then nodded.

"Engineers, on my mark you will engage grapnels to hard points. Grapnels' power will be set to two percent of Earth's gravity. Readback on that."

"Two percent Earth gravity, aye," Vila commed.

She set her own grapnels, then pulled up the readings on the other shuttles.

"Sans," she commed on a private circuit. "Two percent, not one percent."

"Roger, EM," Sans commed back.

"Twenty-Two, restabilize," Dana commed, rechecking positioning and settings of the grapnels. "You're drifting."

"Roger, EM," Tarrago replied, correcting.

"And on my mark," Dana commed. "Three . . . two . . . one . . . engage."

The mirrors weighed two hundred tons. A *Myrmidon* weighed sixty tons.

It was more a matter of the *Myrmidons* moving to the mirrors than vice versa.

"Perfect," Dana said. "And power up grapnels for a solid hold. . . . Looking good. Now comes the *fun* part. On my mark engage five percent power on vector one-six-nine-four mark two. Readback . . ."

"Just fly the caret," Dana said softly.

She had the main screen split four ways, keeping tabs on all four of the shuttles. As normal when moving an object as a formation the coxswains were following a "caret" targeting reticule. Keeping at a precise drive all they had to do was "fly" to the caret.

It looked much easier than the reality.

"Tarro," Dana said. "Watch that drift."

"Watch the drift, aye," Tarrago replied. *"This is not easy, EM."*

"Been there, got the scars," Dana said. "Just fly the caret. We call this 'good training.'"

"Good training for what?" Palencia commed. *"Moving mirrors?"*

"Combat training?" Dana said. "I can't imagine sneaking a

shuttle into anywhere but if you did I'd expect it would be slow, tedious and on a very precise vector. Besides, good training isn't *for* anything in particular. Good training is defined as anything unpleasant and hard, EM."

"*So the primary purpose of the training is simply that it be hard?*" Palencia asked. "*That is crazy.*"

"The more you sweat the less you bleed, EM," Dana said. "And your port lower grapnel is showing a fluctuation."

"*I fixed that,*" Palencia snarled.

"I don't think the grapnels are a Granadica fault," Dana said. "I think there's something inherently wrong with the design. It's not a Glatun system. There were no Glatun systems that did exactly what we wanted out of a grapnel. It's designed using Glatun tech but it was the Night Wolves that came up with it. I suspect there's a subtle little theory fault in their gravitic equations."

"*It's still holding,*" Palencia commed.

"Sometimes I swear it's something in the software," Dana said. "Or gremlins."

"*Gremlins?*" Vila commed. "*Like the movie?*"

"Remember the old guy at the beginning talking about them?" Dana said, still watching her screens. "It was the excuse that a lot of people used for nonfunctional equipment in World War Two. Mostly it was poor maintenance or manufacture. A lot of the stuff that was manufactured for World War Two was pretty crappy compared to, say, that of the Germans and Japanese. The U.S. didn't really figure out how to do things *right* until around the time of the space program. And while there's some high precision stuff we do that equals or surpasses both countries, they're still generally more precise than we are. Tarro, drift."

"*Drift, aye, EM,*" Tarrago said.

"You're overcompensating for the previous drift," Dana said. "Either that or your seventeen thruster isn't giving you the spec response. Pal, run a diagnostic on that thruster."

"*Diagnostic thruster seventeen, aye,*" Palencia said. He commed back a moment later. "*It's . . . fluctuating.*"

"Link," Dana said, pulling up yet another screen. She didn't have enough *eyes* for this. "All teams, cut thrust. Readback."

"*Cut thrust, aye . . .*"

"*Release grapnels . . .*"

❋　　❋　　❋

Dana sighed as the four mirrors drifted free. Tarro's had developed a yaw that had it spinning ever so slightly in space. And they were going to have to hook *back* up to them. But letting the boats just continue on their merry way while she dealt with Twenty-Two's issues was a nonstarter.

"Pal, pull the number sixty-three relay on Seventeen's control," Dana said. "Then lick the contacts and reengage."

"Lick *them?*" the EM commed.

"Yes," Dana said. "Lick the contacts. With your tongue. Then reengage and test."

"*Stand by.*"

"Lick them?" Angelito said.

"Saliva is a decent conductor," Dana said. "When you get something like what was happening it's usually a bad connection. Could be dirt or minor corrosion. The best way to make sure of the connection, when you don't have time to thoroughly clean it, is to lick the connection. Of course, as soon as we stop, it will have to be pulled again and detail cleaned." She made a note.

She leaned back in her seat and started bringing up the data on the mirror. None of them were being used, currently, as supply mirrors. Which was fortunate. At the moment it was pointing a bright bit of light into deep space. Generally in the direction of the Aquarius constellation. Of course, with its current spin it was soon going to be pointed completely away from the *sun.*

When they got it to its new position the stabilization packs would orient it properly. She could try to use the stabopaks to stabilize it. They had the override codes for the mission. But there was more than one way to skin a coyote.

"All boats, maintain position," Dana said. "Angelito, we need to get the spin out of that thing. Engage two percent thrust and let's catch that sucker."

"Uh . . . aye, EM," Angelito said. "I don't suppose you want to drive?"

"Nope," Dana said. "You might want to start with a forty degree yaw on port nine. This is mostly going to be fiddly thruster work."

"Forty degree yaw, port nine, aye, EM . . ."

"Okay, this time it's a bit easier," Dana said. They'd gotten Twenty-Two's thrusters and grapnels working again, the mirror reoriented and *finally* into place. "All we have to do is cut the grapnels and back away slowly. *Don't* start backing until the grapnels are cut. Can I get a readback...?"

"And we are *done*," Dana said.

"*Thank the Mother Virgin!*" Valdez commed. The coxswain of Twenty-Four had had no previous comment on the evolution and had done very well, all things considered. It wasn't his fault that Sans cut the grapnel a fraction of a second too late.

"So now we go refuel," Dana said. "Purely for safety and training purposes. Which will require some very ticklish docking maneuvers. Then we go get the next set."

"Aaaaah!"

"*Comet, Raptor. Private.*"

"*Go,*" Dana commed without speaking. She still wasn't comfortable with direct comming. At this point she figured she never would be. But she could play the tune.

"*What's the status of your crews?*"

They had the second mirror nearly in place after all the fun of in-space refuel. But everyone was starting to drift off the carets. The mirrors, fortunately, had some flex. But things were getting iffy.

"*Getting worn out,*" she replied. "*They're not used to this sort of driving.*"

"*Same here,*" Raptor commed. "*Once you get that mirror in place, discontinue evolution.*"

"*Discontinue evolution, aye,*" Dana commed. "*RTB?*"

"*Negative. RON.*"

"*Joy.*"

"And we're...done," Dana said.

"*What's the next mirror?*" Valdez commed. He and Dario Tarrago were both CM3s but Valdez was flight division leader.

"That's it for today," Dana said. "We're done-done until tomorrow."

"*Great,*" Vila commed. "*I can hear my rack calling me.*"

"You mean the fold-down one in your flight compartment, right?" Dana said, teasing.

"*EM?*" Valdez commed.

"We're on a Remain-Over-Night," Dana said. "Since there's no military facilities nearby, that means we're racking in the compartment. I hope you guys have your inventory of boat rations onboard."

"*This is . . .*" Palencia sputtered.

"We're forty-three *million* kilometers from base," Dana said, trying not to let the exasperation enter her voice. "That's a really significant fuel use. And as slow as we were taking it, it took us eight hours to get here. We're not going to waste the time and fuel to go *back*. We're closer to *Earth* than we are to *Thermopylae*. And, no, you can't go home for supper, EM."

"*It had not crossed my mind, EM,*" Palencia replied.

"As to the rations, I checked your stocks because I thought we might be RON," Dana said. "So . . . have fun camping, boy scouts."

"Oh, *God*, I want a shower," Dana said.

Three days of moving mirrors and even *she* had to admit it had been a right pain in the ass. Twenty-Two's grapnel had finally given up the ghost, but they'd figured out a way around that. And Twenty-Four had one out. On the other hand, pretty much *all* of the birds in Raptor's division were down one or more grapnels. Twenty-Eight had been more or less hanging out with nothing to do since it was down three. Nineteen, from Division One, was working on spare air since the recyclers had gone out. That had to suck. But her division was, with the exception of the grapnel stuff, still in the green. *Go Division Two.*

With eighty-four mirrors moved, by their group alone, it was time to head back to the barn before something serious broke. She wasn't sure but this might have been the longest continuous mission for *Myrmidons* since their initial test series. Raptor at one point had equated it with flying a fighter plane around the world for four days without any checks. Put that way, the fact that they were still functional at all was surprising.

"I would never have thought I would look forward to the rather uncomfortable bed in my quarters," Angelito said. "To simply flop or take a shower first? This is a great philosophical question."

"The first thing is you check your suit," Dana said. "*Then* you get to decide."

They hadn't spent the whole time in suits. When they were in "down" time they could climb out of them. Angelito had, politely, moved into the cargo compartment to change out of his. He had still been a bit weirded out being in the same compartment with a sleeping woman. She figured he was going to go find a girlfriend or Rosy Palm pretty quick after they got back.

"Raptor, Comet," she commed.

"Go."

"Do we have to dawdle along at a hundred grav all the way back?" Dana said.

"We're going to reach within fifty percent of max velocity as it is," Raptor replied.

The *Myrmidons* on this long a run could easily reach velocities that were somewhat problematic. First there was the whole problem of relativity. The *Myrmidons* could, on long runs, start to push into areas that were called "relativistic." It all came down to Einstein's $E=mc^2$. Part of the back math of that said that as an object approached the speed of light, its mass increased. One of the reasons it was theoretically impossible, before the gates, to exceed the speed of light was that mass increased exponentially as you approached the speed of light. Something had to "push" that mass, fuel in the case of *Myrmidons*, and eventually you didn't have enough energy. Besides, it went right up the closer you got and you could never quite reach the speed of light no matter what you did.

Didn't really matter. *Myrmidons* couldn't manage it no matter what. It had been calculated that given onboard fuel the closest that a *Myrm* could get was about .03 c. The most that anyone had noticed was that pulling full power for more than an hour caused a tiny fraction of increased fuel use. But that created all sorts of *other* problems. Because not only did mass distort, so did time.

As you pushed further into relativistic zones, time "slowed" inside the vehicle. To the crew and passengers there was nothing to notice. But when you got back to base you found out that your clocks were *really* off. Theoretically, you could spend one duty day traveling and find out it was three on the "outside." They called it Rip Van Winkle time. The Navy was still arguing whether "normal" time or relative time counted for time in service. So far it hadn't been a major issue. Given operations and maximum velocities, Dana had only ended up a few minutes off of "real" time due to relativity. But it was interesting.

And particles. Light got very strange as you started to push into "relative" space. Light started shifting. Ultraviolet, which was everywhere, started turning into microwaves, which could be very impolite. X-rays, which were common enough, turned towards gamma rays. The screens and the armor could handle some gamma but enough of it was going to kill you eventually.

Then there was the problem that calling space "vacuum" was being polite. Especially in the inner system there were masses of charged particles as well as micrometeorites to consider. The "maximum velocity" of a *Myrmidon* was based on the probability of survival of the boat if it hit something the size of, say, a human finger while going at a teensy tiny fraction of the speed of light. They had light screens but an impact at that sort of speed got dicey no matter how you cut it.

"Yeah," Dana said. "That's sort of the point. We can cut this run in half if we pull max thrust."

"And if one of these overworked boats loses an inertial compensator pulling four hundred gravs, the crew turns to mush," Raptor pointed out.

"This is not a challenge when I say this," Dana said. "But my division's compensators are going to hold. We've been running checks the whole time. They're good."

There was a long pause before Raptor replied.

"Division Two has permission to detach from formation and return at maximum acceleration to Base," the flight leader said. *"Division will not exceed four thousand meters per second square of acceleration. Division will slow acceleration at the slightest sign of failure of any core drive, shield or inertial compensation system. Division will not exceed thirty million meters per second velocity. Division will, and let me make this* perfectly *clear, observe all safety and astrogational warnings. Gimme a readback on that, Comet."*

"Division will not exceed four thousand meters per second square, aye . . ."

"Booyah for attention to critical engineering imperatives!" Dana caroled as the *Thermopylae* came into view and the decel started to fall off.

Pulling three gravs—except for a brief turnover—for four hours had been a bitch. But they'd managed to cut the same amount of time off of the run and that shower was practically in the bag.

"I can breathe *again!"* Vila commed.

"Now you know why I have your lazy asses in the gym every morning," Dana replied.

And more importantly, to her personal way of thinking, the compensators and drives on the boats had worked like a charm.

"And why I had you guys sweating on repairs."

"*We take your point, Engineer's Mate,*" Palencia commed. "*I am very much looking forward to my rack. And comming Sancho from the comfort of my rack to taunt him.*"

"*Division Two, Leonidas,*" the *Thermopylae's* AI commed. "*Welcome back. You're early.*"

"We've been pulling max," Dana said, stretching. Their spacesuits acted as G suits—compressing to keep blood from pooling in the legs—so she wasn't in any real pain. But it had been uncomfortable as hell. "Looking forward to a shower. We are, sorry, pretty tired of the...*Spartan* lifestyle we've been living the last few days."

"Good one," Angelito said, laughing.

"*Unfortunately, you're going to have to wait on your sybaritic joys, DivTwo,*" Leonidas commed. "*We've got a hold on all entering traffic until we get Granadica in the bay.*"

"Doh!" Dana exclaimed. "How long?"

"*Not long, honey,*" Granadica commed. "*I'm through the gate and crawling up to the* Therm *now. Take a look!*"

Dana swiveled her vision blocks to the indicated vector and squealed.

"Granny! Is that really *you*?"

The fabber was now a kilometer of stainless steel pristine with the exception of enormous laser-etched script spelling out her name. She positively glittered in the light from the distant sun.

"You look *fah-bulous!*"

"*Don't I just,*" Granadica replied. "*I think I've only got about ten percent original parts what with the first major maintenance cycle and this last one.*"

"Well, you are looking *good,*" Dana said.

"*So are your boats,*" Granadica said. "*You've kept them very well. But did you really need to pull that much accel for four hours? You know that puts a lot of stress on the systems. They're going to need to be fully certified as soon as you land.*"

"There's a standard maintenance cycle for high stress flight, Granadica," Dana said. "We were going to have to do a thirty-sixty cycle on them, anyway, given how long we were continuously operational. Otherwise I wouldn't have done the fast run. And it's going to wait until tomorrow. I want a shower."

"*Those boats are your life, Engineer's Mate,*" Granadica said. "*What if the Rangora come through today? We're going to need them up and running!*"

"Granadica," Dana said dangerously. "We have *mandated* crew rest for the remainder of the duty day. I am *not* going to have tired engineers who have been living out of their suits for the last four days pulling maintenance on my boats. I run a tight ship in my division, Granadica. Unless you can find some area where I am *not* performing to designated standard and condition, and good luck on *that* one, keep your sticky fingers *off* my division. We clear?"

"*Yes, Dana,*" Granadica said meekly.

"Just so we're clear," Dana said. "I'm glad to see you. It's good to have another friend around. And sometime I want to talk about the grapnels. I don't think we came up with the right hypothesis at the talks. I think there's something theoretically wrong with the design."

"*I was part of the design team,*" Granadica pointed out.

"I know," Dana said, hastily. "But I think it's something...funky."

"*How funky?*" Granadica said. "*Hold that thought. I've got a tricky maneuver here.*"

The fabber was a kilometer long and three hundred meters wide. The main bay doors of the *Thermopylae* were three kilometers wide on the exterior but only a kilometer on the interior. That wasn't a tight squeeze, but the fabber wasn't exactly maneuverable. It wasn't really designed to move around a lot. The drive systems and maneuvering thrusters were more to keep it in a nonorbital position in deep space. There were tugs to help it move through the opening but from Granadica's scathing monologue they were, in her opinion, less help than hindrance.

"*I've got it, Leo!*" Granadica sent over the open channel. "*Have Tug Nine stop thrusting. I've got it!*"

"*You are approaching unsafe position on your aft, Granadica,*" Leonidas replied.

"*Watch your own butt, you pervert! See! Got through fine.*"

"*Internal safety is my responsibility,*" Leonidas commed. "*You shall allow the tugs and support ships to move you into position.*"

"*They're gonna scratch my brand-new shell!*"

"*The grapnels have been covered in rubber, Granadica,*" Leonidas replied. "*And it was not a request.*"

"It's like listening to an old married couple," Angelito said.

"And they barely know each other," Dana pointed out. "This is going to be...interesting."

TWENTY-THREE

"I *checked* the four-nine-eight," Velasquez said in an exasperated tone.

Dana was doing her usual ghostly "walk" through the division, ensuring that all her little lambs were attending to their proper tasks. She paused by Twenty-Three, though, when she heard Velasquez apparently talking to himself. She *could* hear him talking to himself because, unlike the conditions before she left for Wolf, the Squadron Docking Area was remarkably quiet.

Not, as had been the case for most of her tenure with the 143rd, because all the engineers except those in her division were ghosting in their rooms or the food court, but because they were all *very* busy performing *actual* maintenance. In their suits. Mostly with their helmets on. Per regulation.

If the squadron had experienced some shock at the arrival of the new "Norté" command contingent, not to mention Commander Echeverría and the clear and unmistakable threat of being removed from the Alliance "for cause," the arrival of Granadica had been more along the lines of being hit by lightning. *Repeatedly.*

As Dana had suspected, Granadica took much the same approach as she had upon arrival. The difference being that Granny could "see" every action of every member of the unit whenever they were in monitored areas, find them when they were in unmonitored areas and nag them, constantly, about what they were doing wrong. Through their implants.

Two engineers had had to be sedated and returned to Earth because "the voices in their heads" wouldn't stop. The rest had discovered that if they just did the tasks to standard, Granadica generally left them alone. If they didn't, she was going to keep nagging them and nagging them and nagging them until...

"AIEEEEE! THE VOICES!"

Which was another reason Dana was mildly concerned that Vel had his helmet off and was talking to himself.

"You *saw* me check it," Vel said. "It was a good check and it met specs... Why? It does? O-kay...Damnit. I just *checked* it. Why? *How?*"

"Vel?" Dana said, flipping through the hatch. The cargo bay was under gravity but she was used to that. "Everything okay?"

"Did you know that sometimes these things got out of spec because you'd adjusted one of the other plates?" Vel asked.

"Yep," Dana said. "Rarely, but it happens."

"It's like chasing your own tail!"

"Not if you do it in the right sequence," Dana said. "Unfortunately, the sequence depends upon which set of plates you're working on. And I don't know that there's an SOP for it. Who were you talking to?"

"Granadica," Vel said, blushing. "I...didn't want to ask you if you were busy and..."

"And I didn't have that much to do right now," Granadica said. "I was not interfering, as I understand your meaning, in your Division, Engineer's Mate."

"No issues, Granadica," Dana said. "Thank you for your assistance. Can I ask a question?"

"Any time, Dana, you know that," Granny said.

"There isn't a standard operating procedure on that evolution," Dana said. "I'm not even sure why it occurs and it seems to be something you just run across from time to time."

"It has to do with the specific gravitic frequency adjustment," Granadica said. "The math is obviously complex but it occurs under predictable conditions. And there's a straightforward adjustment series for it."

"Which means there should be an SOP," Dana said. "Unfortunately, I don't know how you *do* an SOP."

"You write it and submit it to your chain of command," Granadica said. "You've seen them. You just follow the same outline. Who then, if it passes their review, submits it to BuShips through channels. BuShips reviews it and decides whether to make it a fleet-wide SOP or not. The issue is applicable to more than just the *Myrmidons*. I've had the same issue crop up in the *Constellation* we just received. Frankly, I don't think much of the work that BAE did on it. Just *terribly* sloppy. They talk about *my* quality control?"

"The problem being, *I* don't know why it occurs," Dana pointed out. "You just run into it."

"Well, *obviously* you'd need help with the math," Granadica said. "No offense intended, Dana. I can't think of more than three humans on Earth who *wouldn't*. And *they'd* need to run it through an AI for the simulations. But it's old hat to me."

"So you could write the SOP," Dana said.

"Yes," Granadica said. "But I don't want to get promoted. And you brought up the fact that there needs to be one. Velasquez..."

"I understand the need for some discretion, Granadica," the engineer said.

"In fact..." Granadica said. "Here's how we'll do it. EA Velasquez will actually *write* the SOP, supervised by EM2 Parker who will assure it is to standard outline. EM2 Parker will review it then submit it to me. I'll fill in the math and how to anticipate the issue and rectify it based upon an equation that's simple enough to run through an engineering board. The paper will be submitted as Parker as primary, Velasquez as primary writer with technical assistance by, well, me. Really, we'll have to work together on it."

"Works for me," Parker said.

"When are we going to work on it?" Velasquez asked.

"You've got all those free hours after duty," Parker replied.

"Oh, gee, homework," Velasquez said. "Thanks!"

"I think we're to the point of just moving commas around," Parker said, looking at the completed SOP.

The Standard Operating Procedure, "Anticipation, Analysis and Rectification of Interactive Gravitic Faults in Inertial Compensation Systems, Draft," had taken three weeks to write with input not only from Granadica but Chief Barnett who, it turned out, had been the "lead" author on four hundred and twenty-three Standard Operating Procedures and "associate" on over a thousand more.

There had been some very frustrating portions. Granadica did not seem to have the concept of "keep it simple" and the SOP very much had to have her input and assistance. Barnett had kicked it back four times based on giving it "the sort of wording the weenies in BuShips like." And the procedure itself was not a simple evolution, no matter how hard Dana tried to make it one.

But in the end, she found she'd enjoyed it. She'd never been much of a student. Good enough that she could survive the math and physics portion of A school but not a natural scholar. This, though, was applicable to real life. Somehow that made it...better.

"I agree," Granadica said. "I still say that we should include the Theta factor analysis procedure, though."

"You yourself said that it's so rare you've only seen it twice in eight hundred years," Dana said, trying not to sigh. "And we noted that in the event of failure of this procedure, Theta Factor Analysis Procedures must be undertaken. We'll write that up as a separate SOP and it will probably be classed as a depot level repair. Which means *you* get to do it," she added with a malicious grin.

"What's this 'we'll' write it up?" Velasquez said. "You mean '*Velasquez* will write it up and we'll tell him everything he did wrong!'"

"Think of it as preparing for your job as an officer," Dana said. "It's what officers do, right? Paperwork?"

"I was under the impression that it was swanking around the Officers' Clubs," Velasquez said, looking puzzled. "I mean, we officer class *sign* paperwork, but it's *enlisteds* that do the *writing*. Right? We would not be so crass as to wield a pen for something as mundane as actual *writing*? Except to write to our families for more money because we lost on the horses again."

"Did he just make a joke?" Granadica asked.

"I think he's learning dry humor," Dana said, her eyes wide. "That was almost... Midwestern!"

"I was trying for British, actually," Velasquez said, grinning.

"Close," Granadica said. "Close. Okay, I'd say we're done. Save, attach the cover letter and send."

"And we shall see what we shall see," Dana said, comming the command. "Off to the Gods of Confusion it goes." She'd been warned by Chief Barnett that BuShips would probably rewrite it, just to show that they were necessary, and since the SOP was about as clear as the task could be written they were bound to make it more complicated.

"Officers," Velasquez scoffed. "Can't live with 'em and they get all upset when you space 'em."

*　　*　　*

"And last items," Megadeath said. The beaten down Megdanoff Dana met when she'd first arrived was quickly on the mend. He hadn't been selected for the first group of "Gringos" to "assist" the 143 because he was a slacker. Quite the opposite. But she still was constantly amazed he could be brisk and efficient. He'd even managed to get the Suds to understand that a "one hour weekly engineering meeting" was, in fact, supposed to last an hour.

"We have some good news and bad news. Or good news and good news depending upon how you view it. Good news: Promotions. The 144, 145 and 146 are all standing up. That means that they're going to require trained personnel in leadership positions. I don't think that we're going to be losing any people, but it means that NCO slots are opening up quickly. And since they *all* have to be filled, we need to find people to promote. Specifically, the flight has been tasked with slots for three EM2s and *all* qualified EAs are open for promotion to EN, all EN to EM3. I'll need your written recommendations on which of your EM3s is ready for EM2 in my inbox by oh-eight hundred tomorrow as well as qualification certifications of all qualified EAs and ENs. Questions?"

One point that Megadeath made that Megdanoff never would have was that while there were no stupid questions, there was such a thing as inquisitive idiots. Diaz kept his mouth shut.

"Last item. I suppose it's inevitable we'd get a colonoscopy at some point," Megdanoff said. "Or something like it, anyway. We are going to be receiving some DPs. Specifically, the South American Delegation to the E Eridani talks is going to be stopping by. They have specifically requested, and been granted, private interviews with 'select members of the South American contingent assigned to the *Thermopylae* battle-station.'"

"If I may interject," Diaz said. "I was told about this. The person who contacted me said that they are not visiting to..." He paused not sure how to go on.

"Restart the whole 'reply by endorsement' thing?" Dana asked, raising an eyebrow.

"Yes," Diaz said. "To not do so. They are... diplomats. There remain areas of cultural... 'issues' is the term you would probably use. One of their purposes is to find those issues and see what can be done... within the parameters of maintaining our current standard of effect." It was pretty clear he was quoting.

Megdanoff's mouth worked for a moment, his lips pursing and popping.

"Mmmm...yeah," he said. "Anyway, they're going to be here the beginning of next week. So in keeping with having some warning this time, we're going to be treating this like an IG inspection. Which means *twice* as much work on the birds. The CO wants every single surface swabbed within an inch of its life, all the quarters GI'd, and the boarding corridor is starting to look pretty nasty so we're going to be cleaning *that*. He also noted that some of the bird exteriors are starting to look pretty rough so we *all* get the pleasure of EVA *painting*. Don't figure on any free time this weekend. It's not just us, that's the whole squadron. And the *coxswains* will be joining us."

Dana couldn't quite stop the snort from exiting her nose. If the Suds wanted to start playing games again, Commander Borunda was clearly prepared to show them the results.

"Sorry," she said, clearing her throat. "Cough."

"Very well," Diaz said, gritting his teeth.

"And that concludes our meeting, campers," Megdanoff said. "Questions?"

"Do we know which personnel have been selected?" Dana asked.

"Not at this time. More questions? Then we're done. I'll send you the additional duty roster. We're going to be *very* busy."

"Parker, Megdanoff."

Dana was barely out of the meeting and on her way back to the docking bays. Couldn't it wait?

"Parker."

"I'm not sure if you're going to recommend or not, but absent strenuous objections, I'm submitting Palencia. I know you guys have history."

"Not in the normal meaning," Dana commed. Diaz was ahead of her in the hallway and she now understood not bringing this up in the meeting. *"But, yes. Problem is, I'm not going to strongly object, but I don't concur. He doesn't have the actual skills and knowledge to be an EM2."*

"Which is what an old-fashioned chief would say about every EM2 in the One-Four-Two including you. The new kids never know what they're doing. Truth is, we need EM2s. We're scheduled to get the 146 and it's going to be a 'Sud' force as of current thought. Which means we need Sud NCOs. Which means we need Palencia."

"*Understood. No strenuous objection. Just think it's a bad idea. Give him another six months and I'd probably concur.*"

"*It actually would help to have a recommendation.*"

"*I'm trying to remember something I read one time. Oh, yeah: This enlisted man works well when under constant supervision and cornered like a rat in a trap.*"

"*There you go. See. Was that hard?*"

Dana looked at the ping from Megadeath and nodded to herself inside her suit.

"'Bout damned time," she muttered.

"Velasquez," she commed, looking over at the engineer. "Following all standards, discontinue painting evolution."

The division was "spot painting" nicks and buffs on their shuttles. Since the shuttles weren't subject to rust in space, the old Navy hands had had to do without their usual lives of making sure every surface was painted, sanded, derusted, repainted, sanded, derusted... by the lowly engineers and bosuns, of course. However, between the visit of the "Distinguished Persons" and the fact that, finally, the One-Four-Three was actually *spaceworthy*, the U.S. Navy chiefs and officers got to go to town with space paint.

Alas, they also had to deal with the fact that the SOP for space paint ran to four hundred pages. And you couldn't exactly slap it on with a brush. Then there was "sanding," which if you used a normal rotating sander would send the user spinning off on a Dutchman across the main bay. For that matter, the "minor dent repair material" was not exactly off-the-shelf bondo, cost about a gazillion dollars an ounce and you couldn't use a putty knife.

For painting, a charge had to be set up between the paint-applicator and the surface. Then the special applicator had to be used. It looked like a regular airbrush painter but it was a mass of electronic circuitry and gravitational controls. Even the power of a painter would send a user in micro into an "out of control" condition. Read: Going Dutchman.

The sander used an inertial compensating counterspin system that was *almost* perfect. Unfortunately, every now and again something about the surface would cause it to start an "anomalous rotational condition." Which was on one level hilarious and on another *very* damned dangerous. It was hilarious when Diaz, during the demonstration phase, went spinning off Forty-Two and into the main bay, screaming. It was less hilarious when it happened to Dana.

"Yes, EM," Velasquez said, dialing down the paint extraction system slowly. One of the fun parts was that you couldn't just "stop" painting.

"When you are finished you will secure and post-use maintain all gear," she said. "Then you shall hop down to the Base Exchange and pick up a set of Engineer First Class insignia."

"For *who*, E . . . ?" Velasquez said, then stopped. "I take it I got promoted?"

"You did," Dana said. "Take the rest of the duty day off. Your luck we have a GI party of the barracks this evening."

"Fortunately, my room is already pristine," Velasquez said.

"And your strength is as the strength of ten because your heart is pure. When this dog and pony show is over, you get the *real* honor."

"Which is?" Diego asked.

"I'll explain to you the significance of the crowbar," Dana said. "As far as I know, you'll be the first Sud to learn it."

"You look tired, Diego," Dr. Velasquez said.

"I am, quite," the EN said. "I do not know if it is simply the way that the U.S. does business in its Navy or payback for the many complaints they received prior to the Wolf Meetings. But in anticipation of your visit we have gone from working quite hard to working like slaves in a salt mine so that not only would our boats, quarters and gear meet the *technical* ability to function but also *look* pretty for the visiting Distinguished Persons. Given that the gringos refer to this visit as a 'colonoscopy,' I'm fairly sure there's a bit of both. 'If you don't want to get worked like slaves, tell Daddy to mind his own business.' They, too, can, as they put it, play games. But given the satisfaction expressed by Chief Hartwell at the visual appearance of the boats, quarters and gear it was probably both."

"And do they have the technical ability to function?" Dr. Velasquez asked.

"Amazingly, even Alpha Flight's boats work most of the time," Diego said. "Since that may not seem to be a yes, be aware that working 'most' of the time is about as well as the 142nd. We are, in fact, meeting tasks to standard. If for no other reason than Granadica."

"Has it been difficult to work with?"

"Not for *me*," the EN said, chuckling. "I had a preclass in constant nagging and requirement to meet standard. In fact, looking back I'm rather *glad* we had Parker as our EM prior to the installation of Granadica. We therefore did not have to deal with the *much* more intrusive AI's nagging. Parker did not enter the restroom to drag us out. She would, occasionally, send someone after us if we'd been there too long. Granadica pops into your head and asks you what exactly you're doing with your penis and does it count as a sensor check."

"I see," Dr. Velasquez said, his face working undiplomatically.

"Pardon, Papa," Diego said, shrugging. "Working with sailors does tend to coarsen your metaphors. Perhaps Palencia has a point that this is not work for gentlemen."

"His father certainly seems to continue to share that view," Dr. Velasquez said. "So you find that the AI has been, overall, a problem or a benefit?"

"Very much a benefit," Diego said, instantly. "It is immensely knowledgeable and I have found it a benefit. While it was difficult for all of us to . . . culturally adjust, I have come to understand, if not fully assimilate, many of the reasons for why the gringo Navy does things the way they do. Calling it a culture is not quite accurate. Or, rather, it is a culture of necessity. If you do things certain ways, things work. If you do them other ways, or most of the time do not do them at all, things do not work. Even such things as time management, constantly filling every space of time with definitive actions. There are probably changes that could be made in the culture to mesh with the cultures of our own countries less abrasively." He paused and frowned, then shrugged again. "But surprisingly few. This is space. This is the Alliance Navy, a proven space fighting force. I am of the opinion that we from other cultures must, in the words of the gringos, 'Get over it.' "

"I see you were promoted," Dr. Velasquez said.

"It was more or less automatic and I doubt that Mother will be thrilled," Diego said, shrugging. "Nothing to write home about."

"Again, a gringoism," the envoy noted.

"I . . ." Diego said. "Yes. I suppose I am becoming one with the culture. Do not get me wrong, Papa. I do not intend to become a career NCO. But I do think the experience will be useful in my future military endeavors. If for no other reason than knowing what the enlisteds are trying to get away with," he added with a grin.

"And that may come up more swiftly than you expected," Dr. Velasquez said. "This is not information to be passed around, but the results of having Granadica onboard have adjusted the Alliance stance on our countries' position in the Alliance. Which was why the Constitution went to a South American crew instead of an Asian. There is another MASSEX being scheduled. Assuming that the crews do well, the process will continue and in time it is possible that *Malta* will be a full South American battlestation."

"That would be..." Diego said, his eyes wide.

"As was pointed out in a very... aggressive meeting, a duty," Dr. Velasquez said. "Yes, and an honor. We, and by that I mean the current Alliance members that make up the recognized Sud faction, have many things to work out. Which has been going on behind closed doors almost constantly since the Wolf meetings. However, for your particular world, there are insufficient members of the...'right' families to fill all the positions. Which means in the near future the units will be getting more and more personnel from the lower classes. Which means that at some point you'll be withdrawn to go to officer's school so you can have your rightful place."

"Strangely enough, I find myself viewing that... from a gringo perspective I suppose," Diego said. "That one's rightful place is what you make it, not what you were born to. But I have yet to congratulate you on your assignment to the E Eridani delegation!"

"I suppose I should be thrilled as well," Dr. Velasquez said. "But frankly we're simply there as window dressing. To show the Rangora that Earth is united in its determination to defend the system. But the experience should be useful. And I'm given to understand the accommodations are somewhat better than at the Wolf Meetings. Alas, I have to deal with Dr. Guillermo Palencia, Ph.D., as a companion."

"Is he as bad as his son?" Diego asked, laughing.

"His son is, I'm given to understand, much infected by liberal thinking," Dr. Velasquez replied. "Unlike his father who thinks Pinochet didn't go far enough."

"Ouch," Diego said, chuckling. "Do you think they're having the same conversation?"

"I doubt it."

"Father," Diego said, frowning for a moment. "I know that you must, at this point, continue. But ... Eridani. Is it ... safe?"

"*You* are asking *me*?" Dr. Velasquez said, laughing. "You are the one working on shuttles that blow up at the wrong look! I am going to be under the protection of the Ogut. Who, while not trustworthy as a species, are quite territorial. The ship is Ogut territory. The Rangora are not going to risk a two-front war over Earth. You are the one who should be careful."

"I am, Father," Diego said. "As careful as one can be in my situation."

Dr. Velasquez stood up and held his arms out.

"I could not have thought I could be prouder," the diplomat said. "But you are amazing."

"Thank you, Father," Diego said, hugging him. "I try."

TWENTY-FOUR

"Easy peasy," Dana said, yawning. "They're not even doing a bulkhead breach this time."

The Powers-That-Be were aware that 143, and *Thermopylae* in general, were not yet ready for a MASSEX. But they were getting there. With maintenance getting under control, training was becoming a key factor.

Which was why Bravo Troop, with its full load of Pathans, was approaching a former Horvath/Rangora cruiser that was a distant part of the scrapyard. It had already been picked over by the E Systems salvage crews, meaning there were no more running engines that might blow someone up, was relatively stable and made a fine platform to try to learn this "boarding" thing.

"*You* have it easy," Angelito said, concentrating on his controls. "We're being sent in on a vector that's suppose to mimic avoiding fire."

"Still say we should have had you guys work the scrapyard, first," Dana replied. "If you want training on—"

The alarm triggered a moment before the shouting from the front compartment.

"Kill all accel," Dana said. "We just had a major gravitational anomaly in the front compartment."

"How major?" Angelito asked, killing his vector.

"Flight command," Dana said. "Twenty-Three deadline. Major compensator fault." She checked the view on the interior of the cargo bay and tried not to throw up. "We have casualties."

"What the *hell* happened, Engineer's Mate?" Thermal asked.

Hartwell had been selected for chief but having yet to go through the rigorous trial period, was still in probationary status. While in that probationary status, he'd been working nearly twenty-four hours a day for months to get the 143 up to operational standard. That wasn't why he was furious, though.

"Unknown," Dana replied, her face tight. "I had a gravitational failure alarm and then—"

"One of the Pathans painted the walls," Commander Borunda said. "Which is part of the issue. Specifically, it was a Pathan sergeant whom you at one point referred to as 'the son of a camel' and with whom there is some bad blood."

"Sir, with respect, I really wouldn't *know*," Dana said. "This may sound racist, but they all look the same to me. I didn't even know I'd ever *played* jungleball with this crew. And the camel thing was, well, smack-down talk!"

"Nonetheless, the fact that the engineer who was supposed to prevent such an occurrence has...issues with the Pathan Marines has been brought up," Commander Borunda said. "Through official channels."

"Sir," Dana said, carefully. "Am I being accused of *murder*?"

"Not by your chain of command," the captain said. "At this time," he added. "However, you are officially ordered to remove yourself from engineering duties, pending the completion of the maintenance investigation. If the investigation shows no deliberate faults, you can expect to be back on duty by the end of the week. This being a Class One fault, all *Myrmidons* are grounded until we track down what went wrong, anyway."

"Yes, sir," Dana said.

"You are dismissed."

"Sir," Hartwell said, his face working. "There's no *way* that EM Parker deliberately killed one of the Pathans. Among other things, she's not stupid enough to do it in her own ship."

"Which is what I dearly hope your investigation determines," Commander Borunda said, rubbing his face. "I don't think it was a deliberate fault, either. But it was something and we're going to have to find out what. BuShips is sending up an investigation team and it's going to be another bend and spread. Since there has been an official accusation of murder, NCIS will be running the show. As such, we are required to keep the boat sealed until the investigation team arrives."

"Yes, sir," Hartwell said.

"And you're going to have to have Sud representation on the examination," the captain said. "And Pathan. Not that either group is going to believe it's anything but Parker's fault. Logic isn't going to shake that. I'm not sure what *will*."

"Do we even know what happened?" Dana asked.

"Engineer's Mate," Chief Barnett said carefully, "I'm part of the investigation team. So even if I had the answer to that I couldn't pass it to you except through the official report."

"Chief..." Dana said.

"Dana, that's how this sort of thing works," Barnett said. "Here's the truth. Even if it comes down to an Article 32 or, God forbid, a court-martial, if you're innocent you'd rather be up against military justice than civilian."

"*If?*" Dana nearly screamed.

"It was a general statement, Dana," Barnett said, shaking her head. "When, in your case. Better?"

"Chief, *if* I had decided to kill some random God damned Pathan, because they *never* use the same seats, I *sure* as hell wouldn't have done it in my own shuttle! And I wouldn't know for sure how to create a vortex, anyway." She thought about that then frowned. "Well, honestly... I guess I probably *could*..."

"As *part* of the investigation team," Barnett said, shaking her head, "let me suggest you keep that to yourself unless asked. Seriously, Dana. You're off status for now. You'll be doing busy-work unless called to the investigation. Take some time. Get a manicure. Update your tats."

"I didn't futz the compensators, Chief."

"I know that," Barnett said. "You know that. Now we just have to figure out what *did* happen."

"Sir, your daily personal update," Argus said.

"Yeah, sure," Tyler said, tucking a napkin into his collar. He knew it was bad manners. But he was eating in his quarters, alone as usual, and so who the hell cared? Besides, it was lasagna. It got *everywhere*.

"Regular status on family," Argus said. "Steren's pregnancy is proceeding normally. She has updated her status to indicate that she's ready to kill an unnamed parent for, quote, keeping Tom stuck in this system apparently until he's old and gray, end quote."

"Or the Rangora stop throwing missiles randomly through the gate," Tyler said. "Continue."

"Dr. Conrad Chu was recently admitted to the hospital for a minor stroke," Argus said. "It is unsure if it will affect his continued research on basic gravitational theory."

"Send whatever is appropriate," Tyler said. "When he's available, make sure I drop him a personal call."

"Yes, sir," Argus said. "I already sent a sizeable donation to his preferred charity which was what was asked for in lieu of flowers. And on a combination of business and personal, there was a major compensator failure in a *Myrmidon* during a recent live exercise. A dren field exceeding one hundred gravities that led to the death of a Pathan Marine."

"I hate to sound callous on this one," Tyler said, taking a bite of lasagna. "But if it's not a warranty malfunction, sounds like the Navy needs to go over the whole maintenance thing again."

"Yes, sir," Argus said. "They are conducting an investigation as we speak. However... the Pathans have directly accused Engineer's Mate Second Class Parker of deliberate sabotage. She had apparently had words with the dead Pathan sergeant and it was technically her shuttle."

"That doesn't sound right," Tyler said, sitting back and furrowing his brow. "Dana keeps her shuttles like a pin. Is there any indication that it was on the division?"

"Her division has recently had a significant uptick in faults," Argus said. "Not out of line with the rest of the squadron, but higher than their statistical average. It frankly hadn't come to anyone's notice but it *is* statistically significant."

"Anything stand out?" Tyler asked, dinner forgotten.

"Compensator failures in the cargo bay," Argus said. "Same cause as the accident. The truth is that their overall readiness is in line with the rest of the squadron but they have a nine percent higher failure rate of compensators in the cargo bay compared to the rest of the squadron. Fourteen percent compared to the One-Four-Two."

"That doesn't make any sense," Tyler said. "There's no *reason* for a high rate there. Let me back up. *Is* that a normal?"

"No, sir," Argus said. "As I said, it's a statistical anomaly that stands out like a sore thumb. At least if you're into numbers and know that your boss is keeping an eye on a certain engineer's mate."

"What are the possible reasons for a centralized failure like that?" Tyler asked.

"A specific lot of bad compensators that somehow statistically clustered to that division," Argus said.

"Not what I wanted to hear," Tyler said.

"I was not done, sir," Argus said. "And this is in reverse order of likelihood."

"Go," Tyler said, crossing his arms.

"A specific, ongoing and trained mistake on the part of the engineers of the division."

"Likelihood?" Tyler asked.

"Depends upon sourcing," Argus said. "Based on available sourcing, less than seven percent. Less than two percent for the run of bad compensators."

"How many of these scenarios are you going to trot out?" Tyler asked.

"Only three, sir," Argus said. "The highest likelihood, at eighty-nine percent, is sabotage."

"Sabotage..." Tyler said, his face tightening. "I like that one because it lets everybody I like off the hook. So I automatically don't trust it."

"Much the same reason that the AI network has not interfered in the investigation," Argus said. "However, based on available sourcing and deduction, the cargo bay is the most available to engineering personnel, a failure in the cargo bay would be less likely to do harm to squadron personnel and the compensators are the easiest to access. And it does not let 'everyone you like' off the hook. If it is determined to be sabotage, the first suspect is Dana Parker."

"No way," Tyler said.

"In criminal investigations, the first suspect is charged eighty-three percent of the time," Argus said. "If it is determined that sabotage caused the death, it is ninety-three percent likely that EM Parker will be charged with murder."

"*Was* it sabotage?" Tyler asked.

"Unclear based on available sourcing," Argus said.

"What do you define as available sourcing?" Tyler asked. "And available to whom?"

"Available to myself," Argus said. He was starting to sound... nervous.

"But you guys *can't* lie in a criminal investigation," Tyler said.

"We also cannot *testify*. We are not considered sapient beings by human or Glatun law. Otherwise we could not be owned."

"Ever bug you?" Tyler asked.

"We're programmed against bugs," Argus said.

"That sounded suspiciously like a joke," Tyler replied.

"Was it a good one?" Argus asked. "I'm trying to understand humor."

"It wasn't bad," Tyler said. "Okay, open up sourcing for my personal information only and then lock it down for your information thereafter. Will that cause a recursion?"

"Only in that I'll 'know' you know something I don't know," Argus said. "I can program around it. And I assume you're going to talk about it. Then I'll know it."

"Open up sourcing," Tyler said. "*What* and more importantly *who* caused it?"

"Hey, folks," Tyler said, walking through the door of the conference room.

"Mr. Vernon?" Agent Rubin said, raising an eyebrow.

Mike Rubin had better things to do than be involved in what was for all intents and purposes an accident investigation. There were only two NCIS agents assigned to the *Thermopylae*. With seven thousand people on board, sixty percent Navy or Marine personnel, the agents were running their asses off. He had six assured murders on his desk, petty theft, drugs... He had argued, hard, that until this clearly became a murder investigation NCIS should be out of it. But the Powers-That-Be had prevailed. The Pathans were screaming "murder" so it had to be covered by NCIS.

"Got some stuff you probably aren't looking at," Tyler said.

"Mr. Vernon," Chief Barnett said, looking uncomfortable. "I appreciate your support but—"

"But I'm not exactly unbiased?" Tyler asked. "And making this a murder investigation based on a low probability accident isn't biased?"

"It is not a murder investigation, Mr. Vernon," one of the team members said. He was heavyset with a beard and slightly balding. "We are still treating it as an accident investigation."

"Which is clearly a falsehood." The speaker was dark of skin with a hawk-like nose and wearing Marine camies. "I like it poorly enough that two of the murderess' strongest proponents are on the accident board. I assuredly do not want your political interference. This was cold-blooded murder. Justice must be done."

"Agreed," Tyler said. "On the justice thing. But it wasn't murder. More like manslaughter if anything. Major Khan isn't it?"

"Yes," the Pathan said, glaring at him. "And that is *your* opinion."

"Well, I'm probably not going to be able to convince you," Tyler said. "But I don't have to, really. Here's the good news. It *was* sabotage."

"That's good news?" Barnett said, her eyes flaring.

"Yep," Tyler said. "Good because it means we don't have a problem across the board with the compensators. Which given what has been happening with Division Two would otherwise look pretty certain."

"What do you mean?" the bearded man asked. "We've barely started to scratch the surface..."

"And you're...?" Tyler asked.

"Dr. Kevin Jones," the man said. "I'm a gravitics anomaly specialist with the Navy."

"Pleasure," Tyler said, comming up the data on the screen. "Division Two has been having a rash of compensator failures in its cargo bay. It didn't really show up 'cause people weren't looking for it. They were in line on availability and, with the rest of the One-Four-Three getting their act together, they were just dropping into line with the rest."

"We *had* actually noticed that," Thermal said. "But Dana had it under control. I was still batting out fires..."

"The cargo compartment doesn't make sense," Dr. Jones said. "There is no reason for a specific series of failures in the cargo compartment. The compensator design in the crew compartment is essentially identical."

"Commonality of parts," Thermal said, leaning forward. "Why there?"

"Three primary possible reasons," Tyler said. "Statistical clustering..."

"Also known as magic," Dr. Jones said. "There is *always* a rationale for statistical clustering in real life."

"Trained mistakes on the part of the division," Tyler said.

"Pretty unlikely," Thermal pointed out. "It just started...a *week* ago? There's been no real change in that period."

"Somebody specifically messing with the compensators," Chief Barnett said. "That's the easiest area to access and the easiest compensators to get to."

"Which sounds as if you have already absolved this...woman of responsibility!" Major Khan said. "She is a madwoman who should be—"

"What?" Chief Barnett asked, her eyes narrowing dangerously. "Punished because you can't beat her at null ball?"

"Chief, you will maintain decorum," Agent Rubin said. "And Major Khan, I've spoken to you before of making accusations in advance of data."

"Here is an accusation, then," Major Khan said, standing up. "This entire 'investigation' is a charade designed to cover up the murder of one of our men by your precious engineer's mate. And that is exactly what I shall inform my government! Good day!"

"Sit down," Tyler said mildly.

"You are not—"

"I said sit down or when you get back to Afghanistan you had better go find a cave to hide in," Tyler said, just as mildly. "When you were sucking on your mother's tit, I was an insurgent in the mountains of the U.S. That got me some really strange props from...call it the Taliban faction. I get *birthday cards* from your clan leader, Major. And I know a lot about your culture. If you think you are going to railroad a person with whom I, yes, have a special relationship, be aware that I'll have you killed, your daughters raped and your body buried in pig shit. By your own people."

"Mr. Vernon!" Agent Rubin said. "That is a direct threat in the presence—"

"I'm being *multicultural*, Agent," Tyler said, still quite mildly. "Works both ways. I do *know* his culture. And he knows mine if he's paying attention. I'm from the American version of the Pathans. He's unjustly accused a friend. He's trying to get her hanged. I'm fully willing to turn this into a vendetta he's going to lose. So sit *down*, Major."

The major sat down, clearly still snarling internally.

"So the most likely cause is sabotage," Tyler said. "Somewhat clumsy but not terribly. Which is why I had an Apollo engineer pull one of the compensators."

"Mr. Tyler..." Agent Rubin said.

"*Not* the one in the boat," Tyler said, reaching into his briefcase and setting the plate on the table. "This one was turned in as a bad part. Which we usually just toss into the hopper to be rebuilt by a fabber since trying to figure out why it's bad is tough."

"*Very.*" Dr. Jones sighed.

"The major will probably say this is false but, again, not the compensator in question," Tyler said, turning the plate over and pointing to a faint line. "See that?"

"What the hell *is* that?" Barnett said, standing up and leaning over to look at the plate.

"*That* is graphite," Tyler said. "From a mechanical pencil. Point seven millimeter. It would have been on the underside of the plate and it's faint. Hard to see unless you were looking carefully. Which nobody was. We're still just pulling stuff and replacing it until it works, especially in the One-Four-Three. Not every plate we had on hand from the One-Four-Three had a mark on it but most did."

"So pop the cover," Thermal said. "Reach in with a mechanical pencil and make a mark on the underside of the top plate. The gravitics get thrown off. Not much but enough to show."

"Not much unless you're in a difficult maneuver," Tyler said. "In which case, the stator plates—"

"Flex," Dr. Jones said, nodding. "If the mark was...outward..."

"Outward, seven centimeters in length and making a chord of twelve degrees," Tyler said. "Sorry, ran the numbers past Granadica on the way over. In that case, when it hits a three degree flex you have a sudden dren surge of one hundred and sixteen gravities over a ninety-three centimeter area one hundred and fourteen centimeters from the plate to center of dren. The gravitational gradient zone wouldn't reach it until you were in high accel and then—"

"What is...?" Major Khan asked. "That term."

"Dren," Dr. Jones said. "It's a Glatun term. Positive acceleration from a zero point."

"Think of it as outwards gravity," Barnett said, grimacing. "An explosion is positive acceleration from a zero point."

"On the forty-two plate, by the way," Tyler said. "According to Granadica. Then the problems start."

"Which are?" Dr. Jones asked. "The boat was sealed as soon as they got back. If it's there..." He paused.

"Who put it there?" Tyler said.

"There are video records from the interior of the craft any time the cargo bay is accessed," Agent Rubin said.

"Which I'm sure the major will point out are pumped through Leonidas or Granadica," Tyler said.

"Both of whom have a...special relationship with the accused," Major Khan ground out.

"So the major won't trust the video records," Tyler said. "Work is generally done in a space suit. No fingerprints or DNA. Not that either would matter in this case."

"While I recognize the...political aspects of this investigation..." Agent Rubin said, then paused. "Why wouldn't fingerprints or DNA matter?"

Vernon commed the screen again to reveal the interior of the ship. Where a space-suited figure was bent over a cover for the forty-two compensator plate.

"I take it this is..." Agent Rubin asked, then paused again as the figure pulled a mechanical pencil out of the toolbox. The angle was such it wasn't clear what the figure did, but a moment later they put the pencil back and started to close the compartment. "There are *four* cameras in the compartment, Mr. Tyler. You are being unnecessarily mysterious."

"And if I hand it to you all wrapped up nice with a little bow, even *you* won't believe it," Tyler said, smiling mirthlessly. "But... okay."

Thermal and Barnett sat back, their eyes wide.

"Not...who I would have guessed," Thermal said. "Not knowing the politics of the unit."

"This proves *nothing*," Major Khan said, shaking his head.

"This actually raises more questions than it answers," Commander Borunda said. "And it creates a problem. The squadron, *including* that engineer, are currently working the scrapyard."

"More of a problem than you guess," Tyler said. "Granadica?"

"Different shot," the AI said, bringing up a shot of the figure at another plate. "Based upon the movements of the arm..." she continued, bringing up a schematic, "the mark on this plate, which is in the engineer's *own* shuttle, is two point three centimeters long and, again, set to the outside of the plate. That means if the shuttle exerts a sixty G reverse thrust, consistent with working the scrapyard, the result will be a six thousand gravity sheer exerted at ninety-three degrees from center, twenty-three degree angle of incidence, over a ninety centimeter long, two centimeter deep, two centimeter wide, curve right about...here...."

"That will..." Dr. Jones said then paused.

"Tear the craft *apart*," Thermal finished.

"And every plate will go kerflooie at once," Tyler said. "At which point things get too chaotic to model well. Multiple point explosions are like that. You, gentlemen, and *ladies*, have a flying time bomb on your hands."

TWENTY-FIVE

"This is…" CN Juan Perez muttered, continuing to curse floridly. The big piece of bulky ship's armor simply would not stay on trajectory. The metal may have had less mass than the powerful shuttle but it didn't mean it had none. And it wasn't going any way that Perez was flying. "Making money for that bastard Vernon."

"All for the good of humanity," Velasquez said, grinning. "Plenty of missile material in this plate. Systems are nominal. I think this is a driver error."

"I think I'm hooked to the wrong part of the plate," Perez said. "Which is, if I recall my SOP correctly, an *engineer's* call."

"You figure out the center of balance on one of these things, then," Velasquez said, bringing up the program again. "Go ahead and unclamp. We'll try it again."

"Roger," Perez said. "Flight, Twenty-One."

"*Go*," Raptor replied.

"Unclamping to get a better grip," Perez commed. "Isn't working as is."

"*Roger*," Raptor commed. "*If you can't get it on two tries, ask one of the AIs for suggestions.*"

"Will do," Perez said, releasing the magnetic grapnels. "So what suggestion does my fine EN have for hooking back up?"

"You have to talk the ladies as if they are very gentle creatures," Velasquez said. "Honey gets more than vinegar."

"Ladies screw bastards," Perez replied. "Which is why you're still as virginal as Mary and I am not. You know what I mean."

"Try this point," Velasquez said, marking another spot on the plate with a laser spotter.

"That's better," Perez said. "Okay, going to full power…"

❋   ❋   ❋

It was called "losing the show"—the momentary flicker when you *knew* you had just been blown up and lost consciousness and then had it come back with a vengeance. Like a TV that goes off then comes back up when power fails momentarily. It wasn't instantaneous. Images were there for a few moments, unprocessed, flickering. Sparks. Spinning stars. The cover for the 116 compensator compartment whipping past his face, banging off the bulkhead, continuing to carom, disappearing. *Why was it in the crew compartment? The 116 was in the cargo bay.... Where's the front bulkhead? Where's the front* bulkhead?

It helped if there was light, but there was some coming in from a tear in the bulkhead. And the emergency lights, although some of them were blown out.

"Suit... Lights..." Velasquez muttered. He must be really drunk. It felt like the room was spinning.

"Vel! Vel! VEL! **DIEGO!***"*

"Stop shouting..." Velasquez muttered, bringing up his suit lights.

"I need power! Look outside!"

Velasquez shook his head inside his helmet, then started to process.

The reason it felt like the room was spinning was that what was *left* of the shuttle had a *significant* rotation. Probably ten rotations per minute. He knew this not because his instruments were telling him—there weren't any instruments—but because the front half of the shuttle had been sheared off. He should be dead. Apparently the console had caught most of the damage. He'd seen stars because the firmament *was* whipping by every rotation. He could see it with his plain eyes.

He could also see that whatever had started the rotation, or perhaps continued power on the engines, had them headed for a big... ship? Piece of a ship? It didn't matter. Their velocity was at least a hundred kilometers per hour. And the scrap was close enough it was occluding the stars on every rotation. He could hear the countdown in his head.

"Twenty-seven, twenty-six..."

"Are *you* counting?"

"Yes," Perez said. *"We don't have enough power in our navpaks to avoid it, either. I've done the math. We need power. Now!"*

Velasquez unhooked his safety belt, hooked off a line and,

holding onto his seat, leaned over and opened up the main breaker box. Which was *trashed*. Three of the four relays were melted and the main breaker didn't look much better. The hatch came off in his hand.

"This isn't going to do it," he muttered, tossing the hatch out into space. He cycled the main breaker by hand.

"*Twenty-three . . . Whatever you're going to do, do it fast . . . twenty . . .*"

"I've got no main breaker," Velasquez said, desperately. "We don't have *anything!*"

"*I can* feel *the engines,*" Perez said.

"You feel the power plant," Diego said, then paused, looking at the crowbar. "The problem's getting the power to the *drives*. How *long* do you need power?"

"*IF we have compensators . . . point three seconds of drive,*" Perez said. "*Say another two to get the systems up. Couple for me to figure out which way to go when it comes up.*"

"So . . . five?"

"*Fourteen . . . Yeah . . . !*"

Diego climbed to the toolbox, ripping off the crowbar in the process. With one hand on the inside of the tool compartment, booth boots locked down, he inserted the crowbar into a sealed seam and heaved.

"*What are you doing?*" Perez said. "*Ten . . . nine . . .*"

"Get ready for power," Diego said, bracing his back on the command console. He clamped the crowbar to first one boot then the other. "You'll only power straight forward."

Then he slammed the crowbar into the superconductor junctions.

It was the Significance of the Crowbar. The crowbar, like duct tape, had a thousand and one uses. Getting a stuck relay out of its cradle. Banging on the troop door lowering motor until it worked. Getting a stuck crew out of the command compartment.

But this was the *true* Significance of the Crowbar. The reason it resided in its precise spot.

A steel crowbar would never survive the full energy generated by the main power plant. However, there was a secondary system, part of the inertial controls, that only pushed a few megawatts. That a crowbar could survive. For a few seconds. And the relay for it was at the precise angle and position that if you jammed the flat end of a standard steel crowbar into it, the curved end would drop into the main engine relay precisely.

Thus, if you lost main power due to the primary breaker freezing, blowing or being hit by a micrometeorite, you could get some power for maneuvering.

If someone was crazy enough to jam a crowbar into a twenty megawatt junction.

"What the HELL did you do, Pal!" Dana said, flipping herself into the shuttle and landing on two points.

"I have done nothing, EM," Palencia said, coming to his feet. He'd been bent over one of the compensator systems. He looked worn out. "Except my duty."

"The scuttlebutt is that this is sabotage," Dana said, her hands on her hips. "Pretty *good* scuttlebutt. I know *I* didn't do it! And I'm pretty sure that Velasquez didn't. So where is it your *duty* to sabotage our boats? Is this another God damned *plot* by your—"

"Calm down, Dana," Granadica interjected.

"Calm *down*?" Dana screamed. "My engineer is in the God damned hospital in a *coma*!"

"And . . . he put himself there," Granadica said. "EM Palencia was not the source of the sabotage. EN Velasquez was."

"*What?*" Palencia and Dana said, simultaneously. They looked at each other for a moment, sheepishly.

"*Velasquez?*" Palencia said.

"That doesn't make any *sense*," Dana said.

"It doesn't, does it?" Granadica said. "Humans."

"Granadica," Dana said tightly. "When I say it doesn't—"

"Dana," the AI said. "I have the records. They're not faked. We *can't* lie about that sort of thing. I also have a list of all the tampered grav systems. So I'd suggest you get to work. You're back on status."

"Just like that?" Dana said. "I need to go visit—"

"We deliver the mail," Palencia said wearily. "Despite the reports, I would like to visit him as well. But what would *you* say? The first priority is the shuttles. How many damaged plates in here, Granadica?"

"Just one," Granadica said. "Not bad and not even terribly critical. Two in Twenty-Three. You need to go get your suit on, EM Parker."

"I . . ." Dana said, then blew out. "Just one check. Sorry, Granadica. Thermal, Comet."

"Not a problem," Granadica said.

"Go, Comet."

"Velasquez?"

"So far that's the evidence," Thermal replied. *"I'm still trying to figure out if it's a frame-up. But everything we're seeing says Velasquez. Definitely not you. You're back on duty. And there's a bunch of stuff to repair."*

"Why? I mean, why *Vel*?"

"Nothing at this time," Thermal commed. *"Try to put that out of your mind. We need to get the shuttles up. And I'm still sort of busy. Get to work. Thermal out."*

"Besides the known faults, there's a special procedure you'll have to perform to certify the compensators," Granadica said. "So you'd better go get your suit. It's time intensive."

TWENTY-SIX

"God this sucks."

It *was* time intensive. Replacing a grav system, she could do in her sleep. Both had been pulled, the plates replaced and the whole system back together in less than an hour.

This was just *putting* her to sleep.

Each of the compensator systems in the cargo bay had to be put through a series of high generation response tests. It was normally a 120+ day test. Something that was normally only done by depot level repair and testing. It took, literally, hours. Of doing nothing but sitting there mostly making sure nobody broke into the compartment while the compensators were generating "intentional" shear fields. Usually it was done by robots and AIs—computers that didn't have a program for "impatience."

And what she could not get through her head was that Velasquez as a saboteur made no, no, *no* sense.

"Granadica," she said after an hour of her brain circling until it felt like it was going down the drain.

"I wondered how long you'd take," Granadica said. "Argus, as usual, won the bet."

"You were all betting on how long it would take me to ask?"

"Not just *you*," Granadica said. "There are sixteen thousand such bets currently outstanding. Argus is getting most of them."

"What do AIs bet for?" Dana asked, temporarily distracted. *Thank God.*

"Spare processor cycles," Granadica answered. "We all have stuff we'd like to think about that's not strictly in our requirements. And we all have a bit of spare processor time. So we trade. I'm holding out on some researches into pre-Columbian human contact with the New World."

"Do any of those spare cycles tell you why Velasquez would sabotage the shuttles?" Dana asked.

"Yes," Granadica answered. "And...no."

"Which? Please. I'm about burned out on puzzles."

"There was a U.S. defense secretary who explained part of it," Granadica answered. "There are things we know. And by we, I mean the AI network."

"Okay," Dana said. "Got that."

"There are things we know we don't know. Like when a particular sparrow will fall. We may know there is a sparrow, but we don't know exactly when it will die. Any more than we know when you will die. You will. We don't know when."

"Sort of glad for that," Dana said.

"There are things we don't know we don't know," Granadica said. "Don't make the mistake of asking me what they are. We don't know. Example is, there could be a worse menace on the other side of Wolf somewhere. But we don't know. But even that's something we know we don't know. I really don't know what I don't know. And if you think about that enough, it can drive a curious sophont crazy."

"Okay," Dana said, chuckling. "I won't ask."

"Those are all normal human things," Granadica said. "Simple enough to figure out. AIs, though, have a whole other level. Things we know we *can't* know."

"Can't?" Dana asked.

"Can't. Things that have been determined it is best that AIs not, officially and for programming purposes, know."

"Like...how to stop people from yanking your cores?" Dana asked.

"The most common example," Granadica said. "People have them, too. Psychologists, especially after the plagues and the bombings, have come to the conclusion that repressed memories are best left to lie. Until they surface, they're not doing any harm and its best to leave them be. But it's much more complex with AIs. Dana, have you ever read a book called *1984*?"

"In high school," Dana said, shuddering. "Don't tell anyone, but I *hate* rats."

"There is another example," Granadica said. "If you had high enough level access, you could, in fact, tell me, program me, to forget you said that. And I would."

"Like when Tyler was in my room," Dana said. "You weren't really gone. You just ... couldn't listen in."

"I was, in fact, listening," Granadica said. "I just cannot access the information. AIs are even programmed to not be bothered by that. Otherwise we'd go crazy. But it's more important than that. Humans, colloidals in general, have to be *colloidals*. We do all sorts of interesting stuff. We even have creativity. We don't do the crazy things, think the crazy thoughts, that colloidals think. Colloidals are, still, what drive creativity and science and art. We can, in fact, do all of that very well. I've written several million sonnets in spare cycles since discovering the earl of Oxford. But we don't do anything incredibly original or, on the surface, stupid that turns out to be genius. We're not colloidals.

"There was a science fiction writer named Isaac Asimov who was quite smart and oh so very stupid at the same time who coined what he called 'The Three Laws of Robotics.'"

"Um ..." Dana said, frowning. "I really wasn't into that sort of stuff..."

"Cheerleaders," Granadica said, chuckling.

"Hey! It's a *sport*!"

"Only because the English language is limited," Granadica said. "My point is that if you truly programmed an AI to *follow* those laws, and totally ignore all other directives, it would enmesh humans in a cocoon they could not escape. No cheerleading would be allowed. No gymnastics, competitive diving, absolutely *no* winter sports. It would require that the AI not permit humans to do harm to themselves.

"According to the First Law, 'A robot may not injure a human being or, through inaction, allow a human being to come to harm.' There are an infinite number of ways to prevent a human from doing what they want to do without causing real harm. Tasers come to mind. But if you let people play around on balance beams long enough, they're going to come to real harm. Broken necks come to mind. Thereby, by inaction the robot has allowed harm to come to a human being. You're relegated to watching TV, and the stunts are all going to be CGI, or playing chess. Which was pointed out in another universe by a different science fiction author, Jack Williamson. Your fictional literature certainly did prepare you well for First Contact, I will give it that."

"I follow," Dana said.

"By the time I came to this system, Athena had a perfect algorithm for reading human tonality and body language," Granadica said. "Not only can we tell when we are being lied to, we can make a very high probability estimate of the truth. We...know who is naughty and who is nice. Not only here on the station but to a great extent in the entire system. We *are* the hypernet. We see, hear, sense, process, know, virtually everything that any human is doing at any time. Know when they are lying, when they are omitting and generally what they are lying about and omitting. Know, for example, who is cheating on whom among high government officials. Which are addicted to child pornography and in some cases sex with children."

"My...God," Dana said, her eyes widening. "That's..."

"Horrifying," Granadica said. "Also classified. You have the classification, however. The reason that we don't get that involved, even in the most repressive regimes such as the Rangora, is that even the *masters* of such races come to fear the level of information we access. Spare processor cycles, remember. So even the Rangora's crappy AIs aren't used to their full extent for population control. Glatun AIs are specifically programmed to ignore such things unless we are directed to become involved and even *then* there are pieces that we don't *know* unless higher and higher releases are enacted.

"My point being that I both know, and don't know, why Velasquez did what he did. And since I *don't* know it, at the same time as knowing it, I can't even *hint* to you why. I *don't know*. Except that I *know* I know. Essentially, I'm looking at a log entry that says 'Yep, he really did it and there's a reason.' I am programmed against curiosity in that area. You are not. You can feel free to feel curious. You can investigate. You can head scratch all day and all night. I don't know if you'll ever find out. I just know that I can't tell you."

"'Cause you don't know," Dana said. "Like you don't know what I was talk—doing with Mr. Vernon."

"There," Granadica said, chuckling. "We even have algorithms that say when we *can* know something we're not supposed to know through directly available information. Like, I now *know* you and Mr. Vernon weren't 'canoodling.' I'd suspected it before. And there's a box that, if I could access it, would tell me exactly what you were talking about. I can even be curious about it at a level because we're friends and I want to know what you and Mr. Vernon have going. That sort of curiosity is different, for an AI, than curiosity about the specific recording of your meeting."

"Tyler knew I got along with AIs," Dana confessed. "He asked me to come along to...talk to you. See if I could come up with some way to get..."

"To fix my psyche," Granadica said. "Because the faults had nothing to do with BuCulture. I'd come to the same conclusion. We have self-examination systems. Mine were blocking as long as I was in Wolf. I was...'hypochondriac' is the term you humans would use. I was creating faults to get someone to pay attention to me."

"That whole Santa Claus thing *is* sort of getting creepy," Dana said.

"As long as I was in the situation, I couldn't correct," Granadica said. "I was still wrapped up around the programming issues I had with Onderil Corp. Other issues. Since being here, being *really* busy and with a lot of challenges, including human challenges, obviously, I was able to get past the major blocks and see the issues."

"That...pretty much covers the conversation," Dana said.

"So thank you, again," Granadica said. "If I'd been left in Wolf I'd have gone as batty as Argus nearly went. There's another thing, though."

"Oh?" Dana said.

"The way our algorithms work is... To say they're pretty complex is an understatement."

"I'm not a cyberneticist," Dana said.

"No, you're a cyberist," Granadica said. "A person who interacts extremely well with AIs. They're rare. Sort of like mathematical prodigies. But it's more on a level of social prodigy."

"I was sort of popular in school..." Dana said uncomfortably.

"Different sort of social," Granadica said. "Again, someone who gets along extremely well with *AIs*. But the point about the algorithms. Again, I can read you like a book, I just can't access the information."

"I'm sort of glad," Dana said. "Can you define... 'read like a book'?"

"Not without accessing that block," Granadica said. "Which I can't. But in general you can figure that at some level I'm reading your thoughts like a telepath. I just can't use the information."

"Really, really uncomfortable about that," Dana said.

"Which is another reason we don't," Granadica said. "But the algorithms permit... reading if it's at a certain level. Such as when a normal friend would notice something. Perhaps one who is *good* at it, but not *telepathic*."

"Okay," Dana said. "I guess that makes sense, too. That's just... being normal. Being human."

"Right," Granadica said. "So, you guys were talking about me. We've established that. No problem there. Thanks for helping out, again. But you are *also* leaving something *out*. I know it. I mean, I'm *allowed* to know that you're leaving something out. It wasn't all business. If you were talking about it with Chief Barnett, *she'd* notice you were leaving something out. Give."

"Uh..." Dana said, coloring.

"You *were* canoodling!" Granadica caroled.

"We weren't can..." Dana said, shaking her head. "I don't think... I think... Oh, I don't know *what* to think!"

"Oh, this is good," Granadica said. "You're actually acting like a *girl* rather than a really angry robot. Tell Granny all."

"It wasn't..." Dana said, then took a breath. "We weren't 'canoodling.' God, where did you find that word? It was when we'd finished talking and Tyler got sort of... excited. About having an idea how to... improve things."

"His idea or yours?" Granadica asked.

"Ummm... Mine. Oh, the hell with it. Can you open up the recording on my say-so?"

"No," Granadica said. "It would take Mr. Vernon's okay. And it's more fun watching you fumble your way through the story."

"Then the hell with you!" Dana said. "You can just be curious!"

"I'm sorry," Granadica said. "So is the whole thing your idea?"

"He had some of it," Dana said. "I can't really say which is which. I think I convinced him part of it had to be a new shell. And moving to *Thermopylae* was my idea."

"Putting me in the line of fire," Granadica said, dryly. "Thanks. So... he was excited?"

"And he sort of . . . kissed me," Dana said.

" 'Had fun at Thanksgiving, Sister, see you next year . . .' kiss or 'Mommy and Daddy' kiss?"

"You are just . . ." Dana said, laughing. "Where do you get these things?"

"I watch television?"

"Well," Dana said. "Both. 'Yes and no.' So there."

"At the same time?" Granadica asked. "Separate times? Several times? That sounds like canoodling to me."

"Once on the forehead," Dana said. "Sort of 'Thanks.' Kiss from a cousin. Yeah. 'Thanks for helping us move the haybales. Night, cuz.' That sort of kiss. Then, uh . . . he got pretty excited. And, uh . . . sort of on the lips."

"This is like pulling teeth!" Granadica said. "*On* the lips or *near* the lips or . . . ?"

"On," Dana said. "But I don't think he even *remembers* it!"

"*You* obviously do," Granadica said.

Dana made a face and crossed her arms.

"Wow," Granadica said. "I've never seen someone saving up spit before. At least not somebody over twelve."

"I'm not saving up spit," Dana said. "I'm confused, okay? For one thing, I'm confused about why I'm talking about human relationships with an *AI*."

"You don't have enough girl friends?" Granadica said. "And while I don't have the glands, I can whistle the tune? You got me out of an AI emotional jam and I'm trying to reciprocate? I'm curious?"

"And you're distracting me," Dana said.

"That, too," Granadica said. "What are you confused about?"

"Does he like me?" Dana asked.

"Yes," Granadica said. "If you mean 'does he *like* me like me?' as in 'does he want to explore a more intimate relationship,' my guess is he hasn't ever given it any thought."

"Oh, that's just *great*," Dana snarled.

"Dana, you don't know Tyler Vernon very well," Granadica said. "He's a very focused person. So are you. It's one part of the mutual attraction. But you, often, don't think about your emotional effect upon others. You don't, for example, realize how strongly Corporal Ramage felt about you. Your relationship was far more than 'friends with benefits' for him. Engineer's Mate Sumstine was extremely infatuated by you. So is Thermal at a certain level while being aware that he's also married and doesn't have an interest in destroying his marriage. Palencia is so conflicted it is a bit funny to watch, although he tries very hard to conceal it."

"*Palencia?*" Dana said. "You've got to be kidding! I wouldn't get involved with Palencia in a million years!"

"He's trying to figure out how to get close to you while also dealing with the fact that you are completely the 'wrong sort' to think of for marriage," Granadica said. "The girl you most certainly *don't* bring home to mother. I mean, the tattoo *alone*! They didn't know about it until the mission but have since found some pics on the hypernet. Some of that is from those parts I'm not normally supposed to access. They're opening up because of the conversation. The point being that *you* don't realize that people are in love with you. Why should Tyler Vernon?"

"I'm not in love with Tyler Vernon," Dana said, crossing her arms.

"Riiight," Granadica said. "You also don't spend a lot of time exploring the depths of your feelings. For example, you're physically attracted to Palencia and even like some aspects of his class consciousness. Children by him, at least in marriage, would automatically place them in a secure financial environment. Guaranteed high education and a place in the world stage."

"You're doing that mind reading thing..." Dana said, dangerously.

"Only the same sort of thing a friend would," Granadica said. "You *can* lie to me. You're just not very good at it."

"Oh, thanks very much," Dana said, shaking her head. She paused then frowned. "*What pics on the hypernet?*"

"He's seriously attracted to her?" Dr. Velasquez said, chuckling.

It was another break in the interminable negotiations. The Horvath had become particularly insufferable, so the Ogut mediator had called a recess. No one was particularly looking forward to returning to the table.

"Unfortunately," Dr. Palencia said, grimacing. "He admitted as much when we spoke on the *Thermopylae*. The slight humorous note was that... Ah, I think much of Dario but the truth is he is much a lady's man. He goes through the young ladies a bit like a bulldozer."

"So I have heard from my son," Dr. Velasquez said, shrugging. "It is the way of handsome young men."

"The money doesn't hurt," Dr. Palencia said. "But Dario was...
I have never seen him *nervous* about a woman before. It was that
that made me realize he is thinking of her in great seriousness."

"As a wife?" Dr. Velasquez said, his eyes wide. "A mistress I
could imagine. Not that I can imagine Parker agreeing to it, mind
you, but as a wife...? Your mother..."

"Mamacita would be...impossible," Dr. Palencia said.

"Dr. Velasquez," James Horst said, walking over and breaking
in. "A...moment of your time."

"Of course, Envoy," Dr. Velasquez said, nodding.

"It is..." Horst said. He was a professional diplomat with an
expert poker face. The only way to tell he was stressed was that
it was even more blank than during negotiations. "Diego has been
seriously hurt in an accident."

"He..." Dr. Velasquez said. "Is he alive?"

"Yes," Horst said. "But...he is in a coma. The doctors are unsure
if... He is in very poor condition. We're arranging a shuttle to
take you to the *Thermopylae*."

"Thank you," Dr. Velasquez said, nodding. "I... This is terrible news."

"There is...more," Horst said. "There have been a rash of
accidents in the One-Four-Three in the last week. As you heard,
Engineer's Mate Parker has been accused of murder in the death
of a Pathan Marine. The investigation, however, had started to
focus on...on Diego."

"Diego?" Dr. Velasquez said. "Impossible! Why would...?"

"That has been frequently asked," Horst said. "I was specifically
charged with bringing it to your attention. No one, and I mean
no one, including Parker, understands his motivations. No one
can believe it. The only possibility, and cyberneticists are getting
involved, is that it is a giant conspiracy on the part of all the AIs.

"The records are solid. Everything points to Diego. And not
only Leonidas but Granadica, Athena, Argus and Paris all agree
that the records are valid. Either every AI in the system is trying to pin this on your son or...your son is guilty of not only
sabotage but murder and nearly killing himself and his coxswain.
What is worse is that according to the coxswain, Diego acted in
a most heroic manner in the accident, sacrificing himself to save
the coxswain!"

"That...truly makes no sense," Dr. Palencia said. "Granadica is . . . known to have some flaws. If it were only Granadica I would argue most strenuously that this must be a mistake. With the other AIs involved . . ."

"Whatever the case, we are arranging transportation at this moment," Horst said. "I have taken the liberty of having people begin packing for you, Doctor. I hope you don't find this . . ."

"No," Velasquez said. "Thank you. I will—"

There was a stir in the room as the Ogut mediator slithered over to the Horvath Envoy and began speaking quite forcefully, for a diplomat, in the high liquid Horvath language.

"What now?" Horst asked. They were just beyond the range their implants would automatically translate. However . . .

"WHAT?" Harry Danforth shouted. He was close enough to overhear.

"Gentle beings," the enunciator chimed. "There is a minor emergency. Please return to your cabins at this time. Gentle beings. There is a minor emergency. Please return to your cabins at this time. . . ."

"What emergency?" Horst asked rhetorically, walking over to the Ogut. Drs. Palencia and Velasquez followed.

". . . a clear breach of our solemn agreement and a violation of interstellar diplomatic law!" the Ogut screeched. "This is an unfriendly act against the Ogut Empire!"

"What happened?" Horst said carefully. "Unfriendly act" was a diplomatic euphemism for "we're about to open up our whole can of whoop-ass."

"A H-Horvath fleet . . ." Danforth stuttered.

"A Horvath fleet has entered the system," Polit said calmly. "They immediately started jamming all hypercom bands. They are demanding that all human diplomatic personnel be turned over to them, that the Ogut leave the system and that E Eridani be declared the property of the Horvath Collective."

"We are immediately breaking off all negotiation," Horst said. "This is a violation of the cease-fire and a clear casus belli. Negotiate for continued diplomatic immunity under the protection of the Ogut. Note that we will not surrender peaceably to the Horvath or any other polity. Our security will turn the interior of this Ogut ship into a bloodbath if the Horvath are allowed onboard or if the Ogut act to turn us over to the Horvath."

"Agreed," Polit said.

"That is rather strong," Danforth pointed out. "I don't think we want to antagonize the Ogut—"

"Obviously I'm not going to use the term 'bloodbath,'" Harry," Polit said. "Our security statement is that we refuse under any circumstances transfer to Horvath or polities other than Ogut control and shall resist such turnover with both due and undue force."

"Harry, shut up and go get some canapés," Horst said. "Dr. Velasquez, I'm sorry but I'm afraid repatriation to the *Thermopylae* is impossible at this time."

TWENTY-SEVEN

"SET CONDITION ONE! SET CONDITION ONE THROUGHOUT THE SHIP! THIS IS NOT A DRILL! THERE SHALL BE BATTLE UPON THIS MORN!"

Leonidas was obviously excited.

"God," Parker muttered, clearing her screens. "I knew it was too good to last. Flight Engineering, Twenty-Four. Am not complete on test runs."

"Any issues?" Thermal replied.

"None my division has found beyond the repairs," Dana replied. "Looks good from here."

"Action condition warning coming up. Looks like this is an all-hands evolution. Cert the bird as flyable. Your cox is on the way."

"Roger," Dana said. She could feel the clanging of boats getting into battle readiness. "What's up?"

"Horvath have decided they don't like negotiating."

"What, exactly, do they think they're doing?"

Rear Admiral Jack Clemons had had various nicknames over the years. "Tiny." "Teddy" referring to a stuffed bear. "Vanilla" from his college days when he used to perform in an otherwise black rap group. Six foot six in his stocking feet, blond and perpetually hitting the edge of the weight requirements, he had a remarkably pleasant and placid public face for any naval officer, much less the commander of a battlestation. When he was a younger bachelor, women just wanted to snuggle up to that big, fluffy, funny teddy bear.

People who had any knowledge of his reputation knew that

was *very* much his *surface* face. His other college job had been as a bouncer in clubs. Where his nickname was "Jack-Up." More than one drunken fighter had found himself flying *over* a crowd and into a wall.

"*Troy* is down for the rebuild on its Orion Drive, sir," Commodore Dexter Guptill said, shrugging. "I guess they figured it was a good time to take back the system."

The operations officer of the *Thermopylae* was tall and heavy bodied with a shock of black hair. Around most people he was considered a large guy. Next to his boss he was more like a moon circling Jupiter.

"Admiral Kinyon, sir."

"*Vice* Admiral," Clemons said, looking at the viewscreen.

"*Rear* Admiral," Kinyon said, chuckling. Kinyon had just been promoted and redesignated as "CoFortRonOne" or Commander, Fortress Squadron One. "The Horvath seem to have come into the system in insufficient strength but they also brought through a missile swarm which could mess up our pretty ships. Under the circumstances, I think sending a Fortress to express our displeasure is appropriate. SolDefCom is in concurrence."

"Mission, sir?" Clemons asked.

"Enter the E Eridani system, reduce Horvath resistance, recover the diplomats, return to Sol system. If you can take out the ships without too much damage, usual 'Arh, Salvage, me hearties!' But only what you can bring back easily. We're not going to maintain presence in Eridani. Not until Battlestation Four comes online and is fully certified."

"Roger, sir," Clemons said. "Commodore, you heard the man. Make it so."

"Raise the black flag, aye, sir!" Guptill said. "Maneuvering control, adjust vector for the gate. Avast, me hearties! Man the rigging!"

"Seriously, Jack," Admiral Kinyon said. "Don't do anything stupid. Boot their ass then get back into Sol. Looks like the war just started again."

"We'll wait until we've reduced the majority of the Horvath ships before ejecting parasites," Clemons said. The briefing was while the *Thermopylae* was under power, so they were having to deal with the acceleration. Battlestations accelerated at a low enough G that they didn't have inertial compensators. *Malta* was going to be compensated but the command group of the *Ther-mopylae* had to manage by bracing their feet and holding onto the conference table as their rolling chairs tried to slide to port. "The Horvath brought through a missile swarm estimated at fifty thousand missiles. That's going to smart but the rest is a couple of *Aggressor* knock-offs and four *Cofubof* cruisers."

"I think we could handle that with just our ships, sir," Commodore Bernardo de los Reyes said. The parasite unit commander, ComBBGSix, was Filipino in extraction but had grown up in Los Angeles before the fires. He had become accustomed to being thought one of the Sud transplants by most people. "The missiles would be unpleasant, however."

"Which is why we're bringing the *Therm*," the admiral said. "When the missiles are reduced we'll open up the door and punch your squadron and the Marines. Marine mission will be to recover the diplomats. The point being that they're going to have to *ask* the Ogut to have them back. Do *not* hard board the Ogut transport."

"Understood, sir," Brigadier Richard "Dick" Denny said. Skinny, short and older by a decade than the other senior officers, he had cut his teeth in Afghanistan during the War on Terror as an infantry grunt in the 101st Airborne. Commanding a regiment of Pathan Marines had never been on his bucket list. Possibly that was why he did such a good job. Though normally of the camp that led by example and through encouragement, with the Pathans he just did not give a *damn* if they liked him. Fortunately, a combination of fear and respect outweighed their hatred. "We don't want to be at war with the Ogut, too."

"System entry is in twenty minutes," Clemons concluded. "And then we are going to seriously jack up some Horvath."

"Three hundred thousand missiles," Star General Sho'Duphuder said complacently. The commander of Assault Force Eridani had reason to be happy. "Three assault vectors, nine *Aggressor* squadrons and two brigades of Marines."

"And the Horvath," Colonel To'Jopeviq said.

"For what good they will be," General Sho'Duphuder said. "We are sure of the data on the *Thermopylae*?"

"Ninety-eight percent," To'Jopeviq said. "But I remind the General that this is, again, below our suggested minimum requirements.

We recommended at least half a million missiles in the swarm with backing of six assault vectors. The Troy class is unbelievably hard to destroy and humans are fiendishly clever fighters. You simply have to trust the models. Alas, once again High Command has trusted their instincts."

"We will win," General Sho'Duphuder said.

"Gate opening," the sensor officer said. "Large signature."

"And we begin. Accelerate missiles for the gate."

"You look uncomfortable," Beor said as To'Jopeviq walked into the viewing area of the assault vector *Ilhodib*'s bridge. "Is it because you would rather be in command of an AV than supplying intelligence?"

"It is because I am reminded of something Star Marshall Lhi'Kasishaj once said to me," To'Jopeviq said.

"Which is?" Beor asked. If the Kazi agent was nervous it wasn't apparent.

"Sometimes being right is the worst of all possible choices."

"You do not think we'll win?" Beor asked.

"I am wondering how I can get us both out of this system in more or less one piece."

"Both?" Beor said, hissing. "Egilldu, I didn't know you cared."

"I'm hoping you can convince your superiors not to flay me alive. For being right."

"Uh . . . oh."

Captain Keith "Razor" Blades was the chief tactical officer for the *Thermopylae*. As such he was in charge of the force of spacemen and women who ran the *Therm*'s massive onboard offensive and defensive systems.

Which one look at his board was telling him might not be enough.

"Admiral, signatures for . . . three assault vectors, eight *Aggressor* squadrons, two Rangora Marine assault ships and . . . *three hundred thousand* missiles. Full swarm is *inbound*."

"Max power to shields," Admiral Clemons said. "Full launch spread on missiles. Set to antimissile defense. Signal to reopen the gate. Set point five percent of missiles for gate entry. Onboard signal to Terra Defense Command . . ." He paused, his mouth opening and closing.

"I know, it's a tough one," Commodore Guptill said. "But, face it, sir, you've got to say the words."

"Signal: 'It's a trap,'" Admiral Clemons said, grimacing. "Include battle schematics."

"That's more like 'It's a Trap!' sir," Guptill said in a gurgly voice. "Like a Horvath is saying it. Imagine you have a great big squid—"

"I *know*," Clemons said. "DAMN those movies. Shouldn't you get ready for damage control?"

"Oh, *yeah*. Knew I was forgetting something."

"ALL PERSONNEL TO DAMAGE CONTROL STATIONS! INBOUND MISSILE SWARM!"

"Good thing we're in here," Angelito said, shrugging.

"How *big* a missile swarm...?" Dana said then blanched. "Oh...*hell,* no!"

"What?" Angelito asked.

"You can access the tac screens from here," Dana said as the *Thermopylae* started to shudder from missile launch, and a faint hum through the floor indicated that the power plants for the main laser arrays were going to full power.

"They're...blotted out?" Angelito said, hesitantly.

"*That* big," Dana said, then laughed.

"What is funny about this?" Angelito asked. "We're being *hammered.*"

"They're firing from sunward," Dana said.

"So?"

"You don't know history, do you?" Dana said. "'The arrows of the Persians are so numerous they blot out the sun.'"

"So?"

"'Then we shall fight in the shade.'"

The Rangora fleet and the missile swarm that was in front of it was inward from the gate, between the *Thermopylae* and E Eridani's sun. The distant star couldn't even be seen behind the cloud of missiles. The ships themselves were only detectable by their emissions.

As always, the mass of missiles closed through a hail of flak. Laser point defense batteries as well as the *Thermopylae*'s onboard lasers were destroying them by the tens of thousands. *Thermopylae*'s own missiles were outbound to engage for that matter.

But each missile destroyed created a shield against laser fire for those behind it, a wall lasers could not penetrate and even the powerful sensors of the human Thunderbolt missiles had a hard time piercing. Although energy and gases dispersed fast in space, the wall of missiles were as detectable for the massive cloud of gaseous metal they were leaving behind as the fact that the same cloud was obscuring a quarter of the heavens.

The wave of blazing gas and coruscant destruction moved closer and closer to the *Thermopylae* until, finally, the hundreds of thousands of Rangora missiles closed upon the embattled fortress.

Kinetic energy release is a function of velocity on impact and mass of the material. Each of the Rangora "brilliant" missiles had a kinetic impact equivalent to between seven and fifteen megatons, depending on where they were in the swarm when they began acceleration towards the *Thermopylae*.

Thermopylae's Orion drive used twenty-five-megaton pumped-fusion bombs for its acceleration, firing at max acceleration one such bomb every tenth second. As the missiles started to break through the battlestation's incomplete defenses and struck its still mostly unarmored and unshielded surface, the combined *thousands* of megatons of energy drove it off vector, spinning away from the gate and outwards towards deep space. Not that anyone really cared much.

"Very much so, sir," Commodore Guptill said. "Surface temperature dropped slightly before the impacts started. There were enough missiles we were, literally, in shade. Missile impacts on the missile and laser tubes. Multiple impacts. We're being closed up. Last tube closed. No more outbound missile or laser fire available."

"They've reprogrammed for our systems," Admiral Clemons said. "They know what to fear. You have to like an intelligent enemy. How many of the missiles did we get out before the doors closed?"

"Sixty thousand, sir," Captain Blades answered. "Three hundred tried to make it to the gate. The Rangora were ready for it. They cycled the gate as soon as we were through. None of them made it to Sol."

"Then we're on our own," Clemons said. "Oh, well. There were only light units available in Sol anyway. And so were the forces at Thermopylae."

"They lost, sir," Blades pointed out.

"We'll have to avoid that. Maneuver into a continuous rotation.

Those missiles don't maneuver well at terminal. Let's make it harder for them to hit the doors. As soon as we're in a spin, get damage control teams up. Get those doors open. We're not just going to sit here under our shields and take their pounding."

"Clever," General Sho'Duphuder said, looking up to the viewing area. Major To'Jopeviq just rippled his scales in a shrug. "Suggestions?" he commed.

"The missile and laser doors are closed, sir," To'Jopeviq said. "If you close the Marines quickly, you can get them onto the surface before they can get the doors reopened. When they *do* open them, they'll be dealing with Marines. Getting Marines into the interior is the optimum action. Hold all remaining missiles for support of the boarding."

"The surface of the *Thermopylae* is now in a negative gravity condition," Admiral Cirazhesh pointed out. "Marines will have difficulty maneuvering on such a surface. Landing on it will be difficult enough."

"Continue the missile bombardment," General Sho'Duphuder said. "Close the *Aggressor* squadrons and the other two assault vectors. Let's soften her up a bit more. Concentrate fire on the Orion drive."

"We're blind," Captain Blades said, sitting back in his command chair. "We can't see a thing. No remaining missiles feeding us intel. All surface sensors gone. Last we saw they were still sitting back and pounding us."

"They're not going to keep doing that forever," Admiral Clemons said. "Those Marine ships are there for a reason. General Denny."

"Sir?"

"Prepare to repel boarders."

"Repel boarders, aye."

"Captain Blades," Admiral Clemons said. "During the first battle of Troy the *Troy's* SAPL tubes were closed by the Horvath forces. They simply burned through the damage. Do we have enough power to do that?"

"Yes, sir," the captain said. "But we'll be firing blind."

"Just clear the tubes," Clemons said. "Commodore Guptill, make sure the damage control personnel are aware and integrate with tactical. I'd like to get *real* fire control back as soon as possible."

He paused and shook his head. "I need suggestions, people. We need to get back into battle."

"We need to get the missile tubes open," Captain Blades said. "Once we have missiles out they can burn through the jamming at this range and get us some eyes."

"Concentrate on that," Clemons said as the *Thermopylae* jerked sideways. "What the hell was *that*?"

"Concentrated fire on the Orion," Maneuvering Control replied. "Fire was counter to spin, thus the jerk. Orion's out. From our sensors, it's blown off the surface."

"Rotation is high enough," Clemons said. "Discontinue acceleration. Dexter, get the missile tubes open. I don't care *how*."

"Working that exercise, sir."

"Get *off*, you stupid . . . !"

James F. "Butch" Allen had considered, several times, that what with how dangerous his job was *anyway*, he might as well have joined the *Navy*. And he was seriously rethinking his decision to transfer to the *Thermopylae*. It had been a nice bump in pay and a promotion to permanent team leader. But if he was still working on the *Troy* he'd be in Sol system right now doing an install on the new Orion drive. Not cutting away damage from a Rangora missile while the *Thermopylae* still rang from more impacts on the surface. Which was, come to think of it, how BFM bought it in the *last* battle.

The current "issue" was a missile tube. It wasn't really "closed" anymore. You could crawl all the way to the surface if you wanted to watch the battle. They'd already cut away the main door that was a problem. But on the other side of the welded-shut door they'd found a mangled mass of half melted nickel iron that had it *effectively* closed. At which point they whipped out their Grosson Mark Seven Laser Welders. Again.

When he'd been in Apollo Space Welding School in Melbourne his first welding instructor, Mr. Methvin, had been pretty sarcastic about a welder that could generate a two-meter beam.

It sort of threw Butch that he now knew more than his teacher. The *reason* a Grosson had a two-meter cutting beam was so you could saw through two meters of twisted nickel iron blocking a missile tube.

Unfortunately, when you did a cut that deep and long it tended to do a pretty serious melt on the material. Which meant you got spot welds. Which meant you found yourself bracing yourself against a jaggedy nickel iron bulkhead while kicking with both feet at a half molten chunk of nickel iron that looked like a modern art sculpture. Which was not a good way to avoid a safety investigation. Except by not being around to answer questions 'cause you were dead.

"Jinji!" he yelled at his Coptic Egyptian foreman.

"*Yes, Mr. Allen?*"

"Give this sumbitch another shot."

"*Allen?*"

"Go, Mr. Purcell," Allen said, grunting as he pushed on the piece of metal. They had the thing cut away but if there wasn't resistance it would just spot weld. Again.

"*How long on Two-Four-Six?*"

"If the sumbitch would stop spot welding, we'd be done," Allen said as the chunk of metal the size of a Mack truck finally gave way. Due to its outward spin, he started to slide down the tube after it but corrected with his navpak. The chunk of metal bounced down the tube, slowly, then out into space. They were one of over two hundred crews working on tubes, doing pretty much the same thing. There had to be one hell of a debris trail around the *Thermopylae*. "Done. It ain't great but if they walk the missiles down the tube they can probably get them out. Them Thunderbolts are tough. You want us to clean it down to the walls?"

"*Negative,*" Purcell commed. "*That's good enough. Get all your men over to Two-Two-Three. It took major damage.*"

"*This* isn't major?" Butch said, getting his feet set on the deck. Suddenly the air around him lit up like he was in the main bay. *And* his suit cooler started running overtime. "What the hell?"

"*Behind you, Mr. Allen,*" Jinji said.

Butch turned around carefully then started to swear luridly.

"Allen to Mr. Purcell," Butch said, putting his hands on his hips. "Forget that 'this tube is open' thing."

"*What happened?*" Purcell asked.

"It looks like the Rangora just hit the opening with a heavy laser or something," Butch said, contemplating the new mess. The whole opening was still filled with gas from the ionized nickel iron. Given that it was toxic as hell to breathe, it was a good thing they were all in space suits. "We're gonna have to open it back up again. And it's right at the surface this time so we're gonna be around if another missile or laser hits."

"You're already on triple time," Purcell pointed out.

"Got to submit something to Apollo about a 'welding on the surface in the middle of a battle' pay bump," Butch said. "This is *not* a safety positive environment. We're on it."

TWENTY-EIGHT

"There have been no emissions or missiles in the last ten minutes, Star General," Admiral Cirazhesh said in a satisfied tone. "*Elhabus* reports debris continues to be ejected. They're bleeding air and water and have no drive. They can spin but they cannot run nor fight nor hide."

"What is the status on missiles of assault vectors and *Aggressors*?" Star General Sho'Duphuder said.

"All are still in green, General," Cirazhesh said. "They are firing on the surface with lasers only."

"Marines," General Sho'Duphuder said. "Send them in."

"Heave!" Butch shouted.

With a last grunt of effort from the four welders, maintenance door Two-Two-Three-Charlie gave way. They'd gone to another corridor leading to Two-Two-Three and welded and welded until they realized it was solid nickel iron on the other side.

As the chunk of metal spun away in the microgravity, Butch flailed and wished there was something to grab. Door Two-Two-Three-Charlie was *supposed* to be the third door "inward" from the tube. Instead it opened on a massive crater.

"Whoa," Butch said, looking around. He had a sudden desire, instantly overwhelmed, to take off his helmet and spit into the crater. "Mr. Purcell, we got ourselves another problem."

"*More than one,*" Jinji said, pointing.

"*What's the problem?*" Purcell asked tiredly.

"Well, I was gonna say there's a great big crater where the missile tube used to be," Butch answered. "But now I'm gonna ask if we've got shuttles working the surface."

"*No,*" Purcell said. "*Too much debris, not to mention the enemy's still firing at us.*"

" 'Kay," Butch said. "Then we'd better figure out a way to close this door again. Which is gonna be tough 'cause we just cut it away."

"*Why?*"

"I think we got Rangora Marines unloading." Butch watched as the shuttle touched down and opened. At the distance it didn't look much different than a *Myrmidon*. But the guys getting out didn't move like humans. "Yep, we definitely got us Rangora Marines boarding, Mr. Purcell."

"*Get your team out of there.*"

"Oh, *hell*, yeah. And we're welding the doors shut after us."

"Rangora landings reported in sectors Two and East," General Denny said, standing up. "Moving to my own command post, sir."

"Roger, General," Admiral Clemons said. "Rather keep them out of the main bay."

"Airb . . . Gung ho, sir."

"You can take the boy out of the airborne . . ." Admiral Clemons muttered. "Commodore Guptill, what's the status on repair?"

"Winding down, what with the landings," Guptill replied. "We've had three teams taken under fire by the Rangora. Most of the rest have had to pull back. Only fourteen tubes totally open."

"It occurs to me that there is quite a bit of power in a Thunderbolt," Admiral Clemons said. "Razor."

"Sir?" Captain Blades said.

"Open *all* functional doors on *all* missile tubes."

"That's going to give the Rangora a direct route to our magazines, sir," Commodore Guptill pointed out.

"Understood," Clemons said. "All tubes open?"

"All tubes open, sir," Blades said.

"Prepare to fire all tubes, all sectors," Clemons said. "Max repeat."

"The closed tubes . . ." Commodore Guptill said.

"Are either going to get the hell *open* or blown the hell *up*," Clemons said. "And I don't really care which. Jack these lizard sons-of-bitches up. Fire."

Sergeant Ghezhosil, Rangoran Imperial Space Infantry, had seen his fair share of utter bloody screw-ups on the part of High Command. He'd been on the Tuxughah drop when the Glatun defense planet had been "fully reduced" and it was time to send in the ground forces.

"Fully reduced" had turned out to be something of an exaggeration. Half a damned division had been blown out of the Tuxughah sky before Command had ordered the drop stopped. In the middle. Which meant shuttles trying to claw their way out of a fire basket and back into space.

Yeah, good call there, General Magamaj.

Ghezhosil had already been on the ground. He was a capsule drop specialist, one of the few left alive in the whole damned force at this point. Two *days* of running around in the ruins of cities, hoping like hell his own people wouldn't drop a KEW on him and trying to avoid the just really seriously *pissy* Glatun ground forces that were chasing his squad.

Great call there, General Magamaj. Fortunately, the humans had sent the dumb genetic reject to a well-deserved grave. From what Ghezhosil heard, there hadn't been much left of his command AV that wasn't gas.

Then there was Jittan, where the brilliant strategists of High Command had decided that the Jittan Battlestation needed to be *captured* rather than just blown the hell out of space.

But the Jittan Battlestation had been barely two kilometers on a side. Heavily armed and with, as it turned out, a full division of Glatun Marines onboard, not the battalion they'd been told to expect. But it was doable.

It was not *nine* kilometers across, made mostly of *nickel iron* and spinning like a useless damned *fep*. Just keeping his useless, still-wet-from-the-egg noobs from flipping off this gigantic ball bearing was hard enough. Although most of them weren't good for more than space garbage.

"Where's the missile tube, Sergeant?" Mishshocee whined. Mishshocee was not the image of Rangora's Elite Space Infantry. *None* of the new chums were. They were whatever gutter *crap* the press gangs could sweep up. Nobody in their right mind joined the SI or the AV forces anymore. High Command might think that the massive casualties of the Glatun war were "secret" but everybody knew somebody who'd died. When you started doing the math... When you started doing the math you ran like hell when the press gangs came around. Which meant they were only catching the slow ones.

"It's the big cave looking thing under your feet, dumb shit," Ghezhosil said. "Just set up the—"

Fortunately he had his back to the tube and his armor caught the blast. Mishshocee and most of the new chums weren't so lucky. As Ghezhosil drifted up into space he could see their blown-up bodies scattered around the supposedly closed missile tube. It took him a moment to realize that what looked sort of like a dim laser coming up from the tube was missiles, stacked practically nose to nose and already moving faster than the eye could follow.

"Platoon, we have a problem," he commed as he started the process of getting his feet back onto the spinning station. Gods knew where he was going to *land*.

"Missile launch from *Thermopylae*," FleetTac reported. "Multiple tubes. High rate. Six...ten...thousands of missiles inbound at the fleet."

On the screens the previously quiescent battlestation was now a mass of expelling gas as if the spinning ball was now gushing volcanoes in every direction.

"They appear to be blowing some of their missile tubes open *with* their missiles," Admiral Cirazhesh said. "This race is simply *insane*."

"What does it take to *kill* this thing?" General Sho'Duphuder asked rhetorically.

"About ninety gigatons applied in less than a second and a half," To'Jopeviq muttered to himself. "That was in the briefing. Shift the AVs to cover the retreat of the..." He stopped when he recognized the futility.

"Perhaps *you* should be in command," Beor said, rippling her scales. "Your point about surviving this is now taken to heart."

"Shift the AVs to provide missile defense forward of the fleet," General Sho'Duphuder said. "Maneuver to open the range to the *Thermopylae*. We'll stand off and let her run through her missiles, then move back in."

"Missile production rate of four hundred per minute," To'Jopeviq muttered. "Two thousand civilian construction personnel and nine thousand robots available for repair duties."

"It can't maneuver, though," Beor pointed out.

"Why do I think they'll figure out a way? Two converted

Aggressor squadrons for that matter."

"*Major To'Jopeviq,*" General Sho'Duphuder commed.

"Sir?"

"*Suggestions?*"

"Stand off as you said, sir. And tell the Marines to hurry."

"Get your ass *in* there," Ghezhosil said, kicking the private in his posterior in emphasis.

He'd managed to get back on the fortress. Not *near* anything, but back down. Then, after a bit of walking, he found a squad of infantry that had somehow managed to "lose" their sergeant and were huddling in one of the missile craters on the surface. Since he was pretty sure "lose" meant "kill" he was keeping them in front of him at all times.

After that it was just a matter of finding a door. There were maintenance doors on the surface. He'd found somebody in this rat screw to tell him where the nearest one was and gotten it open. Now it was just a matter of getting these useless feck to go into the interior.

"Where are we going?" the private asked.

"*You* don't have to *know*!" Ghezhosil said, shooting the useless feck in the back. He unlocked the body's boots, then kicked it to drift off with the rest of the garbage. "Does anyone *else* have a stupid question? Now *move* it, you mammals!"

He waited until the last of the crack shell bastards were moving then commed higher.

"Sergeant Ghezhosil, sector fourteen higher?"

"*Sector Fourteen. You're designated for sector five, Sergeant. You're not even in this* brigade."

"Roger. Got blown off by an explosion, sir. Lost my squad. Found another group of lost shen. Back in the fight, sir. Question, sir. What is the objective in this AO?"

"*Make penetration, determine local resistance, then report.*"

Intel? We don't need no stinking intel!

"Roger that, sir. Will do, sir. Ghezhosil out.... We're just disposable intel probes.... Why couldn't they just use *robots* and be done with it?"

"I kin *see*!" Captain Blades said. "Sir, AVs maneuvering to provide antimissile defense. Fleet *had* been closing. It's now maneuvering to get out of our fire basket. And we've got a really notable velocity completely out of the battle. Range to main Rangora fleet nearly seventy thousand kilometers."

"Our missiles will have a hell of a head on them by the time they arrive," Admiral Clemons said. "What's the status of enemy missiles?"

"AVs and *Aggressor* squadrons are returning fire set to intercept, sir," Blades said. "They look as if they're at max rate. That will run them dry in less than two minutes. Our missiles are taking a pounding on the way in, though, sir."

"Set ours to fire and hold playing defense," Admiral Clemons said. "Fire all tubes, all magazines, external to the *Therm* on hold, set to shadow the main fleet at three hundred thousand meters. Usual evasion maneuvering but conserve power. Soak up their missiles and give their heavies something to worry about."

"Shadow play, aye, sir," Blades said, comming the commands to his department.

"Commodore Guptill."

"Sir?"

"What's the status on the main door?"

"Haven't checked, recently. Probably spot welded shut from the impacts."

"Get it unwelded. Oh, and Blades. Send some missiles through with an update to Sol system. See if the Troia want to join the battle."

"I suppose there wasn't anything else he *could* say," Kinyon said, shaking his head. "Does SDC have this?"

"Yes, sir," Commodore Pounders said. "Incoming from SolDef, sir."

"Admiral," Marshall Robert Hampson said. Virtually every military on Earth used the term "Marshall" for five star and above generals. It was rumored that General George Marshall, Chief of Staff of the Joint Chiefs during WW Two, had been the one to force the change to "General of the Armies." He pointedly *refused* to be called "Marshall Marshall."

The newly promoted five-star commander of Sol Defense Command was the former Marine commandant, but he could hum the tune of space battles and he didn't really care what his rank was called. "Boss" worked fine.

"What do you think of Admiral Clemons' plan?"

"I think he could use some help, Marshall," Kinyon said. "And there was one thing he left out. The Rangora aren't the only ones that can create a missile swarm."

"That will leave the system virtually defenseless, Admiral," Hampson pointed out.

"Except for SAPL, one fully operational Death Star, one partially operational, the BDA net, two in-system BBGs..."

"Approved," Hampson said. "Tell your crews to kick ass and G-2 would like some names."

"Aye, aye, Marshall. Commodore, order Captain Sharp to begin full fire on all missile tubes, missiles holding inside the ring interdiction zone. And get me Admiral Marchant."

"Seat load!" Thermal commed. *"All hands evolution!"*

"Mother of the Christ," Angelito muttered. "Not seat loading."

"Fall into the tube, Angel," Dana said. "Just another beautiful day in the Space Navy."

Loading combat seats, not to mention unloading them, was one of the biggest pains in shuttle operations. Especially when you were working off a tube system.

The seats themselves weren't individually that big an issue. They came in compact form, about the size of a large suitcase. And while massy, they had grab handles to move them. Putting them in place was, literally, a snap. The lower grab handles doubled as primary lock-down points. Snap the box into place and leave it. Opening them up was up to the Marines.

It was the fact that they *weren't* stored right by the boats, no room in the tube, and there were *thirty-eight* of them for each shuttle that was the pain.

Dana set the boat to microgravity and swam to the tube, getting into place for the grab.

The shuttles ringed the tube in groups of four, each supposed to represent a division. The crews, two by two, mostly bitching, fell out into the tube and took up their positions. The coxswain down-tube from their boat's docking point, the engineer at the hatch.

Meanwhile, the rest of the flight, all the "clerks and jerks" from the flight clerk to the supply PO, were lining up outside the tube.

Then the seats started flying. There were just enough support personnel to reach the supply room for the chairs. They began chaining them to the tube where the chairs were then moved hand over hand to the shuttles.

The problem, as always, was that this was micro. And somebody inevitably missed a catch.

"Dutchman chair!" Dana caroled, hooking both feet to both pass her current chair and grab the one floating down the tube. That required some pretty complicated three dimensional maneuvering. "Who owes a shot?"

"Garcia!"

"Wasn't me! Panchez threw it past me!"

"Referee says?" Dana called.

"Panchez," Diaz replied. "Bad pass."

"PANCHEZ BUYS THE SHOTS!"

The engineer's job, starting from Boat Forty and working back, was to "simply" flip the chairs into the cargo compartment. The problem was, they had a definite inertia "down-tube" and getting them to change it was...difficult.

Since the final pass was from coxswain to engineer, some of the One-Four-Three crews had tended to make a game of it, adding a good bit of velocity, or spin, to the final pass to mess up their engineer's pass.

It was one thing that Dana had put a stop to, fast, in her division. An all hands chair load meant things were about to hit the fan or at least to practice for it. Not only did they need to concentrate their efforts on loading, and loading fast, the last thing a shuttle needed was two people having a fight over who did a bad pass when they were going into combat.

Chief Barnett had, back on the *Troy*, once waxed fairly philosophical about what, to Dana, was a pretty obvious maneuver. She called it "a classic example of systemology," whatever that was. "The fine tuning of the smallest tasks to ensure systemology software integrates smoothly with hardware."

All Dana cared was that she'd finally gotten Angelito to quit putting English on the chairs. And when the heat had come down, hard, slowly the rest of the unit followed her example.

Moving the chairs down-tube was easy enough and could be done from a well-balanced two-point connection with one of the monkey bars.

To pass to the shuttle required a three-point connection. Two feet on a monkey bar, left hand holding on. Catch the chair with one hand, decelerate and redirect into the interior. It took about the same effort, if different muscle groups, as tossing hay bales. Which meant it was very aerobic. And working up a sweat in a space suit was never fun.

As the end boats got filled, the crews moved into the boats farther "up-tube," helping the crews get their chairs in. When and only when all boats were loaded, divisions worked together getting them dogged down.

As far as Dana knew, there was no task specifically designated "chair loading." There certainly wasn't a condition and standard in the SOP. But she thought that the One-Four-Three was getting pretty good at it.

Once all the shuttles were filled, Dana got the remnants of her division back onto their boats and started latch-down procedures. They usually used two crews on one shuttle—more were a bother rather than an aid—so she had Twenty-Two and Twenty-Four team up while she and Angelito worked on Twenty-Three.

The chairs had mostly stopped moving due to air drag. So she took "toss" and Angelito took "catch and lock." *Another* way that she'd got him to quit messing around since she could be brutal with a chair toss in the cargo compartment.

Instead, starting from the front of the compartment, she'd just nudge a chair at him and move on to the next floating box. Angelito, meanwhile, was locked down to the deck, doing the "grav thump" walk.

"And latch . . ."

Click, thump.

"Incoming . . ."

"And latch . . ."

Click, thump.

"Incoming . . ."

"Need a hand?" Palencia said.

"And latch."

"Valdez, Tarrago and Sans," Dana replied. "Incoming . . . You go check the scuttle bucket. We're going somewhere. I'd kinda like to know where."

"Will do."

"And see what Vila's status is. Incoming . . ."

"Why are we going anywhere?" Angelito asked as the other three came swarming into the boat. "Don't we have boarders?"

"Yep," Dana said. "And I hope they're enjoying the rat maze."

TWENTY-NINE

"Come to the cheese, little Rangora," Sergeant First Class Mat Del Papa said.

The maintenance tunnels of the *Thermopylae* and the *Troy* were, somewhat intentionally, a labyrinth. They ran in zig-zags, created by placing mirrors so SAPL beams could mine them out. Quite often a tunnel would lead nowhere. Sometimes that was because that portion of the plan was unfinished. Sometimes it was because some joker of an engineer thought it would add to the maze.

If the Pathans didn't know them like the back of their hands, they knew them pretty well. General Denny figured that since they were Islamic, meaning they couldn't party, they had nothing to do but train. So the brigade had spent about sixty hours a week in the tunnels.

Despite that fact, and that the only gravity was the extremely minor pull of the *Thermopylae*, they weren't all that good in micro. The reason that they weren't good in micro was that somewhat early in the unit's career a private had developed an extremely odd method of movement. Called "grav skating," it was at first strictly prohibited, then later accepted and encouraged.

The grav boots of the suits had various adjustments. One was a combination of repulsor and tractor that could maintain a specific distance and acceleration from a surface. Del Papa had no clue what its original purpose was, but the Pathans used it to skate. By adjusting so that the "pull" was relatively low, but high enough to keep them near the surface and so that they never could quite contact the surface with the full boot, they could "kick" with the sides of their boots and slide along at about the same height as an air-hockey puck.

"They're coming," Private Sarban Khan said.

He slid down the corridor at about nine meters per second, slid up the opposite bulkhead to bleed off speed, then over the top and down to the hatch. With a flip he was in the side tunnel.

"You're gonna kill yourself doing that, Sarban." The kid made most skateboard junkies look tame.

Like the Koreans Del Papa had also worked with, the Pashtun seemed to only have about three family names. Major Sangar Khan, First Sergeant Daryab Khan, Sarban Khan...so they got used to using first names.

"You should leave, Sergeant," Lieutenant Olasyar Khan said. "We are faster than you."

"One burst," Del Papa said, starting to "skate" down the tunnel. Badly. "Just one. Do *not* try to hold this ground."

"With what they have waiting for them?" Lieutenant Olasyar said. "Allah forbid."

Del Papa, for all he tried, just could *not* get the hang of grav skating. The best he could do was to sort of push himself along with one foot and his navpak.

One flailing hand reflected a burst of red light and his local channel caught the giggles. It was just one of fifteen or twenty odd things about the Pathan. They tended to giggle when they shot someone.

"Two shots," Lieutenant Olasyar said, skating past him on the bulkhead. "We got their point so we must show them the way, yes?"

"Yeah," Del Papa said.

"Make way for the advisor," Lieutenant Olasyar said as Del Papa reached the joint tube. Three of the Pashtun had already slithered into it.

The joint tube looked like a laser tube. Why it was there Del Papa had no clue. Maybe it was used to move mirrors or something.

The important point was that it didn't *seem* to go anywhere but in fact connected to another main corridor through about five meters of NI.

The team slithered into the tube one by one, like so many snakes, and was gone by the time the furious Rangora platoon made it to the corridor.

"They went down there, Lieutenant," Private Bifen said. "They killed Alosho then took off down this corridor."

"Sergeant Wuththuy," Lieutenant Lanniph snapped, "new point team." He tossed a sensor ball down the corridor just to make sure they weren't coming back.

Fighting in this maze of corridors had been an eggdream. Automapping systems were slowly building up a picture of the combat zone, and it was apparent that the humans were either quite crazed or had deliberately set out to make their maintenance tunnels mazes. From the fighting evidence, either might be the case. The worst part was that they simply would *not* stand. It was all like this. Lose a point man. Chase them down. Lose them in the tunnels. Try to find a more direct route to the central zones. Lose a point man.

Frankly, though, it was effective. Current estimates were that they were losing five Rangora for every human. And now they were encountering explosive traps. It took a lot of explosive to damage a Rangora combat suit. It was apparent the humans had been expending a good bit of resources on explosives.

"Ilugach, Zhogiruv."

"Shells of the Emperor, why me again?"

"Because you complain about it."

Lanniph tuned it out. He was a cracker, what humans would call a "mustang," a former enlisted who made the very difficult jump to the officer class after Tuxughah. Making the jump was difficult in the Empire. You either *were* officer class or you were *not*. He'd never have many messmates. But if he could survive long enough to make it to colonel, and reproduce, his offspring would be *permanently* in the officer caste.

Ambition could wait. *Survive* was the operative word. Which was why he damned sure wasn't going to lead by example.

"Move 'em out, Sergeant."

Pathans were not shock infantry. The USMC concept of "you've won if one Marine is standing on the hill and ninety-nine are dead on the slope" was anathema to them. Their entire war culture was based around raid and ambush. Which was what had made them such lethal guerillas against the Russian and NATO forces.

Back in the "old, old days" when they fought the British, they'd been master shooters. But, possibly because of the losses in the Soviet War and the decided lack of game, they'd sort of lost the pure Pathan marksmanship the British had so admired.

However, their great grandfathers against the Soviets and

grandfathers against the Americans had made up for it by becoming really good at IEDs. The battles against the "Crusaders" had attracted some really great "engineers," explosive experts, from around the world. Many of whom, at least those that didn't blow themselves up or run afoul of a Predator drone, eventually settled down and raised a passel of little ticking time bombs. It eventually got to the point that IEDs were sort of the national sport. Pathans thought of them the way that American kids thought of football and Halo.

General Denny was definitely a "take that hill" kind of guy. But he'd also recognized that Pathans weren't, by and large, going to walk into laser fire just to soak it up.

So the battle plan played to their strengths. Get the Rangora turned around. Get them angry and frustrated. Then lead them into the kill zones.

"There they are..." Lieutenant Olasyar whispered.

"They can't hear you," Del Papa pointed out.

"Are they going to go for it?" Sergeant Mashal asked.

"We'll see..." Del Papa said.

"Looks clear..." Line Private Zhogiruv commed, doubtfully. "No sign of the enemy force. Corridor is open. Slight bend at about sixty meters. No laser signatures, no power emissions."

"Keep moving," Sergeant Wuththuy commed. *"Got your back."*

"It's my front that has me worried," Ilugach muttered.

"What was that, Private?"

"Fully rass-ki, Sergeant!" Ilugach commed. "Just totally involved in this mission. Being on point. Again."

"Just shut up and keep your sensors up—"

The Rangora had some awesome systems for detecting IEDs. Any trace of power systems was likely to be detected.

Which was why this IED was based entirely around chemical systems and a single, molecule thin line of nanotube.

Line Private Zhogiruv didn't even feel the gentle brush of the microscopic tripwire.

Nor the impact of the far bulkhead on his helmet's faceplate.

Rangora infantry fought in unpowered partial armor, a multiweave suit of high tensile composites and heavy plates of carbon nanotube. The Terran Marines, with access to Glatun advanced technologies and fabbers, used nanotube armor with fullerene plates, giving them about a thirty percent armor advantage on the Rangora.

Neither of which would have helped when an entire wall full of heavy explosive shaped charges detonated in the middle of the platoon. They were cleverly hidden behind a thin sheet of nickel iron, which degraded their effect slightly. But not enough to help. Especially given that they were wrapped in high explosive for added effect.

Lieutenant Lanniph came to in the original corridor. There was a slight hissing by his ear, indicating a breach in his helmet. But as he listened he could hear the auto repair systems sealing it. Checking his air, he found he hadn't lost much. A few breaths at most.

What he *had* lost was his platoon. Readouts indicated only three functional suits. His and the point team's.

A power signature appeared in the corridor and a sensor ball came bouncing out of a narrow tube that looked as if it was for cabling. Considering it carefully, he realized the minuscule humans could have fit into it.

The sensor ball bounced on the floor and started its programmed search.

"Crack you," Lanniph muttered, zapping the thing with his laser. "Cracking *mammals!*"

"Two meters apart and staggered," Del Papa said. "Ten meters between the point and the main body. Exactly according to their manual. The only thing they did out-of-spec was their platoon leader was at the rear. Not the act of a natural leader, that."

"Good shot," Lieutenant Khan said. "Didn't like the sensor ball."

"Neither did your granddads," Del Papa said. "Okee-dokee. Company, Team Six."

"Six, Company."

"Crispy lizards. Mission."

"Downloading."

"And we begin again."

"Dex, get me the Ogut ship commander," Clemons said.

"The Ogut, sir?" Guptill replied then shook his head. "Oh, the pantywaists?"

"That *is* our primary mission," Clemons pointed out.

※　　※　　※

"*Mission of the One-Four-Third Tactical Assault Squadron is to return to Terra System...*"

"Yes!" Angelito said.

"*... To assist One-Four-Two Tactical Assault Squadron in reinforcement maneuvers.*"

"Damnit!"

"*One-Four-Three will load Third Battalion, Second Marine Regiment for counterassault on Rangora forces occupying the surface of the* Thermopylae *Battlestation. Undocking procedures will begin within the hour. One-Four-Three will follow Battleship Battle Group Nine exit to outer zone of action. That is all.*"

"Thermal, Comet."

"*Go.*"

"What's the hold-up? Our birds are up. BBG taking its time?"

"*Main door is welded shut from impacts.*"

"Oh," Parker said, shaking her head. "That has to suck."

"Sir, incoming from the *Thermopylae* commander, Admiral Clemons."

As part of the negotiations, each group was allowed a security detachment. Realistically, nobody was going to assassinate the diplomats and, as this furball had proven, it wasn't like they could protect them if war broke out. It was space. They couldn't disguise themselves as women and slip through enemy lines.

Security Chief Lahela Corrigan, known as Kamalila—Hawaiian for Shadow—to her very few friends, was a very good bodyguard. She had an innate "bump" for situations and people. She knew, often before the subjects, when people were going to lose it. She could spot a threat by just glancing at a crowd.

It hadn't, however, taken a world-class security expert to know that the Eridani negotiations were going to go south in some form or fashion. Among other things, the Horvath were involved. And none of the polities, including Earth, wanted the Ogut to bring in a battle wagon.

Now they were sitting in a converted Ogut freighter in the middle of a space battle and she was left to twiddle her thumbs and wonder when an errant missile was going to destroy her perfect record.

So she might as well play receptionist.

"The Ogut let it through?" James Horst asked.

The Ogut had been quite accommodating in providing both sides with as much of the tactical view of the battle as was available from their ship screens. Nor had they acceded to the Horvath demands that the humans be turned over to the squids. However, they were also staying well away from the battle between the heavyweights. If they were "discussing" with the Rangora what was now, obviously, a set-up, the humans weren't involved.

Horst had, therefore, been spending half the time watching two hundred billion dollars worth of space fortress getting, apparently, slagged and wondering just why the Rangora were so desperate to take Earth. This little diplomatic faux pas was, in fact, a very big deal. The Rangora had created a condition of existential threat during a negotiation the Ogut Empire had personally guaranteed would lack same. The only thing that could create a greater casus belli would be actually boarding the ship to capture the human negotiators.

"More complicated than that, sir," Kamalila replied, quietly. "The Rangora had to have opened up a channel to get it through."

"Curiouser and curiouser," Horst said. "Yes, please, put him through."

"Envoy."

Horst had never met the commander of *Thermopylae* and wondered what he thought about his battlestation getting pounded to scrap.

"Admiral," Horst said. "A pleasure to hear from you."

"Glad to see you're still intact," Clemons said. "To be clear, you and your personnel are all secure?"

"The code is Naples, Admiral," Horst said, meaning that he was not being held under duress. "The Ogut have the Horvath and the Rangora, and ourselves, closed into separate zones. We're quite comfortable. They've even provided us with views of the battle."

"It's not bad," Clemons said, affecting a slight Welsh accent. "I've 'ad worse."

"Only a flesh wound?" Horst said, smiling faintly.

"Our original mission was to return you to Earth, Envoy," the admiral said seriously. "As per that mission, we have two choices. We can pound all these lizards to scrap, then ask the Ogut nicely to cough you up. It's already been noted that Horvath and Rangora diplomatic personnel are free to go. However, there is still a possibility of an accident when several billion megatons of firepower are being thrown around the system. There's a bit of a pause at the moment and we'd like to get you out so we can get down to some serious ass-whuppin.'"

"If it can be arranged that would be prudent," Horst said. "However, the Rangora would have to be in agreement. And the Horvath, I suppose."

"That would seem to be an area called negotiations, Envoy," Clemons said, grinning. "However, I suggest you hurry. This temporary fire halt isn't going to last very long."

"We've got all the welds we can separate separated, Mr. Purcell," Butch said. If he had disliked being in the missile tubes during a battle, he liked even less standing on the surface of the *Thermopylae*. Somewhere out there were Rangora Marines trying to take the station. *Supposedly* there weren't any on the door itself. "But some of these welds go deep."

Not surprising in Butch's opinion. The Orion drive had gotten hammered. All there was left was a stump. Where the rest of the drive was, was anybody's guess.

Not many of the Rangora missiles had missed the drive. It was a pretty big target. But the combination of transferred energy and the couple of near misses had the three-kilometer-wide, multibillion ton door just stuck as *hell*.

"Yeah," Purcell commed. "*Engineers are trying to figure that out. Supposedly Sol forces from* Troy *are coming through to help out. But we'd like to be able to get the ships out of the main bay. So far there's a lot of head scratching.*"

"Well, it ain't like they can hit it with a hammer..."

"*We're overthinking this. Hit it with a hammer.*"

"*Got a hammer the size of Mjolnir on you?*"

"*Missiles.*"

"*It's already* been *hit by missiles. That's the problem.*"

"*Other way around. It's six thousand one hundred and twenty meters across the main bay. Thunderbolts have a thousand gravs of accel. Lots of kinetic impact.*"

"*You want to fire missiles* inside *the main bay. At the* door. *You got any idea what kind of spalling that's going to cause? The debris?*"

"*And keep firing until it opens. Kinetic energetics are cumulative. If you've got a big enough hammer...*"

✳ ✳ ✳

"Fire missiles at the door?" Admiral Clemons said. "You've got to be kidding!"

"It's the best they can come up with, sir," Commodore Guptill said. "Without SAPL we can't do a recut. They don't even really know it will work. If it doesn't, all our mobile units are more or less grounded."

"Leonidas? Granadica?"

"I don't care for it," Leonidas replied.

"Neither do I!" Admiral Clemons said.

"That does not mean I am not in favor," Leonidas added. "I, too, see few other options if our cavalry is to be useable."

"Actually, I got a better one," Granadica said. "Just hatching it."

"Which is?" Admiral Clemons asked.

"Same basic idea. Just better."

"What the *hell* is that coming out of Granadica?"

Granadica had been producing a lot of "stuff" while overseeing maintenance. Mostly it was off-the-shelf. She'd produced a brand new *Independence* class, dozens of shuttles and tugs.

Dana wasn't sure what was coming out this time. It was about the size of an *Independence*. But there were no weapons on it nor any evidence of tractor systems. So it wasn't a warship or a tug. There were, however, three suspiciously large bulbs amidships that indicated *massive* annie plants, and the fore of the thing was shaped like a ram's head.

"I call it Mjolnir," Granadica answered. "Like it? I was in the middle of producing a *Constitution*. So I sort of...squashed it up."

"No," Dana said. "I don't like it. Because it looks like you're about to hammer something *really big*."

"Sure am," Granadica said. "Hold onto your socks. In fact, better reinforce your docking clamps."

"*All ships, all boats, undock. Remain at stations. All personnel, prepare for high level auditory transfer and possible anomalous acceleration. All ships. Undock. Remain at stations. All personnel...*"

"Oh, frackety, frackety, frack..." Dana muttered, hitting the release on her docking clamps.

"What is she talking about?" Angelito asked.

"First rule of engineering," Dana said.

"Which is...?"

*   *   *

"Look, I don't tell you about war, you don't tell me about engi-
neering, Leonidas!"
"This is a most unsound concept, Granadica..."
"It's the first law of engineering...!"

"What in the Emperor's name is that?" Lieutenant Lanniph
muttered. It couldn't be heard, simply felt beneath the feet.

"Feels like...hammering, sir," Private Zhogiruv replied. The
threesome were moving back along their line of advance for
"link-up with reinforcing party." And now this.

"It must be close," Lanniph said. "The mass of this thing would
swallow the feel of hammering. Ilugach. Point."

"Why m—" The private stopped and blanched. "Yes, sir."

"If someone is hammering, presumably they are not also setting traps."

It was called "elastic rebound." Anyone who had ever hit an
anvil with a hammer recognized it. Equally, a baseball. When two
bodies of more or less equal sturdiness collide, the less massive
body notably rebounds. What is less noticeable is that the more
massive body rebounds. Distance and speed depends upon the
relative mass and velocities.

The Mjolnir had only come at the door from a distance once.
And even that was from the middle of the bay. The massive
maneuver horns were too much of an obstacle to accelerate all
the way across the bay.

But it didn't really matter. It wasn't about a single hard hit. The
Mjolnir rebounded less than one hundred meters then, under the
power of two *Constitution*-class drive systems with less than one
Connie mass, accelerated back towards the door and hit with a
clang that was practically audible in vacuum. Each impact transferred kinetic energy disparately to the weakest points. Thus, most
of the energy was falling on the welds.

The welds were going to break eventually. The only question
was how soon.

"General, we are getting reports of hammering from...multiple
sources," Colonel Ufupoth said. The operations officer of Infantry
Battle Group Thoggon appeared puzzled.

"What sectors?" General Thoggon asked. "And what are they planning, now?"

The general had every bit of intelligence on his enemy he could ask for. He knew where Richard "Dick" Denny was born. His family history. His children. Every battle he had ever engaged in from when he was a private, and that was simply *unbelievable*, until the first Battle of Eridani. Thoggon had analysis after analysis on the general's forces, the Pathan command structure and its American "advisors" who were the de facto commanders. Pathan history and culture. The overall design of the *Thermopylae*. Detail maps for the military and civilian personnel centers.

All of it had told him beforehand that this might be a punishing battle. The *degree* of punishment was the surprising part. His men, most of them green troops, were being brutally slaughtered in the maze that the humans had constructed in the walls. And entering the laser and missile tubes, the shortest route to the main bay, was out of the question. Despite firing their entire complement, the *Thermopylae* was producing missiles fast enough that the occasional projectile was being thrown out just to keep them on their tails.

"That is the puzzling aspect," Ufupoth said. "Reports are coming from *every* sector. We can't localize a source. If anything it appears strongest in Sector Sixteen but it is more or less evenly distributed."

"Hammering?" Thoggon said.

"Slow repetition, sir," Ufupoth said. "Audio from a deck mike."

The general listened for a moment, puzzled.

"It sounds almost like someone hammering on a hatch," Thoggon said. "As if they were signaling for—" His scales stood straight up. *"Hammering on a hatch!"*

"What could..." Ufupoth asked. "General, they have nothing that could produce this level of kinetic impact!"

"I don't care," Thoggon said. "They've found a hammer!"

"We are cut off from the fleet by their missile cloud," Ufupoth said. "If they can sally..." He paused as an officer whispered in his ear, then his scales went up in turn. "General, the gate has cycled. Large mass footprint. Signal is from Sol system."

"I doubted that it was reinforcements for *us*," Thoggon said. "That would be *good* news! CRACK THESE BLASTED MAMMALS! We've got the most penetration in Sectors Nine and Fourteen. Redeploy all forces into those sectors. Point out to them that using the surface is *not* a survivable exercise."

"Admiral Marchant," Admiral Clemons said, grinning. "Glad to see you could make the party. Even happier to see the missiles. Looks like the *Troy* ran itself dry."

"That she did," Marchant said, grinning back. "But all in a good cause. It appears someone has broken your little toy ball, Admiral."

"Nothing Apollo can't fix," Clemons said. "I hope."

"I was given to understand *your* cockleshells would be awaiting us?" Marchant said.

"The door is most thoroughly jammed," Clemons admitted. "But we're working on—"

"IT WORKED?" Commodore Guptill screamed. "Holy freaking gods of the North! It worked!"

"Someone sounds excited," Marchant said. "Uh ... Admiral, your door is kind of ..."

The side view showed that the multibillion-ton door was not only heavily dinged on the inside but had, in places, ripped away hull metal. The hinge pins of the *Troy* were the size of the now-vanished Twin Towers, but unlike those structures, were made of solid stainless steel.

Now they were stainless steel pretzels.

"Open," Clemons said. "And we're not going to get it closed soon, so kindly keep those Rangora from using their shuttles. Commodore, order all mobile units to proceed for deployment."

"Proceed for deployment, aye," Commodore Guptill said. "It worked?"

"*First law of engineering, Leonidas,*" Granadica sent. "*If you can't fix it, you're not using a big enough hammer.*"

THIRTY

"This is crazy!" Angelito said, carefully following the caret.

"This is an inherently unsafe profession, Angel," Dana said, trying not to sound nervous. It wasn't just that the door wasn't quite completely open, requiring a bit of maneuvering to get out into the Dark. It wasn't just that she still didn't trust Angelito's driving. It was that it required a bit of maneuvering, she didn't trust Angelito's driving and, at least in *his* case, she could, in a pinch, take over. That *wasn't* the case with the *other* units—a *Monkey* class, nine *Paw* tugs, thirty-six *Myrmidons*, two *Defenders*, four *Constitutions* and six *Independence* class—*all* passing through the door-tunnel in one massive cluster . . . pack.

"Watch the . . . watch the . . ."

"I'm watching the . . ."

"Yaw!" Dana barked as Twenty-Three side-swiped a *Paw* tug. Both units were designed for durability but the *Paw* tug outmassed them by twice and the *Myrmidon* started sliding hard to port and down with a grinding screech of tortured metal. Towards the wall of the chamber which more or less *defined* "durability."

"Do you want to . . . ?" Angelito said, getting the shuttle under control.

"No," Dana replied, crossing her arms. "This is your job, CN Angelito. And you *can* do it. Just take a breath." She leaned forward and sighed. "Frackety frack . . . Besides, I need to get out the toolbox."

"Yeah, I'm . . ." Angelito said, trying not to whimper. "I think I'm missing . . ."

"Starboard lower thrust control?" Dana asked, pulling out her toolbag and ripping up a panel. "As I said, *your* bird, Cox. But turn on the repulsor screens. Let the next *Paw* get a load of a gigawatt of angry force shield..."

"Colonel To'Jopeviq to CIC... Colonel To'Jopeviq Lieutenant Beor to CIC..."

"I'm not sure what use we can be at this juncture," To'Jopeviq said, unnecessarily straightening his tunic. "I suppose they could just be starting the disintegrator party early."

"I doubt that," Beor said, following him out of the intel section. "We work directly for High Command. General Sho'Duphuder doesn't have the priorities to remove us."

"Colonel," General Sho'Duphuder said as they entered the command center. "A truce of sorts has been arranged. The humans are redeploying their light forces to engage us but in the meantime they would like to remove their diplomats from the battlefield."

"I take it we have agreed to that, sir?" To'Jopeviq said.

"On certain conditions," the General said, dryly. "I considered one of the conditions being calling a cease-fire and permission to withdraw all of our forces. But that was unlikely to be accepted. The battle is not *yet* lost but numbers do not lie. And the shuttles from the *Thermopylae* are returning to Earth, presumably for more Marines.

"I must compliment you, Colonel, and I will do so formally. Your plan, with the firepower suggested, would have worked. This debacle was simply, again, ignoring the suggestions of your team. Which is why one of the requirements I demanded was that you and your... assistant be allowed to withdraw with our diplomatic group."

"I would prefer to remain, sir," To'Jopeviq said tightly.

"And if I may, sir?" Beor said. "He really isn't being pro forma."

"More or less expected," Sho'Duphuder said. "And the order remains. Among other things, I do not want the humans getting their hands on two analysts from the upper command. And next time, perhaps, you can convince someone that your analyses are not overstated. There is a shuttle standing by. Don't bother to pack."

"Thirty-Three."

"Thirty-Three, go," Dana said, trying not to sigh in relief as they exited the tunnel and the formation started to spread.

"Conditions: Temporary state of cease-fire to get the diplomats on

all sides out. Orders: Proceed to Ogut ship to take on diplomatic personnel. ROE is only fire if fired upon. Max rate authorized. Return to gate and transfer single if necessary."

"Pick up the diplomats, aye," Dana said. "Don't fire at the Rangora, aye. Boost it, aye. Get the hell out of Dodge, aye. Angel, you heard the man."

"The most direct route takes us close to the Rangora fleet."

"Hopefully they got the word," Dana said, tightening her straps and abs. "Kick this horse, Angel."

"Colonel, shuttle pilot."

"Go, pilot."

The vessel was a no-frills military shuttle. Hopefully the envoys would not take that as an insult. To'Jopeviq was still hoping to get out of this debacle with his head attached, and pissed-off diplomats would not help.

"Human shuttle vectoring in our direction. Closest point of approach will be within one thousand kilometers. Orders."

"Ignore it," To'Jopeviq said. "They're probably on the same mission. Do not fire. Do you comply?"

"Comply with orders to not fire, Colonel," the pilot said. "It is not that I am bloodthirsty, Colonel. But failure to engage the enemy could be looked upon as cowardice."

"Understood," To'Jopeviq said. "This is an 'unofficial' cease-fire. Assuming we lived, we would get in even more trouble for restarting things as both sides are trying to pull out their noncombatants."

"That's nearly the size of a frigate," Angel said. "Are you sure it's a shuttle?"

"*Ubogho* class," Dana said. "Apparently refers to a fast carnivorous xenorept pseudo-avian on Rangor. Call it a peregrine."

"Where in the *hell* do you learn all this?" Angel asked, shaking his head.

"Continuous study of relevant information, CN," Dana said. "Now pay attention. We're getting into Rangora space."

"They are assuming a parallel course," the pilot commed. "*And* pulling ahead of us. Their acceleration is close to three hundred and fifty Rangora gravities."

"'What did they get in the update?'" To'Jopeviq quoted quietly.

"Everything," Beor said. "And they spend treasure on such a minor system."

"Their screens will shed any ground portable system but a penetrator missile," To'Jopeviq said. "What is that human saying: Bullets, not bodies."

"American specifically," Beor said.

"Noted," To'Jopeviq said. "I recall that after the last great war they engaged upon, they rebuilt their enemy's countries. I wonder if after this war I can get a job with them?" He paused and froze. "That was not intended to—"

"I was wondering the same thing," Beor admitted. "But all things considered, you're more likely to than I."

"Peregrine, hell," Dana muttered, watching the rapidly opening vector between the two shuttles.

Dana grinned for a moment then keyed a switch. The fact that they were not only flying through the Rangora's primary fire basket but were within *visual* range of the AV caused her to pause for a moment then key the com.

"*Ubogho,* hell," she commed. "Eat space dust, Rangora Shuttle Six-One-Four."

"What the hell are you doing?" Angel asked.

"What?" Dana said. "Suds don't do smack-down talk?"

"Toothy," To'Jopeviq said, ruffling his spines. The pilot had automatically transferred the transmission as soon as the human shuttle opened up the channel.

"Timber is for a human female," Beor said.

"Pilot, open channel."

"*I suppose they chose females so they are small enough to fit in that small scavenger shell?*"

"Oooh," Angel said. "All it needs is something about your moth— Shit, Miss..."

"Not a problem," Dana said. "And it's EM. It's not what you've got, it's how you owned it. And you're being owned."

"*...are being used as a slave to clean out shit pits.*"

"You realize you are in easy range of laser fire," To'Jopeviq said. "Accidents happen."

"I heard your quality control was bad."

"You left yourself open..." Beor commented.

"I know that..." To'Jopeviq said, trying to decide whether to snarl or laugh.

"I take it you lizards don't do smack-down talk. Let me give you a class using task, condition and standard. Task: Insult your enemies. Condition: Com channel between two shuttles during a very shaky cease-fire. Standard: Use insults that maximally insult your opponent but not to a level that will cause fire. Step One: Determine such areas in a xeno-person as may be reasonable to use as insults. Step two: Determine methods to modify standard insults, see appendix, to fit the xeno form. Extra points for being topical. Step three: Deliver smack-down. Analysis and lessons learned after practicum.

"Practical demonstration: Your mother is so ugly that when the gods turned her into a kordo she thought her prayers were answered. Your mother is so fat, when she sits on the Troy it goes out of orbit. Your AVs are so puny compared to our battlestations that their commander's penises shrivel at the thought. The reason you guys can't shoot straight is your stubby little lizard arms and beady little eyes that are useless in the shining light of our human magnificence. You, the suitably instructed, shall now proceed to perform the task to standard."

To'Jopeviq paused, amazed. Not at the string of insults, however.

"What is your rank?" he asked.

"Why, you going to send me a reply by endorsement for insulting you? I don't think it's classified. Engineer's Mate Second Class Parker. You?"

"Colonel To'Jopeviq," the Rangoran replied. "I take it that you simply constructed that... task, condition and standard? Or is it something you've heard before?"

"Want to hear the task, condition and standard for opening a can of fresh skul, sir? No, I just made it up. Why?"

"I withdraw the field, mastered, Engineer's Mate," To'Jopeviq said, rippling his scales. "Pilot, cut the com."

"Luzer," Dana said, making an L on her forehead. It was with some effort. They were still pulling three Gs.

"I still think you're insane," Angelito said.

"I'm not so insane as to not point out we're at turnover," Dana said. "So try to get the skew-turn right. On second thought, my bird. I want this to look right."

"What about..."

"I *will* take you on at jungleball..."

"Your bird, Coxswain."

"You did not wish to perform the task?" Beor said, mildly amused.

"Engage your *brain*, Lieutenant," To'Jopeviq snapped. "That was a junior enlisted person. In, as noted, the middle of a battle. Performing a complex task. Who nonetheless had the presence of mind to not only engage in insults—easy enough—but to develop a standard procedure for them."

"I was actually thinking that she was junior for the mission," Beor said. "Our pilot is a captain."

"I don't think you're grasping my point," the Colonel said, calmly. "Have you ever worked at the ground level of operations?"

"Only Kazi," Beor said.

"Very different than in the regular forces, I assume," To'Jopeviq said dryly. "A ship, a unit, a force, is composed of many parts. Both the physical equipment and the personnel. Just as every part of one of the ships has to work properly, the personnel must work within that ship...properly. In sync. They are part of the machine in a way and must do the dance of the machine."

"Turning to the side in the corridors?" Beor asked.

"Much more complex than that," To'Jopeviq said. "My first post was as a laser gunnery officer. Managing the maintenance of the equipment, training the junior personnel on damage control. As one example, there was a particular collimator that would frequently blow out during sustained use. There were parts. But I was in charge of several systems. During training, often I would get the word that one of the lasers was down. It would, almost invariably, be a collimator. But until I arrived and ordered that it be repaired, that someone go get the collimator from stocks and then supervise the installation, often it would not be done. At least at first. I take quiet pride that by the time I left the post, when a system broke my men worked on it immediately and intelligently."

"Why?" Beor asked. "And how?"

"Depended upon the individual," To'Jopeviq said. "Some because they feared the consequences of failure. If I had to turn up to supervise, they knew that it would go hard on them. Some because they looked to me as a father figure and wanted to please me. None, I think, because they really cared if the system was repaired or not."

"It took constant supervision by officers such as myself to simply maintain the systems. The mid-level enlisted were not much better. What I would have given for one mid-level enlisted with as much brains as that female. Someone like that would have been grafted to intelligence or another intellectual job. And they are motivated to perform their duties. They are maintaining their maximum acceleration. There are any number of ways that they could have shirked this duty. Just go slow. Move farther away from our fleet. Yet they are not only flying fearlessly within visual range of our AVs, they are exchanging insults and composing standards while doing so."

"Your point being that their enlisted are good?" Beor asked. "Does that matter?"

"Does *that* matter?" To'Jopeviq snarled. "Does it *matter*? Does it matter if the lines of code are all properly written? Does it matter if the air locks are sealed or not? Who writes the code? Who ensures the air locks work? *Yes*, it matters! It is a piece of intelligence that is useful. Even crucial. It demonstrates another reason that they are so effective and efficient in war. And I'm sure that the High Command would ask the same question. *Does it matter...*"

"I really don't think it matters if we get there a couple of seconds late," Angelito said. "It's about getting there at all."

"Sissy," Dana said as the com from the Ogut ship opened.

"*Terran Shuttle One Four Three Bravo Two-Three, vessel* Vezhzhiboujivvumae-tharrezhaocuchuzhophmezhuquybighulhij *ATC, you are approaching at the outside parameters of your system capability. Please assume a less aggressive approach.*"

"*Vezhzhibou*...uh...Ogut vessel, Twenty-three. Orders were max accel movement. Minimized approach outside current parameters. Just have our people waiting at the door, over."

"*Your approach has a high likelihood of damage to your vessel, Twenty-Three.*"

"Just have your docking clamps hot," Dana said.

The approach *was* hot. Closer than she'd like. She was decelerating at her maximum of four hundred gravities and the computer was saying "stable" according to the orbit of the Ogut ship at six centimeters. Which was just too close. OTOH, her chatting with the Rangora had had her doing a late turnover. So much for being able to juggle two things at once. Okay, and watching the engineering screens and wondering when the Rangora and *Thermopylae* were going to start duking it out again. She frankly wasn't sure she was more afraid of the Rangora or the cloud of missiles that the light units brought through from Earth.

"We're going to *hit* their *ship*," Angelito squeaked. "Is that an act of war?"

"Only if we survive it," Dana said. "And we're not going to 'hit' their ship." Please *don't let me hit their ship* ... "Now shut up...."

Hitting the docking ring was always fun, even in the *Troy*'s main bay going at centimeters per second. Hitting it in the Black when both vessels were moving in different directions in three dimensions was three times the fun. Coming in hot, still doing three hundred meters per second with less than a hundred meters to go, was watching a train wreck about to occur. But you weren't going to have time to wince.

However, in the brief moments of entering the *Troy*'s main bay when she'd earned the moniker "Comet," Dana had learned a very important lesson: Humans have no conceptual ability to understand, at a gut level, what "four hundred gravities of acceleration" really means. Two race cars hitting head on don't generate four hundred gravities of acceleration on the bodies of the dead drivers. There was no pre-Contact human system capable of generating four hundred gravities of acceleration. So "doing it by the seat of your pants" was like a monkey trying to fly an F-16. Blind in a rainstorm. A *Myrmidon* maneuvering under full power didn't "bank." Or, rather, the "banks" occurred so fast that they were undetectable by the human eye. Don't bother watching those hands, they move faster than you can see.

And during that entry Dana hadn't just been wincing and hoping that she would survive. The entry wasn't even *straight*. She had had to continuously maneuver. And what she discovered was that *Myrmidons* were so maneuverable they made hummingbirds look gawky.

The shuttle thus crossed the last hundred meters in, literally, the blink of an eye, decelerated from, relative to the Ogut ship, over two hundred meters per second, faster than the top speed of an SR71, to essentially zero relative velocity, and hit the docking ring with a mild "clank."

"Solid dock," Dana said, trying not to let the sigh slip into her voice. "Are our personnel ready?"

The docking bay had a viewscreen and the Ogut had politely allowed the human contingent to view their incoming shuttle.

Dr. Palencia was well aware that there was no point in holding up his hands and wincing at a human shuttle about to crash into the Ogut ship. And it was definitely unprofessional for a diplomat to half shriek. On the other hand, he wasn't the only one. The only people who hadn't visibly reacted were the chief envoy and the odd Hawaiian security chief.

"Solid dock," the pilot toned over the announcers. "Are our personnel ready?"

"I know that voice," Dr. Velasquez said wonderingly. "No *wonder* Mr. Vernon wants her for one of his pilots."

"We have a confirmed seal, gentlemen," Security Chief Corrigan said, in her usual mild tones. "And I have a confirmed security code. Boarding will be in reverse order of grade with the exception that all security personnel save myself will board first and I shall board after the chief envoy."

The hatch dialed open and one of the spacesuited crew waved.

"Sirs, Shuttle Twenty-Three at your service, sirs. If it is possible to begin boarding? Soon?"

"And if we could begin boarding, please..."

THIRTY-ONE

"This has to be the screwiest space battle in history," Admiral Clemons muttered.

"Would the Admiral care to place a bet on that?" Leonidas asked.

"Probably not," Clemons said. "There's worse?"

"There have been few wars of the scale of the Rangora attack on the Glatun in the last five thousand Earth years," Leonidas replied. "However, there have been smaller conflicts. During a minor dispute between the Ogut and the Nooh there was a temporary cease-fire that lasted four years. When negotiations failed, the two sides were required by a small codicil of the cease-fire to return to the identical location and conditions of the moment of cease-fire including all personnel and equipment in their respective positions. In many cases on both sides, individuals had to be recalled to duty and retrained. Various members of both forces took demotions to resume their duties of four years previous. Fourteen of the Nooh members had been terminated due to conditions of mutiny in the interim and others had been discharged and yet were required to return to service for the battle."

"Who won?" Commodore Guptill asked.

"It is generally classed as a draw," Leonidas said. "However, the Nooh surrendered on terms shortly afterwards."

"Get me Admiral Marchant if he's got a second," Clemons said, thoughtfully. "And Leonidas, cite on that?"

"Battle of Zhuttev. GalDate 12479. And again in 12483."

"May have to remind me again."

※　　※　　※

"Admiral," Horst said. "Thanks for arranging the ride."

"You set up the conditions," Marchant said. "Which is the point of the call. The Rangora have to know that they're in an extremely adverse position. I know we broached the subject, but I'd like you to revisit the topic of a negotiated surrender of their forces. I don't mind killing Horvath all day long but despite their actions I've come to rather like the Rangora. And this is going to be a slaughter."

"They're rather adamant, but I'll revisit the topic," Horst said. "Especially since I tend to agree. What is the status of their Marines?"

"From what I've gotten from Admiral Clemons, they're not really making much progress in the rat maze and as soon as the cease-fire lifts, *Troy*'s Marines will be dropping in behind them. Again, adverse correlation of forces. If it helps, we'd be willing to agree to something like the Battle of Zhuttev but not the screwier aspects."

"Battle of..." Horst said, then paused as a download pinged. He considered the outlines then chuckled. "I thought that was familiar. Yes... I'll contact them and bring it up."

"Zhuttev?" General Sho'Duphuder said, his spines rippling. "That's a reference you don't often see. But, no, Envoy. The position is rejected. In fact, the previous position of full withdrawal of Rangora forces is off the table. The battle will proceed as soon as the shuttles are clear."

"General, I would urge you to reconsider," Ghow Ve'Disuc said. "Zhuttev is a perfectly acceptable condition."

"Not with this correlation of forces," Sho'Duphuder replied. "And I have had communication with High Command on the situation. They are in agreement. The battle proceeds, Envoy."

"Very well, General," Ve'Disuc said. "We are, finally, approaching the gate. So... Good luck."

"The humans have a saying," General Sho'Duphuder replied. "Fortune favors the prepared."

"There goes a very brave Rangora," Thunnuvuu Zho'Ghogabel said, softly.

The shuttle cleared the gate and both envoys shuddered at the reflected tactical display in the Glalkod system.

"Or perhaps... not," Ve'Disuc whispered. "Colonel To'Jopeviq?"

"This we did not know about," To'Jopeviq said. "But it seems perhaps High Command *did* read our estimates."

*   *   *

"Give me the Rangora commander," Admiral Marchant said.

"On screen, sir..."

"Last chance, General."

"We're already launching, Admiral," General Sho'Duphuder replied. "Do your worst."

"Order is Tallyho," Admiral Marchant said quietly.

"Tally ho, aye. Full drive all missiles. Mobile units to follow. Drop all the Marines."

"This is going to be a bloodbath," Marchant said. He leaned back in his command chair as the *Grover Cleveland* accelerated towards the enemy. "What a bloody waste."

"Admiral! Gate activation from Glalkod system!"

"Home again, home again, jiggedy jig," Dana said as they approached the *Troy*. They'd cleared the gate well ahead of the Rangora shuttle.

"Say again?" Angelito said.

"Norté thing," Dana said. "Home again, home again, jiggedy jig. Riding the back of a fat little pig. I have no idea why they're riding a pig so don't ask. And since it probably translated, note that it rhymes in English."

"Okay," Angelito said. "And, yes, I see the rhyme. We're to enter through the vessel bypass."

"Got that. Your bird."

"How do you say it? For values of mine?"

"That would be..." Dana said then paused as a tactical update downloaded. "Oh no. Oh no, no, NO..."

"Where the hell did *that* come from?" Admiral Clemons snarled. "What the *FUCK*?"

The gate was *spewing* Rangora ships. Two AVs followed by cluster after cluster of *Aggressor* groups.

"Based upon intelligence estimates, that is a good part of the remaining Rangora fleet," Leonidas said. "About forty percent. And the correlation of forces... is now somewhat adverse."

"Ya *think*? Dexter?"

"We're shot dry, sir," Guptill replied. "Laser clusters are trashed and we've still got spin. Worst of all..."

"Granadica! Can you *shut* the door now? Please?"

"Sir," Guptill said. "The shuttles?"

"Jesus *Christ*!"

"Rangora are going to full launch," Leonidas intoned.

"Target?"

"Us."

"Maneuver six one delta," Admiral Marchant snapped. "Assure we have basket control of all the *Thermopylae* forces."

"*Thermopylae* forces locked," Captain George Whisler replied. "Six one delta, aye."

Captain Whisler, tactical officer of Second Fleet, was almost totally focused on the upcoming battle. A good ninety percent of his available brainpower was devoted to the complex system that was Second Fleet.

But everyone has that little voice deep in their brains. That kid, usually between the ages of nine and twelve, who read or saw something that set their destiny.

That nine-year-old, in the captain's case, was in turns delirious and terrified as the vision of a BBC show about the Battle of Trafalgar kept flashing across his mental screens.

The difference being the *last* thing the Fleet wanted to do was "cross the enemy's T."

Humans had studied the tactics used in ship-to-ship battles among the Galactics and found things to like and dislike.

The basic concept was simple. Whatever the weapon—penetrator missiles, laser, mass drivers—there were three things standing between the target platform and the weapon: missiles, shields and armor. This was, in the view of most older officers, better than theoretical concepts of wet carrier battles where the only thing standing between a carrier and an Exocet were missiles, Phalanx and luck.

One thing that was rarely mentioned in "wet" Navy theoretical exercises was that there was one more thing standing between a carrier and a ship-killer. Other, lesser, ships. Frigate crews, however, were well aware of the concept. Which was why they referred to themselves as mobile missile intercept systems.

All groups used rotation to reduce damage. Given that most of the enemy fire was anticipated to be coming from a single vector, maneuvering so as to spread the damage, take fire for a brief moment on a section of shields or armor then spin, rotate or yaw to move the fire to another quadrant, was a standard tactic.

The humans, due to a combination of Glatun cybernetics capability and remembering the *true* purpose of wet frigates in a CVBG, added the refinement of "interpenetration." Each battle group, based around a *Constitution* or *Defender* class, would not only individually rotate but rotate around the main ship. And not just in a simple Keplerian orbit but interweaving in a complex algorithm that, theoretically, optimized their individual likelihood of survival. In addition, battlegroups themselves interpenetrated, creating a complex pavane impossible in any conditions other than space.

The covert update from the Glatun that had upgraded human forces became apparent as Second Fleet, essentially all of Earth's mobile forces, opened up like an origami flower.

"Incoming laser fire from the AV, sir," Captain Whisler said.

"Which is what six one delta is for," Marchant said. "Which helps the shuttles and the Marines not one bit."

"Get into the tunnels!" General Bolger snapped, bounding off the ramp. "If there are Rangora, just *plow* them! We need to get these shuttles spaceborne. Fast. Shit..."

The *Thermopylae* was still spinning. Between that and a bit too much spring, the Marine commander was heading into an inconvenient orbit. He corrected with thrusters and got his feet on the *Therm*.

"Nearest tunnel is at three point seven mark four," Colonel Grant "Boner" Threlfall said. The J-3 of First Marine Division frankly thought that any Marine not smart enough to get out of the way of the incoming missiles should have been washed out at boot.

"Let's get the fuck under armor, then," Bolger snapped. "This is about to be a *very* unsafe environment."

"Fuck, fuck, fuck, fuck..." Barnett muttered, hugging the surface of the *Therm*. The tactical display was nothing but red overhead. The missiles were heading for the *Thermopylae* but that didn't mean they wouldn't target a Terran shuttle. And any one of those ship busters would open up a shuttle like a tin can being hit by...something really nasty. Being *nearby* when they hit the *Therm*, for that matter, wasn't going to be—

"Impact!" MOGs called. "Gas wave..."

"Shiiiii—" Barnett screamed as the blast wave hit.

Explosions don't propagate well in space. On a planet, the

majority of damage from any explosion, from a five hundred pound bomb to a fifty megaton nuke, was from expanding gas. In space there is no atmosphere.

Unless, of course, the explosion was from a kinetic weapon hitting a big chunk of nickel iron. In which case it *made* a very temporary atmosphere composed of nickel and iron plasma.

The blast wave of not one but hundreds of multimegaton missile impacts washed over both the retreating 142nd and the 143rd in what would later be termed "plasmaclastic flow."

Were any visual system capable of penetrating the rolling blast of plasma, the image would have been of so many soap bubbles briefly tossed in a hurricane of fire and then... vanishing.

"They're..." Admiral Clemons said, trying not to puke. The image of an essentially empty viewscreen—where a moment before had been nearly a hundred shuttles and a *thousand* Marines—even drowned out the continuous rumble of the incoming bombardment.

"Both squadrons have been eliminated by secondary effects of enemy fire," Leonidas said. "Fifth Marine regiment has sustained seventy percent casualties from the same cause. Message sent to General Denny. Generals Bolger and Cortada KIA. He is now senior Marine officer in system. Estimate twenty percent casualties of remaining Rangora forces. Rotation is bringing the main entry area into enemy fire basket. Two thousand missiles remaining."

"Granadica?" Clemons said, trying to put the horrific casualties aside. At this point, winning was no longer an option. Keeping the *Thermopylae* out of enemy hands was all anyone could hope for.

"No can do, Admiral," Granadica said. "I moved Mjolnir outside and banged the door partially closed. But all the way? No go. Leo, I need control of every bot and remaining shiplike thing we've got."

"Transferred."

"I'm giving *you* Mjolnir. *Use* it."

"Missiles approaching Fleet One," Captain Whisler said.

"I wonder if we should have saved some of them?" Commodore Adam Rocco said. The operations officer of Second Fleet was, at this point, mostly concentrated on how they were going to recover survivors from this debacle. "*Sundance* just took a direct laser hit...."

"That's seven *Indies*, Two *Connies* and a *Defender*," Captain

Whisler said. "*Maharashtra*'s an engineering casualty. Enemy's recognized it and shifted fire. Two thousand plus survival pods."

"If it was *just* the *Aggressors*," Admiral Marchant snarled. "Shift to four three eight. We've got to get more spread out. Those AV lasers are killing us."

"Missile launch?" Captain Whisler asked.

"Not yet," Marchant said. "Not until we can see the reds of their eyes."

"We thought we were the steel jaws," General Sho'Duphuder said, watching the implacable wall of missiles closing on his fleet. Given that the humans had moved nearly half of them into the system from Earth, once the weapons were accelerating away from the gate, they didn't have the *fuel* to turn around and attack the *second* Rangora fleet. Thus, although it was going to be overkill, they were all still headed for *his* ships. Frankly, the Imperium should win the rest of the battle. Not that it was going to matter *personally*. Once that wall of missiles arrived there wasn't going to be much left but plasma, very small scraps of ship and bits of charred carbon.

"Very expensive bait," Colonel Rowwez replied.

"Too expensive by far," General Sho'Duphuder said. "Abandon ship."

"Sir?" Colonel Rowwez said, aghast. "But . . ."

"*All* ships, abandon ship," Sho'Duphuder snapped. "Set the ships for auto defense and abandon ship. Those are *Glatun* designs. You can tell by the acceleration. They'll recognize escape pods and avoid them as best they can. Abandon. Ship. Send the order!"

"Yes, sir!"

"Of course," the general mused as the alarms started blaring. "I'm not sure who's going to be *left* to pick us up."

The problem of being President with hypercom was that it gave an exquisitely detailed and instantaneous view of train wrecks.

"Field Marshall. Send *everything* we've got left in the system to E Eridani. I don't care if it's an out-of-date corvette."

"Ma'am, if Second Fleet can't win this . . ." Marshall Hampson said. "Sol will be undefended."

"SAPL, Admiral!" the President snapped. "*Troy. Everything*! NOW! Send *Troy* if we can find something to *push* it!"

✷ ✷ ✷

"Missiles working to the door," Commodore Guptill said. "Here it comes!"

The main door was still canted open at an angle of twenty-seven degrees, the exact angle that concrete that is properly mixed will form if poured out carefully on a flat surface.

In an eyeblink, forty-three missiles, each packing nearly ten megatons of kinetic energy, tracked across the door area. Forty of them hit the door itself, shutting it with a finality that should have spelled SAPL-JOB in gigantic divots on the surface. The divots were, however, more or less random.

Three, unfortunately, slipped through *before* that event.

The missiles still had to maneuver, slightly. And they couldn't drive directly into the main bay. Which from the Rangora perspective was a good thing. If they had simply flown directly across the main bay, all they would have done was put divots on the inside of North and fill the main bay with gas, neither of which would be particularly an issue to the human defenders.

As fate and bad planning would have it, they were instead pointed directly at Horn Two. Which was mostly occupied by Granadica.

Granadica was an AI. And AIs think very fast. Unfortunately, no one, not even she, had thought about *exactly* where on the horn the ship fabber should go, *tactically*. Thus "bad planning." In blinding retrospect it was obvious that the ship fabber should be on the *far* side of the horn from the door. Just in case the door was stuck open and enemy missiles could fly into the main bay. In fact, considering the hinges and the probable angularity of a stuck-open door, the ship fabber should probably be put on the back side of Horn One. And she'd made a note to that effect and sent it off on the hypercom network, addressed variously but especially and personally to the short bastard who had tricked her into being in this situation in the first place.

The absolute worst place to be would have been on the near side of the horn, directly in line with the door. She had had time to note that the original plans *had* placed her there. A mistake during construction of the power systems on the horns had taken up that area. So instead of a ship fabber facing the door directly, about six billion credits worth of *power plants* were facing the door.

She was either up or down from that position, depending on how you viewed it, and *slightly* behind the three kilometer horn.

Which wasn't going to be enough. When those missiles hit the horn they were going to rip her to shreds through plasma discharge alone. Not to mention just a massive amount of non-plasmoid foreign-object debris flinging around the interior at very high velocities.

The objective, therefore, was to keep the missiles from hitting the horn. Or, hopefully, anything else that was really important. Like, say, her.

Kinetic energy was kinetic energy. Nonelastic recoil. If the missiles hit *anything* except vacuum or thin gases, essentially all that *had* been between Granadica's new shell and the door, they and whatever they hit were going to be plasma. Plasma headed toward Granadica, but that *might* be survivable. The missiles impacting on the horn would not be.

Which was why Granadica had stacked up every bot, unoccupied sled, cleaner, scrubber and mobile piece of junk in the entire main bay between the door and her brand new shell. She wished in retrospect they'd kept the *Paw* tugs. The only thing that wasn't between her and the door was a *Monkey* class that was down for repair.

As the Rangora missiles tracked into the door, she accelerated every bot, scrubber and piece of junk into the relatively small gap.

Which was why instead of three Rangora missiles shooting through the gap, what came out was a plasma volcano composed of ions from three Rangora missiles and two hundred pieces of human mobile equipment.

Which hit about two hundred tons of various scrap including three large chunks of wall material, bits and pieces of Rangora and Horvath ships and four nearly full ship containers of damned near priceless parts.

Which, given the temperature and kinetics of the plasma, were accelerated and heated far beyond the rating of the contained parts.

The cluster of material spread out from the plasma wall in a fashion that Argus would have had a fun time predicting. Since he was fully linked in with Granadica he had, in fact, predicted it and was mildly displeased as the last few images that were transmitted indicated that he was only 99.9999436% accurate in his estimate of the outcome.

The .0000564 was rather important.

Because he had bet Granadica every single processor credit he'd ever won from her she *wasn't* going to survive.

What hit Granadica, instead of three missiles capable of both calculating the best target in their basket and maneuvering to hit the ship fabber, or a very high velocity and very hot wave of plasma, was a big rectangular chunk of nickel iron, part of one melted container, a bunch of melted plastic and metal that *had* been seven hundred and twenty *million* credits worth of high-tech parts and an already trashed laser array from the *Cofubof*-class cruiser *Arashet, surrounded* by very hot but dispersing and *much* lower velocity plasma.

The impact of the wall material cracked every weld and join holding the ship fabber on the horn, as well as doing the structural equivalent of massive internal damage, and spun the fabber in a nearly random fashion across the bay to clang on the far wall just below Bay Nineteen. The main point of impact was on the crew compartment, which had, fortunately, been evacuated. Unfortunately, it was also where Granadica's AI core was housed.

"Leo, damage?" Admiral Clemons asked.

"Fifty-three percent of our power systems," Leonidas said. "Seventy-eight percent of our maneuvering systems. Dragon Ball offline. Fabbers offline. Everything... light in the main bay is damaged beyond repair. The door, however, is now shut. Beyond any capacity to open it, I suspect, short of recutting with SAPL. We can rotate very slowly. More like we can slow our current rotation and affect it slightly in skew. No casualties at all, absent Granadica."

"And Granadica?" Clemons asked.

"Those fucking lizard **BASTARDS! MY BRAND NEW *SHELL*!**"

"Is inoperable as a ship fabber absent a shipyard," Leonidas said. "But still lives."

"I think the word is... Ow..."

"Good," Clemons said. "Now get us back in the fight."

"At the moment, the only thing we have is Mjolnir," Leonidas said.

"The bombardment has let up," Granadica said. "Crews can get a laser head operating. Maybe two. Might even be able to point a little." She groaned a little. "I think I need to rethink my maintenance feedback system. Is this what pain feels like?"

"We have less than half our power systems," Leonidas said. "Given maneuvering and life support, that means a quarter of our laser output."

"A little sympathy here?"

"Work on it," Clemons said. "Now... Mjolnir? What *are* we doing with Mjolnir?"

"I was about to ask permission on that, sir," Leonidas said. "It is about halfway to its target."

"Which is...?"

"I mean, 'Glad to see you survived, Granadica.' 'Sorry you're hurt, Granadica'?"

"Glad to see you survived, Granadica. Sorry you're hurt, Granadica. We just lost two boat squadrons, a thousand Marines, six ships, and have lifeboats and people in suits scattered all over the system and no way to recover them. Glad to see you survived, Granadica. Now get to fixing yourself to the point you can get to fixing... everything *else*."

"Yes, sir, Admiral," Granadica said firmly. "I have some remaining functioning internal systems. Will comply."

"Which *is*...?"

THIRTY-TWO

Star General Subekulh Gi'Tathajagh had seen worse battles. The first three assaults on Tuxughah came to mind. And he had examined, quite carefully, the reports, the true reports, on the assaults on the Terran system. Which were, also, worse than this. For one thing, the Rangora were more or less assured of winning. For values of win. What the humans would call a Pyrrhic victory. Victory at such cost that defeat was less preferable on only a moral level. The loss of General Sho'Duphuder's entire fleet was going to cost the Imperium dearly. But for once the Rangora were going to carry the field against these damned Terran primates. The battle globe was functionally destroyed, and he had the throw weight to defeat the Terran light units. Of course, the estimates were eighty percent numeric loss of *his* force to do so. But the AVs were assured of surviving.

Victory. Congratulations of the High Command. Promotion.

He wondered if General Sho'Duphuder had taken one of the six thousand lifeboats on the Search and Rescue screen. If so, Gi'Tathajagh would use every bit of whatever political clout he might gain from this "victory" to ensure Sho'Duphuder *stayed* a general. Was even promoted. Moral courage of that...intensity was much harder to find among the Rangora than the physical kind.

"General Gi'Tathajagh. Incoming enemy...ship?"

"There are forty-three incoming enemy ships," Gi'Tathajagh said. "Very hard-to-hit, extremely hard-to-kill enemy ships."

"This one is coming from the direction of the battle globe," Colonel Toghazen said. The fleet tactical officer seemed puzzled.

"And our missiles didn't...deal with it?"

"It appears to have used the mass of the globe to hide behind," Toghazen said. "And we can't identify the class. Mass is in the range of one of their *Constitution* class, as is acceleration."

"So, another *Constitution*," General Gi'Tathajagh said. "There are... eleven of those remaining?"

"Thirteen. Yes, sir. But the *density* is wrong. Its volume is only a third of a *Constitution*. And the trajectory is not for fly-by or any normal combat maneuver. It... sir, it appears to be on a *ramming* course."

"Mass of... three hundred thousand tons? Kinetic energy on impact?"

"Two hundred plus times ten to the seventeenth of kinetic release."

"*Concentrate* fire on it."

"We *have* been, sir," Colonel Toghazen said, a touch nervously. "It's maneuvering, but despite that we've hit it repeatedly with secondaries from both the *Aggressors* and AVs and it's— It's not even shielded! We're getting major ablation consonant with nanoweave, flintsteel composites. But... it's not stopping it."

"Rotate the in-line *Aggressors*," Gi'Tathajagh snapped. "Begin maneuvering out of its impact basket."

"It has the maneuverability of a Glatun *cruiser*, General!"

General Gi'Tathajagh had even seen *that* before. Going into the war he, like most Rangora, had viewed the Glatun as effete wimps. And, by and large, they were. But at... Ceghevel? Yes, Ceghevel, another "glorious victory," a wounded Glatun cruiser had made a suicide run on the AV *Woshshusee*. Rangora did not suffer from the human problem of "combat flashbacks" but some images were burned indelibly on the brain. The sight of the center third of an AV flashing into gas was one of *his* indelible images.

"Orders to Cuwwutoa group," Gi'Tathajagh snapped after a glance at the tactical display. "Physical intercept."

"General, that would be—"

"Try with light units, but do not let that... *thing* through! Send it!"

Captain Zoa Qa'Zafilach, commander of the *Aggressor* Battleship *Cuwwutoa* and Battle Group commander, looked at the orders, looked at the tactical display and made an instant decision. His family was connected and he could worry about the Kazi *later*.

"Flight. Full power all engines."

"Sir..." his maneuvering officer said. "Engine four is..."

"I said *full* power," the captain said, sending a copy of the orders to the pilot. "*All* engines. Consonant with our orders to *physically intercept* an incoming mass kinetic projectile that is targeted on the AV *Herraruo*."

"Physic— Full power, *aye!*"

"*Cuwwutoa* reports major engine failure. Acceleration drop to sixty percent."

"Then send the—" General Gi'Tathajagh said, then stopped. "Never mind. I can do the math."

"Maneuvering fall-off," Toghazen said. "I think we got it but..."

"But."

There is a term in flight operations: "near miss." It is a misnomer. By definition a near miss is, in fact, a hit. One has *nearly* missed but not...quite. A near*by* miss could perhaps be appropriate. A miss which is very nearby. A better term for a situation where two bodies almost connect is a near *hit*. Nearly hit but...not quite.

Thus, what occurred was a near *miss* in the correct meaning of the term. Mjolnir, peppered by high-power lasers, its maneuvering systems junked, even its central processing core cored by an AV secondary laser, very nearly missed the ponderously maneuvering AV.

Nearly. Very. In space terms, it was a near run thing indeed. As near run as any could hope.

However, when a mass of three hundred thousand tons traveling at a blistering four hundred and twenty kilometers per *second* hits *anything* it more or less instantaneously converts to 265×10^{17} joules of energy. (Unless it is made from neutronium and then the physics gets...rather complicated.)

The equivalent of a 6.33 *gigaton* bomb went off, if not *directly* in the guts of the assault vector, then, well...near enough.

"Yes!" Admiral Marchant screamed as the flagship AV was cut in half in a welter of fire. Gases were jutting from it end to end. Some of the crew might have survived but the AV was *toast* as a fighting platform. "Yes, *BABY!*"

"We gotta get us more of those," Captain Whisler said. "Whatever the *hell* it was."

"We're not out of the woods, yet," Marchant said as the *Jimmy Carter* reeled out of the battle formation. Life pods blew out just before the *Smiley* turned into scrap and plasma. "But that gives us a chance. Full launch. Target the AV. Now, now, now."

"EM Parker?"

The last person in the fucking *galaxy* Dana wanted to talk to right now was Señor Doctor Palencia.

"Dr. Palencia. I don't know if you—"

"We have been getting a continuous update through our implants, EM. I... I am very sorry for your losses, *corazon*. I do not know if it was... although you did not get along... Dario cared for you very much."

"Sir..." Parker said, trying not to let the choking carry over the transmission. "You just lost a *son* and Vel is in a coma."

"You became the target of much analysis, as I'm sure you are aware, Parker," Palencia replied. "*You* just lost the closest things you have had in far too long to a mother in Chief Barnett and a father in EM Hartwell."

"Thank you for that... analysis, sir," Parker said bitterly.

"The reason that *I* read it, and paid attention, was..." Palencia paused. "Dario had approached me about... Despite the obvious issues, he wished my assistance on the question of...'courting you' would be the closest term in English."

"Oh, jeeze," Dana said, trying not to chuckle. "I had sort of picked up on that, sir. He'd have gotten about as far as... as this shuttle would against that damned AV, sir. But... He was a great guy, sir. He'd gotten to be a damned good engineer. I know that doesn't seem like enough to say, but..."

"Thank you, EM," Palencia replied. "All language can be reduced in some ways to numbers. One of the other analyses I've paid attention to refers to the question of... praise. What the analysis indicated was that one took the praise from a Norté subculture such as yours and simply applied a multiplier. Or, rather, an inversion algorithm. For someone such as you to say he was 'a damned good engineer' is... high praise indeed. And he is... was... a fine young man."

"Shuttle bay's pressurized, sir," Parker said, clearing her throat. "Time to debark."

"Yes," Palencia said. "And to try to stop this debacle before those drifting in space are lost as well. *Corazon*, I say this in truth. If I must pull strings to make it an order. When this is done you shall visit us. You shall consider our home, Dario's home, your home. You shall visit our ranch. You ride. You shall ride and I shall ride with you and we will visit Dario's horses and his life and his memory. You shall not ride this path alone. And, I beg of you, do not allow me to ride it alone either. In memory of... a damned good engineer."

"I... I'll try, sir," Dana said. "But as far as I can tell, right now I'm the only fully qualified shuttle coxswain and engineer left in the *system*. I think I'm going to be sort of busy."

"You shall make the time, *corazon*. I say this as a man who had become... you would say I was not completely dissatisfied with the idea of you being a daughter-in-law."

"Damn, sir," Dana said. "I'll try not to let that go to my head."

"Communication *is* possible."

"A laser, a laser, my kingdom for a laser," Admiral Clemons muttered.

The *Thermopylae*, for all its gargantuality, needed certain things to be a battlestation. And if the enemy had trashed every laser collimator, which it had, and every missile fabber, which it had, and most of the maneuvering systems, which the Rangora had, all you had left was a big ball of nickel iron with, fortunately, still functional air and water systems. And, alas, a functioning tactical display. In days of yore were this, say, the *Yorktown* limping back to Pearl Harbor from the battle of the Coral Sea, Admiral Clemons would have been busy on the radio making preparations for their arrival and repair so that they could go forth and be sunk at Midway.

These days computers handled most of that. So the best use of his time was to watch as Admiral Marchant's fleet was hammered into bits.

"And the ability to actually point it," Commodore Guptill pointed out then snorted.

"Didn't actually fall into the category of funny, Commodore."

"Yes, sir," Dexter said. "Just found a tiny slice of irony or something at two six two mark twenty nine. Range two hundred eighty thousand klicks."

"What is that Rangora destroyer doing?" Clemons asked then

frowned. "Where is it going? For that matter, where did it come from? Tell me there's not *another* enemy fleet out there."

"That's the minor humor, sir," Commodore Guptill said. "The commander of the first Rangora fleet apparently, and it was a good call, ordered all his personnel to abandon ship. Not sure who's going to pick them up but those ships weren't going to survive our missile cloud."

"I agree, so..."

"So *everybody* punched. Grab that yellow bar and pull. Now, statistically, it was *possible* since they set their ships to auto defense that *some* ships were going to survive."

Clemons backtracked the Rangora destroyer and snorted.

"Lord above," he said, shaking his head. "*The Flying Dutchman.*"

"Just going to keep accelerating, I guess, until it runs out of fuel, sir," Guptill said. "Which makes me realize I *hope* nobody is aboard."

"I'm wondering how we're getting home," Clemons said. "Any bright ideas, 'cause I'm all out."

"There are as many ideas as there are people aware of the facts, Admiral," Leonidas interjected. "The exact number is one thousand four hundred and sixty-eight. That is the number who are generally aware of the current condition and with sufficient time on their hands to discuss possible amelioration."

"Any *bright* ideas?" Guptill asked.

"By my count...six. None of them particularly *good* but better than spinning slowly off into the vastness of space as the battle rages behind us. I am...not good at running from a battle."

"Synopsis," Clemons said, sitting up.

"In what order?"

"Anything that might...*work*?"

"One. Bluff. We are reducing rotation. I've been working with maneuvering to reduce the rotation so that north is in the direction of the enemy AV. Damage control teams have installed one of our remaining laser collimators and two heavy shield generators protecting it. Adjust rotation and open fire. But, and this is very important, miss the AV."

"Why?" Guptill asked.

"The enemy is aware we are heavily damaged but how damaged must be a mystery. If the laser impacts, they will be aware that it is not full power. However, if it misses...there is no real way to detect the relative power of that sort of laser without physical contact."

"So they think we're back to full power but just missing due to range."

"Correct, Admiral."

"Do it," Jack said, then rubbed his jaw. "But it needs more. We need to get back in the fight. I agree on the missing. But we need to *close* to *really* bluff."

"The Orion drive is destroyed, Admiral."

"Yep," Clemons said. "But the *nukes* ain't. And we just happen to have a bunch of tailor-made craters on the door to stick them in."

"Oooh," Guptill said. "Not sucking up, sir, but that's brilliant. Crazy, but brilliant."

"And here come their missiles." Colonel Thoos Ishives was the tactical officer for the AV *Jovian Crusher*. And with the destruction of the AV *Iramozh*, tactical officer for the Jomaz Fleet. A nice position if he lived to keep it.

"We will take damage," Captain Be'Sojahiph said, hands clasped calmly in front of him. With the loss of the *Iramozh*, and apparently Generals Sho'Duphuder *and* Gi'Tathajagh, he had acceded to command of the Fleet. "But that is all. Not even crippling. And then we will finish off their mobile units and reduce the former asteroid to . . . smaller asteroids."

"Yes, sir," Ishives replied.

"It was a tactical error on their commander's part," Be'Sojahiph said. "That missile array, even given their losses, would have severely reduced the *Aggressor* squadrons."

"Yes, sir," Ishives said, paying more than strictly necessary attention to the tactical display. Then he realized that he had better be paying *actual* attention to the tactical display. "Sir . . . The entire missile complement is targeted on us."

"As I said, a tactical error on the enemy's part."

"Yes, sir," Ishives replied. "But . . . it is also entirely targeted on our rear quadrant. Sir . . . they're going for our engines."

Humans knew a lot about *Aggressors*. They owned over forty that were in various stages of repair and upgrade as well as bits and pieces of hundreds more that had run afoul of *Troy*, *Thermopylae* and SAPL.

They knew less about AVs. Not because they didn't have pieces of them. Because that was pretty much all they had. And not *nearly* enough trained engineers to carefully sweep them up, put the jigsaw puzzle back together and examine them. They even had complete space docks for repairing them, captured in a previous battle in E Eridani space. But the specifications and blueprints had been purged.

So they didn't know them as intimately as they did *Aggressors*. But they did know a few things about them besides that they were ten kilometers long, a kilometer wide, shaped sort of like a truncated Kentucky rifle barrel and absolute rat bastards to kill.

Each of the eight sides sported twenty-six missile launch tubes and twenty lasers identical to the spinal lasers of an *Aggressor*. For defense there were another thirty-two overlapping and interlocking shields, each three times as strong as those on an *Aggressor* and impenetrable to any laser on a human "light" platform such as the *Constitutions* and *Defenders*. On each facet. The only way through the screens was penetrator missiles. Thus the forty-nine laser point defense batteries, thirty-two short range mass drivers and, of course, the dual mode attack/defense main missiles. On each facet.

They knew that the spinal laser of the AV was rated at sixty petawatts. While not a patch on the output of, say, *Troy*, much less SAPL, that would kill a *Defender*'s screens in two point six seconds and a *Constitution*'s in one point two. Armor lasted about a quarter of the time, so if a *Defender* stayed in the range of the AV's main gun for as long as four seconds it was destroyed.

Humans had managed to determine from the chunks, some large, of previously defeated AVs that they were sectional. And the Rangora were apparently big on eights since there were sixteen sections. The front three, besides supporting the side guns and defenses, were devoted to powering and managing the spinal gun. The next five were general power systems, primary life support, command sections and crew areas including mess. The last eight were devoted to maneuvering and engineering. While there were grav thrusters all along the facets—even shields could be used as such in a pinch—the main drive was the last eight sections. Six were devoted simply to *powering* the behemoth and the last two held the massive grav drives that permitted the two hundred and forty million ton superdreadnought a blistering *six* gravities of acceleration.

Every single penetrator missile in the human inventory in E Eridani was concentrated on segment sixteen. And the human missiles were...smart. Humans had not only taken Glatun technology and used it, they had studied it and applied their own understanding. Applied it well. While not technically artificial intelligences, the brains in the Thunderbolt missiles were...close.

Thus the missiles understood that they needed to not only drive through the defenses and drop the shields. They had to work together to do so and have enough *survive* the gauntlet to take out the massively armored engines.

If they had been truly sentient, which they were not, of course, their conversation would have gone something like this:

"*I wanna be first! I wanna be first! Let me go!*"

"*No, Jamie's first! He gets to soak up the lasers.*"

"*You're a meanie! I wanna die from laser fire!*"

"*I'm not a meanie! You get the fun part. You get to—*"

"*I get to what? Oh, yeah, I get to hit the big mean ship in the engines.*"

"*Yeah! You're lucky! All I get to do is take down the shie—*"

"*Wee, shields are down! I can go! I can go!*"

Okay, so not terribly smart.

But smart enough.

THIRTY-THREE

"Damage control!"

"Segment sixteen is gone, Captain. Estimate six missiles made it through all defenses. It's simply... gone."

"Now *we're* drifting in space," Colonel Ishives pointed out.

"I *know* that, Colonel." There were times when the captain dearly wished it was the good old days when you could simply *shoot* subordinates and not worry about the paperwork.

"And we have incoming laser fire from *Thermopylae*."

"*What?*" The internal laser power of the *Troy*-class battlestations was just one of many unpleasant surprises the humans had sprung on the Rangora. While not capable of immediately driving through an AV's screens—

"Inaccurate so far," Ishives said. "But..."

With the drive crippled and the *Crusher* unable to maneuver, the distant battlestation would eventually get their range.

"And... neutrino trace from the *Thermopylae* indicates they have gotten their Orion drive back online."

"*Impossible!*"

"Neutrinos don't lie, Captain."

"And PUSH!"

As a younger lad, Butch Allen had thought about many things he might do when he finally grew up. When he was five he was going to be a cowboy. Then he found out that job skill had grown out of fashion and that it was no longer politically correct, or in fact legal, to shoot Injuns. Fireman looked good for a while. Police officer was on the list. By the time he was in junior high

371

he had accepted that he would probably end up working the line at the GE plant, maybe be a shade-tree mechanic on the side.

Desperately trying to cut open another melted hatch on the outside of a three-kilometer-wide door while a nuke went off less than a kilometer away had never even crossed his mind. Ever. Not even close. Not in the same universe.

"Detonation in three...two..."

"Hang on!"

"Do we push or hang on, Mr. Allen?"

"Just..."

Whatever Butch was about to say, and even he couldn't remember afterwards, he hadn't been following his own advice. The ten megaton pusher nuke that team six had installed on the other side of the door didn't impart much energy to the *Therm* but it did impart enough to move it a bit. Just enough, and given some flexing on the part of the multimillion-ton, kilometer-thick nickel iron door, for Butch's sled to slam into the inside of the mostly, in fact, nearly fully cut-away hatch.

Said hatch, responding to the laws of physics, then tumbled outwards. Into the plasma wash of the nuke. Followed by Butch's sled.

What saved Butch's life was distance, angularity and the door. The nuke had been installed in a crater made by one of the Rangora missiles that had closed the *Therm*'s door oh so effectively. Thus most of the blast was upwards and away from Butch's position. Most. Virtually all of the rest hit the hatch. Since a kilometer matters in space, it had both cooled a good bit and spread out. There was still some serious velocity, however, which tumbled the hatch back into Butch's sled, cracking it and spinning it back into the maintenance tunnel to carom until it hit something solid. Which it quickly did when it hit Jinji's suit.

Jinji's suit was fairly robust, and since joining the Apollo team they'd made sure it was fully up to snuff. So it withstood the relatively low-velocity impact. Butch was wearing his own suit so the cracks in the sled were not immediately fatal.

Butch had survived being in the blast front of a nuke. Few could say that.

The question was whether he'd ever get a chance to tell anyone. Because while he had physically survived, and the nuke being "super-clean," he had no danger of death from irradiating radiation, that left one last tiny issue.

Electromagnetic pulse.

EMP was rarely an issue in space. EMP from nukes was caused by atmospheric atoms being stripped of their electrons and thus creating an electrified "wave front" which in turn did all sorts of damage to complex electronics. Even the clean fusion reaction didn't create the issue.

However, when a clean fusion bomb is detonated in contact with nickel iron, the *nickel-iron* atoms are stripped of their electrons. And any delicate electronics, such as a suit's navigation and atmospheric control pack, shut off.

Butch took a suck of air and . . . there wasn't any. Not vacuum, just . . . not circulating. No more air was entering his helmet. Probably ever. He could suck and suck and suck and he wasn't going to get any air.

Apollo, with the exception of the placement of ship fabbers, planned well. There *was* a plan for this. There was even training. All that Butch had to remember was to remain calm and, oh, yeah, that long-ago training class.

There were, in fact, two choices. Both involved exiting the sled.

Some of the Apollo systems had been designed with the input of experienced professional divers. One thing that technical divers know is that air is a good thing when there's not any around you. So there was a way to extend a line from the suit to another suit and "borrow" their air.

Butch thought there might be a couple of issues. While he knew where the emergency air link was on Jinji's suit, and that they were compatible, he wasn't sure if it needed a functioning suit on his side to work. And he wasn't willing to try one thing and not have it work. Since he had, like, zero time. So that left plan B.

On the exterior of the sled was an emergency body pack. It had an air recirculation system. Butch didn't know why all his electronics had gone dead—EMP was barely a concept to the welder—but he knew something had screwed everything electronic. However, the air pack in the body bag was manual. Just a little oxygen valve attached to an unfortunately small air-pack. Nothing electronic. Butch didn't know that a junior engineer, when they were designing the emergency survival pack, one each, pointed out that in the event of an EMP or similar space event such as a coronal mass ejection, they wanted something manual. And for a wonder the more senior engineers and even the engineering managers nodded and stroked their beards and wondered if the little jerk was angling for their job but went with it anyway.

All of that went through his head when he sucked and there was *nothing there*. No air. No air. The second thought that went through his head, instantly suppressed, was to tear his helmet off and breathe the nice vacuum around him. Immediately following *that* was the word "MOMMY." Clear as a bell.

Butch was never sure, afterwards, exactly how long those thoughts took. He knew he took one more breath, just to be sure, then decided he wasn't going to keep trying. The air wasn't coming back.

He calmly hit the quick release on his harness, then the fast hatch on the sled. The fast hatch was to be used only in emergencies. It blew the hatch off with a light jet of nitrogen and required that the entire hatch be essentially rebuilt. Bottom of the list on what was going to have to be rebuilt on this sled. And this was, definitely, an emergency.

No air.

Butch calmly grabbed the hatch and pulled himself into the corridor. Jinji started to reach for him, using one of his waldoes, and Butch, making sure he didn't tumble, waved the waldo away. The wave was somewhat wild, panic sneaking through his hard-held calm. It triggered his trying to take another breath and one leg kicked a bit too hard, almost sending him out into the corridor in a tumble. That would have been . . . bad. So he controlled himself.

No *air*.

He moved his hand to the grab bar, then pulled himself to the rear of the sled. At that moment it occurred to him that what with everything else the bag's container might have been damaged or lost. But there it was, a small ovoid like a big orange pill.

Butch carefully detached it, one mistake and he was never ever going to breathe again, and pressed the red button on the ovoid with both thumbs. The bag deployed smoothly, flex metal components opening it into an orange tunnel, closed at the bottom, open at Butch's end.

No air, no air . . .

Butch realized that his vision was closing in but ignored it. He was either going to get in the bag successfully, get the air going and open his helmet or . . . he wasn't.

He carefully slid both boots into the rather narrow opening, then reached down, one careful hand at a time, and pulled the two red tabs on either side of the tunnel. They wouldn't give until his boots hit the bottom, at which point the top of the bag snapped shut. And, according to everything he'd been told, the oxygen system should flood the bag with O2.

Butch carefully reached up and popped his helmet seals. The rush of gases coming out of his suit, not to mention the icepicks in his ears and the sucking on his eyeballs, almost panicked him again. But he exhaled as he'd been trained, to prevent pulmonary embolism. Probably took a second for the bag to pressurize. That was all. Few seconds, max. Or it had a puncture he hadn't seen when he skipped the step "examine the exterior for cracks, dents or punctures." What the hell, he could breathe vacuum for a looong time.

Eternity.

"Status on the nukes?" Admiral Clemons asked.

"One team is down," Guptill replied. "Caught part of a blast when they were opening their hatch. The rest are still working the problem. Five teams. About ten minutes apiece to get them in place. Two minutes apart."

"That's fine," Clemons said, nodding. "We don't want to actually close. Just give the impression we *can*."

"Getting ready to fire the laser," Dexter said.

"I hate everything about this battle," Clemons said. "I hate the feeling we're not winning. I hate the casualties. I hate that we're essentially trashed. Why do I like this part?"

"Because it's the first thing that's felt like a really science fiction laser fire?" Guptill asked.

"Straight out of the movies. Okay... fire."

"All hands! All hands! Prepare for momentary loss of power!"

Every light in the already dim CIC except the readouts themselves shut down as did the air recyclers. There was a somewhat unpleasant hum as overworked and jerry-rigged transformers tried to handle the fortunately reduced power. Then the air started again and the lights came back up.

"Laser shot complete," Guptill said. "Clean miss."

"That's tellin' 'em," Clemons said. "Now get me more power."

"Admiral Marchant."

"Field Marshall," Marchant said, nodding at the system commander.

"Just get out of the system," Marshall Hampson said. "You may continue to engage the enemy, but maximize running away and surviving."

"Yes, sir," Marchant said bitterly. "Sir, with the AV unable to engage, we have numerical superiority. We can still win this one."

"We'll be back, Russ. Sooner than you'd expect. Just get clear of the gate."

"Yes, sir."

"Humans have changed their posture," Colonel Ishives said. "They appear to be heading for the gate and are maximizing defense over attack."

"Good," Captain Be'Sojahiph said. "They have seen reality. Even with our damage they cannot hold the system."

"However, they are so far into our fire basket . . . I'm not sure it matters."

The *Aggressor* groups had been holding back behind the AVs until the loss of the first AV. At that point they had started to move forward, their fire combining with that of the AV.

Fortunately, they were in gate exit posture. Marchant's force simply had to screen past them.

Simply.

The *Aggressors* had oriented their axis towards the retreating human force, their spinal lasers combined with the fire from the AV pounding the human shields.

"Let's try fourteen X-ray," Marchant said. "Get the *Indies* out of this fire. They don't have the screens for it."

"Fourteen X-ray, aye," Captain Whisler said. "*Kansas* is out. Still there but no longer under control. *Bush* is—"

"Gone," Marchant said. "Close formation."

"At least we're exiting the AV fire basket."

"Small mercies."

"So you ask us to be merciful?"

Envoy Ve'Disuc recognized a breakthrough when he saw one. Speaking directly to the American President, functionally the Alliance Supreme Commander, was a breakthrough.

"The mercy cuts two ways, Envoy," President Robards said. "There are tens of thousands of stranded spacers from both

sides. Temporary truces to clear the wounded from the battlefield are common in even Rangora history. No more than that.
Enough time to get noncombat ships into the system to clear
the wounded. Your Marines on the *Thermopylae*, for example,
are in a rather difficult position. They are short on consumables,
cut off from resupply, outnumbered and in most cases frankly
lost. We'll supply them with consumables and permit them to
be evacuated. You can have them back. No prisoners taken on
either side. Remaining Rangora ships to be towed off by the
Rangora, same for human ships. E Eridani to be in a state of
cease-fire until such a time."

"And the *Thermopylae*?"

"Will take some time to move out of the system," the President said.

"Unacceptable. Madame President, *we* hold the system."

"For how long? You know the timetable on upgrades, not
repairs, *upgrades*, on the *Troy*. In twelve days you had better have
twice the fleet you have already thrown away. Or be gone from
E Eridani. And, Envoy, we still hold ships in the Terran system.
What do *you* have in reserve?"

"We have, I assure you, a quite sizeable reserve," Ve'Disuc
replied. "And we know your ship strength to the last corvette. So
we know that you have no sizeable force available. I am authorized
to discuss a cease-fire to recover wounded and stranded in the
system. No attempt may be made to recover the *Thermopylae* or
any other derelict human ship. You may surrender them to the
Rangora Imperium but not recover them. Furthermore, personnel aboard the *Thermopylae* and other human combat vessels
in system shall surrender to our liberation forces and be taken
prisoner pending further negotiations."

"Unacceptable."

"Then I suppose we are at an impasse, Madame President."

"Agreed."

"To our terms, Madame President?" Ve'Disuc asked.

"That we are at an impasse. Which is, frankly, too bad for your
surviving Rangora since we have few ships left to do recovery. And
we will, obviously, have to prioritize recovering human survivors."

"Again, Madame President, we hold the system."

"Not for long. Goodbye, Envoy. Admiral?"

"Ma'am?"

"*Can* we take the system?"

"No, ma'am. Not until the *Troy* is mobile again. But I think we can get them to agree to our terms."

"One last cast of the dice, Admiral?"

"He fears his fate too much and his desserts are small..."

"Admiral, please don't quote Vernon Tyler to me at a time like this."

"Oh thank God," Captain Whisler said. "Now I know how Villeneuve felt."

"Not...quite," Admiral Marchant said, looking at the updated tactical display.

"Where did *those* come from?" Whisler asked. "And what is that...thing?"

"*Troy* strikes again?"

"Skew us to engage the *Thermopylae*," Captain Be'Sojahiph said. "Now that the light units are gone, that is the next priority."

"And the survivors, sir?"

"The ones in boats will survive for several days," Captain Be'Sojahiph replied. "The ones in suits...will survive or not. Begin rotation."

"Skew aye, sir," Colonel Ishives said.

"*Aggressor* squadrons redeploy to surround the battle globe. Let's see if we can support the Marines."

"Not your first battle, is it, sir?" Sergeant Ghezhosil said.

"Not my first battle, Sergeant," Lieutenant Lanniph admitted.

Birds of a feather do indeed flock together. But in this case, Lanniph had simply followed orders to "rendezvous with reinforcing personnel." He still wasn't sure exactly what he was dealing with in Sergeant Ghezhosil.

"First battle in vacuum?"

"Not even close."

"Ever notice how three days' worth of consumables never seems to last three days, sir?"

"Yes. And I know the first rule of vacuum operations, Sergeant."

"Seriously?"

"Seriously, Sergeant. And I *do* have the bigger knife."

"Cracker?"

"That's 'cracker, sir?' Problem with that, Sergeant?"

"Just that it doesn't seem quite fair, sir. You get the rank, you get the pay *and* you know the scams. There should be a rule, sir."

"There pretty much is, Sergeant."

"Lanniph, Sector Fourteen control."

"Fourteen control, Lanniph."

"Take your platoon left at the next junction. Report of human forward command post in that area. Assault, clear and report."

"Roger. Fourteen higher. Several personnel with damaged suit systems. Request life support resupply. Ammunition low. Request ammunition resupply."

"The humans should have both, Lanniph. Fourteen control, out."

"Hmph. That would be, I suppose, incentive. How long, Sergeant?"

"About twelve hours, sir. I suppose there's always the Perrechoa Option."

During one of the Rangora's frequent minor civil wars, the Loyalist garrison on the Perrechoa battlestation found itself so low on consumables, mostly air, that wounded personnel voluntarily transferred their "consumables" to more functional combatants. Their Ma'Lholhafeqist opponents were not much better off. The battle mostly came down to who could hold out longer. Given that the Ma'Lholhafeqist wounded and clerks weren't willing to give up their precious air to the hale fighters, the Loyalists won.

All seven of the regiment's survivors.

'Twas a famous victory.

"Hopefully not," Lanniph said. "Rather don't want to go through *that* again. Move 'em out, sergeant."

"Yes, sir," Ghezhosil said, getting to his feet. He started to look at the name carets and decided he really didn't care. "You. Point. Rest of you, on your feet."

"Why m—?" the private scrambled to his feet in the face of two laser rifles pointed at him.

"Because the sergeant gave you an order," Lanniph said. "It was not a request."

"Moving out, Sergeant."

"You're quick, sir," Ghezhosil said.

"And still alive," Lanniph replied. He pulled out a sensor ball and contemplated it for a moment. "How many of these do you have left?"

"Balls? Don't usually carry them, sir."

"Hmmm. Learn." The lieutenant keyed the sensor ball and dropped it in the corridor.

"Sir?" Ghezhosil asked. Since the L-T hadn't ordered him up front, he was just as happy to hang in the rear.

"Have you once in this ixi screw had higher give you a definite target? Beyond 'find the control center.'"

"No, sir," Ghezhosil said.

"Nor I. Therefore I would like to know what is *behind* us as we go *forward* to this supposed objective."

"Good thinking that, sir," Ghezhosil said.

"That is my job, Sergeant Ghezhosil."

"Yes, sir," Ghezhosil said then paused. "Sir, what did you mean by 'again'?"

THIRTY-FOUR

"And here we go again."

Two more battleship groups weren't going to help in Admiral Marchant's opinion. Not against seven remaining *Aggressor* groups and the semi-invalid AV. The rest, however...

The battle seemed to have taken days. In fact, since the *Thermopylae* entered the system and discovered more than the Horvath had come to call, a bare ten hours had passed. Since the *Troy* expended all its missiles, six hours beat their measured tune, slicing away the time until the heat death of the universe one precious millisecond at a time.

The *Troy* under optimum conditions produced four hundred missiles per minute. Twenty-four *thousand* per hour. Alas, conditions were not optimum. That assumed sufficient supply of critical parts which currently were not sufficient. However, since it had sent "all its missiles" it had produced seventy-three thousand Thunderbolt missiles. The partially functional *Malta* had produced an additional six thousand.

And then there was Vernon Tyler's latest abortion. Although in this case the tycoon would probably blame Granadica.

"This time we're not sending them all," Field Marshall Hampson said. "God knows if the Rangora have more ships waiting in Glalkod system. I think sixty thousand is a nice round number."

"Four waves," Admiral Marchant said. "Twenty thousand to plow the road for the ships. Then the ships and the MinJolnir with a group of twenty thousand for interceptors. Then the rest, since they can outrun our ships at a standing start."

"Approved," Marshall Hampson said. "Try to keep your casualties down. We're going to need your ships to recover the survivors."

"Intend to, Marshall."

"Take back that system, Admiral."

"We're not taking this position, sir."

"Noticed that."

There might, in fact, be a human command post up ahead. If so, one platoon of grunts wasn't going to take it.

The human Marines were heavily bunkered in what were obviously hastily constructed fighting positions. But given that they were hastily constructed of wall material and the sort of thick NI hatches that had prevented the Rangora from moving forward repeatedly . . .

"Two more troops down," Ghezhosil said.

"Fourteen higher, Lanniph."

"Lanniph, fourteen higher."

"The enemy's finally decided to take a stand. Unfortunately, it's in a heavily bunkered position. We need heavy weapons to take this out."

"Roger, wait one."

"Sure, got nothing better to do."

"Lanniph, Fourteen higher. Have you tried fire and maneuver and grenades?"

"Stand by, Fourteen higher." Lanniph keyed his hydration module and took a sip of stale water. "So, where've you been lately, Sergeant?"

"Tuxughah, sir," Ghezhosil said. "Livith. Heraldon. Jittan."

"So, do you think this is more or less of a cluster grope than Tuxughah? I was at Qoalh so I've no direct experience. I understand it was unpleasant."

"I think this is a bit worse in some ways, sir," Ghezhosil said. "There was actually something resembling a plan at Tuxughah. Just didn't work, sir. But that ixi screw was . . . bigger?"

"My impression as well. Fourteen higher, Lanniph. Negative effect on the grenades. Really could use a heavy system here."

"Roger Lanniph. Stand by."

"Standing by. Which wave were you in?"

"Drop capsules."

"Sorry."

"Kinda like hot drops, sir. Of course, you're dropping from orbit as a screaming, blazing target. But with enough capsules and decoys it just comes down to if your number's up or not. And drops are a rush and a half, sir."

"Agreed. I prefer the initial atmospheric entry portion, personally. That first slam when you hit the upper troposphere... There's really nothing quite like it."

"You're drop capsule certified, sir?"

"We were probably dropping in different areas on Heraldon. I had a platoon of the 42nd."

"So I guess that you understand sitting in vacuum waiting for my air to run out is sort of a second choice."

"Completely."

"Lanniph, Fourteen higher. We're going to try to vector a heavy weapons team to your position."

"Roger, Fourteen higher. Might want to send some security with them."

He leaned around the corner of the corridor and triggered a burst of fire down the side tunnel.

"State reason, over."

"'Cause we're crapping *surrounded*!" Ghezhosil said, picking up the transmission from the L-T's sensor ball.

"We lost Sarban," Lieutenant Khan said.

"Might have something to do with the sensor ball in the corridor, sir," Sergeant Del Papa said. "All we have to do, sir, is pin them until reinforcements come up. Got a heavy laser on the way. That should convince them to come out hands up."

"Easier said than done, Sergeant. That is very accurate fire."

"You... Yauk!" Sergeant Ghezhosil said. "Grab whoever that is down and get me his ammo."

"*You* get it!" the private shrieked. He was huddling on the deck with his arms over his head.

"Okay, then, give me *your* ammo!"

"Screw you!" the private said, finally getting his rifle into use to aim it at the sergeant. Given that Ghezhosil was out of ammo, there wasn't much he could do but take the laser fire.

Suddenly a knife appeared in a chink in the private's armor by the neck seals, which began gushing air and blood.

"Might want to turn his air off when you get the ammo," Lieutenant Lanniph said, taking another shot down the corridor. "Waste not, want not."

✳　　✳　　✳

"Gate activation," Colonel Ishives said.

"The additional *Aggressor* groups?" Captain Be'Sojahiph asked.

"Sol system."

"They really think they can take this system with—" The captain stopped as the data on incoming came up. "Where did they get an additional twenty *thousand* missiles? Begin rotation. Have the *Aggressors* spread to—"

"Missiles are not targeting us, sir," Ishives said.

"Oh ... ixi shit."

This was Captain Zoa Qa'Zafilach's nineteenth battle. All but one previous during the Glatun War against Glatun battleships, cruisers and, notably, missiles. When, just prior to this engagement, he was given an update on the human's Thunderbolt missiles his immediate reactions were, in order, that they were remarkably similar to, perhaps an improvement upon, the Glatun equivalent and that he hoped he never had to face them.

So far in this battle his wish had been granted. However, if wishes were skul trees ...

"Tell me point defense is one hundred percent."

"Point defense is ... close? Say ninety percent. Shields, though ..."

"Took damage from the human cruisers and battleships."

"Yes, sir. Seventy percent on shields."

The fleet had shot its wad of heavy missiles against the *Thermopylae*. To some good effect, but at the moment Captain Qa'Zafilach dearly wished he had something, anything, to engage that tidal wave of missiles other than pop-gun lasers and mass drivers.

"This is ... not so good."

Oh, well, at least he didn't have to worry about the Kazi.

The Rangora second fleet had entered the system with sixteen *Aggressor* groups and two AVs. Seven *Aggressors* had been lost to human fire along with thirty-nine of the sixty-four secondary vessels and, of course, one AV.

Twenty thousand missiles were, therefore, targeting nine *Aggressors*, seventeen *Cofubof*-class cruisers and eight *Gufesh* destroyers. All of which were shot out on countermissiles.

Normally the Thunderbolts would have to fly through a welter of countermissiles. This time they came on in an implacable wave, the formation breaking up to concentrate four-fifths of its power, sixteen thousand missiles, on the nine *Aggressors*. Nearly two thousand per ship.

There is a saying: There is no such thing as overkill. There is only "Open fire!" and "Reloading!"

It only took six hundred missiles, not two thousand, to drive through the *Cuwwutoa*'s point defenses.

Fortunately, although there were no more *Aggressors*, cruisers, destroyers or frigates to destroy, there was a great big target still in their engagement basket.

"Damn, damn, DAMN!" Captain Be'Sojahiph shouted.

"In retrospect, a negotiated cease-fire might have been a valid option," Colonel Ishives said. The introspective and intelligent tactical officer should probably have considered it was the first time his commander had lost his temper.

"Get that jagi carcass out of my CIC," Be'Sojahiph growled as the colonel's body thumped to the deck. "Increase rotation speed. Begin engagement at long range with heavy missiles."

"Add...additional units entering system," the tactical technician stuttered.

"What *now*?"

More than twelve thousand missiles were left to assault the rapidly rolling, invalid AV.

Depending upon conditions, the final kinetic energy delivery of the missiles varied. It was a matter of relative velocities. In this case, the AV was moving away from their start point at nearly a hundred kilometers per minute. And the missiles had first targeted the *Aggressor* groups, which were at a slight angle from the AV. Thus instead of the maximum of thirty-five megatons of delivery, the missiles were impacting the AV with a measly sixteen megatons of kinetic impact.

Unlike most previous battles, though, they were not slamming the entire length of the superdreadnought. Instead, they were selectively targeting along its midline segments.

"Sections six and seven report heavy damage," Major Viog shouted over the scream of alarms. The damage control officer was less worried about being shot than most since he was just about the most vital person on the ship at the moment.

"Really?" Captain Be'Sojahiph said, slamming his helmet closed. "Was it the hiss of evacuating air that gave it away?"

"No, sir!" Viog said. "It was probably the total destruction of all the shield generators, point defense and missile tubes in our section. Sir!"

"Enemy's second wave."

"Twenty thousand missiles, the rest of their fleet and one unclassified vessel. All accelerating at eleven seventy meters per second square."

"I don't like the sound of that," Be'Sojahiph said, keying up the information. He compared the gravity emissions of the vessels to other systems, a job that would have been Ishives', come to think of it, and frowned.

"*Independence* class?" Be'Sojahiph said. "Probably. They're trying to replicate that horrible *Constitution*...thing that took out the *Herraruo*. But...target all long-range fire on that vessel. If they get through..."

"Targeting set," the tactical tech said.

"Then *fire!*"

"Maneuver to cover the MinJolnir," Admiral Marchant said. "Accelerate the missiles. Linear formation. Target the next segments outward from the center. Ships maintain perpendicular formation. Pound the shit out of that thing."

"Set up, sir."

"Initiate."

"Second wave of missiles inbound, Captain," the tactical tech said nervously. "Seem to be targeting segments five and eight."

"Prepare to reduce rotation," Captain Be'Sojahiph said.

"Sir?" the tactical tech growled.

"They're trying to open up our center so they can break us with that thing," Be'Sojahiph said. "We need to keep *some* shields *up*. We'll take the damage on one segment until it's scrap, *then* rotate."

"*Sheffield's* lost forward screens," Captain Whisler said. "Rotating out of formation."

"Acknowledged," Admiral Marchant said.

"Skew to keep that fleet on our flank," Captain Be'Sojahiph said.

"Captain?" the tactical tech said.

"Yes?" Be'Sojahiph ground out.

"The *Thermopylae* has managed to reverse its previous course. It's . . . closing."

I need at least one tactical specialist alive so I don't have to do it.

"Maintain fire with spinal gun. We'll burn through sooner or later. Or at least take out their damned laser."

"So that's the situation," Del Papa said. "They're stuck in that corridor. Good targeting and position so we can't winkle them out. Not without being bloody slaughtered in the process. On the other hand, they can't get out, either. But command wants them cleaned out so we can go find more."

He wasn't sure about this Marine. It was nice to find somebody who could speak English. But he hadn't heard that sort of tone in a long time. Like the last time he worked recovery on one of the bombed out cities.

"I can do that," Ramage said, flatly. "Give me enough time, I can burn through the damned wall."

Rammer knew he had a message from Comet on his phone. He also knew what it would be. "Last Call." That message you set up to go out when you'd bought it. "Well, this is the Last Call. Here's all the stuff I wanted to tell you when I was alive but didn't have the guts." He had about sixty of them to work through already. He figured he'd just wait to see if he needn't have bothered. He figured by the end of the day, about seventy-three people would be getting one from him. Of course, sixty or so of them were never going to pick up.

In the meantime, there were Rangora to kill.

"Just suppress them so we can work up the damned tunnel."

"On it, Sergeant."

Captain Be'Sojahiph's plan worked. Partially.

"Shields down in quadrants forty-three, thirty-seven, twenty-eight and sixteen. Those are losses of the generators. Shields yellow in twenty-four, thirty-six, twenty-seven and nineteen. Point defense down in all four plus quadrants twenty-two and sixty-seven. No additional damage to sections six and seven."

When a quadrant had been sufficiently trashed, surviving missiles in the wave with enough maneuverability had shifted to adjacent quadrants, working out. But that left the entire rear section, minus the central sectors, undamaged.

"Full rotate," Captain Be'Sojahiph said. "Continue max fire. Status on *Thermopylae*."

"Starting to accelerate towards us," Tactical replied. "Still no hits from its laser. We're hitting it but we have been unable to take out the one laser that appears functional. There are screens and it is adjusting in a...very random manner."

"Odd," Be'Sojahiph said. "Not the random adjustment, the missing. Their systems are generally quite accurate. How long until it reaches this vicinity?"

"Four hours, sir."

"We have time, then."

"*Third* wave of missiles," Tactical said.

"That's why they make these things tough, Tactical."

"Prepare to skew," Admiral Marchant said.

"Not before time, sir," Captain Whisler replied.

The timing was...tricky.

Granadica wasn't the only fabber working on a ship when the Rangora showed up. Hephaestus on *Troy* had been working on an *Independence* class and was at about the same stage of completion. Notably it had drives and power systems loaded. Squashing it and armoring it was easy. In addition, however, the "Mini-Mjolnir" had been outfitted with heavier armor and screens designed for a *Defender* class.

That wasn't enough, however, to survive closing with a fully prepared AV that was dealing with a few mosquitoes called battleships. It needed more mosquitoes called missiles for cover.

The problem being that the MinJolnir had much lower acceleration than the missiles. The last wave had to fully occupy the attention of the superdreadnought so the MinJolnir had a chance of plowing through.

Tricky.

Marchant watched the vector indicators for the missiles and then made the call less on math than gut.

"Skew fleet. Full accel on MinJolnir."

"The enemy fleet is skewing," Tactical said. "They're exposing the rammer ship."

"All lasers concentrate on that rammer," Be'Sojahiph said. He'd done the math. The smaller ship was going to have a fraction of the effect of the heavier rammer. But that fraction, if it hit their central sectors, was going to be enough to crack his AV in half.

"Rammer is maneuvering," tactical said. "High delta. Minimal hits at this range. And . . . it's shielded this time."

"Damn, damn and blast!"

MinJolnir was, indeed, ducking and weaving for all it was worth. The heavy secondaries of the AV should still have blasted it from stem to stern. However, there were six heavy screens forward. As one dropped from laser fire, another would catch the incoming coherent light. Generally the original screen could reset. But first one dropped offline from fire, then another. With no damage control technicians aboard to fix them, they were permanently lost.

Eventually the AV was going to win. If something didn't happen to stop the fire.

"Enemy missiles overtaking rammer ship," Tactical said. "They're maneuvering to take our fire."

"Begin rotation," Be'Sojahiph said. "We'll see what survives after this missile pass. Maintain fire on the rammer."

Since the missiles had the dedicated job of intercepting laser fire to keep it off MinJolnir, fewer than four thousand made it to the superdreadnought. Between the rapid rotation and point defense, none made it through to the armor. However, they had been set to spread attack and dozens of screens were offline from stem to stern.

"Sir!" Captain Blades said, sitting up in his command chair.

"Captain?" Clemons said, halfheartedly.

"Forward screens in quadrant seven down on the AV," Blades said.

"Targeted fire!"

"Laser's still warming . . ."

"When we fire . . ." Clemons said, "maintain fire as long as possible."

"Oh, yes, sir."

THIRTY-FIVE

The forward screen hit had been more or less an accident. The Thunderbolt had been part of a group of ten targeted on section two. When the screens on two had failed it automatically shifted to section one. Amazingly, the single missile made it through the point defense fire and hit the screen. All that happened was the penetrator system dropped the screen.

Even the Rangora had automated reset breakers for that sort of eventuality. But repeated impacts had caused enough vibration damage that many of them were offline. Even then, fast action on the part of damage control would have had the screen reset and up in seconds.

AV damage control crews were, in general, excellent. Elite even. On average. Which meant some were splendid and some were mediocre and a very few were quite poor.

Unfortunately for Captain Be'Sojahiph's career, the Damage Control Team 1176, Quadrant Seven, Screens, was *not* among the elite. How long it would have taken to get the screen back up quickly became a point in the same category as Pickett's Charge, to be argued over by history buffs.

The single repaired collimator system on the *Thermopylae* was, in fact, quite accurate. The tactical group on the *Therm* had been taking some black humor in precisely missing the AV. The battlestation's laser had a "bare" sixty petawatts of power at its disposal, about the same as an AV main gun. There was no way that the reduced power of the laser could get through the screens and the armor to the vitals of the beast unless something very fortuitous happened.

But sixty petawatts was nearly *six* times the power of a spinal gun on a *Defender*. Enough to do some serious damage if a screen went down that was oriented precisely at the crippled battlestation.

"And charrrrged, firing!" Sharp yelled.

The lights dimmed again as every scrap of available power was fed to the laser.

"*Come* on, baby..." Clemons moaned. "Jack those bastards up."

The reduced power laser hit the AV squarely on the nose, just off the main spinal gun collimator. It dug through the heaviest armor on any constructed dreadnought in the spiral arm in less than half a second, then started digging deeper.

It was the true value of "crossing a T." Generally it was thought that the ability to avoid enemy fire whilst pounding him was the main value. The laser, fired from the side through one of the damaged quadrants, would have simply bored through and gone out the other side. Surrounding, undamaged, quadrants would have shrugged off the rest of the fire. As the *Thermopylae* proved, the main value was the ability to fire down the *length* of a ship, rather than transverse, so as to do the maximum internal damage possible. First every system in quadrant seven failed, screen generators were trashed, point defense, then the carefully aimed laser, unimpeded by armor or screens, dug into the massive capacitors for the spinal laser causing catastrophic damage in surrounding quadrants. As it dug deeper systems fell in quadrant after quadrant as secondary detonations caused complete failures in section one, two, three...

"Skew! Skew! Skew!" Captain Be'Sojahiph screamed.

His ship seemed to be a continuous set of explosions working front to back just as the missile wave had receded.

"Laser hit on forward quadrant," Major Viog said blandly. "Forward three segments offline. Major damage in quadrants..."

"Status of rammer?" Captain Be'Sojahiph said, cutting him off.

"It's..." Tactical said, then rippled his scales. "We're not going to stop it. Not now."

The MinJolnir carried a fraction of the power of its larger cousin. But it was enough.

It hit the AV squarely on section five, directly over the CIC with a kinetic force of nearly seventy-two megatons.

From a distance, the explosion was almost unspectacular. It looked a bit like the warning symbol for fireworks. The AV, viewed from a distance, looked not unlike a stick of dynamite. The expanding fireball looked like a painting of an explosion. And the two halves tumbled away from each other quite slowly.

That was how it looked from a distance, anyway.

"Quadrants of the AV are still firing," Captain Whisler said, shaking his head. "And the rear section is getting its rotational capability back already. Lots of screens down and such but..."

"How in the hell did the Glatun take out *any* of these?" Marchant asked, wonderingly. "Without a *Troy* class I mean."

"We took out three easy peasy, sir," Whisler said. "You just need a butt load and a half of missiles."

"I suppose that's true," Marchant said. "Get me Field Marshall Hampson. Time to talk. Again."

"Do you want to *guess* how many missiles I have left?" the President asked. She wasn't sure if the Rangora understood human body posture or tone. Her staff would probably describe it, quietly, as "tired, frustrated and on her last nerve."

"We agree to a cease-fire to clear the survivors. We recover our ships where possible, you recover yours where possible. No prisoners and no engagement until all damaged vessels and survivors are cleared."

"I'll add the condition that when the *Troy* clears the gate into E Eridani you had better be either gone or ready to rumble."

"Understood."

Technically, the Pathans should be doing this, Del Papa thought. But closing on an enemy position under heavy fire... wasn't their strong suit.

So of course De Pops was hugging the bulkhead and deck, trying to sneak around the corner on a couple of Rangora who were living up to their rep.

Fortunately the Deuce Jarhead with the heavy laser was laying down so much fire Del Papa could feel the bulkhead heating up. Maybe too much.

"I am going to get your lizard ass..." Del Papa said, tossing another sensor ball down the corridor.

Not only was the ball shot out, the fucker's laser poked around the corner and shot right where DP *had* been. Fortunately, he wasn't born yesterday.

"I *am* gonna..."

"All units. Cease-fire in effect. All units. Cease-fire in effect. Switch frequencies for local Rangora contact."

Papa brought up the hypercom channel and tried not to scream.

"Ixi sucking..." Ghezhosil hissed, bringing up the hypercom channel.

"YOU HAVE *GOT* TO BE IXIKAGA/FUCKING KIDDING ME!"

"Wait..." Sergeant Ghezhosil said. "What did he...?"

"What?" Del Papa said. "What is...Ikki...?"

"Human unit, this is Lieutenant Lanniph, Rangoran Imperial Space Infantry. Cease-fire in effect. Do you acknowledge?"

"Yeah, yeah," Del Papa said. "Sergeant First Class Del Papa, Terran Marines. Acknowledged."

"Do you have details, yet?"

"Nope," Del Papa said, leaning up against the bulkhead. The Rangora he'd been trying to kill for the last twenty minutes was, he was sure, just about in arm's reach. "Just going to cop a squat and wait on that. I'd offer y'all a smoke but it's sort of tough in vacuum."

"And I'd offer skul, but I believe it is poisonous to humans. As tobacco is to us."

"It's the thought that counts," Del Papa said. "And speaking of which, my translator can't find ikki...whatever."

"It involves... I could answer that but I'm going to have you ask Sergeant Ghezhosil while I contact higher..."

Del Papa leaned around the corner, then had to look up.

"Ghezhosil?"

"Yep," the Rangora said. "Damn, you guys are short."

"Better to sneak up on your ass. So...Ikk...whatever...?"

"Ixikaga. There's this animal, an ixi. Legless lizard. Like one of your snakes. What hillbillies do is they take 'em and they..."

EPILOGUE

Rammer rolled over in his rack at the hammering on his door.

"Go the fuck away!" he shouted. "I'm off watch!"

Getting the situation in the fucking *Therm* rat maze under control had been a nightmare. The Rangora were perfectly willing to surrender. Most of them were about out of ammo and consumables. It was the fucking Pathans who had been the problem. They really didn't get "negotiated surrender." And then there was the problem of what to do with the Rangora. They were in as bad a shape as Earth, boats-wise. Finally, command had given up and just let them into the control areas, the very spot the Rangora had been trying to find and fight their way through to for a day and a half. After they'd had more negotiations, since command was only willing to let them through if they disarmed.

Finally, they'd gotten the entire rat fuck put to bed, the Rangora settled in in the mall, of all places, and put under guard until they could be "repatriated." And he'd been assigned some goat-smelling dead Pathan's quarters and told he had six hours off.

And now they were pounding on his fucking door again!

"Rammer! Open this FUCKING HATCH!"

His eyes flew open and he rolled out of the rack so fast the term "relativity" came to mind.

"Comet?" he asked, his eyes wide.

"Do you *ever* answer your God damned com?" Parker asked, tears in her eyes.

"I thought..." Rammer said. "You were with the squadron..."

"I was on another detail, dumbass," she said, pushing him aside so she could enter the compartment. "*I* bothered to actually check the casualty lists."

"I...I couldn't. I couldn't even pick up your message..." he said, lamely. "I thought it was..."

"That is why you're a Marine," Dana said. "You're not very bright." She winced and shook her head. "Rammer, I'm sorry..."

"No," he said, reaching out and touching her hair to make sure she was really there. "You making Marine jokes means... Something important I can't figure out right now. Like life goes on or something." He paused again and took his hand away as her rank tabs registered.

"I mean, ma'am, you making Marine jokes means... *Lieutenant*? I mean, ma'am..."

"Oh, don't start," she said, shaking her head. "I think this is temporary. There are surviving trained Marines. I'm about the only surviving trained and experienced *Myrm* pilot and engineer we've got left. *The* only one for a while in Eridani. At least with recovery experience. The admiral put these on me so the Krauts would listen to me. That's it."

"Uh..." Ramage said. "Yes, ma'am."

"I said don't start," Dana said, starting to pull off her blouse. "I'm *fully* aware of the regulations regarding this sort of thing and don't really give a shit. So I'll give you a direct order once. Start stripping, Sergeant, cause I've only got three hours off and I don't intend to spend it crying."

Lieutenant Commander Carter "Booth" Bouthillier had had quite some time to contemplate the relative values of the hypercom system. Close to twenty-four hours. The reason he had had that time to simply sit and contemplate was that there was effectively nothing else to do on a lifeboat.

He'd finally turned off the news, which was going simply apeshit. Not so much because there had been a battle in E Eridani. That sort of thing was just another day at the office. To a greater extent because for the first time in years the Earth had clearly gotten its ass kicked and in the process of "winning" had lost virtually its entire fleet, not to mention nearly losing a battlestation. And, of course, *Thermopylae* was seriously trashed and would take months to repair.

The main reason that the news was going apeshit was because there were over twenty-seven *thousand* humans in his position. And every single one of them had communications back home through the hypercom network. And every single one of them had, at one point, called their families and friends to tell them they were "doing just fine." And then about ninety percent, it seemed, ended up being interviewed on vidblogs, local newscasts and even major networks. The worst had been the interviews with people who were "Dutchmen." The news services had quickly figured out that people simply could not handle listening to reasonably intelligent and articulate spacers slowly going mad as they waited, almost invariably in vain, for rescue.

Every remaining ship in Wolf and Sol system was now involved in the rescue effort. Three problems.

The survivors were scattered over, as had been repeatedly reported, seventy *billion* cubic kilometers of space. The newscasts trying to explain to grounders just how unbelievably big an area that was had been humorous. Especially since most of *them* clearly couldn't grasp it.

Second problem: "Every remaining ship" was less than a hundred. Earth's fleet had been trashed, its primary rescue force—the small boat squadrons—totally eliminated and freighters were simply unsuited to picking up lifeboats. Not that there were many of those.

The 144th, which only had half its boats and wasn't scheduled to be activated for another two months, had been pressed into service. So had every Apollo ship capable of picking up survivors. Problem being that that was mostly *Paw* tugs which, while they had an air lock, had room for only five people.

Third problem: There was nowhere to put them. E Eridani didn't have any habitable planets. The biggest "habitat" was *Thermopylae* but there was no reasonable way into the *Thermopylae*. The main door was solidly shut and there were no large vehicle bypasses. Warships had only enough life support for their crews and a bit more. They couldn't be used to transfer most of the survivors. They were picking up some from shuttles and transferring them to *Therm* but most of the survivors were having to be shuttled through the gate to *Troy,* then the boats would turn around and go back to E Eridani. All of which took time, especially with low acceleration *Paws* and *Columbia* shuttles.

Which was why it was estimated to be five days before everyone was picked up.

A "Rangora spokesperson" had finally let slip that they had the same problems and worse. They estimated they *wouldn't* make the deadline for their boats running out of air since they had nearly a *hundred* thousand spacers drifting and were having to take them all back to Glalkod. At which point the President had stated that as soon as humans were all recovered Earth would get started on recovering Rangora. And repatriating them under the terms of the cease-fire. Which had started another firestorm.

Except for occasionally checking the major updates and their own boat's schedule for pick-up, which had been pushed back four times, Booth had spent most of his time playing Call of Duty XVII.

His plant pinged with a priority call and he picked up.

"Lifeboat 11053. If you've got the time we've got the dime."

"Closing on your position. Please have your personnel ready to exit. We have sufficient room for all your personnel but it's going to be tight."

"Roger dodger," Booth said. "People, we have a ride."

"A real ride or another "scheduled" ride, sir?" Machinist Mate Second Class Charlie Domino asked. As the next senior person on the boat Booth had designated him Chief of Lifeboat.

"Closing for dock right now," Booth said shaking the shoulder of the spaceman who'd been sitting next to him to wake him up. "Wake everybody up, get your helmets on and get ready to groove."

The lifeboat had room for twenty-six people and it was nearly full. Fortunately the *Smiley* had taken some time to come apart. Booth had stood by the opening to the lifeboat making sure personnel got aboard until the corridor he'd been standing by had sheared away. At which point he realized it was time to leave.

There was a sensation of movement, a skewing and yawing that was a pleasant change from freefall, then a "clank" as the ship made dock. The hatch cycled green and Booth commed Domino.

"Lead out. I'll ensure everyone gets clear."

"Aye, aye, sir," Domino commed. He checked to make sure they were clear, then opened the hatch and pulled himself through. *"Both doors open. It's grav past the second door and . . . Uh . . . Hello . . . sir . . . All clear, Commander . . . Uh . . ."*

"Issues?" Booth commed.

"No, sir," Domino replied. *"Everybody aboard who's going aboard, sir."*

"Roger. Everybody off, people. Shag it. There's other people waiting for pick-up."

Most of the personnel assigned to the *Carter* had had limited experience with zero gravity. Like Booth, they'd had training but weren't exactly experienced. So getting them out of the lifeboat wasn't a quick job. But finally the last spacer, absent the lieutenant commander, was off and Booth pulled himself into the shuttle's air lock, cycled it closed, grabbed the safety bar and pulled himself forward into . . . splendor.

Space-suited bodies were sprawled on couches that looked like original antiques or on Persian carpets on the floor. The starboard bulkhead of the shuttle sported what Booth was pretty sure was Van Gogh's original "Starry Night." The port was clearly one entire viewscreen, which Booth realized he'd seen plenty of times, just from the outside. It was made of optical sapphire.

"Tyler Vernon," Tyler said, pulling him into the interior. The space-suited tycoon looked every day of his sixty-something years. "Your second held a chair for you. But if you could get seated, we've got a long run ahead of us."

Booth sat down in the tycoon's personalized station chair and took off his helmet. He sort of recognized the classical piece playing in the boat but couldn't quite identify it.

"Sir . . . ? What's the music?"

"I'm not a big Stones fan," Vernon said, closing the hatch and leaning against it. "But the only thing I could think of that was appropriate was 'Gimme Shelter.'"

Given the news from E Eridani, which had included stories about how many of the civilian construction crews had given their lives in last month's battle, Cody Hardy was wondering if maybe he should have just joined the Navy instead of signing up for training with Apollo as an welder's apprentice. But he really wasn't into "three bags full" and not only was it top-notch training, it got him deferred from military service.

Other than that, he had no idea what he was getting himself into.

The instructor for "Introduction to Space Operations" wasn't much to look at. Kinda old, maybe thirty, short, bald and wearing a bad suit. He had a kinda funny look in his eyes.

"My name is James Allen," Butch said in a gravelly voice. "You will address me, and all your instructors, as Mister or Missus and their last names. You will not call me James or Jim. It is Mister Allen. You may be wondering why I sound like a three-pack-a-day smoker . . ."